STUFFED
LIVES

STUFFED
LIVES

ALASTAIR SCOTT

www.vitalspark.co.uk

Other books by the same author:

Scot Free
A Scot Goes South
A Scot Returns
Tracks Across Alaska
Native Stranger

For George & Gillian Woods (keep a good grip on your teeth, Seoras!), and all SKAT supporters.

My thanks to George Woods for the best bits of the artwork, Neil Wilson for giving this book life and Morven Dooner for her inspired suggestions and deft editing. Also to Sallie Moffat for tying off all the loose ends.

I'm grateful to Faber & Faber for permission to quote parts of This Be The Verse from *Collected Poems* by Philip Larkin, on page 88.

Published by

an imprint of
Neil Wilson Publishing
303 The Pentagon Centre
36 Washington Street
GLASGOW
G3 8AZ
Tel: 0141-221-1117
Fax: 0141-221-5363
E-mail: info@nwp.co.uk
www.nwp.co.uk

A catalogue record for this
book is available from the
British Library.

ISBN 1 903238 25 0

Typeset in Utopia
Designed by Sallie Moffat

Printed in Poland

CONTENTS

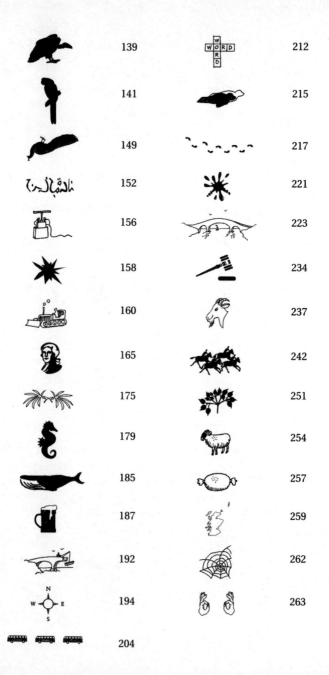

Angela Cleghorn sat filing her nails and thought of rubber. Spongy, warm, clingy rubber. She paused her abrasions and imagined her body tightly gripped in it. Black rubber. She slipped her free hand through her dressing gown and along one thigh. Back and forth. Feeling rubber. Sensuous rubber. *Rub-aaah!* Following every curve of her body. Left and right. Up and down. Her fingers tracing a seam, wandering abstractly across this deliciousness of latex, describing little circles spiralling bigger, and bigger still, her pulse rising, thumping, her muscles tightening, her skin tingling in ripples, growing and growing …

The phone rang.

Her mother:
Weather.
Coffee mornings.
House repairs: pending, completed.
Friends: ill, recently-passed-on.
Grandchildren's utterances: update.
Lots of love.

A wasted hour. Angela thought of love. She hadn't ever really known it. Not with a man. Certainly not with Farquhar. She'd been a Co-op check-out girl dreaming of drama school when they first met. At that moment a stage name was her most pressing problem and she'd just decided on Angel Ewe, when he entered her vision. His smile was radiant. Thereafter totting up his weekly stack of beans was the high point of her shifts. No, it wasn't love for Farquhar. It was convenience, an escape. And not just from a dull life. From Ramsbottom. Such a cruel, cruel name. To grow up a Ramsbottom in a farming community had been as much as a teenager could take, so she'd married the first boy to take an interest in her, Police Cadet Cleghorn, at seventeen.

He'd only just scraped in. She could remember praying they'd take him, and every detail of what had happened. The minimum requirements to enter the force had been a height of five-foot eight-inches and three O-Levels – if she remembered correctly – or six-foot one inches and a degree in Sociology.

English, Divinity and a low pass in Mathematics had combined with his narrow clearance under the measuring stick to permit his acceptance. His first posting had been to Glasgow Gorbals. The flush of being newly-weds carried them through this disappointment and they made the best of it. They went dancing. Farquhar metamorphosed on a dance floor, exhibiting a delicate nimbleness which anyone chancing upon his stationary footwear would not have believed possible. Then she recalled his dark mood when she announced she'd enrolled at the RSAMD. She hadn't noticed it then but his possessive nature was starting to emerge. It exploded the night of her first performance, when Farquhar discovered Angel Ewe naked in the lead role of Hair! He'd made a terrifying spectacle, forbidden any more involvement and shortly afterwards they were transferred to Flabbay.

Why had she accepted this? What had happened to the spirited Ramsbottom she'd been? Somehow she'd acquiesced, and even meekly accepted his sop – offered years later when the issue had cooled – of joining Flabbay Amateur Dramatic Society with him. Perhaps, she reflected, she could have accepted the curtailment of her ambition if she could have supported his. But a diminutive stature and a dedicated allegiance to incompetence had halted his career at Sergeant. Three-quarters of an inch too short for the Force, a couple of inches and a candlewatt too short for her.

Angela resumed her filing, while a fleeting image of the newly-incumbent priest trespassed on her thoughts.

She glanced at a photograph of her husband on last year's summer holiday. Framed. His birthday present to her. Aberdeen beach. Even in wellies his legs looked frail. He'd developed a marsupial belly and his crew-cut looked positively criminal. Yet, she admitted, he still had lovely teeth. She pulled the picture close and tried to be more forgiving, eventually conceding that few people look their best in a Force Six.

Farquhar. Such a romantic name! Farqu-har. From the Gaelic, *fearachar*, meaning 'manly'. She'd looked it up when they'd first met. And now the irony made her weep. She looked back at the photo. In a world where size and position meant a lot to her, he'd proved a disappointment. Sergeant Cleghorn would never match up to her scale or ambition. Her vision of a steam-driven High Commissioner had long dissipated, in a puncture-like hiss.

They were too different. She daring and impulsive, he frumpish and cautious. She longing for excitement in her life, he for peace in retirement. She Pisces, he Gemini. She vegetarian, he carnivore. She dynamite, he damp match. It was not a happy marriage, and was ceasing to be convenient.

There was only one thing worse than being miserably married to a policeman, she bemoaned, and that was living next door to the police-station.

Inspector Farquhar Cleghorn.

Sergeant Cleghorn imagined the words engraved in brass on his door. Sometimes, when nothing much was happening, he passed hours immersed in the vicarious joy of polishing them with Brasso. At other times, in particularly boring periods when they already gleamed, he experimented with font, size and case.

Inspector Farquhar Cleghorn

INSPECTOR Farquhar Cleghorn

INSPECTOR FARQUHAR CLEGHORN

INSPECTOR FARQUHAR CLEGHORN

Ινσπεχτορ Φαρθυηαρ Χλεγηορν

One day the plaque would be there. He'd screw it on himself, he vowed. At forty-two, there was time yet.

He surveyed his fiefdom. Forty-eight square feet of contiboard desk. Phone (blue). Fax (white). Wooden keyboard with labelled hooks (Cell, Car, Handcuffs, Armoury, Kennel).

He lingered on the last two hooks, which were empty, and wondered if they were conditional on rank.

INSPECTOR F CLEGHORN

LICENSED TO KILL

BEWARE OF THE DOG

Two filing cabinets (one empty). Cupboards. A shelf supporting boxed reports, regulations, manuals and his personal library: *The Complete Ruth Rendell*, *Great Unsolved Crimes of the World* (Readers Digest) and *OJ Simpson, The Trial – A Concise Summary* in six volumes.

He looked at the wall map of the island. Muckle Flabbay represented the antithesis of his roots and upbringing in Cowdenbeath. 'The Chicago of Fife' they'd called it in his father's day when the coalfields were throwing up prodigiously and everyone could afford a regular massacre at the pubs. He recalled his childhood in smoke-laden streets, his brief apprenticeship with Fife Window Cleaners, his first pint in the Rabid Dug and first steps at Miss Gillespie's School of Ballroom Dancing. He'd gone to appease Miss

Gillespie after trying to clean her windows and breaking three of them with his ladder. To his astonishment he found he had a flair for dancing and each week eagerly attended her classes.

His other love was football. The Blue Brazil! No one knew how the club had earned its nickname. Well, he for one would always be a Beath supporter even though team, pubs, work and spirit had all withered. The town had sunk lower than the pits, and he might have gone with them had Angela and the Force not saved him. They'd offered him Dunfermline as a first posting. *Dunfermline! The Blue Brazil's arch-rivals!* Naturally he declined, so it had been the Gorbals until the need to save Angela from that depraved stage cult became imperative. Muckle Flabbay had seemed like paradise. And Angela had loved it too, once she'd found new interests. In an effort to belong, she'd thrown herself wholeheartedly into home baking, church choir, line dancing and sheep identification.

Flabbay's map showed a lump of land shaped like an H fallen on its side. Twenty-five miles long from top to bottom, twenty miles at its widest (at both top and bottom) but narrowing to eight miles in the middle. Yet every mile felt doubled in length on singletrack roads rambling round bogs and skirting below the central obstruction of Ben Stac Mor. With klaxon warbling a police car could drive from end to end in an hour, though this depended entirely on a persistent refugee sheep crisis.

From his desk, when the windows weren't sheathed in condensation, Sergeant Cleghorn could watch Lysline freighters tramping their weekly passages between Liverpool and Bergen. They used the Sound of Pluck, a slender arm of sea separating Muckle Flabbay from the mainland, as a sheltered shortcut through the Minch. Further up Flabbay's coast in the direction of Dundreary Castle, just out of his line of vision, the sound narrowed to 400 metres and the island of Mickle Flabbay lay in centre channel. Ships had to pick a careful route using cardinal buoys and the Mickle Flabbay lighthouse. Cleghorn wished an occasional one would screw up. It would make a welcome change from drunk driving and witless tourists losing credit cards.

A mile away the ferry was leaving Pluckton. The Flabbay-Pluckton ferry. Quite a tongue-twister, that one.

I'm not a Flabbay-Plucker I'm a Flabbay-Plucker's son ...

God, it was a tedious day!

Every hour on the hour, 8am to 6pm, the *Flucker*, as it was more commonly known, left the mainland and brought a fresh wave of imports, and most journeys were observed by Her Majesty's Police Service. Cleghorn watched the passengers disgorge, clog the street, buy postcards and drive to Claddach Beach. On the way they always stalled at a viewpoint overlooking Dundreary. Seat of Clan MacFie. A hideous pile, in his opinion, a Hollywood-esque display of crenellations and turrets to which a swarm of oafish gargoyles had been given quarter. Yet, he conceded, under the right light, preferably lightning, it could look imposing.

Claddach Beach, tea at the Stac Hotel, ferry to the Western Isles. That was the format. The Western Isles ferry left from Muckle Flabbay's only other settlement, the fishing village of Grimport, situated in the north. Two white-fish trawlers, a small fleet of lobster and crab boats and a fish farm – which seemed to rear nothing but lice and Infectious Salmon Anaemia – were all that was left of the once-mighty herring industry. The Silver Darlings. Vamoosed. Grimport was lucky to have its ferry link with Craigmuir in Benbecula, though if Cleghorn had his way he'd close it down, and Grimport with it. His day book, where it was filled at all, was mostly filled with Grimport 'incidents'. Bloody noses and petty vendettas.

No, wouldn't have the guts for manslaughter, that bunch.

Paradise! Well, it had seemed that way at first. He fingered the Tourist Board's latest issue of *The Hebrides*. Despite having been down-sized and down-graded, it still devoted an entire page of bleeding ink to Muckle Flabbay. 'The Jewel of the Minch' ran the heading. Claddach Beach looked tropical despite haemorrhaging badly. The greatest praise was heaped on Ben Stac Mor. It was, apparently, '3,236 feet of Munro-bagging delight, its black gabbro arête offering the finest rock climbing in Europe.'

'Munro-buggering, more like,' he chortled, if the drop-out rate was anything to go by. Ben Stac Mor did an alarming trade in body bags.

Cleghorn idly rewrote the copy.

Muckle Flabbay: Golden Weekend Away Breaks on Ben Stac Mor!

3,236 feet of mass-murdering gabbro – come test your adhesion against a REAL mountain!

No, he reflected, perhaps that wouldn't do much for the island's ailing guesthouse trade.

Not much else for the visitor really. They could pick up a scrap of Gaelic here and there. Be verbally abused and legally ripped-off at Miss Oliphant's

Emporium. Dine out at the Birtwhistle's Indian Restaurant, The Ganesh Gnashery, which closed during the Highland monsoon (September 20-April 15) and was ethnically closer to Lancashire. Try a spot of fishing. Flabbay's trout lochs witnessed the migratory passage of retired majors and the breeding antics of red-throated divers – *and,* he had no doubt, *sometimes vice-versa.* Such was the Jewel's lot. Paradise to through traffic, a damp way of life to 600 residents and 6000 sheep. The sheep ate grass and bog myrtle. The crofters ate sheep and dabbled in cottage crafts or cyber businesses. Service industries consumed pretty well everyone else.

It wasn't much, but it was at least all his. A one-officer post on twenty-four-hour call. Not every policeman could claim to be a force unto himself. (Or to have his own Fiat Uno.) But what really kept him going – more than going, *dynamically dutiful* – was his belief that Muckle Flabbay had *Vice.*

Vice Vice **VICE**

He had his pet theories. The long dark winters contributed to these. So did the long light summers. And isolation. And boredom. And the monotonous predictability of the island's faces. And Gulf War Syndrome (from Culloden, still unrecognised). He had not the slightest doubt that there thrived a sizzling hotbed of orgies and wife-swappers and sex-aids-by-mail aficionados (let's face it, not much choice with Miss Oliphant at the helm of the only shop). Anything could happen. It was also reasonable to expect that Mairi Ban the Byke, the local prostitute, would provide the means for an escalation in crime, though this side of her business appeared patchy outwith the Klondiking season. And there were always strong possibilities that something might go violently awry among the Masons, Gaelic mafia or, as a fail-safe, the Churches.

Yes, he reassured himself, there was hope. It was perhaps too much to look forward to someone being murdered in cryptic logic that only Cleghorn *savoir-faire* could deduce, but if he could crack a big one – a yacht with a sack of heroin up her heads, a pornography ring (*especially a pornography ring*) or even a couple of decent-sized embezzlements, then INSPECTOR could be in the bag.

Another idea occurred to him. The MacFies ... his fingers were running along files ... always strange goings-on in that family. Yes, he'd start with the MacFies.

7

Hamish MacFie stood by the chapel putting the finishing touches to his mother. A final pat of mortar secured Marietta to the firmament. She hadn't turned out quite the way he'd expected. He'd asked for tenderness, serenity and love. Hugh the Mason had excelled. She stood there looking beatific, smiling, head slightly askance, her arms in the act of reaching out to receive and comfort some of life's damaged goods. Beyond that the figure bore little resemblance to the person he remembered. To have recreated her unnaturally long legs would have looked ridiculous, but Marietta never had fat thighs or big hips. And he didn't remember her nipples protruding quite so much. Though cleverly executed within the folds of her chemise, they were downright offensive. He'd asked for them to be removed but Hugh had turned apoplectic and wittered about perspective, angles and stress fractures. He would have to start again, he remonstrated, and he'd want double the fee. So Hamish settled for a mother with fat thighs, big hips and sexually-charged nipples.

She'd died ten years earlier when he was sixteen. A sudden and tragic end which left him inconsolable. He'd wept hogsheads. Ten years was somewhat tardy for erecting a memorial but it had taken him four to decide on its form, and Hugh six to complete it. By West Highland standards, he supposed, ten clients in a lifetime was reasonably brisk business.

'I do hope, daaarling, you'll put one up for me when I'm gone.'

Hamish turned to find his stepmother watching him over a bunch of wild flowers gathered in her arms. Given her diminutive height and the bush in the way, all he could see was her face. His father seemed to go for women with permanent smiles, but Fran's was a bit different from Marietta's …

'Which'll probably be fairly soon, the way I'm feeling,' she added, drifting off in a dreamy lilt.

Hamish watched her with the disbelief her wardrobe had provoked for the past nine and three-quarter years (his father never having been one to waste time). A loose twin-set replicating a zebra. Skin-tight ponyskin trousers. Her hair resembled an extrovert selection of curls you'd usually only find in a drag outfitter's, but it was all real except the colour – fair, today. To be so small and have so much hair! She was always immaculate, even wore her wellies well, as if any day the call might come:

'Mrs Fran MacFie? BBC. Could you possibly read the news tonight?'

Apart from brutalising 'daaarling' she did have perfect articulation.

He recognised the small yellow flowers, one of her customary harvests.

'More agrimony, then, is it?'

'Yes. And I'm after honeysuckle. Should I get you some too?'

'No, thanks. That's fairly far down my list at the moment.'

Incense sticks and Bach Flower Remedies, he thought. The only things we have in common. So different from his mother. She never needed agrimony. For *Mental Torture Behind Cheerful Face*. Or honeysuckle. *To Escape Living in the Past*. Marietta wore a smile for everyone, especially for him, but also for the ghillies, the servants, door-to-door salesmen, Mormons, Jehovah's Witnesses and – most magnanimously – her husband, 'Rapsy'.

He thought of his father, an immutable pudding from the army's mould and already forty-six when Hamish was born. He'd always craved his father's recognition, and probably always would even though their values appeared irreconcilable. As a child he'd nursed injured birds back to health, and saved worms from drowning in puddles. In those days he'd wanted to be a big-game warden in Africa. His mother's influence, of course. His father was the cause of the injured birds and would be the one Hamish would be protecting Africa's game from. By quirks of fate he'd ended up an unemployed social anthropologist, ashamed both of his drawling accent and privileged background. Prime material for Greenpeace, he admitted with an ironic chuckle, but a bit of a waste in a fish farm labourer.

He plucked some scleranthus. *Inability To Choose Between Alternatives*. Ah well, he mused, roll on the social revolution and, please, dear gods, let me be somewhere near the front.

He stared at the effigy of his mother again. How could the astute daughter of a Morningside bank manager have ended up with a Hebridean blimp still steeped in the Raj? Even the certifiably optimistic must have had doubts about the suitability of the match, but somehow it had held together. Her gift to the marriage had been shrewd housekeeping, Hamish's long legs and a supply of oil for troubled waters. Homicidal flare-ups among the staff, upwardly mobile damp, downwardly mobile masonry, Rapsy's extravagant losses on horses and evidence of his latest libidinous dalliances ... her smile and placid demeanour confronted them all. What she really felt inside, Hamish had no idea. Maybe she could have used agrimony after all. He'd thought the world of her. As her features faded in his mind, so her sweetness grew and engulfed the fragments that remained. Within this aura her stiltiness contracted, ampleness reshaped what had been lean, and plainness was redrawn into prettiness. Gradually she turned into a roadside shrine. With sharp boobs.

Not that she didn't have faults. Hypocrisy surely had to be one of them, smiling at infidelity when a handful of shrapnel and a charge in the ancestral blunderbuss would have been a more natural reaction. And she was a dervish for work. Never stopped. Never adjusted to having servants. Spent most of her time trying to make life easy for them. And obsessive about cleanliness. In the end it killed her. Not for the first time he tried to imagine how it felt, butter knife in hand, being electrocuted while extracting crumbs from a toaster.

The accident was freakish enough to make it into all the papers. Then the National Safety Council contacted his father after what it considered a tactful period – two weeks – to ask if it could feature the incident in their new series of TV adverts, *Home Hazards*. For the Benefit of The Nation. An inducement was offered. Two hundred pounds (and a replacement toaster). Hamish and his father were horrified. After considering legal action the colonel eventually thought better of it, and accepted. For twelve consecutive weeks *Coronation Street* was prefaced by the ritualised execution of his mother until the series moved on to the case of farmer Donald Martin and a two-ton bale of runaway silage.

On the housekeeping front, Fran was the total opposite of his mother. But, he reflected, Fran was alive and his mother was not. A moral might be construed to illustrate the deadliness of high principles but such would be a denigration of his mother's sacrifice. He preferred to believe she'd been admirable for striving towards perfection, unfortunate that two hundred and forty volts were attached to a near-miss.

* * *

Dr Edward Bach perfected his flower remedies in 1934. He made a mint, although not from Fran, who had a small witchery in the castle. Here she extracted her own mother tinctures (the very phrase used by Dr Bach). Depending on the species, she either boiled, squashed, steeped or partially cremated and then drank, swallowed, inhaled or rubbed on. The witchery flagged black on the fire-risk scale but provided a pleasant alternative to the smell of rot.

Fran had added honeysuckle to her gleanings and was now, as an afterthought, on her way for willow. *Self Pity and Resentment.*

Hamish was still lost in thought, and hadn't moved since she'd left him.

'I do wish he'd let me in,' she murmured. Too loudly.

'I beg your pardon?'

'Your tan, daaarling. I was just remarking on how strong it is. Must be three weeks since you got back.' She inhaled yellow petals. 'You never really told me what you did on your trip to India?'

Hamish sighed. 'A combination of travelling and industrial sabotage.'

'How utterly delicious. Sounds a perfect antidote for when the beach gets boring or overrun by Germans. I'm so out of touch. I never knew travel agents organised those sorts of things.'

'They don't. I went with Greenpeace. We were protesting about organophosphates being dumped in the river Cauvery, in the Western Ghats.'

Fran wanted to rush up and throw her arms around him. Show him she understood. Be a mother again, something she'd been only briefly – her partner had absconded to the States with their six-month-old twins. Mothering cut short inflicted a desperate deficiency. Hamish was so close … but the frigid decorum of the MacFies exercised a powerful forcefield and once more she felt helpless before it. One day, she vowed, she'd break out, stop participating in the charade.

Poor lost Fran, she thought. Poor lost boy. She could sympathise with him. She'd recently heard a word that might describe him perfectly – Trustafarian. But how sad to be so impoverished; a Trustafarian without a trust. He did all the other bits like play reggae, tool around on two-tone bongos and wear Rajasthani cast-offs but he had to work. And it couldn't be easy being a part-time fish farm worker when you were the only one smelling of patchouli oil.

'Greenpeace! Daaarling! I'm so glad my money's put to good use.'

It took time for her meaning to sink home.

'You support Greenpeace?'

Must have been a milkman baby, she thought. Had nothing of his father in him, except perhaps the over-wrought correctness and superiority of the public school voice. Long, lean, sharp. Black hair, matching hers for crimp and curl, to the shoulders. Beads encircling neck and wrists. Gentle, feminine movements. No wonder his father despaired, she smirked. She couldn't work out if he was gay or not. He never talked of girls, never had a girlfriend. Yet he didn't talk of boys either. And that postcard he'd sent them from some place with a preposterous name. Something like Sanaravabellagola! A sixty-foot statue of a naked man! Was that just to wind his father up, or …

'Yes, but to postpone World War Three, daaarling, don't tell your old man.'

Surprise, surprise, mused Hamish.

Back to concentrated sulphuric masculinity, mused Fran. Adjusting her mask, she disappeared through dangling screens of *Self Pity and Resentment*.

The morning of 26 August 2003 marked the inauguration of change for Colonel R A P MacFie, relic of Clan and Colonialism. Crows and clouds gathered over the twenty-third anniversary of his retirement from a lifetime of privileged idleness as, on this fateful morning, he stepped out of red silk pyjamas and into senility.

Corbies, cras, craws, crows ...

... gargling their names as they jostled for supremacy on the castle's corbie-steps. Old hierarchical games on an old battle site. Another morning chorus of power struggles. Claws rattling like guilt on conscience.

Below – pyjama-less and guiltless – Colonel MacFie never heard them.

He stared at the mist roiling around the glen beyond his window and noted with alarm that chunks of his mountains had been stolen. Mistaking the salty infusion of Hebridean air that percolated his moustache for gun smoke, he thought of deserts, heard camels snorting and went down to breakfast – with a rough draft of orders for his troops, but without his trousers.

'Damn cold,' he muttered.

When his wife failed to acknowledge his presence he endeavoured to distinguish her from the taxidermy and furnishings, although it was seldom that all the ornaments in the castle were silent at once.

Fran occupied her territory, the southern ten feet of dining-room table, their morning battleground. She sat immobile, tightly wrapped in a mauve and apricot kimono streaked with green, like a bundle of her wild flowers awaiting arrangement. Her features had disappeared under a face mask that imposed a fifteen-minute retreat from the world.

Dalrymple appeared. Batman. Gamekeeper. Ghillie. Grateful Dog's Body. His brogues sent tremors across the floorboards as he served salted porridge. He had already peppered the outside corners of the castle to discourage stray dogs from piddling on them, as he did punctually at seven every morning. From his customary stance on the edge of the room he stared at his master's bare legs in a state of shock.

MacFie slowly raised his bowl of porridge. He crouched until his nose lay level with the steaming gruel, eyes transfixed on the turbaned Sikh about to storm the trench before him. All around lay the silent vastness of the Thar desert. His moment of glory had come. *Now* ... and he flung the bowl at the enemy.

Fran let out a scream as a trail of scalding glue dripped down her head. Fortunately her face mask insulated her from the lingering wrath of husband and Empire.

Dalrymple rushed forward. 'ARE YOU ALL RIGHT, MA'AM?'

'Godsakes, Dalrymple. It's like having tiffin in a waxworks here.' MacFie smiled horribly, as if the duplicity might jolt some dignity into a figure gnarled by a lifetime of fawning. 'Where's that indolent bastard? Still abed, eh? Godsakes. Wife's a clown, batman's a dummy and son's a waster.'

Ever since deafness had partially closed his ears (an inevitable consequence of five decades' intimacy with gunpowder) Angus Dalrymple had perfected the art of lip reading. What he'd just read caused him to react like a ferret watching a gin trap close underfoot. He swallowed. Squirmed. The Change. The Flouting of Decorum. The End of Tradition.

'I ... DON'T UNDERSTAND, SIR?' No longer able to judge volume, he erred on the quiet side of shouting. But the colonel had ambled off.

So he's finally gone, Fran thought. Colonel Rudyard Apsley Prendergast MacFie. Hereditary Chief of Clan MacFie. Twenty-third Laird of Dundreary. 'Rapsy' to his friends. No longer solid in the turret.

'He's flipped,' she hissed into the confidence of the phone later that morning.

'How badly?' The voice belonged to her Gestalt therapist in Tobermory.

'Seriously.'

'Certifiably?'

'Tricky. It's patchy. There seem to be spells when he's perfectly normal. At least as normal as he's ever been.' She stroked Ming, her shih tzu, who lay in her lap like a pile of unravelled knitting. 'What on earth can I do?'

'Very little. Just old age. Natural degeneration ... '

'No ... to accelerate the process?'

A two-dimensional Rapsy looked on. Like his relations in this gallery of life-sized portraits he was young and discreditably handsome. His paunch and chest had swapped positions and he bulged excessive musculature through a uniform decked with medals. Fiction, not fact – art, not history – had always been important to the MacFies. Fourteen framed lies decorated the great hall along with a disembodied herd of deer. Here and there something exotic like an oryx peeped through as self-consciously as fancy dress at a drab party. The zoologically-gifted would also recognise a kudu, gnu, dikdik, ibex and perhaps even the grizzly whose mould had turned to alopecia at the hands of the local laundry, unused as it was to dry-cleaning American carnivores.

Hamish MacFie shuffled sleepily across the room, instinctively weaving a course through a landscape of Victorian leviathans. Eight-foot mock-Chinese vases. Sofas like boats stranded on a shallow carpet. A hardwood forest of tables. Lacquer this. Gilt that. A jaded world. Cracked. Peeling. Warped. Leaking feathers.

'Should get this place fumigated.' Out of habit he spoke to himself. He rolled a fag. 'Even a smoke's beginning to taste of rot.' He threw back his head, exhaled a blue trail, and immersed himself in a conundrum. Darwin; right or wrong? Wrong, he believed. Man was not evolved ape, but stuck-in-rut ape. Chimpanzee, however, having transcended tantrum and attained total contentment through a fistful of bananas and two acres of trees, was the perfection of man. Therefore …

Auld MacFie, inconspicuous against a wine stain on leather, gazed over the battlements of an armchair: his wife, permanently plugged into the telephone socket; his son, prospective Clan Chief and Twenty-Fourth Laird of Dundreary, a lanky runt fading into a blue cloud. MacFie smelled patchouli. Viewed the bare feet. Saffron dhoti. Then the T-shirt: *Only when the Last Tree has Died and the Last River been Poisoned and the Last Fish been Caught will we Realise that we cannot eat MONEY*. His lips quivered. To think he'd produced an *environmentalist*. A meddling Greenpeace hooligan. Why the Indian Army didn't shoot the lot of them, he'd never understand. River pollution! Show him an Indian river that wasn't polluted! Stiffs were chock-a-block in the Ganges so why not the Cauvery? And how good for the farmers, with all that organophosphate flowing by. Save a fortune on sheep dip. *Greenpeace* … and his blood rose in a flush.

'REARED A FLAMING CUCKOO,' he bawled. Not a waxwork moved except Fran's lips. 'To hell with you. I'm off to the hill.'

'Happy killing.' Blue words.

Only when the Last Tree … Cree words.

'Hmmm, yes. I heard. Terrible.' Telephone words.

Slats of sunlight had fallen from the sky and lay aslant, one end hinged behind the clouds, the other supported by Earth. The island of Muckle Flabbay occupied a site of celestial subsidence. The heavens frequently fell in on it.

On the braes of Ben Stac Mor three red deer stood silhouetted against the brightness of Loch Papil. Two hinds and a stag, the latter pouting arrogance. Sunlight seeped towards them, infusing the orange glow of autumn grasses with warmth. The blaeberry leaves were at their finest and emulated a miniature canopy of Canadian maple. Red-yellow. Vermilion. Crimson. Heart-wringingly beautiful. The stag deposited a steaming turd on the scene and walked off.

'Damnation,' snorted the Colonel, lowering his rifle. 'Bastard,' he added as his disappointment deepened. 'Jittery bastard … '

Angus Dalrymple, now clad in outdoor plus-fours, remained mute. Anxiety from the morning's events still puckered his face. His lip-reading surely hadn't deceived him? His craft was infallible. Words had become solid objects sculpted by lips. The subtlest movement incised meaning. At first he'd had to concentrate, but now it was effortless. He could listen to distant conversations through a telescope. No, he hadn't confused the master's words that morning. *Dummy*, he'd called him. And his crackpot behaviour. These could only mean one thing. Forty-three years of service and it could end tomorrow. If the old man snuffed it, he'd be up the creek. The Boy wouldn't keep him.

He turned to look at his demented benefactor. Red-faced. Ranting. Porcupinely dangerous.

Gypped-up cowardly little bugger, he read. VICHY COLLABORATOR.

'ACH THERE'S PLEN-TY MORE WHERE HE CAME FROM, SIR.' His Lewis accent, given feathers, would have described the flight pattern of a meadow pipit. By contrast, the laird's Etonian bombast was the pine-shattering blunderings of a capercaillie.

Dalrymple's words were kind. He'd become used to the increasing length of time the old man required to steady his sights on a target. More time than any but the most accident-prone creature was prepared to give him. Muckle Flabbay's deer had entered a golden period. It would become platinum if The Boy inherited.

The colonel lay back in the grass and looked out over a capitulated France where treachery and Huns lay concealed beyond every contour. He worded commands to his artillery to obliterate every possible refuge, especially the police station with its execrable pock-pudding of a sergeant, and Miss Oliphant's shop, both of which were just visible. He then ordered them to turn their sights on the spectre of a bridge that had haunted him for decades. They'd never defile his island with a bridge! No, never. Saw the explosion, limbs of twisted metal hurled sizzling into the sea. Yes, he'd show them. Sort out the sheep from the goats. Rid the vermin from MacFie land. They'd all had it too good for too long.

'Home, Dalrymple, my man. Can't hang about here all day. Work to do.'

Just short of their goal they came across another unexpected alteration to the landscape. A battered camper van, painted with a flower, was parked on MacFie land close to the castle entrance. Close to a sign intended to exhibit the Colonel's command of languages as well as its particular message:

> NO CAMPING
> KAMPING VERBOTEN
> NON CAMPÉ

A home-made yurt had been erected on the machair above a gentle slope to the sea. MacFie wood was smoking and heating a kettle.

'GOOD GOD,' thundered the Colonel. 'What the hell … '

'TINKS, SIR. I'LL BE GOING RIGHT AWAY TO MOVE THEM.'

The Colonel raised his eyeglass. On either side of the flower he could discern two words. 'Grout.' 'Loony.' Below them, a love heart and 'Dunfermline'.

'No, no, Dalrymple. Hold fire. They're one of us.' He winked. 'Undercover.' He turned and gave a friendly wave to the figures.

'VIVRE LA FRANCE LIBRE. UP DE GAULLE,' he yelled, and entered the castle.

Fran was on the phone. As he passed he cut her extension with his gralloching knife. Once in his office, now the line was free, he called Hamilton, Gerund, Nayers & Filigree. He was connected to Gerund.

'George, old boy. We'll need to meet. I want to change my will.'

'Certainly, Rapsy. I'll come at once.'

'Strange auld critter, eh?' Grout poked the fire.

'Whit the fuck wis he oan aboot? Up de Gaulle.'

'Vivre la France! Must hiv spent tae long in the sun. Brain's addled.' He skewered a sausage on a stick and propped it over the embers. 'Here y'ar, Rastafarian.' A raw sausage made the short flight from the packet to slathering jaws.

'Been meanin tae ask ye, Grout. If yer dug started life as a Hungarian Pulli, like ye said, how come he's grown intae a Lassie crossed wi shredded wheat?'

'Ah hope ye didnae hear that, Rastafarian. That, fer yer information, Loon, is whit a Hungarian Pulli's supposed tae be like when its nae dolled up fer Crufts.'

They ate sausages and smoked a joint. Rastafarian chased rabbits, unaware that Pullis had been bred to startle Hungarian sheep, not to overhaul Highland rodents. In the evening Grout and Loony picked whelks until their backs ached and their hands were numb. They ate a bucket of mussels for supper.

'Ye realise, Loon, if we wis in France noo, we'd jist hae eaten aboot eighty fuckin quid's worth o mussels? Nae bad livin, eh?'

'Ah wish ah *wis* in France noo. Chillin oot. Soakin up some sun an aw that. Drinkin a drap o wine.' He stared down to the sea which was creeping up on their orange sack of whelks. 'Still, nae bad haul fer the furst day. Quarter a hunnerweight at sixty quid.'

They smoked another joint. 'Where ye reckon the night life's at?'

'Nightlife? Ah reckon nightlife went oot eftir Culloden.'

'Think we should sorta re-educate em then. Ken, show em a good time.'

'Yea. Least we kin dae. Jist a wee thankye fer the whelks.'

'Aye, we owe it tae the system an aw. If ye dinnae shak it noo an again it gits stuck an gaes aff. Let's awa an check oot Dracula's castle.'

They strolled down the driveway that rhododendrons had all but converted into a tunnel.

'Moat's weel-maintained,' remarked Loony, as they splashed through a two-hundred-yard puddle.

'Evenin, David.' Grout greeted a Roman standing on one leg atop a plinth. He'd lost his other leg, both arms and head. 'Soberin message, eh Loon? That's whit hangin aboot here daes tae ye.'

The castle towered gloomily above them, slightly darker than dusk. Three windows were illuminated. Somewhere at the end of the lawn a peacock laughed.

'Fucksakes! S'like *The Exorcist!*'

They approached an open basement window and heard voices.

'No, Angus. It's not like the old days, that's for sure. Not like when the Colonel's father was here. He was a *real* gentleman, so he was.'

'AYE, IT'S TRUE, WOMAN. HE'D HAVE DONE THE RIGHT THING BY US. THE BOY'LL THROW US ON THE MIDDEN. SURE AS COD'S COD.'

The voices continued to reminisce on the late Sir Hector MacFie, twenty-first of that Ilk. How he never charged them for coal. How he paid Angus extra when he played his pipes for the gentry and ladies. How the gamekeeper's right to hooves and bones was never flouted. And Effie recalled how her ladyship, Hectorina, had always consulted her on arrangements for the Burns Night Fancy Dress. How she'd been blessed by gifts of her mistress's cast-offs. Had been treated like family. And Lady Marietta had been the same. Even cleaned her own toaster – God rest her soul. Quite unlike the new one – uppity tramp. Life had been more like a partnership in the old days, they agreed. Honour. Yes, that was it. There'd been honour. And respect. Everyone knew their place and respected everyone else's. There was no respect now.

'NOW IT'S ALL ABOUT MONEY. TREAT US LIKE DEBTS. WELL, EFFIE, WE'VE A RIGHT TO BE HERE. THAT'S THE WAY OF IT. WE'LL NOT BE MOVING.'

Feet away, Grout and Loony shimmied up a drainpipe and shuffled along a cantilevered rim to reach the next window.

'Djaysus! Whit fuckin planet's this?'

Shadows conspired to triple the number of severed heads arraigned like a disapproving jury. Three armchairs, strategically placed to maintain the greatest distance from each other, cradled three figures in various poses. A young man with dark tangles of hair sat across one chair with his legs draped over an arm, reading. He was wearing a kaftan and looked – to Loony – as if he might have fallen from Tintoretto's *The Last Supper* and been saved by the chair. The cover of the book he was reading was familiar to both Grout and Loony – *Zen and the Art of Motorcycle Maintenance*. In the furthest chair Fran was curled into the foetal position. Well used to her husband's maliciousness, she'd replaced the severed line from her stock of BT cables and was chatting away on the receiver. Her face was yellow and she'd hennaed her hair.

'Weel there's hope fer yer man. An she looks right oan the pulse. Cute little raver, fer sixty summin.'

'Oi, look! It's de Gaulle.'

'Shitabrick. Snuffed it. Bet it'll be a month fore oany bastard notices.'

But the Colonel was very much alive. In fact he'd never felt better. He was rearranging his memories. Tweaking exaggeration here, fine-tuning glory there. Adding bar to the DSO that got away. Art, not history. It was 1956. There was work to be done. Principles to be upheld. Arabs to whip. Smack it up! Tally-ho! Happiest days of his life. Those, and a childhood in the Punjab in the last days of the Raj. Under his father, His Excellency, Sir Hector MacFie, Governor General of Punjab and Haryana. By Jove, they knew a thing or two about titles in those days! And order! At the drop of a topi his father could muster a thousand sepoys to bring insurgents to their knees. Sir Hector had been a hard act to follow. Brother Hannibal, twenty-second Laird, hadn't even tried, succumbing to a bent elbow and pickled liver. End of a long line. MacFies had distinguished themselves in all the great knees-up of recent history: Balaclava, Mafeking, Magersfontein, Somme; and of course he'd graced the rearguard of the Suez Crisis. Too bad he couldn't have shipped The Boy off to the Gulf, Bosnia … anywhere. A ripping dander would have done him the world of good.

He pulled the ends of his moustache and retwisted them into points.

'Moved.' Grout sounded disappointed.

'Ye realise whit we're lookin at here? Last o the dinosaurs, man. Missin link. Half lizard, half ape. An aw his relatives wi big teeth an horns oan the wa. Early *homo sapiens* wi fuddled brains an nae free will. Born an boxed. Ah bet his fuckin portrait wis painted an his obituary written afore he slipped oot the birth canal. Poor sod.'

The Colonel had slipped a few years further back and up the leg of Italy to the Bernese Alps where he'd enjoyed impregnating chalet waitresses galore as part of a Cambridge mountaineering expedition. Rock climbing had been one of his youthful frolics, and reminiscing on the Jungfrau's tight chimneys always brought a smile to his lips. Of course, The Boy had inherited his mother's vertigo and, even more alarmingly, had shown no interest in crumpet. The only mitigating circumstance that had averted patricide was that The Boy appeared not to be queer.

'Ahhh,' MacFie sighed. It was all vexing. The family's history mirrored the decline of Empire. First India, then Africa, then the Commonwealth. First Sutherland, then Inverness-shire, then Ross-shire. All gone. God alone knew what would happen in the next generation. The Boy was an air-head, an idealist. Indeed, a degree in social anthropology was confirmation of a wonky tappet. Yes, should have been him at the wrong end of the toaster, not Marietta.

'Whit's that fuckin hairy thing in the punk's lap?'

Grout scrutinised the object. 'Beats me. Either the old codger's sporran, or an ancestor's scrotum.'

'Aye, ye need a fuckin thermometer tae work oot who's at ninety-eight point six an who's extinct.'

At that moment Hamish suddenly looked up from *Zen* and stared straight at them.

' … That one's alive. We'd better beam airsels oot o here.'

By the time Grout and Loony had descended to gravel and gazed upwards, the fallen Apostle was struggling to prise open the window and they could hear the ancestral scrotum barking.

They walked back through the moat as far as the Roman monopede and noticed a side-track branching to the right. They followed it for several hundred yards until they came to a clearing, where they could discern a figure standing motionless in front of them. They stopped dead, hearts pounding. Grout fumbled for his maglite. Slow movements. Adrenaline pumping. The same thought struck them simultaneously; *the fuckin keeper, wi a shotgun …*

'Arrrrrrrrrrggggh,' Grout screamed, flicking on the torch while throwing himself sideways to the ground, rolling, trying to glimpse the keeper in the beam without allowing himself to become an easy target. The shot never came. He lay on the ground, panting, looking up at the Virgin Mary.

She held out her arms. Had both her legs. And her head.

Loony began laughing and fell down beside Grout and together they lay helpless in hysterics. Eventually Grout regained control.

'Fucksakes. First time ah've been felled by a miracle. Auld David there's doon tae his prick an one leg an she hisnae even lost a nipple.'

Beyond the statue was a chapel with a portico and lancet windows. Grout shone his torch up one of the pillars.

'Corinthian.'

Loony nodded thoughtfully, trying the handle of the door. Locked. 'See whin ah win the lottery. Ah'll build a mansion wi hunners o these fuckin pillars. Doric, mind. Dinnae want tae be ostentatious.'

They wandered round the building, pulling on a rope draped down the far gable. The rope gave. They felt tension, heard a dull thud high above in the darkness and pulled harder till the rope snagged.

'Three, two, one … ' They let go.

Strident clangs shattered the night in couplets. A peacock shrieked.

'Teach the bastard fer laughin at us.'

They discovered an open window and squeezed through.

Loony whistled as Grout's beam illuminated marble saints, gold stations of the cross and a colossal altar of some variegated stone.

'Onyx,' Grout confirmed. 'Nae bad, eh? Hivin a mini Vatican fer yer private worship.'

'Ye kid git fifty in here, nae bother. Wunner where they keep the priest.'

'Locked in there, nae doot.'

They entered the vestry.

'Loony fer Pope,' crowed Grout, as Loony donned a purple cassock and a mitre embroidered with silver. He flunked the sign of the cross.

'Ah used tae be Catholic,' Grout confided. 'Far as Christians go, lot tae be said fer it. Absolution frae sin, aw they pictures an idols, fitba on a Sunday an aw that.'

'Whit made ye become Baha'i then?'

'Cudnae hack that nae contraception crap. An nae free will. If yer Catholic ye hiv tae produce Catholics. Nae ifs, buts or mebbes.'

'Ah went through a Jainist spell, masel.'

'Whit the fuck's a Jainist?'

'It's sorta extremist non-violence. Ah wis hangin oot in India at the time. They Jains winnae kill oanythin. They's the folk whit sweeps the path aheida em soze they winnae step oan a bug. Ah gaed alang wi that, man, till ah thought aboot it. Bein a Jain, ye kidnae kill Cowdenbeath scum. That wisnae right.'

'Naw. Ye kid hiv reverted tae Christianity. They're aye killin folk.'

'Tae sanctimonious fer me, man. Tae insecure. They've aye tae drag in converts tae mak themselves feel ok 'boot themselves.'

'Ye should try the Baha'is. Ye tak the best bits oot o aw religions.'

'Disnae dae a thing fer me. Ah'm intae animism. Life's aw aboot vibes. Energy. Tae me, there's nae god cos we're aw gods.' Loony flung out an arm in an extravagant gesture. 'Cept in Beath.'

They examined a chalice and sniffed a bag of incense. Grout played with the censer, swinging it while thinking.

'Ah've jist hid an idea.'

He laid the censer on the altar and opened it. With the torch clamped between his teeth, he withdrew a pouch from his pocket and stuffed a wad of the finest grass into the silver semi-sphere, then sprinkled on a covering of incense.

'C'moan. Bit fuckin generous, innit?'

'Aw in a good cause.'

In the castle they heard the bell toll. It wasn't until the next morning, long after his porridge had congealed, that Colonel Rudyard Apsley Prendergast MacFie was discovered dead in his armchair, still smiling.

* * *

Several days later Sergeant Cleghorn's phone rang.

'Police station.'

As he listened he felt his blood drain to his feet and surge up again in one giddying rush.

'I'll be over at once. Don't touch anything.'

The voice had been muffled, in such an emotional state that he'd been unable to determine whether the caller was a man or a woman. But the message was clear enough. A body had been discovered on Grimport pier.

Sergeant Cleghorn's tyres drew black lines on Grimport pier as he jolted to a halt. He glanced at his watch. Fifty-nine minutes, and with the loss of only one sheep. A record! Grabbing a body blanket and red/white cordoning tape he leapt out, walked briskly round some containers that were blocking his way, then slipped on a discarded skate. His view suddenly upended and filled with sky, and he found himself lying in a slime of decomposing fish. With a shake of the head he raised himself and used the blanket to wipe off the mess. He retrieved his cap, pulled his shoulders back and resumed what he regarded, despite the reek of fish, as his purposeful and dignified gait. His boots imitated a plague of crickets.

The only body on the pier was upright and full of vigour, gesticulating at a departing ship. Not the slightest evidence of death or incident could be seen. He wondered if the ship was the key ... *I immediately knew, Your Honour, that the accused was taking the body to be dumped at sea.* Then he recognised the figure at the end of the pier. The tight leather trousers, long silver hair. Her top-heaviness always made him queasy, reminding him of how dangerously unbalanced life was.

'So, Mairi MacLeod, I might've guessed *you'd* be involved.' He withdrew his black book and snapped back the elastic. 'Unnecessary as it may be, I have to remind you that anything you say may be used in a Court of Law as evidence against you.'

Mairi Ban ignored him and continued waving to the *Spodra*, an unexpected windfall of mackerel processors from the Black Sea delivered to her though the mysterious workings of destiny, in this case a failed bilge pump. The main Klondiking season was several months off – January to March usually – and the continuing low prices for cod, whiting, haddock and megrim were depressing her own trade – fisherman processing – among itinerant trawlers. The *Spodra* had come as such a surprise that its departure, as she waved with one hand and fingered a wad of £20 notes with the other, was making her uncharacteristically emotional.

'Just waving farewell to some friends.' Then the smell reached her. *'Ej pie velna,'* she swore. 'You'll need to change deodorant, Sergeant

Cleghorn.' She reached towards him and removed a set of monkfish jaws that had attached themselves to his shoulder.

'Just stick to answering my questions, Mairi. Now, time is 1615. Where's the body you reported?'

'There's just been eleven beautiful bodies here, Sergeant, but I'm afraid you've missed them. Lepaya. That's where they're going.' She read his perplexed expression. 'Latvia. Beyond Finland and down a bit.'

'You reported a body, a dead body, on this pier … '

'I did no such thing, Sergeant. How dare you suggest I'm a necrophiliac. I'll have you stripped for slander if you persist with that outrageous lie.' She plucked a backbone dangling from his sleeve and held it to his face. 'Clean up your own act, Sergeant, and let innocent people get on with their private business in peace.' She flung the bone at his feet. '*Pazûdi,*' and strode off.

The harbour master knew nothing about the matter and after pursuing a few more lines of enquiry, Cleghorn had to concede that it had been a malicious hoax. He'd file a report and request a trace on all future calls to the station.

'Cowards! Perverts!' he ranted, driving home in a chowder of putrefied smells. Approaching the junction to Dundreary Castle, he decided to reap some benefit from the wasted journey and call in to see the Colonel. He'd been meaning to have a word with him about stalking on Sundays. This was a relatively recent transgression and while not actually against the law, it contravened accepted custom and was deeply upsetting to the more devout members of the community. He would appeal to the Colonel's sense of decency.

'Bloody hell … ' The yurt and painted van came into view. A goat was tethered to the NO CAMPING sign. 'Damned hippies. Louts. I'll soon give them a piece of my mind.'

'And just what d'you think you're doing here,' he growled.

Grout and Loony looked up from their books. Rastafarian woke up from his slumber and expanded into a dervish of hair, fangs and bark. The goat stopped eating. Cleghorn stopped dead in his tracks. Dogs terrified him. LICENSED TO KILL was what he craved. BEWARE OF THE DOG was a bluff. Grout called out and Rastafarian dropped to the ground, a bathmat with panther's eyes.

'At the moment, ah'm readin. An ma friend, he's readin tae.'

'Don't you come smart with me, son. If you're so keen on reading, how come you can't read that sign?'

'We kin read it fine.'

'Nae sure aboot the German,' added Loony, 'but the French's aw wrang. Dayfonce de camper. That's whit it should be.'

'Right. Give me your names.'

'Grout.'

'Grout?'

'Grout.'

'That's not a real name. Give me your real names, full names.'

'Grout's aw ah hiv. Deed poll. Suit yersel. Tak it or leave it.'

Grudgingly, he recorded 'Grout'.

'You?'

'Loony.'

'Loony?' He took a deep breath and wrote 'Loony'. 'Addresses?'

'Here.'

'Ye like fish?'

Cleghorn failed to comprehend Loony's question until he saw their concertina-ed faces. 'Emergency. Have to get in and get our hands dirty in this job.' As happened so often, he felt his authority slipping away.

'Occupations?' He paused for effect and resharpened his voice. 'What do you do to justify your places on this planet?'

'Ah tread carefully an tak sma breaths. How aboot yersel?'

'Any more of your lip and I'll book you for insolence, as well as loitering.'

He felt a tug at his ankle and looked down to see a goat's head clamped to his trousers. Angrily he kicked at the animal, heard the sound of shearing cloth as he stormed off. Revving the car into an exaggerated display he hurtled past the camp, where the goat was busily masticating a sizeable portion of trouser leg, and entered the gates of Dundreary.

'Fuckin Beath-ite. Smell em a mile aff.'

Grout and Loony waited for the sounds, imagined the wave that would rise from the flooded pothole, the jolt which would split the suspension asunder. *Schlasssssh, Hraah-ruck.*

Visibly shaken, festering in fish, one leg showing through tattered trousers, Cleghorn hammered on the castle door. When no-one came, he kicked it and wished he hadn't as he was forced to hop about to disperse the pain searing up from his toecap. 'Damn these bloody siege-proof dungeons,' he cursed, unaware that the door had opened slightly.

Dalrymple looked out through a two-inch gap as if expecting a hostile army.

Cleghorn pulled himself to attention. 'I'd like to see the Colonel.'

Dalrymple said nothing. His eyes ran down and then up this extraordinary apparition.

'Well on with it, man. Haven't all day.'

'AND WOULD YOU BE HAVING AN APPOINTMENT?' The policeman's state took him so much by surprise that Dalrymple subconsciously reverted to habit before realising what he'd done.

'Appointment. I'm an Officer of the Law. I don't need appointments.'

'WELL, YOU CAN'T BE SEEING HIM FOR ALL THAT. HE'S DEAD.'

'Dead?' Cleghorn's eyes slowly brightened. 'Dead! Well, well. I'd better see his son then.'

Dalrymple closed the door. When it next opened, Hamish stood there.

'Ah, good afternoon, Mr MacFie. So sorry to trouble you. I've just heard the sad news about your father's departure.'

Hamish took a moment as he absorbed the true scale of Cleghorn's state. Dalrymple's warning hadn't remotely prepared him for such a mess. 'His death, you mean. You make it sound like he's just caught the *Flucker*.'

'Quite so, quite so. His death.' The word eased off Cleghorn's tongue with disquieting relish. 'I just happened to be passing,' he indicated his disrepair as if divulging a confidence, 'been involved in a few unpleasant incidents, but all in the nature of the business. I was wondering if you might be able to assist me with a particular line of enquiry I'm pursuing at the current moment in time, sir?'

'I'll try.'

'Very good of you, sir. Won't take long. Now, your father – I mean, your *late* father – hasn't by any chance been on Grimport pier during the last, say, six hours?'

'He died three days ago. Saturday night.'

'I see. Of course, he couldn't have gone there of his own accord then but … it's possible … I mean … no-one happened to take him up there maybe for sentimental reasons and leave him lying about for a while, eh?'

'Sergeant. My father died on Saturday and his body's been here ever since. I've been sorting out his funeral which, correct me if I'm wrong, is the usual practice, rather than littering stiffs around the country on sightseeing tours. What's all this about?'

'Oh nothing, nothing.' Cleghorn stroked his chin. 'While I'm here … ' he sucked in his cheeks as he conjured up an acceptable weighting of words. Clearly his choice of 'departure' hadn't gone down well. 'I don't suppose there were any, what you might call, suspicious circumstances concerning your father's death?'

'Suspicious circumstances?' Hamish repeated blankly.

'Quite so,' continued the sergeant. 'No knife in the back, so to speak.'

'Definitely not.'

'No unusual shot wounds?'

'No, Sergeant. He died peacefully *and naturally.*'

'*Digitalis?*'

'I beg your pardon.'

'*Digitalis.* Very hard to spot. Foxglove in common parlance, sir. You obviously haven't been following the Gypsy Murders case in New York. Easy to acquire, easy to administer … '

The door slammed in his face.

Funny family, he thought as he returned to his car. Touchy. All to do with in-breeding, no doubt. Of course he'd have to attend the funeral. Protocol.

Grout and Loony watched him drive away, listing to one side.

'Damn hoax call,' he lamented when he got home.

'Really!' exclaimed Angela, looking up from her watersports catalogue. 'What *is* this island coming to?' She returned to the pictures. 'Darling. If you're looking for a little surprise for my birthday, I've marked one on page forty-six and written my measurements alongside.'

Involuntarily, a gorgeous shiver fluttered down her spine.

* * *

Angela rode her eighteen-speed mountain bike out of town, auburn hair flowing. She passed the Fundamentalist Church and adjoining manse, and a monotony of council houses whose minimalist architecture was contrasted by a sprawl of fussy suburban kithouses. The last was occupied by the new priest.

'Afternoon, Father.'

Father Benedict looked round from a row of underwear he was hanging on the line, confused as to where the voice was coming from. He blushed when he spotted Angela.

'Afternoon Mrs ... um ... '

'Cleghorn,' she yelled.

Y-fronts, she thought.

A few golfers were battling the irregularities of Flabbay's nine holes as she cruised by in high gear and spirits. She noticed a foursome in wellies poking dejectedly into flooding on the eighth until one plunged a hand down and let out a jubilant shout. Just off the fourth Archie Oliphant, the Mad Professor, was niblicking among the whins with a prototype iron. She was in the open moorland when she heard a corncrake somewhere to her left utter a sound like amplified indigestion, and spotted in fairly quick succession a Cheviot, Suffolk-Soay cross and a dozen or so Black Faces. A long uphill made her pant, then she reached a crest and free-wheeled round the disused quarry where the Mad Professor had his house and laboratory. When the road levelled she braked, dismounted and hid her bike in some bushes where a path led down to the sea.

Relaxing in a clump of heather she panned her binoculars across Mickle Flabbay until the door of the lighthouse filled the lenses. She raised them until, at the top of the column that she imagined veined and throbbing, through criss-crossed panes, he appeared. His hands moved slowly up and down as if playing, *dolce* and *appassionato*, a piano.

Good, she breathed. Lawrence Brodie was at his laptop.

Arunk returned to the cave earlier than expected. All day during the hunt he'd been dreaming of the beautiful Bohair. So much had his thoughts dwelled on her he'd scarcely been in control of his spear.

'Good one,' Lawrence chuckled. 'Nice double-entendre.'

Fortunately Moak had noticed his predicament and intervened, saving the day, the hunt and his reputation. They'd all eat tonight.

'Don't worry,' Moak had said cheerfully, slapping him on the back. 'Your ardour will soon subside. Mark my words, my friend, love is just like ichthyosaur jaws. Once closed, you're trapped. Bohair will prove no different. A merycopotamus nag.'

Arunk smarted at these words. He knew Bohair was different. There was nothing merycopotamus about her. She loved him and he loved her. Together their love would grow and know no bounds, soar high on the wings of an archaeopteryx.

He'd been planning their evening together. First he thought they'd have diplodocus kebabs with spinach, then he'd give her the sabre-tooth earrings he'd carved, and then, he'd carry her off to the gorgosaur pelts that had cost him so dearly in barter, and they'd make love.

But.

Can you say 'But' on its own like that, he wondered?

But.

As Arunk approached their home, a semi-detached, 3 [lfl] The Crags, he noticed strange footprints. Readjusting his spear which was proving awkward again, he knelt to examine them. They were two hours old. Foreign feet. Left little toe missing. Bad posture. Over-weight. Possibly athlete's foot. A bad omen. Strangers always meant trouble.

When he entered the cave and called her name, no reply came. Bohair was gone. The neighbours who occupied the adjoining tunnel (3 [lfr]) were out. Therefore, there had been no witnesses.

Mournfully he slumped on the gorgosaurs and released an anguished wail. Bohair adored their home. She never wandered. She must have been kidnapped. Sorrow tore at his heart.

Tomorrow, he resolved, he'd begin the search for her. He'd leave no stone of Hibernia unturned. And as his plan took shape, gradually he pulled himself together. Life had to go on.

Shit! he thought, times were so tough in the late Pleistocene-early Palaeolithic. Yet again it would be diplodocus on his own tonight.

Lawrence paused and nodded. It was shaping up OK. But two things, quite unconnected, were troubling him. Automation and Neanderthal sex. He'd been Mickle Flabbay lighthousekeeper for six months and loved the place. Simple cleaning duties and general maintenance in the morning, and the rest of the time off to write. He'd installed a desk in the dome and made it his daytime office. The views up and down the Sound of Pluck were breathtaking. And he'd worked in some of the great beauty spots – Flannan, Ailsa, Treshnish and awesome Skerryvore – yet none could compare with Mickle Flabbay. On a clear day he could see forty miles beyond Dundreary Castle to Eaval, the highest mountain of North Uist, and in the opposite direction, to Ardnamurchan. But the Northern Lighthouse Board had warned him that it was only a matter of time before Mickle Flabbay would be automated. One year, two years at the most. The Board reviewed his contract annually. At forty-eight, he'd be on the rocks. Unemployed. Unemployable. Wrecked. Which was where the bestseller came in. Arunk and Bohair and their clan were going to make him rich! Rich enough to buy the redundant cottage when automation came.

Neanderthal sex was a more pressing problem. How would Pithecanthropus man and the Neanderthals have *done it*? What would their range have been? What degree of finesse? How strong their libido? Did they observe taboos? Circumcise? Fake orgasms? Have headaches? Toys? What about sexuality?

Naturally fiction was fiction but he didn't want to destroy reader credibility by introducing *soixante-neuf* if this wasn't a realistic possibility, neither did he want to become boring by playing safe with every Neanderthal rooting in the dinosaur position. As if this plethora of uncertainties wasn't enough, it was now so long since he himself had actually *done it* that he could no longer visualise the sensations or describe the subtleties from Arunk's point of view, far less imagine how Bohair might find the experience.

The problem was assuming greater urgency because he couldn't put off the act indefinitely. It had been a masterstroke to have Bohair misappropriated on what was, in effect, her wedding night, just when Arunk was all worked up and ready to go, but Bohair couldn't keep on going AWOL every time a randy Arunk appeared. Sooner or later they'd have to have it off. The great saga spanning 500,000 years would be a non-starter if the Brodies died out in the early Palaeolithic.

A possible solution had occurred to him a fortnight earlier while reading an old copy of *Knave*.

Beaver Fever Aids by Lovecare Ltd. TOP QUALITY SEX DOLLS now featuring a new real feel vibratory pleasure pussy. Life-sized. Durable. Special love lubricant included. Buy one and receive a Magi-sex stud sleeve set FREE … and perform like a stud! All orders discretely wrapped.

The accompanying photographs were small and of poor quality. Sharon Party Doll looked a bargain at £14.95 but he doubted that her seams would last, and Susi, at £34.95, while presumably more robust, had ridiculous tufts of hair. If he was going to do this at all it was only worth doing properly. He opted for Vibrating Greta, the most expensive, though he could only imagine what hidden extras she must have at £99.95. *Allow ten days for delivery.* Today was the fourteenth.

Lawrence picked up his binoculars and swung round to see if Calum the Post had been. His mail was delivered to a box on the jetty opposite. The box was large enough to hold parcels and groceries, and a red flag was raised when it contained something to be collected. He examined the state of the tide; at low tide the sand between Muckle and Mickle Flabbay dried to form a narrow spit four hundred yards long.

It was just right. His twice daily miracle, the parting of the Sound of Pluck. He'd be spared the guddle of launching and rowing the Lighthouse Board's rubber dingy.

His binoculars located the box and to his disappointment he could see the flag was down. A movement caught his eye and he was astonished to make out a figure lying in the heather with binoculars, *watching him*. Like a clawed lizard, panic scuttled across his chest. It desisted the moment he realised the figure was a woman. Further scrutiny revealed her identity.

'Mrs Cleghorn! Well, well.'

She had now changed her posture and appeared engrossed in an oyster-catcher strutting along the waterline. He glanced up in case there

happened to be an albatross or some errant species on his roof, but there wasn't.

His watch pipped four. Perhaps it was a little early yet for Calum. He'd take a stroll to the box. He could use some fresh air. He pressed 'Save' and 'Close', and scribbled a note in his IDEAS pad. *Like a clawed lizard, panic scuttled across his chest.* Yes, he could use that. With all the bounce of a lover heading for the tryst, he skipped down one hundred and sixty-four steps, grabbed his Goretex and was out the door.

He soon realised it was a mistake to have assumed Mrs Cleghorn would have headed off to the eider colony. She was intensely observing some clusters of feathers as he approached, having delayed his arrival for as long as possible.

'Oh hallo! Such squabblesome birds, sparrows!' Angela extended her hand. 'Angela.'

'Lawrence.'

'Cleghorn.'

'Brodie.'

They smiled and fell silent.

'That was all a bit back to front, wasn't it?' She gave a little laugh.

'I came to collect my mail.'

'Oh, how interesting!' The words were out before it struck her that it wasn't really interesting at all. 'I hear you're a writer.'

Lawrence flushed, 'Well, Keeper of the Light officially, but a Writer of the Heart.'

'Of the Heart. That's so poetic. I adore romance. Mills and Boon. I must have devoured them all. So you … write romance?'

'Not exactly romance, but of course romance comes into it. I'm currently working on what you might call a historical thriller.'

'History fascinates me too. The Crusades, King Arthur. Medieval, mainly.'

'I … ' He noticed what gorgeous eyes she had. Orange-brown, like seaweed. Auburn hair. And a curious gesture of tossing a hand as she spoke. He filed them in his memory.

Bohair's eyes sparkled like sunlight dancing on bladderwort. Her hair was a shield of bronze … Damn, he realised, too early for bronze … *of radiant brown, the likes of which would remain a secret of the gods for countless millennia …*

'You were saying … '

'Oh yes. My book goes back a little further. It's a great saga of the Brodie family from the days of primitive man to the present, spanning 500,000 years. Naturally I'm only selecting a few Brodies from each age.'

'Gosh!' Her enthusiasm faded. 'It sounds terribly ambitious.' Angela was conscious that she sounded like a schoolgirl. 'How many novels have you written?'

'Five.'

'Five!' Adoration made Angela melt. She felt her legs wobble and thought she might have to fling her arms round Lawrence to avoid complete collapse. Unfortunately the sensation passed and her strength returned. 'Five!' she repeated, slightly higher and with more vigour.

This made Lawrence uncomfortable. 'They haven't actually been published yet, but, well, I'm hopeful.'

'I'm sure it's only a matter of time. Why, it must be so exciting with all those launch parties coming up.'

'Yes, the thought is really quite stimulating … '

'STIMULATING,' Angela interrupted, excitement getting the better of her, 'I'LL SAY … ' and she fainted, grabbing Lawrence's Fair Isle jumper as she slithered down him.

Lawrence was pulled off balance and collapsed under her, fortuitously breaking her fall but, less fortuitously, bruising his knee. As he crawled free and bent over her, checking her air passages were free and she was still breathing, he heard a cough.

'Don't mean to interrupt, sir, but here's your mail. Be happy to get rid of this one.' Calum clasped a large parcel to his chest.

'She's fainted.'

'Well, some it affects that way but none of my business, I'm sure. Now I'm needing a signature for this one … '

'Calum, she's not well. Help me make her comfortable.'

'*A shìorraidh!*'

He dropped the parcel and rushed over to Lawrence. As they straightened Angela's body and eased her onto some grass, she opened her eyes. Lawrence was supporting her head and looking into her face. Her gaze seemed unnaturally steady. Her eyes widened until the whites were showing all around. Then she screamed.

Aware that the cause of her distress had to be lurking behind them, Lawrence and Calum cautiously turned round. A woman's hand was

coming out of the parcel, and it was reaching further and further out as the seconds crept on.

'*Murt! Murt mhòr!*'

The journey from Bognor Regis had been extremely hard on Vibrating Greta. She'd been shaken, squeezed and crushed the whole way. The worst ordeal had been during the change-over from the 1845 Virgin Express to the 2300 GNER Edinburgh Sleeper when she'd been dumped on the edge of a Kings Cross puddle for forty minutes. One corner of her box had been reduced to mulch and when she was rudely thrown ten feet to a butter-fingered guard, the corner came off altogether. Rattling throughout the remainder of the journey had forced a label through the hole. Calum the Post had refrained from reading it – he was as strict as a Sabbatarian about prying into private mail – though the words were clear enough.

SEXUAL SENSATIONS! CONGRATULATIONS ON YOUR PURCHASE WHICH WE KNOW WILL GIVE YOU HOURS OF PLEASURE! VIBRATING GRETA HAS SUCCULENT BREASTS, SKIN LIKE VELVET AND SILKY HAIR! SHE CRAVES ONLY YOU! SHE'S FULL OF SURPRISES AND THE FIRST IS THAT SHE'S SELF-INFLATING! **HOT UP YOUR ROD AND GET YOUR ROCKS OFF!**

It was only later that Lawrence realised how unfortunate (indeed, ironical) the wording turned out to be. It was the rocks that had got Greta off. Calum's final act of disrespect, dropping her onto a lump of Torridonian sandstone, was what had detonated her gas canister well ahead of Lawrence's rod being hot. As Lawrence and Calum watched – Angela had fainted again – there was a hiss like a firework rocket taking off, and Vibrating Greta's arm shot out the hole to full extension.

Lawrence leapt to his feet before any further cardboard fatigue could occur and grabbed the parcel, bending the arm down one side and tucking it out of sight as he gripped the parcel against his chest.

'I'll run back and phone for a doctor. You stay with her.'

He began to run towards the lighthouse.

'*Hoigh*! Mister Brodie.'

Lawrence turned to see Calum holding up something.

'A signature, if you'd be kind enough.'

Lawrence turned and walked meekly back.

'S-Survival suit,' he stammered.

'With hands?'

'Built in gloves.'

Calum held out the pad and a biro. Lawrence looked at them. He felt the parcel expand and bulge. Nothing would induce him to let go of it. His desperation mounted. Silently he cursed not having gone for the Sharon Party Doll whose sides would have blown by now.

'Don't look like gloves to me. More like hands. Ladies' hands at that.'

'THEY'RE NOT LADIES' HANDS,' Lawrence snapped. He regained control. 'They're gloves. Slender gloves. Most likely too small. I'll probably have to return the suit. Just put the pad on the parcel and the biro in my mouth and I'll scratch a signature.' Lawrence felt his arms weakening against the strain.

Calum pulled a look of disgust, wiped the biro's stem on his jacket and did as instructed.

'*Ghia*! Hairy armpits too.'

Greta's head was now peeping out. Lawrence threw down the pad and spat out the pen. 'Doctor,' he uttered, turning and fleeing as another *rip* and *hiss* rent the air and Greta's other arm unfurled with a rollicking *THWOK*. Halfway along the spit the parcel disintegrated completely and Greta exploded into full magnificence, legs and arms akimbo.

Calum stood and watched. 'Queer bloke. Suppose it must be lonely out there.'

Angela stirred. 'Rubber!' she exclaimed.

'Beg your pardon, Mrs Cleghorn?'

'Rather, I said. Rather lonely.'

'I'll give you a lift back.'

'No, it's all right. I've got my bike. I was out cycling and stopped to admire the view. Then I came over a bit dizzy. I'm fine now thanks, Calum.'

Miss Grinella Oliphant pulled out six stops, nudged her occasional friend and regular Scrabble opponent, Miss Dilly MacDonald, as a sign to crank up the bellows, and plunged her hands into the keyboard. An asthmatic wheeze sent puffs of dust from the pipes, and reeds wobbled into confidence as Bach's *Toccata & Fugue in D Minor* began to dominate the elements. Cyril Braithwaite, the choirboy, looking positively cherubic (Dilly thought) in his red and white robes, was struggling to light the tallest candles with a broken taper. Father Benedict was having difficulty in getting the incense to ignite but it eventually took and was soon going splendidly. He handed the censer to Cyril to swing up and down the aisle while the pews were filling.

'What a hat,' tittered Dilly, 'have you ever seen the like! At her husband's funeral too. Opprobrious, I'd call it. Like a toadstool. Ascot-ish, right enough.'

Miss Oliphant adjusted her mirror to open up the view. She understood exactly what Dilly meant. 'Profoundly unmeritorious,' she agreed.

The two women constantly tried to outwit the other with words, even off the Scrabble board.

She examined Fran MacFie's lid more closely. A white fungus dotted on a sweep of crimson. Dilly was quite right. *Amanita muscaria.* 'Fly Agaric,' she whispered, and knew Dilly had understood because she felt the air supply slacken and the keys soften.

'Never seen Young MacFie looking so smart before. Very dapper. He suits the kilt.' This was Miss Oliphant again.

'By Jove, the Bees Knees. Such a sartorial nightmare usually.'

'Nidicolous' – [*adj (of young birds) staying long in the nest*] – 'I've always thought. It's a problem with young aristocracy. Does them no good.'

'Yes, but nidifugous' – [*adj (of young birds) leaving the nest soon after hatching*] – youth can experience problems too, aristocracy or not.'

'Well, whatever the cause, he's a good-looking nincompoop.'

'What on earth's that smell? It's utterly nidorous' – [*a strong smell or fume, esp of animal substances cooking or burning*] – 'Must be some new brand of incense. Italian, no doubt. Just like their sauces.'

'I rather like it.' Miss Oliphant was feeling exceptionally jolly.

'Slow down, Grinella. It's not meant to be played that fast.'

'Oh go sclaff a goose, Dilly.'

Dilly tittered. Grinella had her there. She'd have to look that one up. [*sclaff: to strike with a light slap.*]

They watched the chapel fill with mourners. Hamish and Fran sat on their own in the first row. Angus and Effie Dalrymple were in the second. Beside them, and in the rows behind, were a host of strangers, presumably fragments of the MacFie family, some wearing the black and white sett, others in the gaudier red and yellow. It suddenly occurred to Grinella that perhaps Fran's hat, given her otherwise black appearance, was a token gesture to MacFie colours, and she felt a tinge of guilt at having judged her so hastily. It passed in a moment and she let rip a snorter of *prestissimo acciaccatura* that ran down two feet of keyboard and surprised even herself.

Really, she thought, I've never played so well, and unaware that every eye was on her, she broke into an *accelerando* version of *The Entertainer*, one of her favourites, embellishing it with extra *tremolo*. Dilly, forced into the new pace, had broken sweat and was beginning to fear for her heart. Fortunately, Grinella, too, was suffering for her exertions and she lapsed *rallentando* into *The Bridal March* as a stopgap.

'Is that … Good God … ' Dilly's heart fluttered again, this time at the sight of the man who had just entered. She stopped pumping. Grinella tried to follow her friend's gaze through the twisted logic of her mirror and then she spotted him. Her fingers became lumps of lead as the organ's voice withered *diminuendo* on her last chord. She turned round to confirm the reflection.

She turned back and she and Dilly exchanged yawning goldfish smirks and resumed their tasks.

'Can you believe it! Lord MacArthur of Flashcairn! Crossing a Papist doormat.'

'*Scandalum magnatum*. It's like … like … ' she was struggling for a cataclysmic simile …

'The Pope going to Mecca!' chimed Grinella, insensitively loudly.

' ... Jesus caught insider-trading on the Stock Exchange!'

In the history of the Fundamentalist Church, never had one of its members ever entered a Catholic premises, let alone participated in one of its ceremonies. And here, before everyone's eyes was not just any old Fundamentalist but Lord MacArthur of Flashcairn, the Church's highest-ranking office-bearer, its incumbent Moderator.

'There'll be a merry rumpus about this.'

'Merry rumpus! What a simply luscious oxymoron, Dilly.'

Grinella absentmindedly played *God Save the Queen* and was startled to see everyone stand. She caught sight of the doctor, and Captain MacQuarrie, senior skipper of the *Flucker*, and then, just as the room was disappearing in a swirl of blue, two scruffy strangers at the back. Dog food, she recalled. They'd been in her shop and bought dog food. Her fingers had recovered and she took it upon herself to get things going with the first hymn, jazzing up Augustus Montague Toplady's classic *Rock of Ages* into an *animatissimo* funk which, if he hadn't intended it, he jolly well should have.

Whoooopee, she called to Dilly.

Jeeeoooooch, Dilly replied.

Grinella was about to try a slow, sultry version of *In the Summertime* when the mirror threw up Father Benedict's image gesticulating for silence.

'Brothers and Sisters,' he began, walking from the altar towards the assembly of mourners.

Halfway down the church, Angela couldn't take her eyes off him. All that purple. She wondered what colour his underwear was. The black ones, she hoped. An Emperor in black Y-fronts. What a transformation! One moment hanging out his washing like everyone else, the next all togged up, saving souls and launching them into eternity. Such a responsibility on his young shoulders. He looked just a boy. But that hat really did things for him! There was no doubt. Purple was his colour.

Father Benedict was overcome by a coughing fit. 'Cyril, put that infernal thing out,' he spluttered, and the next moment a violent clanking issued from the vestry where, apparently, Cyril was trying to extinguish the censer by knocking it against a pillar. Every now and then he shrieked with laughter. A flutter of giggles travelled along the pews. Revitalised by the activity, more smoke than ever was flooding into the room.

'Sisters and Friends,' he tried again, but tripped on an edge of carpet and fell headlong into the obscurity. For a full minute he remained hidden from view but a whooping laugh traced his crawl to the base of the lectern. He appeared, hands first, hauling himself up the stem. For safety's sake, he decided to entwine himself round this for the rest of the ceremony.

'Sinners and Fiends, we're gathered here today to bury ... to bury ... someone whose name temporarily eludes me,' he continued bravely, and remarkably coherently, 'and God knows who he is. *But* God knows who he is, I mean.'

Gradually, bits of his prepared address were coming back to him. 'Though he strayed from the path of his Faith on several occasions ... ' He faltered, knowing he hadn't quite got that right. ' ... Though much of his life was spent searching for the path of his Faith ... '

'QUITE AGREE,' interrupted Dalrymple, at a volume only the deaf could fail to appreciate, 'HOPELESS SENSE OF DIRECTION. NEVER KNEW WHERE HE WAS.'

' ... he remained a true friend and benefactor of this church, and was far from being a heretic ... '

'EROTIC! I'LL SAY HE WAS. BLOODY SEX MANIAC.'

Father Benedict was feeling high enough to be God. If he half-closed his eyes and stared at a candle, the chapel tilted to such a degree he thought they might all end up in a heap in the vestry. He hadn't the faintest idea what SEX had to do with anything but it was very pleasant to have someone else do some talking. What would God do under the circumstances, he wondered? He'd let the people be God, for a while.

'Now would anyone like to add a few kind words about the late whoever he was before we get to the digging part?'

Sniggers shivered through the ranks. Bodies rustled in the discomfort of suppressed hilarity. Eyes sunk, heads bowed, they suffered their paroxysms in silence. Someone passed wind, but no one spoke.

'Come, come.' Father Benedict was suddenly extremely lucid. What in the Good Lord's name was happening? This was a funeral. 'You are Colonel MacFie's kith ... '

'ALWAYS AT IT. SURPRISED HIS LIPS NEVER WORE OUT.'

' ... and kin, his friends ... ' he felt himself losing it again.

' ... and relativities, his tenants and serfs ... what about you in the funny hat, weren't you the old so-and-so's wife, or at least, one of them?'

Fran gave a coy wave. When she realised more was expected of her she leapt to her feet and flung her toadstool in the air.

'*Whoooopee,*' she shrieked.

'*Whoooopee,*' echoed Grinella and the organ erupted into *For She's A Jolly Good Fellow* for several bars until the organ ran out of breath as the pumper was asleep.

'I insist someone says a good word for the diseased before I go on.'

'A GOOD WORD ... GOOD GOD! THAT'S A TALL ORDER. HA!' He slapped his hymn book on the shelf 'HA-HA-HA-HA-HA-HA-HA-AAAA ... '

'Thank you, Mr Dullpimple. We'd be much obliged.'

Through the haze Angus saw a vision of a leering Colonel. For days he'd been nursing his bitterness at the old goat. And now he was being forced to make public homage to his tormentor. It was as much as he could bear. He saw no way out, got to his feet and shuffled up the aisle.

He removed his deerstalker and for a reason that no one could fathom, set fire to it on the altar. He watched it flare up and collapse into a shrunken black effigy of itself.

My life, he thought.

Then he turned and shuffled on the spot, gazing at his feet with his hands sunk deep in his plus-fours. A minute passed. He raised his head, closed his eyes and took a deep breath.

'HIS BROTHER ... ' he swallowed, ' ... WIS WURSE!'

'To the sandpit,' announced Father Benedict, disentangling himself from the lectern and staggering down the aisle to the door where he anchored himself to the handle and attempted to stay upright while dispensing bonhomie.

Lord MacArthur of Flashcairn approached Father Benedict grinning. 'Most intitilating service. Rapsy would have been proud of you.'

'Never realised what a pervert he was,' remarked Sergeant Cleghorn, clinging to the priests cassock. 'Should have arrested the bugger years ago. Menace to society. Good work, son.'

'Marvellous funeral,' exclaimed Angela, 'quite mesmerising. If you're always this good, I could come more often.' She gave her most enchanting smile and watched his expression change as she deftly slid a hand through the priest's cassock and gave his penis a playful squeeze.

'Nice,' said Grout.

'Ace,' added Loony.

* * *

Only a handful of the assembly made it to the family mausoleum, situated half-a-mile away, overlooking the sea, and the late Colonel R A P MacFie was not among them.

Lord MacArthur had a plane to catch and the Cleghorns had to collect the police car from repairs at the garage. Miss MacDonald and Miss Oliphant respectively pumped and played for several more hours. Fran made an unexpected departure in pursuit of her hat which the wind wheeled towards Loch Papil, and many seemed to be lost in fertility rites around the base of the Roman monopede.

Colonel MacFie, in his coffin, had been placed on a cart pulled by his favourite garron, Josephine, a sack-coloured mare with a douce nature and an unnatural appetite for sugarbeet. The idea of using Josephine had been proposed by Mr Gerund, of Hamilton, Gerund, Nayers & Filigree, who recalled his late client having been very taken with an account of Sir Walter Scott's funeral in which the author's favourite horse was used to touching effect. Fran liked the idea and Hamish realised that a hearse would never make it through the bogs and the estate tractor was temporarily defunct. Josephine was clearly alarmed by the sight of so many skew-whiff humans and in mounting panic, she bolted.

It proved a long wait for the dedicated few who made it to the deceased's chosen resting place.

'Some good scramblin there, eh Loon?' Grout was looking over the balcony of the MacFie necropolis which was built on the edge of a cliff. He dropped a stone and watched its splash two hundred feet below.

'Looks crumbly tae me. Widnae touch it masel.'

Hamish overheard them and felt woozy. Just listening to the talk of heights and cliffs and falls was enough to spin his head. So many strange faces had converged on Dundreary Castle for the funeral that it had taken him a while to realise that this pair were the ones he'd seen through the window the night his father died. They'd been on the ledge looking in. *On the ledge.* The words made him giddy.

Effie misread his wistfulness. 'Your father'll be here soon,' the mother in her said reassuringly. 'He was always late.'

Father Benedict was having difficulty in keeping his cassock from flying up around his head, and was shivering with cold.

'I think we'll just have to go on.' He felt as if he was somewhere between heaven and the arctic.

'Dear Lord, please accept this premature ceremony of the interment of the temporarily absent and accept the mortal remains, whenever we find them, of the late Colonel ... '

That night the predicted Force nine from Iceland, Faeroes and Rockall arrived. In the yurt, only Gertrude the goat slept well. In the castle, draughts whined, doors banged, slates rattled and another twenty-eight feet of roan came down to earth. Angus suffered nightmares for the first time since he'd fallen asleep while whitening spats during the assault on Port Said. In his dreams the previous day's reality was undone with horrible consequences. Instead of finding Josephine in the sugarbeet store, retrieving the Colonel from the West Wing rhododendrons and burying him in his allocated spot, the Colonel had sprung out from his box and forced Angus to take his place. Trapped in the darkness as *Rock of Ages* sounded through the cart's rumbling, he was haunted by that last glimpse of the Colonel's spiked moustache and those horrible *kissing* lips. Then the motion stopped, the patter of soil hit the coffin, and he knew he was being buried alive in the hole dug by his own hands ... The sound of shattering roan woke him.

The following afternoon it was discovered that there had been a landslip. Where the necropolis had stood for almost two hundred years was a ragged corrie in the cliffs. Far below, the Atlantic swell nibbled at a new reef where a couple of shags were drying their wings.

Grout and Loony drove to the village and parked their van just out of sight of the police station. Carrying a chain they'd found on the beach, they approached the building and checked the windows. The soles of two black, size eleven, Northern Constabulary shoes were visible on Sergeant Cleghorn's desk. Assuming Muckle Flabbay's police force was attached to them, they walked up the drive to where a fluorescent-flashed Uno was parked conveniently close to a fence. Grout tied a round-turn-and-two-half-hitches to the nearest strainer, while Loony went for a bowline round the axle. The excess chain, a generous twenty feet to allow momentum to build up, they slaked under the car and covered with grass.

'Mak the bastard hamesick fer Beath, eh?'

Within four minutes they were back in their van heading for Miss Oliphant's Emporium, unaware that Angela had been watching from the house opposite.

Public Notices, read a glass-fronted board at the entrance to the Emporium.

Thursday 8 October, 7.30pm, at Muckle Flabbay Community Hall
'The Corncrake (*Crex Crex*), Our Charming Resident – Its Life-cycle and Importance'. An illustrated talk by Amulree Shaw of Scottish Natural Heritage. Tea and Home Baking. All Welcome. Entry 50p.

Kittens – Free to a good home. Also geriatric budgerigar, and kitchen table £10. No time-wasters. Tel Pluckton 386.

Diving Lessons by qualified BSAC instructor. £15 per hour inc hire of tank and demand valve. Own wet/drysuits required. Tel Lawrence Brodie, Flabbay 202.

To be, or not to be? Actors wanted. Grimport Amateur Dramatic Society, last year's runners-up in the Inner Minch Thespian Oscars, urgently seeking Peter for this year's pantomime, Peter Pan & The Seven Dwarfs. Dwarfs also wanted (any size). Tel Grimport 447.

'There y'are, Grout. Made tae measure fer ye. Dopey, mebbe. Or Baldie. Ah kin jist picture ye haudin up ane o they Inner Minch Oscars.'

'Aw dry up. Ye kin play Grumpy wi'oot oany actin. Naw, but ah dae fancy this next ane.'

> **Handel's Messiah:** Choir practices begin this Wednesday, 7 October, at 7pm in the Church of Scotland, Flabbay, to rehearse for the Christmas Eve concert. Non-denominational! All Welcome. We're always short of bases and tenors. Don't be shy!

'Singin! Ah didnae ken ye hid a voice?'

'Ah'm nae fuckin Pavaroti like, but ah kin haud a note an ah've a rare ear fer it. Aye, think ah'll daunder up an tak a look see.'

They entered the shop.

26 Across: Telling-off for wearing casual clothes? (8,4)

Miss Oliphant stood behind her counter in a flour-white apron, a biro prodding her lips as she contemplated twenty-six Across. Until all the squares were filled customers were always unwelcome intrusions.

'No dogs. It states it perfectly clearly on the door.'

Miss Oliphant viewed the tousled clod of curls with as much disgust as she did its owners. It looked as rabid as they did. The small one with his shaven head and Afghan woollen hat, his tie-dye T-shirt and leather jacket. The other in a blue denim uniform like a jailbird's, blond shoulder-length-hair like a girl's, and that ridiculous earring of pink and blue feathers. Honestly! Dangle him over a boat and you could catch mackerel. She laughed silently at her own joke, neatly inserted *DRESSING DOWN,* and turned serious again. Savage Frown.

'No dogs, unless you're registered blind.'

Grout adapted his own exterior. Oscar Charm. 'Naturally ma dug widnae wish tae cause oany offence an he'd be delighted tae wait ootside. But he widnae like tae be judged unner any misunnerstandin that he's jist oany auld dug, oany ill-mannered disobedient mongrel. An ah think ah'd be failin im as his owner an guardian if ah didnae attempt tae shaw ye his qualities, whit gie's im his distinction.'

Not used to having her authority questioned, Miss Oliphant listened dumbfounded.

'Sit.'

Rastafarian sat.

'Lie.'

Rastafarian lay down.

'Heid.'

Rastafarian lowered his head and pressed it to the ground.

Grout withdrew a Shape™ and tossed it to the dog. It bounced twice and rolled to within an inch of Rastafarian's nose. His eyes had followed the biscuit and were now transfixed on it. Somewhere within his fur he swallowed, but otherwise remained motionless.

'Here.'

Rastafarian rose, picked up the biscuit and carried it to Grout, laying it at his feet. He then looked up at his master and waited.

'OK.'

He ducked and snaffled the biscuit.

'This is his pee-ess daraz-east-ance.'

Grout held up three fingers.

Rastafarian held out one leg, his rear right, stiffly behind him and stood on three legs.

Grout folded down one finger.

Rastafarian gingerly raised his front left leg and stood balancing on the remaining two.

'Good boy.' Grout bent down and rubbed the dogs head.

'It's quite against trading regulations but he can have a blind dog's dispensation.'

Miss Oliphant then returned to her crossword. She was stuck on three Across. *Bury cat in Spain with note (6).* Bury cat … she thought back to the Colonel's funeral. If she'd known what fun it was going to be, she thought, she'd have been much nicer to him when he was alive. She cast a look around to make sure the louts weren't shoplifting. They were in the fishing section. Probably sizing up more earrings, she didn't doubt.

The bell jangled again.

ENTOMB, she wrote.

She looked up to see Miss Stewart shuffling towards her, and tried fifteen Across, while waiting for the clatter of upset tins that would preserve Miss Stewart's record of carelessness intact. Sometimes she wondered whether the argumentative old bat didn't do it on purpose so she could buy the dented tins at a discount on her next visit.

*Ice-axe – **not** a holding of breakfast cereal! (10)*. Well, breakfast cereals ought to be in her department …

'Busy today I see, Grinella.'

… *ALPENSTOCK.*

'Busy? Ha! The trouble with tourists,' declared Miss Oliphant, 'is that they need half an hour to make up their minds that they can't decide what to buy.' She leaned closer to Miss Stewart, Flabbay's eldest citizen who could still manage a surprising 2mph behind her zimmer, and dropped her voice so that everyone in the shop had to concentrate on what she said. '*Soft* in the head to boot, if you ask me. From the way they carry on you'd think it would be the end of the world if I run out of Tunnock's Caramels! Ha!'

She laughed. The sort of sound Miss Stewart imagined you'd hear, after a long wait, from a vulture espying its next meal crawling in the distance.

'And you'd think their children were being precipitated halfway through death's door if they can't get their Super Soft Pampers, or some such.'

Miss Stewart's sympathy lay with the tourists. The shopkeeper – for that's all Miss Oliphant was, aside from being Flabbay's councillor – wore her sanctimony as ostentatiously as tarts' rings. She fervently hoped the stuck-up prude would lose the impending council elections. Miss Hoighty-Toighty Oliphant gave the impression of having been *Chosen* to conduct a crusade for the moral edification of those poor city-softened tourists who were *Sent* to Muckle Flabbay Emporium. The Miss Oliphant School of Hard Knocks (and Nappy Rash). Her method was to inflict crushing disappointments on those whose list of essential consumerables did not correspond with that of her own. Her shop window was chock-a-block with the empty packagings of forbidden merchandise, mostly health aids, or 'medical mollycoddling' as she termed them. Lured by the apparent promise of Pampers, Amber Solaire, Disprin, Durex and such things, the visitor was thus set up for the humbling denial that would force abstinence and – just possibly – Damascan *Light*.

She bent herself once more towards Miss Stewart's nearest dysfunctional ear. 'And as for Durex, well, you'd think it was one of life's staples. Of course I've nothing against birth control as long as it's not used for pleasure … '

'But what else is it used for?' Miss Stewart interrupted. She had a disarming way of suddenly abandoning her pose as a listening post, mute and safe.

Miss Oliphant flushed, her eyes secretly scanning the room. 'Really, Daphne,' she whispered reproachfully, 'this is hardly the time or place to discuss such delicate matters.'

'I'VE ALWAYS WONDERED WHY YOU STOCK CONDOMS,' Miss Stewart retorted loudly.

Miss Oliphant rose to the attack. Rumour had it that Daphne Stewart had spent at least fifty years consoling herself over the loss of her fiancé at Dunkirk with an ageing series of look-alikes. 'I DON'T. And I'd prefer to be engaged in conversation with someone not only less interested in the subject, but also less familiar with it.'

Miss Stewart chortled with delight. At ninety-four she was fully immune to Miss Oliphant's barbs and she always enjoyed the banter, even though she considered Miss Oliphant, almost fifty years her junior, somewhat callow and poorly equipped in their battles. She refrained from wiping out her adversary, which she could quite easily have done with one howitzer reference to the barren sterility of virginity, and bought half a pound of sausages and some lard.

Miss Stewart jauntily zimmered through the door, though not before the corner of her shopping bag had caught the lowest row of a pyramid of baked beans.

4 Down. Dogs pee a lot! (7) That'll be right, she thought anxiously, and immediately regretted her leniency over the louts' pet.

Another door jangle. Hamish MacFie entered. He looked down at Rastafarian in surprise, bent down to pat the dog and removed two tins of beans from his tail. He glanced quizzically at Miss Oliphant.

'Blind dog,' she explained, and then stiffened as the dog's owners approached with armfuls of groceries.

'Oany Durex?' Grout enquired. 'Preferably Featherlite or Mates, coloured, ribbed an sensitol lubricated.'

Miss Oliphant braced herself against the counter. 'No.' A whisper. She turned to look for some semblance of security and the old order and, for want of better, settled on the Young MacFie.

'Good morning, Mr MacFie. Wonderful funeral.' She grimaced as a waft of patchouli oil assailed her.

'Morning, Miss Oliphant. You heard about the storm damage though?'

'Yes, terrible. But he always loved the sea, didn't he?'

'Not that much, I don't think.' He glanced at the shelf of newspapers.

The irregularities of rail and ferry timetables meant that newspapers always arrived a day late in Flabbay. He'd been awaiting these ones with some trepidation. Dundreary's phone had been jammed by reporters since his father's funeral. The headlines were worse than he'd feared.

Church Split Over Funeral, said *The Herald*.

Flashcairn Fury, said *The Press & Journal*.

Moderator 'Traitor', said *The West Highland Free Press*

MacFie, MacFoe, said *The Daily Mail*.

Stuff This Up Your Presbytery! said *The Sun*.

'My family can never just die quietly,' Hamish bemoaned.

'Lord MacArthur's appearance has certainly caused quite a kerfuffle,' Miss Oliphant replied cheerfully.

'By the way, thanks for giving the organ a dust-off.'

'Aye, it wis grand,' affirmed Grout. 'Ya kin sure belt oot a rhythm.'

Miss Oliphant reluctantly turned her attention back to the reprobates and began totalling their goods.

'Even Rastafarian wis impressed.'

'Thank you,' replied Miss Oliphant coldly. 'I suppose your dog is concert trained too.'

She took the proffered notes and returned the change.

'Poodles,' said Loony.

'I beg your pardon?'

'Four doon. Ah think ye'll find it's *POODLES*.'

Grout and Loony drove home, staying within the 30mph speed limit for the first half mile, then accelerated to 65mph as they approached the police station. Grout sounded the bullhorn to give Sergeant Cleghorn plenty of warning, while Loony leant out the window and yahooooed and Rastafarian barked.

'Ye in fer a spot o climbin, Loon?' Grout suggested when they reached their camp.

'Yea. How aboot the North Face?'

Hamish was delayed on his way back to Dundreary. A tractor was dragging a disembowelled Uno from the middle of the road where it lay grounded like a war victim among a tangle of wire and fence posts. Its plight looked all the more pitiful for its self-indulgent paintwork. A stripe waved at him. *Help!* It seemed to say.

Sergeant Cleghorn watched the proceedings and, to Hamish, he looked close to meltdown: swollen, crimson, convulsing. Hamish hoped the policeman wouldn't notice him but he did and grasshopped towards the landrover.

'THOSE BASTARDS DID THIS,' he screamed, his breath resembling smoke in the cold air.

Hamish lowered his window. 'Which bastards, Cleghorn?'

'Scuse my language, sir. Those ... those useless hippies camping at your castle. Booby-trapped my car, they did. By hell, I'll get the scum. Terrorists, that's what they are.'

Hamish pondered this while driving home. He'd never liked Cleghorn. He was a bigot ... megalomaniac ... dullard ... sadist ... The invectives flowed more quickly than passing places. ... state henchman ... a Mussolini's laundrette. Processing someone else's dirty linen. History was full of them. Self-aggrandising cowards justifying privilege through duty to the highest power. No, he did not like Cleghorn.

It followed, therefore – he was now descending the quarry hill, opening into a view of Mickle Flabbay, and was momentarily distracted by the sight of a small black boat floating with apparently no one on board, but the twistiness of the road quickly blocked the view again – it followed, therefore, that anything or anyone who upset Cleghorn was to be encouraged. But – and this was the crunch – he resented his privacy being invaded by these strangers. How was he to reconcile the opposing forces tugging him apart – the desire to implement a different system of land management based on community involvement, and the reluctance to give up the peaceful life of a laird? The Marxist in him shrieked at social conscience, while the sloth in him gilded the easy option of apathy. *Laissez-faire*! It sounded just and democratic as long as you turned a blind eye to the fact that individual foundations were never equal. So, now he had to decide. Up until his father's death he could posture the socialist because he was never in a position to follow it up with deeds. On the off-chance his father had left him the estate, he might soon be called to climb down from his fence.

Loony and Grout's goat was munching a hole in a dwarf ginko as Hamish rounded the castle and parked the landrover by the outhouses on the north side. Hearing tapping above his head, he looked up and was surprised to see the two men, joined by a rope, halfway up the tower. Grout was leading, hammering a piton into loose stonework below the Master Bedroom, while Loony manned a belay at a drainpipe outside Fran's Dressing Room. A lump of mortar landed at Hamish's feet. He felt his balance waver.

'Are you all right up there?' he enquired.

Grout looked down. Concentrating on the next pitch, he hadn't heard the landrover arrive.

'Aye, thanks. See yon bag doon there. Ah'm short o a few pegs. Ye kin pass em through this windie.'

Marxist or Colonel … tolerance, indignation … the dilemma held Hamish rooted to the spot for a moment. Marx won. The thought of turning into his father was the most painful image of degeneration. He gathered the pegs, went inside and strode up the stairs.

'Here.' He held them out of the Master Bedroom window, his eyes clenched shut.

'Doon a bit. Ah cannae reach.'

'I … I don't like heights.' He felt a hand remove the pegs.

'Ta.'

'I'm … I'm Hamish.'

51

'Grout.'

'If you make it to the top window, that's the attic. You're welcome to drop in for tea.'

'Ah hope we dinnae drop oanywhere.'

They arrived through the sash and case twenty minutes later. First Grout, then Loony, separated by fifteen metres of rope. Hardware clanked around their waists. Grout did the introductions.

'Hamish, this is ma pal, Loon.'

'Pleased to meet you.'

'That's a risky assumption,' he grinned, then took in the smell of mildew, petrified leather and damp paper. 'Fucksakes, kid dae wi a good airin, this place. Ye dinnae gae in fer chuckin things oot, ah see.' His eyes took in cobwebs dangling from cobwebs, boxes of paper lying about like anti-tank defences, green piles of petrified leather, taxidermy savaged by mice, military trunks, a camp-bed which had recoiled into a double-jointed knot, unrecognisable objects poking through shrouds ...

'The boxes contain diaries, estate accounts, that sort of thing. A priceless record of exploitation.' Hamish lit an incense stick and raised what looked like a starched net shopping bag. 'A MacFie bridal, from Sebastopol ... '

'1854-55,' interrupted Loony.

'Absolutely right. Sebastopol ... ' he gave a mocking laugh, ' ... if you can believe family tradition, that is. Which you can't. I checked. None of our family was ever there.'

'Mebbe they jist sent their cuddies. Mair sensible.'

Hamish led them down six storeys. Loose floorboards and echoes turned their feet into a marching regiment. The walls bore a miscellany of trophies from the predictable crossed pikes, patterned broadswords and studded targes to the less explicable snowshoes and framed Zambian currency which, Grout noted, consisted of a hundred ngwees to the kwatcha. Embroidery samplers insulated at least eighty yards of corridor.

'Iver git lost here, or whit?'

'Yes, when I was a boy. The place used to terrify me. All the dead animals and creepy sounds. At night the place really comes alive. You get used to it. Like a hotel, you just accept strange comings and goings. Dundreary has fourteen bedrooms, six bathrooms, eight reception rooms, kitchen, billiard room, and a suite of service areas and servants quarters in the basement.'

'Fucksakes, tak a keek in there Grout.'

'That's the library.'

'Ah didnae think it wis the laundry. Djaysus. Fuckin books frae flair tae ceiling. Ye kid lock me awa here fer life an ah'd be happy. Quite a reader wis yer auld man, eh?'

'No. I don't think he ever read anything, except these. His favourites.' He removed two companion books from a shelf and handed them to Grout.

'*The Leadership Secrets of Atilla the Hun* and *The Perfumed Garden*.' Grout flicked open the latter and read, 'Property of Sloane Club Library, Return by 12 October 1948.'

'Most of these are archives of trapped air. Like the antarctic ice shelf. Some day when they want to discover the ambient pollen count of the Inner Hebrides in 1866, they'll analyse these books.'

'The Writins o Plato, Socrates oan Pleasure … whit a fuckin waste. Tae hiv aw this an nae read it. Whit wis he like, yer auld man?'

'Putting it mildly, he was racist, narrow-minded, short-tempered and over-sexed. A solid grounding in ignorance entitled him to strong views on everything.'

They entered the Drawing Room which Grout and Loony had already seen from the outside. The furnishings were even more mountainous than they remembered.

Fran sat glaikit in a leather throne, worn out after a morning in the witchery. Hamish ignored her. The shih tzu appeared, skimming over the carpet towards them, yapping, then sheared off under a chaise-longue.

'Whit the fuck wis that, Grout?'

'Jist a rat, ah think.'

'Whit's up wi the Punk?' Loony asked.

'My stepmother's not very well. She's always been a bit tetchy when she's detached from a phone and the lines are now constantly jammed with journalists trying to find out what went on between my father and Lord MacArthur … '

'An whit did gae oan?'

'I've no idea. They probably gambled together.' He motioned towards Fran again. 'She's also upset about my father's death. Worried sick about her inheritance. We all are.'

'Wid ye want this heap?'

'For a long time I wanted nothing to do with it. I'd have given it away sooner than look at it. But then I realised it could be an opportunity to do something very different, give something back to the community which, for centuries, has given to us. But I doubt I'll get the chance. I reckon my father will have left everything to some mistress or gambling crony. And perhaps that's what's making me want it all the more. The fact it might now be taken from me.'

He rang a bell. Dalrymple appeared.

'Tea for three, please, Angus.'

Grout and Loony exchanged smiles.

'High fuckin ideals, eh, an screw the servants.'

'I hate this as much as you. But the sad fact is, it's Angus's life. I'd pay him off tomorrow, pension him for life, but I know he'd just wilt away.'

'Whit aboot the Punk? Keep er doped tae the eyeballs tae keep er oot the inheritance deal?'

'She's been like that for years. She married my father ten years ago. She was a chatshow host. Ratings slumped ... stardom truncated ... damaged goods.'

Dalrymple brought tea in silverware bearing the MacFie Coat-of-Arms and motto. A demi-lion rampant, proper, below 'Pro Rege'. Loony bent forward to examine it.

'Ah'm intae reggae an aw. But yer cat looks pished.'

Dalrymple scowled.

'For the King,' explained Hamish.

Dalrymple stiffened and clicked his heels together. 'I WAS WONDERING IF I COULD HAVE A WORD WITH YOU, SIR?'

'Of course, Angus. Go ahead.'

'IN PRIVATE, SIR.'

'Oh I'm tired of secrets. Just speak. None of us have anything to hide.'

Dalrymple smothered his sense of impropriety. 'WELL, SIR. YOU'LL BE AWARE I'VE SERVED YOUR FAMILY FOR FORTY-THREE YEARS, AND MY WIFE'S DONE THIRTY-NINE. THAT'S EIGHTY-TWO YEARS' DEVOTED DUTY. WHY, SIR, IF YOU DON'T MIND MY SAYING SO, I'VE BEEN PART OF THIS FAMILY FOR LONGER THAN YOURSELF. AND NOW THE COLONEL'S GONE ... WELL, I KNOW YOU DON'T SEE THINGS THE WAY HE DID ... AND HOWEVER MUCH YOU'RE GOING TO CHANGE THINGS HERE, EFFIE AND I ... WELL, WE'RE NOT LEAVING. YOU'VE NO RIGHT TO GET RID OF US.'

'I've no intention of getting rid of you, Angus. But it may not be my choice. This whole place may be given to someone else who doesn't give a toss about tradition. This may be the end. We'll know on Wednesday. We've all to go to the solicitors.'

Dalrymple looked crestfallen. 'YOU'LL PUT IN A GOOD WORD FOR US, SIR?'

'Of course. But it may not do any good. There's usually little sentiment involved where wills and lawyers are concerned.' He began pouring tea and made a mental note to rearrange his fish farm shift. 'By the way, Angus. I'd like to introduce you to some friends. They'll be moving into the West Wing – at least for as long as we have a West Wing, or any other wing for that matter.' He turned to Grout and Loony. 'I assume you'd like to? It is getting a bit cold for camping.'

'An Rastafarian? He's ma dug.'

'As long as he doesn't eat the Dundreary rat – whose name, by the way, is Ming – I'm sure he'll be welcome.'

'Naw, Rast disnae like Chinese.'

Dalrymple's eyes slipped sideways as he gave a slight bow, and reversed into the shadows.

'There's just one thing, though.' Hamish continued. 'Would you kindly keep that goat out of the ginko tree. I raised it myself. It's very rare.'

'Aye, ye mind that, Grout. They ginkos are livin fossils. Japanese. Ah read aw aboot em.'

In the orb of the lighthouse, the Brodie tribe was still mired in the late Pleistocene. By this stage of his endeavours Lawrence had hoped to be in the Mesolithic so that, as planned, he'd be in the Bronze for Christmas. But events had conspired against him. Things were not going well between him and Vibrating Greta. The incident with Calum the Post had been such a traumatic affair that he hadn't wanted anything to do with her for a while and pretended she hadn't happened by locking her in the bulb store. It was only yesterday evening that he'd checked the coast was clear and taken her out. She was a brunette, just like Angela: a thought he found both dangerous and exciting. Despite several other redeeming features he had sudden doubts about Greta's ability to stand in for the beautiful Bohair and usefully contribute to the story. After all, she was so lifeless, notwithstanding her eponymous efficacy in the ability to vibrate. He found her fixed grin debilitating, and her naked vulnerability – especially laid out on the kitchen table under a hundred-watt bulb – made him want to fall to his knees and apologise for her manufacture. And he needed the light for reading her instructions. It was only after studying these that he understood why a certain section of skin was hazardously prickly and that a bag of accessories contained a selection of hair backed by Velcro. Frankly, Vibrating Greta was an embarrassment, but at £99.95 he wasn't prepared to write her off completely. He stuffed her back in the bulb cupboard and closed the door on the preliminary stage of what he feared was going to be a very slow process of familiarisation.

His routine was also upset by the disappearance of his inflatable dingy during the weekend storm. He'd spent hours wandering the coast but had failed to find it. The Lighthouse Board would take a very dim view of the loss, and the evidence of bad luck – a frayed rope still secured to the anchor – would not appease them. All in all, it had not been a good week, and the Pleistocene was feeling interminable.

He consulted his notes and launched into a new chapter:

Though he couldn't pin the blame on his neighbours (3 [lfr]), Arunk suspected they had stolen his precious gorgosaur duvets during his long

absence to find and rescue the beautiful Bohair from her kidnapper. He'd *managed to catch a couple of exceptionally large elasmosaurs which had been hell to skin, but these had not proved successful substitutes. Bohair was allergic to elasmosaur, she complained. And that wasn't the end of it: atlantosaur was too prickly, plesiosaur creased, brachiosaur shrank in the wash, and he needn't even think of trying pelycosaurs – they caused static with her nightie. Finally, his spear almost shrunk to nothing, Arunk managed to please her with a fine brace of mosasaurus pelts. There having been no time to let them cure properly, long and frequent arguments erupted as to whose turn it was to sleep on the wet patches. Bohair protested that she always ended up in them. Arunk refuted this. They argued incessantly.*

How different things had been since that fateful day of her disappearance. Bohair had changed almost beyond recognition during her time with those homo sapien savages and their weird ideas of equality and progress. Just look at her. Carrying a handbag! Who did she think she was? He was the laughing stock of the clan.

'Mark my words,' Moak had ridiculed. 'You'll be bartering for woad next!'

Things were not looking good for the future Brodies, lining up to take their place in history as, amongst other things, groom to Mary Queen of Scots and profiteers in Glasgow's tobacco trade.

Risky, thought Lawrence. Melodramatic foresight. Disruptive. He'd decide whether to cut it later. Now there was nothing to do but get on with it. Put some spunk into Arunk.

Yet her beauty still beguiled him. Still made him want to raise his spear and please her every desire, be it mosasaurus, woad or a shiny piece of mica for her handbag. Bohair's eyes sparkled like sunlight dancing on bladderwort. Her hair was a shield of radiant brown, the likes of which would remain a secret of the gods for countless millennia. That evening, as the creodont-fat lamp flickered, he was seized by an irresistible desire to possess her. It had been his turn for the dry spot but he had volunteered for a double-shift on the wet to placate her. Artifice. He knew only too well how the future well-being of generations of Brodies depended on him holding his nerve, and his aim true.

'Bohair, my love,' he whispered tenderly.

'No you can't.'

'No …?' Like a clawed lizard, a mini dimetrodon to be exact, panic scuttled across his chest.

Their pet miacis had been squabbling with the neighbour's, making a fiendish racket and keeping her awake. She was irritable, and a bit merycopotamus.

'You chose the wet, so it's your own fault. I'm not moving.'

Arunk realised he'd have to experiment with a metaphysical idea he'd recently been contemplating during sentinel duty at the rhamphorhynchus trap, and which he'd termed, loosely, 'Foreplay'. He kissed her shoulders ten times in succession, slowly moving a measured distance down her arm each time, then, judging the time to be right, seized her wrist, wrenched her round and adroitly pinned her against the mosasaurus while he flung himself over her ...

A black object floating between Mickle and Muckle Flabbay caught Lawrence's eye. He peered at it.

'It can't be ... Good God, it is ... ' He leapt up and cascaded down the steps at full tilt. He ran to the edge of the rocks to watch his dingy, which the tide was returning from out of nowhere. His elation soon turned to panic as he realised there was no hope of it grounding. The ebbing flow would carry it clean past him and south into open water. A wetsuit, he thought. Flippers. Buoyancy. He might just be able to intercept it. ... *wetsuit ... flippers ... buoyancy ...*

'Sergeant, this is entirely between you and me,' confided Calum the Post. 'But I've been meaning to tell you about something odd that happened the other day. When would it have been? Thursday, I think. Yes, Thursday afternoon.'

Calum was an inveterate carrier of gossip and hearsay, most of which turned out to be true but unconvictable. He was the Rural Eye, part of a smug clique whose only consolation for the poverty or inertia which had rooted them to Muckle Flabbay's earth for five generations was to cultivate resentment against smug English Incomers whose B&B had cost them the price of a Home Counties garage. Despite this distinct bias, Cleghorn listened with enthusiasm.

'Had to deliver this parcel to that lighthouse keeper, Brodie. Right queer fellow, if you ask me. Well, as I was handing it over it sort of erupted and hissed.'

'What on earth do you mean, erupted and hissed?'

'Just that, Sergeant.' Calum wondered whether he should mention Mrs Cleghorn but decided against it. 'This parcel sort of came alive and made noises and fell apart and out of a corner a hand appeared. A woman's hand … '

Cleghorn's eyes widened and he bent forwards. 'D'you mean …?'

'*Daingead*! Not a real hand, no, no, not a human hand.'

'But you just said it was a woman's hand, so you're contradicting yourself.' He reached inside his jacket for his notebook. Calum became slightly alarmed.

'Shouldn't have mentioned it, Sergeant. Probably just a glove.'

'I'm very glad you did mention it. Doesn't sound like *you* thought it was a glove, or why would you think it unusual?'

'Well, I admit it did look like a woman's hand to me, but of course I could have been mistaken. *Òbh, òbh*! Must be getting on now … '

Cleghorn had started to insist on specific times and places but was unable to get Calum to elucidate further. Then those anarchist thugs had destroyed his car and half the garden, preventing him from getting onto the case at once. Now the wreckage had been cleared, he thought he'd investigate the matter.

It was, however, still three hours to low tide. Still, it wouldn't hurt to go and look.

Angela glared at her husband tottering uncertainly on her bike, clearly in too-high a gear.

As Cleghorn coasted down to the final slope he was greeted by such a sight he dropped his binoculars. When he eventually managed to refocus them, there, quite clearly, were two figures swimming, one naked, the other in black. Further examination revealed the black figure kicking a strong wake while trying to drown the naked one. The latter, he ascertained, was definitely a woman, and a brunette. Disconcertingly like Angela, he thought. He focussed in on her breasts. Definitely not Angela, he decided. In fact, definitely not human. No one could float that defiantly under such brute force. Then he spotted the dingy.

'Perverted bastard. Takes his … his … ' he could hardly bring himself to put words to the disgusting images running through his mind, ' … *sordid dummy* out swimming. In broad daylight … Thank you, Calum.' He licked his lips.

VICE

'I wouldn't mind betting there's a fetish ring at the bottom of this.'

He continued watching until the filthy creature had returned to his boat and towed his toy ashore.

On Sunday mornings Angela packed herself and a few dreams into lace underwear, a red tracksuit and trainers edged – like her husband's car – with reflectors, and went jogging. In her mind she was running in slow motion, forcing herself against the treadmill of fantasy, striving towards someone who was never defined beyond a radiance of warmth and longing. The slow undulating rhythm of her movement caused her hair to rise and fall, caressing her neck. She luxuriated in the touch, like a lover's hands cradling her, and felt little shocks of loneliness each time they disappeared. Mile after mile, caught between illusions, she ran for the comfort of embrace.

She always took the same route. First along a shore path to the golf course. Along this stretch the tangy smell of drying seaweed added weight to the air and resistance to the treadmill. Until her breathing grew noisier and drowned other sounds, she heard curlews wittering and the abusive mutterings of seagulls. Then she crossed the main road to Dundreary and side-stepped through a kissing gate onto the ninth fairway. She circumscribed the other eight holes, relishing the absence of missiles and humanity ('NO GOLF ON SUNDAYS'). Here the air lightened and changed character, carrying the earthy fecundity of wet grass which soothed her soul. *Ashes to ashes and earth to earth*, she thought, not morbidly but with gentle acceptance of the universality of matter. Odd rabbits bounced about at erratic tangents and suddenly disappeared, reminding her of a fluky shot on a pool table.

She thought back to the only pool session she'd played, famously pissed, at the Ben Stac Bar last Hogmanay. Farquhar could have easily enjoyed a drink too and they could have taken a taxi back, but he'd set himself against the evening. Farquhar the Martyr. That had driven her to enjoy herself all the more and she'd accepted an invitation to play pool with Mairi Ban the Byke to spite him. What a ball they'd had! Dozens, in fact! They must have played five or six games before she'd mistimed a shot, driven her cue into the felt, ripped a two-foot slash, sent several balls bouncing across the floor and ended up flat on the table herself, howling with laughter. And Mairi had leapt up beside her and announced a special offer of two for the price of one! Even now, while running, Angela could reduce herself to cross-legged helplessness at the memory of that night.

She felt a mysterious magnetism around Mairi, some attraction so powerful it was intimidating. Perhaps, Angela reflected, what frightened her was that Mairi's fullness was the measure of her own emptiness. And how it needn't be like that, for in reality, deep down, Angel Ewe *was* Mairi Ban ... and the thought was so engrossing, and disturbing, she forgot to look out for Beltex, Charolais and Mule, three rare types of sheep the Braithwaites kept as curiosities for their Bed & Breakfast trade.

Once round the golf course, she returned to Flabbay by the main road and passed the priest's house.

Father Benedict's washing line was always a disappointment on Sundays. Although neither he nor His Holiness The Pope had anything against flying one's laundry on the Sabbath – Father Benedict had admitted to her in one of their fence-top exchanges – he deferred to the island Protestant custom that insisted on concealing all evidence of work on the Day of Rest. Angela never usually saw him because he was inside doing whatever priests do before their service, but today he was surreptitiously hiding from Sabbatarians while out feeding birds.

'Failed loaf,' he explained, the memory of Angela's hand at the funeral causing him to smile excessively.

'Manna for the fowls,' responded Angela, the flush of exercise concealing her embarrassment and confusion over whether she had actually reached into his cassock or just imagined doing it.

'I ... '

'Must fly. Bye!' Somehow the image of Father Benedict as the source of radiant warmth and longing seemed too fraught with complexities and Papal bulls.

The next moment she heard a bellow of exhaust and was almost choked by the emissions of a blue hurricane. The thugs, she realised. Farquhar's words. *Fucking thugs*. He'd been very annoyed.

She recalled how she'd watched them, the hippies, attaching the chain to Farquhar's car. She thought the fence post would have held the QEII but it had given instantly. Rotten to the core. Just like her life. Clean and wholesome on the outside while being eaten away from within.

The hippies were parked outside the Fundamentalist Church. One gave her a friendly wave. The other wolf-whistled and grinned. How long was it since anyone had whistled at her? Too long, too long. She straightened her posture and – realising she must have run faster this morning and was passing the Church as the last of the congregation was arriving – accelerated. Five unfortunate minutes had put back the cause of acceptance on the island by six generations. Of all the Churches, the Fundamentalists were the most averse to forgiveness. Latecomers eyed her malevolently as they hirpled on sticks or, arm in arm, slummocked and shauchled through geriatric contortions. She felt their gaze, felt her skin bruise and bleed, her bones break as their stones struck, volley after volley, a sinner's punishment on Zion's desert.

The Reverend Murdo MacLeod threw the largest stone as he stood at his vestry window and invoked the wrath of God to smite down this red obscenity flouting the Sabbath. Already shaken to the core by that week's sacrilege, his carefully nurtured fury increased as yet another example of Sodom and Gomorrah passed before his eyes. With one concerted glower he contrived to reduce Mrs Cleghorn to a pile of salt on the B827 Flabbay to Grimport loop extension before turning to enter the nave.

'Hae tae watch yer pees an kyews here, pal. Hame o hellfire an wretchedness.'

'Life's jist one big headumacation, eh Loon? Whit's sae special aboot em?'

'Ah call 'em the Old Testymentals. They're undiluted Calvinism an jist an altar cushion short o the Spanish Inquisition. Ye kin jist aboot breathe oan the Sabbath, but fer fucksakes dinnae enjoy it.'

Loony and Grout sat on varnished pine below a varnished pine ceiling. The walls were white and unadorned; nowhere for an angel or devil to sit, nothing to distract the mind from Hard Faith. Grout counted the congregation and tallied twenty-six of whom over three-quarters could be imagined as imminent daisy fodder. Most of the rest were underage. A cluster of black-suited men occupied benches around a two-tier pulpit.

'Who's they apostles up front?'

'Elders,' explained Loony, who knew about these things as a result of his Masters thesis, *Contemporary Christianity – A Study of Artful Ritual and Divisive Dogma as Crusades Towards the Highest Ideal of Cult Idiosyncrasy.* 'That guy in front's the precentor. He's like the organ. Leads the singin. Nae music allowed.'

Everyone rose as the minister appeared through a side door and climbed the steps to the upper tier. Below him the precentor raised a book, his face contorted as if he'd chopped a pungent onion, and sang contralto. A psalm. Everyone joined in. A prayer followed, in which the Reverend MacLeod asked for peace for the righteous, and wailing and gnashing for everyone else, especially idolaters and joggers. They sang another psalm. The Reverend MacLeod's reading was from a third psalm. He expanded on its meaning, which – and it came as no surprise to Grout – extolled some of the joys of heaven and touched on some particularly unpleasant practices in hell, and then everyone sang it.

'They kid dae wi incense,' Grout whispered during a held refrain.

'Naw, they'd jist refuse tae breathe.'

As the psalm ended, the Reverend MacLeod cleared his throat for the sermon. Loony detected an unusual electricity flowing. Tension. Something Divisive Brewing.

'I have taken for my text today, Exodus' – he unleashed the word like a curse – 'chapter twenty-one, verse twenty-three. *And if any mischief follow, then thou shalt give life for life. Eye for eye, tooth for tooth, hand for hand, foot for foot. Burning for burning, wound for wound, stripe for stripe.*'

Grout looked up the passage in one of the Bibles scattered along the pews and wondered what wound the minister had suffered and who was going to cop it. Then the voice faded to a monotonous drawl and Grout became more interested in other quaint Israelite laws which the Lord apparently gave Moses, in small print, following the Ten Commandments. In the early part of the chapter he read:

2 If thou buy an Hebrew servant, six years he shall serve: and in the seventh he shall go out free for nothing. 3 If he came in by himself, he shall go out by himself: if he were married, then his wife shall go out with him. 4 If his master hath given him a wife, and she hath born him sons or daughters; the wife and her children shall be her master's, and he shall go out by himself.

Grout considered this in the light of sexual equality, political correctness, trade unionism and the European Court of Human Rights. Worse was to come:

5 And if the servant shall plainly say, I love my master, my wife, and my children; I will not go out free: 6 Then his master shall bring him unto the judges: he shall also bring him to the door, or unto the door post; and his master shall bore his ear through with an awl; and he shall serve him forever.

Grout fingered his earring. Maybe they thought *he'd* been awled to a doorpost, and defected! He browsed on. Chapter 30 made him smile. Triumphantly, he nudged Loony and tapped the page.

1 AND thou shalt make an altar to burn incense upon: of shittim wood shalt thou make it.

'Shittim? Whit the fuck's shittim?'

'Acacia.'

The Reverend MacLeod was hotting up. He too had moved on, to Exodus 32.

'Here we go,' whispered Loony. He cranked an imaginary handle. 'Ah jist knew he kidnae resist yon golden calf affair, ken.' He could see exactly where this was leading. Then he registered Grout's blank expression. 'Idolatry. Aaron's big cock-up. Blew his career as a prophet.'

'And Aaron said unto them, "Break off the golden earrings which are in the ears of your wives, of your sons, and of your daughters, and bring them unto me". And all the people broke off the golden earrings which were in their ears and brought them unto Aaron. And he received them at their hand, and fashioned it with a graving tool, after he had made it a molten calf; and they said, "These be thy gods, O Israel, which brought thee up out of the land of Egypt".'

The minister raised his eyes from his reading and closed the Bible noisily.

'The golden calves are still with us, brethren, herded by the devil. And their barns are many. Their barns are the Catholic Church.' He began fomenting himself into a frenzy. 'We of the Chosen Faith are forbidden to enter such dens of iniquity and devilry, forbidden to mix with idolaters on whom God's wrath will one day fall with all the fury of the Apocalypse as prescribed in Revelations … and yet … and yet … we have been shamed this week to witness the fall of one of our members, one we held in the highest esteem, indeed a banner-holder of our Church, and one who refuses to repent. I refer to Lord MacArthur who has sold his soul to Satan. If the Fundamentalist Church refuses to expel him as the heretic he's shown himself to be, then I can no longer be a part of that Church. Today, all across Scotland, we ministers of the True Faith are creating a new institution to uphold the sanctity of God's worship. Henceforth we will be a part of the new True Fundamentalist Church and I ask you all to answer the call of your consciences and stay with us.'

He paused and drew a deep breath. 'And I will ask more. That anyone who wishes to leave, does so now, and never darkens the door of this building again.'

Calum the Post was the first to rise. He held the minister's eyes. 'It was an act of brotherly love, and that's no sin,' he said, turned and walked out. Captain MacQuarrie followed and then others did likewise. Grout and Loony were tempted to stay out of curiosity but their arses felt misshapen and cramped, and it was time for Rastafarian's dinner.

'Very apt choice o text, ah thought,' remarked Grout. 'Exodus.'

Loony's eyes were still wide with surprise. 'Grout,' he breathed, 'we jist witnessed history. Tae bad it wisnae three years ago, in time fer ma thesis.'

Angela checked for her husband's feet. They were visible, slightly magnified, through two sets of double glazing; her living-room's and the police station's. She went to the phone and dialled Flabbay 202.

Lawrence was bent over his kitchen table with a can of WD40 and an assortment of screwdrivers laid out in a semicircle. Closer to hand were nuts, washers, grommets, bolts, springs, cogs, pistons and a small electric motor arranged in a precise sequence: Vibrating Greta's vibrator. It was only when he was well out to sea with Greta that he remembered that she wasn't an average doll and came with hidden extras which would corrode and seize in salt water. By deflating Greta he'd managed to remove her vital mechanism, which he'd dismantled, treated and was in the process of reassembling when the phone rang. Worried that he might lose the final component yet to be fitted, he slipped a grommet over his little finger before answering the phone.

'Hallo Lawrence. It's Angela. You remember we met the other day by your postbox?'

Lawrence almost dropped the receiver at the memory. He swallowed and tried to sound uncertain.

'Erm, did we?'

'Yes. I wasn't feeling well and had to lie down and then Calum the Post came along with a parcel of gloves which gave us quite a start … surely you remember?'

'Oh yes, yes of course. A box of gloves. One goes through so many, being a lighthouse keeper.' He was dismayed to hear Angela burst out laughing.

'And we thought it looked like a woman's hand!'

Lawrence made a show of mild humour while his alarm increased. What on earth did the woman want? It could only mean trouble. Blackmail, perhaps?

He listened to her laughter until it thinned and he could no longer bear the suspense. 'What can I do for you?'

'I rang about your advert?'

'Advert?'

'For diving lessons.'

The sign had been up for several months without producing any interest and consequently Lawrence had forgotten about it. 'Diving lessons …!' Now it was his turn to laugh.

'What's so funny?'

'Nothing. It's just that it's getting a bit cold for most people.'

'I adore the cold. It gives me an appetite.'

'Quite. Well, when would you like to start. I can be very flexible.'

Flexible. Angela liked the sound of the word and the way he said it. It sounded strong and gentle. She glanced up and checked the feet. Still there. 'How about this afternoon. Two-thirty?'

'Make it three and you should be right for the tide.'

'I'll bring my bikini and snorkel.'

Lawrence was so busy picturing her in a bikini that it was a while before he realised how inappropriate it would be. 'We won't be taking to the water for several sessions yet, and not without proper gear. To begin with we'll just stick to theory. See how you like it. I won't charge until we come to the practical part.'

'See you at three then.' What a lovely man, she thought. *Flexible … the practical part.*

He immediately tidied his workspace and began preparing some notes. She arrived punctually. Mid-afternoon dusk was already falling.

'Hallo Lawrence.'

'Hallo Angela.'

He beckoned her in, through a porch bulging with oilskins. She took in his Sou'wester and wellies, more manly wellies than Farquhar's, she thought. They looked used, as if they'd battled with barnacles and possibly giant squid. Such a dangerous life, she imagined, thinking of Grace Darling, the *Marie Celeste* and *Moby Dick*. She'd always loved *Moby Dick*. She entered the kitchen where a stove hummed and crackled while sending heat up into a pulley of jerseys interspersed with gaps where underpants might have been but, she noticed with disappointment, were not. A neat row of dishes were draining beside a porcelain sink, and the work surfaces had been wiped clean. Clusters of dried thrift hung inverted from curtain rails and cupboard handles. A stuffed bird watched her from a window ledge.

'Kittiwake,' he explained.

'Do you stuff things too?'

'No. It's the legacy of a previous keeper. I dry flowers, though. I like to have nature's colours year round.' He pulled out a chair for her. The legs scratched along bare flagstones. She remained standing. In that moment, now that he was better acquainted with Greta, he was struck by the astonishing similarity of their features. Angela's height, thick russet hair and delicate wrists were so similar to Greta's. She held her head at the same slightly tilted angle. Those wistful eyes were different, of course, dark amber instead of ghastly green.

'Do you eat meat?'

Lawrence was thrown by this diversion. 'Do I eat …?'

'Meat. I see you've got Rose Elliot's cookery books.'

'Oh I see! No, I'm vegetarian.'

'What a coincidence,' Angela beamed. 'So am I!'

Another silence and exchange of smiles ensued while Lawrence struggled to recall how the lesson should begin. 'Well … '

'May I see the light?'

His mind blanked again. 'The light? Yes, of course.' He looked up at the bulb hanging from the ceiling, wondering what on earth …

'The big light,' she laughed, 'the one you're the Keeper of.'

He felt such a fool! He laid a hand on her shoulder and laughed too. 'To the light. I hope you're feeling fit. There's a hundred and sixty-four steps. Clockwise. Some lighthouses are anticlockwise. Takes you ages to adjust.'

They tramped up the spiral. He led. For one hundred and sixty-four steps she enjoyed the view. Tight swivelling bulges of denim. By the time she reached the top, she was breathless.

'I'm not as fit as I thought,' she gasped.

'You're just new to lighthouses. You'd soon get used to it.' He opened the door which led into the dome. Seconds later she was blinded.

'Two hundred and four thousand candlewatts. Four flashes every twenty seconds. The stack of lights is divided into four rows, each offset at a different angle and screened by blinkers. It revolves once every twenty seconds. Out at sea you only ever see one set of lights at a time, and only briefly. It looks like it's flashing but it's not. The lights run continuously but you only glimpse them through the blinkers. On a clear night a tanker can see us from thirty-six miles away.'

'Wow!'

'It's not the best time to visit. No view, and being blinded twelve times a minute!'

She saw his desk. 'This is where you write?'

'Oh, yes. During the day. I like the view.'

Flash.

'Bohair, my love,' he whispered tenderly. She managed to read before the light dazzled her.

Flash.

'Foreplay'. He kissed her shoulders ten times ...

'Well, that's about all there is to see.'

Flash.

he flung himself over her ...

'Romance ... thrillers ... ' she whispered, and let him lead her back through the door.

Down in the kitchen the first lesson got underway. Lawrence began by explaining how human lungs work. Angela took notes.

Freckles. Weather-beaten. Great tufty eyebrows meeting in the middle, giving him a serious, thoughtful look. A gentle face, not fierce or roguish, and fair hair, wavy like the sea – how appropriate! – Neptune, without the scales and trident. I hope!

Lawrence had progressed to the effects of increased pressure and the saturation of gases absorbed in the bloodstream.

'What an unusual ring. It looks like rubber.'

Thrown off track Lawrence looked up and followed her gaze back to his hand, and Greta's grommet. 'Oh that! Silly me. A bit of engine I was repairing. Lighthouse gasket, sort of.'

Angela took more notes. It was important, he stressed, to understand the physical effects of diving, and to avoid such hazards as the bends and bone narcosis. Angela added large asterisks alongside the key points, and looked less enthusiastic.

'It all sounds terribly dangerous. Maybe it would be better if we switched to drying flowers? I don't mind paying the same rates.'

'No, don't lose heart. It sounds bad but as long as you don't knowingly take risks, these things never happen. And it's the most wonderful world down there.' He described the way light refracted and danced underwater, the colours of anemones, coral and gardens of undulating seaweed, the graceful flight of rays and such curiosities as the tiny lumpsucker which looked like a sulking Toby jug, the silence and sensations of three-dimensional movement, until Angela felt enchanted once more and had to excuse herself. All that water was making her need the loo …

'May I use the … er …?'

'Oh yes, of course. It's through that door, second on the right.'

He smiled, watched her leave the room and heard the bathroom door hinges squeak open. He felt his smile drop as his jaw fell … the bathroom door didn't squeak. She'd opened the first door which was the bulb store … OH MY GOD … THE DOLL …

He leapt up and hurtled after her, found her halfway through the doorway groping in the dark for the light switch. As he moved he expected at any moment for her to look up and see Vibrating Greta drying and airing, suspended by strings, deflated, naked and, beyond any doubt, *not* a survival suit.

'NOT that door,' he shouted, as he slipped round her and ushered her out.

'What a fright you gave me … '

'I'm so sorry. Awkward floor in that room. No light. Easy to twist an ankle. *Urnph Urnph!*' He forced a chuckle which made Angela think of piglets. 'You'll have to get simple instructions right before we go diving.'

Angela wondered if she really was cut out for diving after all. His strange behaviour had unnerved her. That was twice now he'd suddenly gone a bit cuckoo. She'd be on her guard in future. He was so nice, though, and looking around the gallery of framed lighthouses that decorated the bathroom, she soon felt reaffirmed in her mission.

'Well, till the next time,' he concluded, when the hour was up. 'I'll need to teach you about decompression.'

'I'll look forward to it.' She tossed a hand in a wave. 'To being decompressed.'

Grinella Oliphant surveyed the Scrabble board with concealed displeasure. The game had started well for her with the leading hand and letters D, R, L, C, O, O, E. She'd laid down 'croodle' and *Chambers 20th Century Dictionary* – her and Dilly's agreed arbitrator – corroborated the word: *croodle [v.i. to murmur like a dove].* This had scored her seventy, but her lead was short-lived for Dilly retaliated with a steady series of thirties and forties against her low teens. Once she'd even been forced to lay down 'lee' for a pathetic three. Her worst ever score! Dilly, it seemed, was spoilt for choice, drawing on her full allowance of five minutes. Grinella got bored.

'Schism,' she said, topping up Dilly's tea.

'I beg your pardon?'

'Schism,' she repeated. 'They've suffered a schism.'

'Who have?'

'The Fundamentalists. Always been prone to them, these breakaway Churches. 1843, you know. Big mistake.' As she and Dilly were both National Presbyterian Church – the *broken-away-from* in 1843 – she knew she was on safe ground. 'Once they get a taste for schisming, they just keep on. Splits them right up the middle it does, nave to pulpit, *chhhrrrrrrrrriiiiiiip.*' Grinella intoned Velcro. '*Chhhrrrrrrrrriiiiiiip,*' she repeated, savouring onomatopoeia while buttering a ginger slice.

'Shibboleth,' countered Dilly.

'I didn't quite catch that.'

'Shibboleth. That's what they'll need from now on. Each to their own. So they can tell who's who.'

'Quite,' agreed Grinella. They were both used to these conversations in which, only later with the help of a dictionary, could they work out what they'd been talking about. [*shib' -leth, n. the Gileadite test-word for an Ephraimite, who could not pronounce sh (Judg xii 5-6; B): any such test: a peculiarity of speech: the criterion or catchword of a group: a cant phrase.*]

Dilly added 'knaggy' to the end of 'lee', making 'leek' and extending her lead to eighty-four. 'Check it if you want but it means "rugged" or "knotty" as in wood.'

'I'm well aware of what "knaggy" means,' retorted Grinella, who had never heard of the word. With five vowels and a couple of worthless consonants, she realised she was out of this game. Nothing short of a miracle could save her.

Dilly looked round Grinella's room. She knew Grinella was forty-nine, eight years younger than herself, but she looked eight years older. She hadn't really had much of a life, poor Grinella, inheriting her uncle's shop like that. Of course she could have sold it instead of doing a crash course in bookkeeping and slaving herself to the Emporium for twenty years. But one could never live other people's lives for them, never know how they saw life. And what an unfortunate experience for an eight-year old, getting lost on the last tour to Edinburgh Castle's dungeons, with a father too absent-minded to notice. So soon after losing her mother too. No wonder she lived a cloistered life. Her room was immaculately neat. Washed and ironed doilies on the chairs. Voyeur-proof curtains. Sensible furniture. Mute colours. Safe pictures. The largest cupboard in the house, she knew, contained appliances and accoutrements in a state of alert for the twenty-four hour persecution of dirt. Sometimes Dilly herself felt like contamination.

'So you think we're immune to schisms ourselves?' she queried, not averse to the tit for tat spoiling of Grinella's concentration.

'We? You mean the National Presbyterians?'

'Quite. I thought you were going to blow a blood vessel during the interval at the Messiah rehearsal when that … that hippy … what was his name? … told you he was a Baha'i.'

'Oh him. Yes, most unsavoury character. Something to do with bathrooms … Mastick … no … Grout, that was it. Most peculiar name. Well, it did give me quite a turn. I don't know exactly what a Baha'i is. One of those Moony-type cults, I imagine. Next we'll hear they've persuaded what's left of the MacFie tribe to commit hara-kiri all over the castle. Cleghorn would love it.'

'Don't be absurd, Grinella. Ignorance and intolerance are bigger crimes against humanity. The Baha'is recognise all religions as paths to world unity. I think they're a most interesting group. Followers of Bahá´u´lláh. It's just the punctuation that puts people off.'

Out of pique, Grinella played 'grout' – four.

'Well, I don't think Reverend Murray will be too pleased to have an Indian mystic singing the *Messiah* in his church.'

'Persian. Not Indian. And that's precisely my point. Schism.'

STUFFED LIVES *ALASTAIR SCOTT*

Dilly played 'ovary' which surprised Grinella as it opened up a triple and seemed a waste of a Y. But with her formidable lead and only a few letters remaining in the bag, it didn't really matter how or what she played. Grinella just wanted the game to end. She got eighteen with a cleverly placed W and T, and delved into the bag. The last two letters.

'No more letters,' she said, and looked at the two she'd drawn. Q and U. She sighed. C, T, Q, U, X, I, I. It was insult to injury. Now she'd be left with thumping penalty points if Dilly managed to get out.

Dilly checked her lead, which had risen to a hundred and twenty-seven, and smiled. 'I suppose you'll be seeking re-election as councillor in next month's ballot?'

'Of course. I consider my record to be rather exemplary. I owe it to the people of Flabbay to stand again.'

'I hear Mairi MacLeod is proposing to stand. And she's certainly got her admirers.'

'Stand,' scoffed Grinella, irked by what was clearly a jibe, 'I thought lying down was her forté.' She watched Dilly play, and still retain three letters. 'What a cheek she has. The tart. Any admirers she has pay and leave, and certainly wouldn't admit it.'

'Well there are some who feel she'd be tough, tougher than you were over the hospital cuts – though of course I understand how your hands were tied.'

Grinella thought of tossing the board in the air and putting Dilly in her place …

… then suddenly she saw it. The O of 'ovary'. The space beside 'leek'. Her C would fit there, on the triple word. 'Cleek' [*a narrow-faced iron-head golf club*] would give her thirty-three, and that was just the score across.

'Well I'm a fighter, Dilly. And I can be tough too.'

Her X she noted with dizzying glee, would fall on the double. She laid down the letters, slowly and heavily, in the top left corner of the board.

Dilly rocked back in her chair, aghast.

Quixotic.

It took Grinella some time to work out her score. Thirty-four multiplied by six – 'quixotic' spanned two triple-word bonuses, plus the thirty-three of 'cleek', plus fifty for using all her letters: two hundred and eighty-seven!

Grinella beamed triumphantly. It was undoubtedly a favourable portent for the elections.

'An excellent game, didn't you think?'

'Y'know, maybe he'll surprise us,' remarked Hamish, trying to make conversation and lighten the mood as they drove to Inverness, 'with hidden foresight and generosity.'

From the outside the office of Hamilton, Gerund, Nayers & Filigree (*Solicitors and Notaries Public*) gave the impression of being in the twenty-first century, sandwiched as it was on Church Street between Azad Video and What Everyone Wants but once inside, Hamish realised it was host to the same class of woodworm, and on the same diet, as those of Dundreary. Indeed, it transpired that Hamilton and Nayers had not made it through the Great War but their names had been retained as marks of respect. Framed certificates showed they'd been replaced first by Gullfodder and Ambrose, and most recently, by Gizzard and Salmon. Hamish wondered whether solicitors, like saints, changed their names for professional reasons, or whether the appellationally-challenged were particularly attracted to the job?

'Ah! Mrs MacFie, Mr MacFie and Mr Dalrymple, a good morning to you. Do please come this way.' George Gerund gave an old-fashioned bow and studied his shoes as they trooped past. Fran's chameleon-green hat fanned wisps of his hair.

Hamish supported Fran's arm, fearful that she should faint. She'd already collapsed twice that morning. Once on the *Flucker* as the ticket collector bantered with a fisherman about herring, and once as they approached Inverness and saw a sign for the ring road. On each occasion the trigger was the word 'ring'. Hamish was fed up hearing about it. All Fran wanted from her husband's estate was the Udaipur solitaire he'd given her on their wedding day, and repossessed a week later. Hamish tried to console her without lying. Ever since he'd come off the breast and was safely on the bottle, his father had fed him the tradition that the MacFies never released the ring to their womenfolk on anything other than the strictest short-term loan; and this had been the practice ever since acquiring the priceless gem from a down-on-his-uppers maharaja during the Relief of Lucknow. There again, you never could be sure in his family. The ring may well be a fake from a Castle Street pawnshop.

They sat on creaky red leather antiques. Mr Gerund had set them opposite his mahogany fortress, two in front and one at the back for Angus.

He withdrew a polka-dot hanky and blew his nose, ran a hand over his bald pate and repositioned half-moon spectacles that had been dislodged by the blowing. He coughed. Looked up. Smiled. Interlocked fingers. Leant forwards.

His sinuses were clear, his catarrh under control, his ritual completed.

So this is Rapsy's domestic troupe, he thought. Wife looks frail and neurotic, and ghoulish in that hat. Son looks just as he described him. A *namby*, that's the term his father always used. *Long-haired idealist vermin.* Gerund felt a surge of envy at all that hair. Probably used curlers. Young men did that sort of thing nowadays. He read the T-shirt: *Greenpeace Saves Lives – Yours and Our Planet's,* and his smile increased on realising how Young MacFie was going to need more than Greenpeace's help once he'd heard the will. And the servant Dalrymple. Wonder if he and the Colonel were having it off? Colonels did that sort of thing with their batmen.

'As you will be aware, I've called you here today to hear the last will and testament of, respectively, your late husband, father and employer, Colonel Rudyard Apsley Prendergast MacFie … '

Fran let out a long moan, flushed a hanky from a sleeve and dabbed her running mascara.

' … his legacies, bequests and the division of his estates … '

'WE'RE NOT LEAVING, SIR.' Angus stood up and glared threateningly. 'EFFIE AND ME, WE'RE NOT GOING NO MATTER WHAT. WE'VE … '

'Sit down, Mr Dalrymple. I must advise you all, that as executor I have the legal obligation to ensure that this will is carried out to the letter, whether you like it or not … '

'I'll sue for the ring, it's mine, he promised it to me … '

'If you'll let me continue.' He frowned and dickered with his glasses, his pupils undergoing lunatic distortions. 'I'll deal with you first, Mr Dalrymple, seeing as you aren't family and the rest of the will is a family concern.' He cleared his throat. 'Your late employer has explicitly stated that you and your wife are to retain the use of your current apartment in Dundreary Castle for the rest of your natural lives … '

'OH, GOD BLESS THE GENTLEMAN, OH THANK YOU, SIR, OH FINE, FINE MAN … '

' … AND your services are to be retained at the current wage of two hundred pounds sterling a week for as long as you wish, decreasing to fifty pounds sterling on your retirement or death, in the latter case, the money being paid to your widow.'

Angus had removed his deerstalker and was down on one knee. 'MOST GRATEFUL THAT WE ARE, SIR. THANK YOU SO MUCH AND BEST WISHES TO YOUR WIFE IF YOU HAVE ONE.'

'However,' continued the lawyer, 'I must warn you that this may change in two years.'

'TWO YEARS?' Angus slowly rose and replaced his hat.

'Yes. The situation is dependent on certain conditions which will be reviewed in exactly two years. Your retention at the castle is to be safeguarded only if those conditions have been met in full.'

'WHAT CONDITIONS, SIR?'

'I'm afraid that's no business of yours.' He turned a wry smile towards Hamish. 'It is a private arrangement between Father and Son. I will be the adjudicator in the matter and I will let you know whether you may stay or must leave at the appropriate time. In two years. You may leave now, Mr Dalrymple, and a good day to you.'

Hamish watched Angus balance himself shakily against the chair before moving to the door. It opened and closed quietly, as if only having entertained an apology. Hamish nodded to himself. He'd known there'd be *certain conditions*. There had been all his life. Inside the cage his father had so carefully constructed, with bars of *certain conditions*. Hamish felt a tear grow, flood the rim, gather and then fall, tracing warmth down his cheek. A tear for the man who had practised so much loving, but never known love.

'And now to your part, Mrs MacFie.' Mr Gerund changed voice as he did for his most expensive and difficult clients. It was a trick he'd mastered during his traineeship. You imagined yourself in charge of a class of five-year-olds. Of average intelligence but emotionally unstable and easily bored. You had to speak slowly, simply and with lots of modulation.

'About the ring, you mean. You can call me Fran, if you like.'

'Thank you, so kind.' He ran his finger down the text. 'Here we are. Er, perhaps it would be prudent to remind you, as I'm sure you're aware, that although you are legally the closest next of kin to the deceased, the

MacFies traditionally favoured very strongly the concept of male *primogeniture*. That means that the eldest or only son tends to inherit the greater part of the estate. It would therefore be unrealistic to hold very high expectations … '

Fran leapt to her feet and threw herself over Mr Gerund's desk. 'The ring … just tell me … did he leave me the Udaipur … did he give me my ring back?'

'Please, try to remain calm, Mrs MacFie. We endeavour to conduct these proceedings with dignity. There is, I'm afraid, no mention of a ring.'

Fran screamed and fell back into her chair, clutching her mouth. Her eyes agog. Her chest ceased to move. She'd stopped breathing.

'I think I know which ring you're referring to and if I'm not mistaken, the Colonel had to sell it recently, with much regret of course, to settle an outstanding debt with our company in connection with some paternity suits … which of course proved utterly unfounded but nevertheless had to be defended. I'm sure you'd agree that the protection of your husband's honour … '

Hamish leapt up as Fran gasped and spluttered, her body racked by contractions. 'You've given her a panic attack.' He whipped off her hat and had it inverted as a bowl to catch her vomit. To Gerund's disgust, he crammed the soiled hat into the wastepaper basket and led Fran off to the bathroom. Half an hour, three gin and tonics and twenty milligrams of Valium later, Fran was escorted back into the room. She looked as if she'd been filled with candle wax. Hamish held her hand. In the meantime Mr Gerund had fumigated the place with lavender.

'"To my beloved wife,"' Mr Gerund started, then realised he'd misread it. 'I'm sorry, that's been deleted and initialled. I'll start again. "To my wife, Fran, I leave the life rent of my stocks and shares … "'

'How much's that worth?' Fran seemed to have made a startling recovery.

'Er, I'm afraid he subsequently had to sell most of them, but there's very good news coming up. I'll continue … '

He paused to inflate his hanky with a hawking snort. Fran whimpered impatiently.

' … and also Turner's *The Frosty Evening* currently in my study.' He looked up cheerfully.

'It's got mould.'

'But it's a Turner!'

'And mildew, creeping mildew at that.'

'But Mrs MacFie, a mouldy and mildewed Turner is better than no Turner at all. In fact, Mrs MacFie, I trust it will not be construed as an indiscretion if I were to add, off the record, you understand, that I believe you have the most to celebrate of all Colonel MacFie's beneficiaries.' He subtly transposed the smile for the widow into a sneer for the son.

Fran had lapsed into a trance and Hamish could only revive her with several squirts of Bach's Rescue Remedy – *Calming Peace in the Face of Anxiety and Panic* – which he found in her handbag. He led her outside and left her under the ministration of Mr Gerund's bodyguard. Mrs Speirs wore her hair in a bun shot through with skewers, and a long red cardigan over the body of a Sumo wrestler. He'd rather face her, Hamish thought, than his father disguised as Gerund. Wearily, and for the last time, he went to collect his *certain conditions.*

* * *

'As you will be aware, Mr MacFie, your father entertained several reservations about … ' A nose wipe failed to disguise the internal grappling for tact.

'About what, Mr Gerund?'

' … about your *suitability* to inherit the Dundreary estate.'

'Why not just say it. We're talking big-time disappointment here. He despised me.'

'If you prefer to put it that way, it does appear so. The first consideration is that, unfortunately, no provision was made to offset Death Duties, and the Inland Revenue has assessed these at £687,028.'

Hamish felt his lungs collapse. His dream of an experimental estate promoting philanthropic land-use evaporated. Now, he realised, he'd be lucky to end up with his own potato plot.

'Current debts amount to £26,303 making a total liability of £713,331. I assume you do not have sufficient private means to pay that?'

Hamish just stared ahead.

'In which case part of the estate will have to be sold. I will instruct surveyors and the estate accountants to draw up a firm proposal to raise this sum, but a preliminary assessment suggests that Fitful Lodge and the northern estate will have to be sold, and the largest part of your southern holdings. At this stage I'm confident we should be able to exclude Dundreary Castle, and perhaps an area of roughly eight to ten miles in radius from it, including Loch Papil but excluding your remaining holdings in Flabbay township. I'm sorry but this is the only practicable way forward.'

Hamish watched this man impassively boxing people's lives into parcels tied with red tape, imagined wax dripping onto knots, seeping, receiving the imprint of Hamilton, Gerund, Nayers & Filigree's signet, hearing the safe door close. A hollow, resounding *thrummp*. Then he closed his eyes. He said nothing.

'On your father's death the estate passed into the custodianship of a Trust. The Trustees are myself, Mr Filigree and Lord MacArthur of Flashcairn. We are to check the annual accounts and, if necessary, we may take any action we deem necessary to avoid bankruptcy. In effect, if you are willing, you are to be the manager of Dundreary Castle and what remains of the estate, answerable to the Trust. Thus, although you occupy the building, you hold no legal title to it or its assets, and may not dispose of anything without the Trust's consent. A thorough inventory will be prepared.' For a moment he wondered if Hamish had gone to sleep. 'You are following all this, I take it?'

'Every word, every insinuation, every threat.'

'At the end of two years the Trust is instructed to relinquish control and hand over full title to you, if – and only if – the following four conditions have been met.'

'Here we go. The rub. Fire away. I'm all ears.'

'Your father used to pride himself on his athletic ability. Your apparent deficiency in this area caused him concern, particularly your poor head for heights. "If a man looks low, he aims low" is how he's worded it here. "Climbing develops manly qualities, helps a fellow set his goals high and boosts testosterone levels no end." So the first condition is a climbing challenge … '

'Oh Jesus. Not the fucking Jungfrau?'

'No. The Mickle Flabbay lighthouse.'

'What? Climb that? A condition of the will … it's impossible, its tall … and … vertical.' His brains slopped at the thought. 'Jesus.'

'I'm only reading what's here. Condition One: climb the Mickle Flabbay lighthouse.'

'And just supposing I am part orang-utan. How would I prove it?'

'Quite simple. Your father thought of that.' Gerund opened a drawer and pulled out a compact video camera. 'Zoom in and out for close-ups. Your features must be visible. No cuts. Continuous sequence only.'

'I bet you both had a ball plotting all this.'

Gerund ignored the remark. 'The next is a more personal affair. The Colonel had a difference of opinion with the local policeman, one Sergeant Cleghorn. Condition Two: You are required to bring about Sergeant Cleghorn's public humiliation.'

'At least that one's feasible.' Hamish considered the proposition further. 'A gift, actually.' His spirits rose slightly.

'Condition Three: You are to maintain the buildings, statues and policies in good repair, and restore the estate finances to a viable concern.'

'Oh Hallefuckingllujah.' Hamish got to his feet. 'That's a joke, when he was the one who ruined them. Next time you're communing with the old fart, tell him to stuff his conditions and his estate. He didn't want a son, he wanted a super-human to offset all his failures.'

'I admit the terms of the will are extreme and far from fair. Quite to the contrary of your accusation of conspiring against you, I wish to point out that I did my utmost to persuade him to alter the most unreasonable clauses.'

'Unreasonable! You call them unreasonable? You're as bad as him. They're insane. He was an out and out nutter.'

A sudden idea occurred to Hamish, and he resumed his seat. 'When did he make this will?'

'It was most coincidental, really. He changed everything the day he died.'

'Don't you have to be *of sound mind* to change a will? He flipped that day. Everyone in the house'll testify to that. We'll contest the will on grounds of insanity. That way it would revert to his previous will.'

'There is *no* previous will. He threw the old one in the fire that afternoon. I and my colleague, Mr Filigree, witnessed it. And we're both of the opinion that your father was *of sound mind*. There would be nothing to contest, Mr MacFie. Naturally you are free to decline these conditions and vacate the estate, but perhaps you'd care to hear the last condition before making your decision?'

'Oh, go ahead. *Do* tell me his final wish, the missing item for the old bastard's everlasting happiness.'

'Condition Four is more of a hypothetical nature. You will be aware that for many years there's been talk of connecting the island to the mainland by a bridge. Recent speculation in the press suggests this may soon become a reality. Your father was strongly opposed to such an intrusion into the life and character of the island. If such a proposal is implemented in the next two years, you are, and I quote, "to oppose the construction of a bridge to the bitter end."'

'What the hell does that mean? Doing a Tiananmen Square job before a squadron of cement mixers?'

'I don't take his meaning to be *your* bitter end. I think we can infer that open and vigorous opposition, or possibly something criminal, would suffice.'

'Terrific! I'll remind the court of your advice at my trial.'

'I'm not advising you to do anything, Mr MacFie, I'm simply trying to interpret your father's wishes. Moreover, it may prove entirely irrelevant because at the moment there is no proposal for a bridge.'

So, that was it. Four Herculean Tasks. Hamish thought he might as well go home and pack. Not even in his blackest assessment could he have pictured his father compiling such a vindictive list. And yet, strangely, the one condition he would have predicted as a cert wasn't there. 'You mean there's nothing about sons and heirs? No mandatory requirement to breed at least a couple of sons a year for the period?'

'I haven't finished yet.'

'But you said there were only four conditions.'

'Four has two parts to it. 4b stipulates: You are to produce a son.'

Hamish slumped back in his chair and laughed. He laughed and laughed until the upholstery pinheads digging into his back were about to draw blood. Then he remained silent for a while, lost in thought.

'So, tell me, Mr Gerund … ' Hamish leant forward and rested his arms on the mahogany table and fixed his gaze on the lawyer's eyes, 'what happens if I fail, if I don't quite manage to blow up the bridge, or talk the castle out of suicide? What happens then?'

'Failing the fulfilment of these conditions the Trust is instructed to sell it to the highest bidder and donate the proceeds to the Rajput Lower Caste Orphans Mission.'

Hamish rose.

'Just one more thing, Mr MacFie. There is one proviso to all the above. If you should turn out to be homosexual, the agreement is nullified and the estate will be sold.'

Hamish was grateful for the silence that descended on the car as he drove Fran and Angus back to Flabbay. Part of him was already listing clothes to stuff into a backpack as Dundreary's cursed image faded into the pages of *Trailfinders Winter Brochure*. The Maldives, maybe, or Goa, or Bali. Anywhere, really. If he got in quickly he could flog off a few antiques before Gerund's vulture squad got their talons into them and have enough money to hang out on some beach for a year or two. No ideals, no ambitions, no worries.

'HE SAID WE CAN STAY FOR THE REST OF OUR NATURAL LIVES, DIDN'T HE, SIR?' Angus suddenly asked as they passed Loch Ness.

'That's right, Angus, as long as I manage to do the impossible in the next two years. If not, we'll all have to leave and it'll be sold from under our feet.'

'WE'VE EVERY CONFIDENCE IN YOU, SIR.'

Hamish could feel hot crushed coral parting his toes, massaging them as he walked, could inhale the soothing fragrance of bougainvillaea, sense the rhythmic arrival of surf banish time and lull him into the eternal ... and now Angus and Effie were trespassing into the picture, standing on the same bloody beach, he in his plus-fours, she in her apron, arms folded, watching his every move with the open hostility of the betrayed. 'Thank you, Angus.'

Ice shattered as they drove up Dundreary's frozen drive. Gertrude, Hamish noted, was tethered to the podium of the Roman monopede with insufficient rope to reach the ginko. She raised her head from a bowl of pony nuts and blinked into the glare of the headlights.

'I'm going for a walk. Need some exercise to clear my head.' Hamish pulled on a trench coat – Russian, allegedly, a witness of the Siege of Leningrad – and a scarf – his own and uncontaminated by his family's past – and set off into the moonlight.

He avoided the chapel, which gave him the creeps in daylight and represented the holiest of horrors by night. He took another path, leading through the overgrown walled garden. Some late-grubbing blackbirds were scrabbling through layers of dead leaves like odd inventions of Caribbean percussion. A peacock stood on a wall snoring. Hamish let himself through a gate that opened onto the moor. He walked past the ragged precipice where the mausoleum had stood, and for a moment contemplated stepping over the edge. Had it been any other part of the coastline where he could have established his own private death site, he might have done it, but the very thought of crashing in on his relatives was repellent enough to defy gravity. He walked on until he came to a boulder where he could sit and look down on Dundreary.

Ancestral seat of his family! A MacFie had sat there since 1396, supposedly. Part of the original keep was authentically dated as late sixteenth-century but the building had undergone radical alteration. True to the fallibility of *nouvelle-richesse* and aristocratic insecurity, the Victorian MacFies – newly rich on the industries of kelp and sheep – had 'improved' their ancestral home by turning it into a monstrosity. Had any of them been happy there? Was history worth anything? Or was it just a grim lesson we refused to learn? Tradition equals guilt equals misery. Inheritance equals chains. Family unity equals inseparability.

From where *he* sat, on this boulder, he saw the family seat for what it was. So small. So self-important and isolated. Adrift in its own carefully constructed world. It's just a joke, he thought. A bad joke. And he laughed.

Back at the edge of the cliff, overlooking the reef of MacFie bones and débris, he removed his coat. The night was windless. The match lit at once. He waited until the coat's resistance was consumed in a frenzy of flames, and walked away.

As was the custom, Dalrymple had lit fires in the hall, dining-room and living-room by the time Hamish got back. The extravagance alarmed Hamish, yet he was glad to warm himself and even gladder of their cheer. Funny, he thought, he'd never considered the extravagance before. Responsibility brought a sense of dislocation. The whole place felt different. The smell of mould was stronger than he remembered even from that morning. The air of neglect, more menacing. Yet its brazen eccentricity had increased in charm. Out of habit he checked his father's armchair, and its continuing emptiness brought him a sense of hope and peace he couldn't remember having experienced in Dundreary before.

'I think we'll have to restrict ourselves to one fire in future, Angus. Just the living-room. We can set up a table and eat there too. And you can stop peppering the castle. Costing us a fortune. I'm sorry, but thank you for all your work in that quarter over the years.'

'YES, SIR.' Angus muttered into his tweeds and left.

'How's it coming along?' Hamish grimaced as he realised what Fran was doing. 'I think that's a job for the experts. You may do more harm than good.'

Set out before Fran was an array of rags and bottles. She was rubbing beaverishly at a corner of *The Frosty Evening*.

'Got to try and get it looking its best. Do you think it's worth much?'

'Oh, probably about thirty thousand without mould, but perhaps only thirty without paint.'

Fran looked up in alarm. 'You think I'm removing paint?'

'That does tend to be the function of Jif and nail varnish remover.'

He turned to the framed fox-hunting prints on the walls, riders gliding over hedges on elongated mounts and for the hundredth time imagined himself among them … the thrill of the dash, the unity of man and animal, the achievement of mythical flight …

'Penny for your thoughts, daaarling. You often stare at those *cheap* prints.'

'I'd love to be able to ride,' Hamish confessed. 'I've thought of taking lessons but I doubt my vertigo would let me.'

Fran gave him such a heartfelt look that he felt he had to escape, and went to look for Grout and Loony.

They were in the attic reading their way through boxes. Hamish followed the smell of a joint to Loony's hand and took a puff. They looked remarkably at home here, he thought: Grout in his camel-driver's hat and woollen waistcoat, and Loony in his orange dhoti; like Oriental curios picked up in a second-hand shop. Like the rest of the junk in the castle. They were all mishmash orphans.

'Wid ye listen tae this,' announced Grout. 'Letter frae MacFie, 15th July 1768:

Dear Sir,
I am in receipt of your letter of 8th inst in which you fulfil your feudal obligation by requesting my permission for your betrothal to your fiancée, one Miss Mary Colquhon of Grimport, on this Lammas coming, in the afternoon. Following my enquiries and satisfaction that the above-named is held to be

chaste and pure I hereby register my interest. I am prepared to give you my consent on condition that the wedding is held in the morning. This through consideration of the distance from the church to Dundreary, which, if the wedding were to be held at the time you request, would result in the excessively late arrival of the lady into my chamber, doubtlessly fatigued and therefore unlikely to provide nuptial pleasure with any degree of enthusiasm ... '

Grout lowered the letter and pulled a face. 'Git a load o that! Fuckin laird's right tae screw the bride afore the groom gits in.'

'I'm afraid that was the custom. It was barbaric.'

'Ah bet ye'd like that wee number reinstated,' Loony prodded. 'Jus primae noctis,' he added. 'Ah read aboot that tae.'

Hamish raised his eyebrows. 'You're certainly well-informed.'

'Aye, ye'll find posh schools dinnae hae a monopoly oan knowledge, ken.'

Hamish flinched. 'I wasn't expressing surprise that you had an education, I was lamenting the fact that I didn't.' Images played in his mind: being forced away at the age of eight, dormitories in an all-boys institution run like a commando camp, the struggle to find a fit in a life that was a faceless jigsaw ...

The dinner gong went. They descended to the dining-room and ate diluted tinned soup (*Baxters* Royal Game) followed by mince and dumplings.

'We get a lot of mince and dumplings,' Hamish explained. 'I think it was a favourite of Effie's mother.'

'Life's nae fair, eh?' remarked Grout. 'One family passes doon insanity, anither mince an dumplins.'

'So what did you inherit?' asked Hamish.

'Aw nae much. Jist an inferiority complex, a pathy-logical fear o water an a clinical dependency on fush suppers.'

'An inferiority complex? You?'

'Aye, it jist manifests itsel as up-yer-nose self-assertion.'

'I wish my flaws came out as their opposites. And you, Loony?'

'Ma family's motto wis that intellectualism wis a contagious disease toffs died frae, an usin yer brain wis a defection frae yer class an roots. Ah've hid tae battle that oot aw ma days. Oh aye, ah wis also born wi an allergy tae Cowdenbeath, but ah kin live wi that.'

'You ever read that Philip Larkin poem, This Be The Verse? *They fuck you up, your mum and dad ...* '

'Aye, says it aw. *Man hands on misery tae man ...* '

'Wonderful meal,' interjected Fran, looking towards her husband's empty seat, the Head of Table seat that Hamish had avoided like one of Loony's upper-class contagions, though the last thing he could have caught from it was intellectualism.

'Nae mince an dumplings fer you, eh, darlin?' remarked Loony. But Fran had once again faded into the furnishings and made no reply.

'She has a special diet,' Hamish explained. 'An aduki bean salad, taramasalata and marmalade on toast. A Shinto repast, apparently. She claims she picked it up in Japan.'

'Did ye spend much time in Japan?'

Fran looked up and smiled vacantly.

'She was never anywhere near the place.'

Grout nodded thoughtfully. 'Ah git it.'

They finished the meal in silence.

Later, with Rastafarian laid out long and splendid in front of the fire, Hamish broached the subject that had been worrying him all day.

'I may need your help to do something, and I'd like your opinion.'

Grout and Loony looked up from bound pockets of nineteenth-century air: Grout from a first edition of Dickens's *Hard Times*; Loony from *The Leadership Secrets of Atilla the Hun*.

'Do you think, if you were at the bottom of a vertical cliff with a blind man, you two could get him to the top?'

'Very odd thky thith evening,' observed Captain MacQuarrie.

Calum the Post hadn't noticed anything unusual. His mind was focused on their current mission and working out what they would do if they found the church locked. He turned to the west. Clouds hovered darkly on the horizon and turned the setting sun into a Halloween lantern. It rested briefly on the horizon and pulled faces at them.

'Aye, tis that.'

'Forecatht'th for a Forth Five out of Lewith.'

Calum was relieved to be drawn out of this messy church business and found himself smiling. He always found MacQuarrie's lisp a secret source of entertainment. Distorting, blurring edges, the artistry of a new perspective. Like an Impressionist painting. He always imagined his favourite artists, Monet and Manet, had lisps and painted the way they spoke. *Thtill Life – Appleth and Grapeth.*

MacQuarrie was breathing heavily, more used to a life of weasely observation from the bridge of the *Flucker* than exercise. Calum paused to let him catch his breath.

'*Thighearna*! All right for you pothtieth,' he grumbled. 'Too thtrenuoth for a thea dog like me.'

'Under the circumstances, blasphemy is unlikely to help. You just take your time, Thkip.'

Thkip, Thkipper, Skipper, Skip. A childhood nickname emanating from the brutality of the playground. MacQuarrie had been ragged mercilessly for his speech impediment, but he'd always known he'd be a skipper. His father had been one (until his unfortunate timing in striking Sgeir Mhor rock, his distress flares provoking gasps and applause in one of Oban's most enjoyable Guy Fawkes displays). And a damn good skipper MacQuarrie Junior had turned out to be. No one dared make fun of him now, such was his stature. Only he could joke about his impediment, and, perversely, his self-deprecation only served to increase his immunity and enhance his reputation. Calum held his friend in great respect. The story he treasured above many was the day MacQuarrie was on the Tarbert to Port Askaig run when a mayday was received from a yacht. MacQuarrie immediately notified Oban coastguard that he was diverting to render assistance. Some time later his vessel rounded a headland and came across a yacht half-submerged with the crew waving from the deck. MacQuarrie approached and picked up his loud hailer.

'Whath wrong wi' you?' he bellowed.

'We're sinking,' came the reply.

A period of silence followed before the loud hailer spoke again.

'And what are you thinking about?'

Calum chortled as he thought about it.

'Whath tho funny?'

'Oh nothing. I was just imagining God looking down on us from heaven and laughing at the absurdity of it all. Do you think he'll help us pick the lock if we can't get in?'

'It'th a good quethtion. I dunno. When'th a cruthade a crime, eh?'

'Well, we'll soon find out.'

They reached the former Fundamentalist Church ten minutes later and were alarmed to see that the sign had been covered with a crudely painted replacement.

'The True Fundamentalitht Church,' read Thkip. *'Mac an diabhail*! Why the little bathtard ... '

They tried the door.

Locked.

'*Gu sealladh sealbh orm*! It's never been locked before. Never, in all my fifty-one years.' Calum felt rage prick his skin. 'He's no bloody authority. It's our church too. We've a right to worship here.'

'What'll we do? We won't be able to have tomorrow'th thervith here.'

'We'll see about that. This is a legal matter now. We'll go to Cleghorn.'

Dark. At four forty-five. It always depressed Sergeant Cleghorn. Robbed him of his view. His outlook on life. Made him feel as lethargic as a salamander.

INSPECTOR SALAMANDER   BEWARE OF THE NEWT

God, what another tedious day! Sometimes he began doubting his sanity.

And unfortunately he wasn't the only one. He'd spent the early part of the week contemplating how to frame his claim for recent expenditures.

No matter how he tried to prettify the list, it was bound to raise eyebrows.

One pair regulation issue trousers, shredded	*30.00*
One regulation issue jacket, incurably stained	*58.00*
Two sets offside suspension, parts & labour	*246.00*
Replacement of rear axle, mountings, suspension, drive shaft, rear & side panels, chassis repair, filling, retouching, parts & labour	*1842.00*
10m new fencing, retensioning existing fence	*125.00*
Total	*£ 2301.00*

And it had raised eyebrows. And hackles. Only yesterday he'd received a dressing down by HQ Inverness. He'd never heard a Chief Inspector use such language before. Maybe he wasn't cut out for The Force after all? More than ever he needed to bust Brodie's porn ring.

He glanced at the clock. Fifteen minutes left, then home. He dreaded finding Angela in front of the telly again, as he had every day last week, wearing a set of diving goggles.

'Just getting them used to the set of my face,' she'd explained. 'Have to acclimatise the rubber to get a perfect seal.'

This diving nonsense was really going too far. But it might be worth tolerating if Angela could infiltrate Brodie's den.

He browsed through his Digitalis Murders cuttings. There was a knock at the door.

'Come in.'

'Thergeant,' Thkip began, 'it'th a grave bithneth.'

Cleghorn found his brain momentarily stunned by this sudden intrusion of activity into his solitude. It was bad enough to have MacQuarrie's bear-like frame burst through the door like some ghoulish escapee from the walls of Dundreary, let alone having to decipher his lingo and weigh up an out-of-hours postman all at the same time. Cleghorn marvelled at how the captain could speak without moving his lips. At least, there was little knowing what went on in the deeper recesses of MacQuarrie's beard. It wasn't surprising some words came out shredded through such an entanglement. *Bithneth* was too badly gone to be recognisable.

'Grave,' repeated Calum, with the Gael's easy evocation of doom.

'A grave?' Cleghorn's brain was moving up a gear. ... *body on Grimport Pier ... the seventh victim of the digitalis murderers was found in a shallow grave ...*

'Business,' reaffirmed Calum. 'At the church.'

'I'm not quite with you. You've found a grave at a church ... '

'*Thalla ith cac*! It'th nothing to do with a grave, you thtupid fool. It'th the minithter. MacLeod. He'th locked uth out. It'th a thin. And unlawful.'

Cleghorn stiffened at MacQuarrie's insult. *Inthult*, he thought, and deftly defused his indignation. 'Calm yourself, captain. There's no need to raise your voice. I never understand why you people can't state simply and clearly what your problem is without expecting me to be clairvoyant. You burst in here and mumble about graves and churches and then inthult me ... '

The word slipped out unawares and Cleghorn stalled as he caught sight of MacQuarrie's narrowing eyes.

'The problem, Sergeant, is this.' He explained the problem. 'What we want you to do is force Murdo MacLeod to open the church and let our congregation conduct its own services at mutually convenient times. He's no right to take possession of that church. It's common property.'

Cleghorn blanched at the thought of the confrontation. 'Well naturally I'll do what I can, Calum, but it's a grey area. Legally, I mean. More an internal church affair.'

'Nonthenth,' retorted Thkip. 'You have a rethponthibility to uphold the peath.'

'What do you suggest, then?' Cleghorn asked.

'That we meet at the church at ten tomorrow, which is an hour before the morning service. That's when MacLeod gets the church ready, and we can sort this out. We've told our congregation to meet at two.'

Cleghorn passed a fretful night. He barely noticed Angela's flippers. In his dreams, tall and lank, his features withered and hollowed by the constant suck of misery, there towered the Reverend MacLeod as Goliath, the fire-hardened remains of recrimination pointing an accusatory finger, a gnarled talon on a scrawny limb. Mad eyes. Rapier voice. Violent halitosis. Volley after volley of deadly invectives. And standing opposite, Farquhar Cleghorn with his empty sling.

* * *

They met at ten. Lights brightened the dusty matrix of panes in the lancet windows, and a soft squelch of base and alto emanated in the form of the 23rd psalm.

… Thou preparest a table before me in the presence of mine enemies …

Cleghorn heard the words and pictured the Reverend MacLeod filing his teeth into points.

'*Mac na Galla,*' swore MacQuarrie. 'They've thtarted early.'

'We'll just wait until they've finished,' suggested Cleghorn, 'and then we'll have a private word with MacLeod. We'll do this in a dignified manner.'

Ten minutes later the oak door opened. The Reverend MacLeod appeared, glowered at them, and then turned sideways while his congregation departed. It appeared from the way they poured out in a solid phalanx that they'd prepared for this moment and consolidated their ranks before MacLeod opened the door. As the last person left, MacLeod briskly closed the door and locked it.

'Good morning, Reverend.' Cleghorn kept his voice light and absentmindedly fingered his truncheon, the very latest in multi-use immobilisation. 'Not a bad one for the time of year.'

'It's never a good one in the company of the God-less.'

'Funny you should mention it. That's exactly why we're here. Not actually God-less, but church-less. Calum and the captain here have reported that you've locked the church, thereby preventing them and others from engaging in the lawful pursuit of worship.'

MacLeod looked down on Cleghorn with a height advantage of four-and-a-half inches. 'This building belongs to the True Fundamentalist Church and I am its rightful minister. No heathen dolt is going to tell me what to do. I answer to God's law, and to hell with you, you immoral, impertinent little runt.'

'How dare you address me like that … why you … badgery blowbag … '

' … sanctimonious prat, hypocrit,' Calum interjected.

'*Pit! A mhic ifrinn!*' shouted MacQuarrie. 'Judath, arrogant thhit … thheep-thhagger … '

MacLeod's face reddened and bulged. He cut a crude cross in the air. '*Mach as mo rathad.* May the Devil burn your souls and disembowel your progeny, castrate your sons, purge your daughters' wombs … '

'Good morning, gentlemen.'

They turned to see Mairi Ban the Byke approaching silently on high-heeled boots that stabbed the turf, leaving a trail of marks like a one-sided sheep. She was wearing a skirt which looked as heavy and weather-proof as a tarpaulin and a rope-patterned pullover interwoven with silver lamé. Her matching silver hair hung down from a sporty jockey cap. She held a wad of leaflets.

'Full of the joys of Christian love, are we?'

MacQuarrie automatically touched his cap, Cleghorn blinked in disbelief and Calum the Post took a step back. MacLeod registered her arrival by deepening the curl on his lips.

'And what would you know of love that's not besmirched with lust,' he spat, flinching and making the keys in his hand jangle.

'You keep out of this, Mairi,' Cleghorn warned sternly. 'We're just discussing the church's opening hours.'

'Sounds more like World War Three. And on the Sabbath too! Well, well. If you need an independent arbitrator, may I offer my services?' She smiled through a sculpted smear of Elizabeth Arden *sunset tropicana*.

MacQuarrie thought she looked magnificent. 'The minithter'th locked uth out of the church,' he explained. 'Thinkth he ownth it. Thplit the congregation.'

'It's our church too,' added Calum. 'We just want to be allowed to worship here.'

Mairi nodded reflectively. 'And is this your understanding of the matter, Sergeant?'

'Yes, I would say that is a satisfactory summary of the situation. But I'm cautioning you ... '

'And what do you intend doing about it?'

Mairi's directness caught him off guard. 'Well ... I'm just conducting a few interviews and collecting a few more facts.'

Mairi moved forwards to face the minister. She looked up into his eyes and held his gaze. 'And what do you have to say for yourself?'

'You mind your own business,' he snarled. 'Jezebel. *A nighean an diabhail.*'

'This *is* my business now, Mr MacLeod.'

In an instant, quicker than anyone could follow, she spun round and kneed the minister in the groin.

He folded, clutching his crotch and twisting his head to one side as he sank, his face distorted by pain. Cleghorn was struck by the way his pupils disappeared and left white slits instead of eyes. MacQuarrie later confessed that the strangulated soprano wail sounded so sweet to him, like a heavenly choir, in fact. Calum could only think: *how are the Mighty fallen.*

Mairi watched impassively as the minister rocked on the spot, whimpering, doubled over like a preening flamingo. When he altered his position slightly a set of keys appeared in a clenched fist. Mairi bent down and took them, the hand yielding without resistance.

'Is this what you're after?'

She handed the keys to Calum who accepted them gleefully.

'*Dia gam shàbhaladh!* We're, um, most grateful to you, Mairi.'

She handed them leaflets, and another burst of *sunset tropicana* graced her presence in acknowledgement of a fine start to her election campaign.

'Wha the fuck's that?'

Grout couldn't take his eyes off her. His fantasy goddess heralded before a wall of malts. He felt his leathers contract around him.

'That's Mairi Ban The Byke,' Hamish told him. '"Fair-haired Mairi". At least, she used to be. Looks like they'll have to rename her. She's changed her image.' Formerly of straight silver hair, prospective councillor Mairi MacLeod was now sporting an Afro-frizz of revolutionary red. 'The surprising thing about her,' he added, 'is she's Conservative-turned-New Labour.'

'Same difference,' Loony observed, and winked at his friend. 'Up de Gaulle, eh!'

Grout rallied to her defence. 'It's nae incurable. Ah think she's gorgeous an' she disnae shave her airmpits. That really turns ma oan.'

'You must be the only one then. The locals once got up a petition campaigning for her to shave.'

'Whit happened?'

No-one knew who started the petition, Hamish recounted, but Mairi found it one morning pinned to the dartboard. She immediately took out a quarter-page advert in the *West Highland Free Press* in which she thanked her most recent customers, listing the names on the petition. 'Then she sent each of them a condom and told them to go fuck themselves.'

Grout groaned in admiration.

The Sailor's Arms, known more accurately, if not affectionately, as the Barmaid's Armpits, was situated opposite Flabbay Pier, adjacent to Miss Oliphant's Emporium. Mairi had held the lease for five years and carefully reorientated the reputation from quiet family pub to ripsnorting hooley venue. She seemed at her happiest when fiddlers were standing on tables stamping out a beat and drunken dancers, gripped by the infamous centrifugal forces of Strip The Willow, were being despatched into splintering furniture, plate glass and air ambulances. The refurbishing costs had to be enormous but this never worried Mairi, nor did the dwindling stocks of kegs resulting from unsettled accounts. Mairi Ban simply never suffered from anxiety. Undoubtedly it helped that she had the power of Second Sight – and was widely held in reverence for it – but this extended to foreseeing *other* people's futures, never her own. Paradoxically everyone else could foresee hers and were only surprised at how long she managed to hold off the inevitable fate at the hands of receivers, Health and Safety or the Licensing Board.

'Ah've jist goat tae tell er she's fuckin gorgeous,' Grout suddenly announced, and he went off to the bar.

'Yer fuckin gorgeous.'

He imagined her handling all those condoms. Opening one. Bubbles frothing along the tear. He stared into her mascara and found little green pools in the middle. Like algae, he thought.

'Yer eyes are like algae.'

'*Ej trīs mājas tālak*. Algae!' Mairi raised herself straight and folded her arms. Her biceps hardened. 'If you've any more compliments, sonny, save them for a fight with someone else. *Atšujies.*'

Grout looked crestfallen. 'Ah didnae mean it like that.'

She leant forwards until all he could smell was garlic. 'And how *did* you mean it, then?'

'Ah muddled ma words. Ah think ah'm in love wi ya.'

'Well that's different then, isn't it. ¡*Que te jodas!* A far cry from telling me I've got slimy eyes.'

She looked him up and down, as much as she could see of him over the counter. No beer belly. Muscular chest. Flashy earring. Confident. Decisive. Unpredictable. He appeared to be his own man, and that was rare in the Highlands where the predominant clans were MacGod, MacMother or MacDrink. So where, she wondered, was the catch? A screwball?

Grout looked at her tits. They were enormous. Big enough for cushions.

'Yev great tits, tae.'

'I know.'

'Ah'm Grout.' He held out a hand. She ignored it. He took it back. 'Whit's *edge trees marge talc* whin it's at hame?'

'Well, literally it means "go three houses away". OK, it may not be much of an insult to you or me but, boy, it's a touchy business for a Latvian. *Atšujies* is much stronger. Means "go unravel yourself".'

'Yer kiddin? Gae unravel yersel!'

'Latvians are not really big on swearing. But their words sound great. Latvian and Spanish are languages without peers when it comes to invectives. They're words with teeth.'

'How many languages d'ye speak?'

'Six. Not exactly fluently, you understand, but conversant with the technical terms of my trade. Portuguese, Bulgarian, Lithuanian and, as I've already mentioned, Spanish and Latvian.' Mairi abstractly twisted strands of her hair and gazed up at a framed print of a man-o'-war. Wistfully she added: 'The sea and sea-faring nations have always had a profound influence on my life.'

Grout expected another broadside of Latvian, nevertheless he asked: 'Jist ae thing … why yer called "the Byke"?'

'Because, sonny, I'm a great ride. And besides, I'm bi. Byke rhymes with Dyke.'

She was also known *internationally*, she emphasised, as 'Queen of the Klondike' and 'the Silver Darling'. Of course, she admitted, the latter was a bit of a misnomer now she'd dyed her hair.

'Prostitution's a shite o a profession fer a dyke, innit?'

'Sonny, in this age, you gotta be ambidextrous, so to speak. I prefer women. Always have. Women know where and how to touch. If you ask me, men are on the way out. If the specimens of manhood I come into contact with are anything to go by, the human species'll be extinct by 2050. 2075 at the latest. Regressed. Muckle flabby, indeed.'

Grout seemed to have slumped. She thought even his earring had wilted. 'You'll have to excuse me' – someone gesticulating caught her eye – 'got to go and give someone a change of breath.'

When she returned, the conversation turned naturally to politics.

'If yer sae smart, how come ye wis Conservative?'

'*¡Me cago en la puta que te parió!*' She leaned over, grabbed the lapels of his jacket and hauled Grout level with her face. 'I remind people once, and only once, to say that word with a little more reverence next time.'

She released him and Grout dropped five inches back to ground level. He straightened out his creases.

'Because Thatcher was my type of woman.'

Grout stepped back and said: 'Fuckin megalomaniac. Overdosed on testosterone.'

Mairi appeared not to hear. She'd gone dreamy. Maggie! The Iron Lady! The very one who'd inspired Mairi's entrepreneurial undertakings and done so much to promote business. *GET ON YOUR BIKE!* So she'd voted Conservative. It wasn't the same with John Major despite being the son of high wire trapeze artists! To have a mother and father who used to fly through the air and catch each other by the hair *without a safety net* ... what must that do to a young mind! What independence and creativity must it spawn! Yet clearly it had traumatised him. The reality was a wash-out. You couldn't imagine John Major twenty feet up a rope ladder without wetting himself. Then along comes Tony BLiar. A whip-cracker! Anti-unions, anti-state-ownership. An Amazonia of sound bytes and spunk. The first irrefutably sexually-capable prime minister for a hundred and fifty years. Yes, Tony had become her man and his politics her tune. Yet, she was beginning to have doubts.

'I'm devoted to New Labour, but I don't like this talk about a bridge they're wanting to push through.'

'Bridge?'

'A bridge to Flabbay. Building it with private money. Private Finance Initiative, they call it. And they'll charge a toll to pay back the investors. If New Labour do that, I'm out. I'll fight it tooth and nail. Join the Socialists. Actually, I don't reckon New labour's going to hack it. The Lib Dems are on the up. If Kennedy gets in, liberalisation'll ruin me. He'll probably legalise prostitution, give it its own union even, and that'll be the end. Have to pay tax.' If that happened, she explained, she'd look for a new job. 'And the only other professions I reckon I'm qualified for, aside from pulling taps, is a diplomat or politician.'

'Diplomat! Yer aff yer heid. Draggin innocent men aff their feet ... ye call that diplomacy?'

'I haven't met an innocent man yet. And if it's one thing I understand, honey, it's people. Yes, the more I think about it, the new parliament's for me. Mairi MacLeod, MSP. Being a punter never did anyone any good. If you believe in something, you got to get out there and fight.'

'Ah changed ma mind, a bit. Yer still gorgeous but ye dinnae deserve a good man like me. But ye kin hae ma vote. Ah like fighters. Ah'm ane masel.'

'You call that a fight?'

'Naw. Ah wis jist observin. Great tits.'

He returned to Hamish and Loony who were discussing lighthouses.

* * *

For some time after Grout had disappeared Hamish and Loony had sat in silence. Loony pulled a curved pipe from a pocket and packed it with Sweet Apricot, an aromatic blend that drove the occupants of two adjacent tables to seek oxygen elsewhere. Hamish sat steeped in his own concoction of internal conflict. He hated this self-administered sabotage that wrecked any form of resolve or direction in his life. All his conscious days, it seemed, he'd been torn between opposites. He idolised Bill Gates and the Dalai Lama; he was a Greenpeace activist and yet lived off the proceeds of exploitation; and now he was a socialist landlord under homage to the late Atilla the Hun …

He was deafened by his own confusion.

'Yer lookin like a snail.'

Hamish was pulled to the present and noticed Loony staring at him through a swath of smoke.

'Like ye want tae crawl somewhere an hide.'

'That's just how I feel. I was thinking about this lighthouse business. It's absurd. I know I can't do it. And I'm not going to let the old bastard kill me.'

It was shortly after this that Grout returned.

Loony brought him up to date. 'Ah've been reassurin oor mate here, auld altophobic Hame, that we kin git him up the light nae bother. Well, a lot o bother but we kin dae it.'

'Aye, we'll need a block an tackle wi a good ratio, if yer gaunnae be dead weight tae us.'

Hamish blanched, visualising himself in free-fall, then lying at the base of the lighthouse like a toad run-over on the road. 'I don't want to be a dead anything.'

'Did ye ring em fer permission?'

He nodded. 'Northern Lighthouse Board. Edinburgh.' His mind, however, was still falling. He wondered at what point a plummeting body lost consciousness, and prayed it would be before impact.

'Weel. Whit did they say?'

'Not a hope.'

'Kid we nae try the charity fund-raiser number? Sponsored abseil frae the light – good publicity an aw that sorta shite?'

'I did. They said their purpose, since 1756, has been to promote saving lives at sea, not losing them on land.'

'Weel, tae hell. They kin gae unravel themsels.'

Loony turned to him. 'Gae unravel themsels?'

'*Artsoogies*. Jist a wee Latvian turn o phrase. Mairi's gien me lessons.' He smirked. 'Weel, aboot this climb. We'll jist hae tae dae it secretly.'

'I think we'd best forget it.'

'Naw.' Grout banged the table with his fist and pinned Hamish with his stare. 'Ye goat tae leap intae the dark, intae the hole nae kennin whaur ye'll end up. An a hale new way o life opens up. Things ye niver thought kid happen. An ye ken whit, it sorta returns a pairt o ye tae yersel. But ye goat tae jump. Ye goat tae believe, pal. That's ma faith. Tae mony folk hiv forgotten how tae jump.'

Hamish remained silent, absorbing the challenge. 'OK.'

'We'll tak care o ye, pal.'

'How?'

Grout scratched his stubble, pulled at an ear. 'Loon an ah'll hae tae gae up furst. Bein an early Stevenson it's nae been plastered smooth which maks aw the difference. Ah cased the joint last week. We kin use pins in the joints fer belays. Worst bit's a wee overhang unner the balcony. Then we kin fix the pulley tae the railin an haul ye up. An ye kin jist pretend tae be walkin up. Like a spider.'

Hamish emitted an anguished moan.

'Ah wis thinkin aboot the filum,' Loony added. 'If we wis tae use twelve frames a minute an nae twenny-four, we double the sensitivity tae light. An if we use infra-red, an the tae o us, Grout, wear green, and we use green rope, we'd be invisible. Infra-red disnae pick up green. That's how they filumed they Superman stunts whin he flies. He wis jist lyin oan a green support.'

'Aye? Niver kent that. Superman, eh?' He jabbed Hamish. 'We'll need a low tide. Ah cannae cross water.'

'Aye, an moonlight tae.'

They consulted tide tables and a calendar.

'A week on Friday. Full moon. Low tide midnight.'

Mairi Ban flicked a tap and caught a peat-stained trickle of Red Cuillin in a tilted glass, raising and lowering it until the froth teetered on the rim. Her other hand plunged into the optics and milked a Grouse for Angus Dalrymple and a rum for the captain, who was already on his fourth shipwreck of the evening.

'Aye, that wath thome thtorm, tho it wath. That Thouthern Othean'th a mean thon of a bitch. Oneth it wath tho bad we wath on the thame wave for three weekth.'

'WELL, I'M THINKING, THKIP,' responded Angus the Castle, 'THAT YOU DON'T NEED TO GO TO THE SOUTHERN OCEAN FOR STORMS. THERE ARE STORMS APLENTY HERE ON FLABBAY.'

'*Gu sealladh sealbh orm*! What on earth d'you suppose they're doing?' They followed Calum's gaze. Above a spilt gin and tonic and a floating raft of lemon, Angela Cleghorn sat with her mouth agape, urgently pointing down her throat.

'*O mo chridhe* … she's swallowed her tongue. And that damn fool Brodie, hasn't realised. Look at the idiot.'

Lawrence held out his fist and twisted it sharply into the thumbs up.

Angela responded with thumbs down.

'*Taigh na Galla* … mutht be trouble … '

'WAIT, THKIP,' advised Angus. '"GOOD." THAT'S WHAT HE'S JUST SAID TO HER. NOW HE'S SAYING, "IMMEDIATE ASSISTANCE REQUIRED".'

'Told you,' retorted Thkip. 'Why doethn't the damn fool shout?'

'SHE'S SAYING, "I CAN'T REMEMBER THAT ONE."'

'HE'S SAYING, "THINK. IT WAS THE ONE THAT SPILT YOUR GIN."'

'SHE'S LAUGHING.'

'We can see she's laughing,' said Calum, grumpily. He wasn't happy that he'd been trumped by Angus's lip-reading. They watched Angela hold up her clenched fist and peck the air. Lawrence responded with thumb and index finger forming a circle, other fingers raised straight.

'Very thtrange. Are they imitating birdth?'

'Do you think they're … they're … carnally involved?'

'NOT A BIT OF IT,' Angus replied sharply, struggling to cope with the short-sighted conversation again. 'THEY SAY SHE'S STRICTLY VEGETAR-IAN.'

Calum and Thkip flashed smirks.

'AS I WAS SAYING,' Angus drawled the words heavily. 'FORGET THE HIGH SEAS, THKIP. THERE'S ROUGH TIMES AHEAD ON THE ISLAND.'

'True enough,' agreed Calum the Post, 'there's Murdo MacLeod for one.' He took a slug of Cuillin, wiped off a cream moustache. '*Ochan, ochan.* It looks like everything's changing.'

Angus the Castle pounced on the cue. 'THE COLONEL SHOULD NEVER HAVE DIED ON US LIKE THAT. SO SUDDEN. LOOK AT ALL THOSE FOR SALE SIGNS. EVERYWHERE YOU LOOK.' He leaned forward and jerked his head towards the back of the bar. 'WE'LL BE OVERRUN BY MORE OF THOSE.'

Thkip and Calum turned to follow his gesture. Bill Braithwaite. They could hear a growling Yorkshire accent churning hard words. Calum thought of a tumble drier with loose change escaped from a pocket.

'US LOCALS CAN'T AFFORD TO BUY ANYTHING HERE.'

Mairi Ban overheard them and bristled. 'You bloody racists. You piss me off with your prejudices. People are people.'

Obscenities cut deeply into Calum, like stigmata. Suffering a rib wound, he retorted: 'No, he's got a point, Mairi. Prices here are geared to making the most profit from Southerners. And they come here with no sensitivity to our ways. Just bulldoze in. And they're forever forming committees to reorganise things. I hear that Braithwaite man's been changing rival guest house signs from "Vacancies" to "No Vacancies" so he'll get more business. Only last week … '

'Bullshit, Calum. He's only doing it because others have done it to him. You get good and bad incomers just like you get good and bad locals.'

'Theeth more Chrithtian than all of uth put together.'

Calum remained defiant. 'I hear, Mairi, that *your friend*, Mr Braithwaite, has put in an application to reopen the quarry. *Daingead!* My uncle used to run that quarry. You see, they come in and steal our jobs.'

'If the locals weren't so sodding lazy, they'd open up the quarry themselves. Half the time it's the incomers who've got the energy and gumption to make businesses work here. Look at the facts, you pillocks. They create jobs.'

'Because they've got money.'

'ENOUGH FOR HELICOPTERS,' added Angus. 'NEVER SEEN SO MANY HELICOPTERS SINCE THOSE ADS CAME OUT. ROMANTIC RUBBISH. YOU'D THINK BONNIE PRINCE CHARLIE WAS STILL KNOCKING UP FLORA MACDONALD HERE FROM THE WAY THEY WRITE.'

'I'm told Scottish Natural Heritage is bidding for South Flabbay.'

Thkip, whose croft, like Calum's, was in South Flabbay, looked stunned. He unreefed a sigh worthy of the Southern Ocean. 'Eth N H?'

'They want to make it a corncrake sanctuary.'

'Thanktuary? What good'th a fuckin corncrake? You can't eat it, can't theer it … can you get a grant for it?'

'They say they'll introduce one.'

'That might be OK then.'

Mairi handed them a sheet of paper. 'Just make a list of your worries here. I'll see if I can incorporate them into my manifesto.' She went off to collect glasses.

'Well, hi, darling.' She'd been meaning to work her way over to Angela for some time, and now she'd left it too late. Angela was leaving. Unusual to see her in the pub, Mairi reflected. And with Lawrence Brodie, of all people! That would set the gossip-mongers going!

She ran her eyes over Angela's body. Tight. Athletic. Tingling with electricity. An aura of girlish innocence compared to Mairi's swampish sexuality. Opposite currents, she thought, and felt the pull.

'Hallo, Mairi. I love the hair.'

'Yea, new image. How're things? Haven't seen you for ages. Not since we shared the snooker table at the Ben Stac.'

Angela giggled. 'Oh yes, that was a great night. I'm fine. Fine really.'

'Good. I see you've got to know the hermit. What's he like?'

'Hermit? Oh, you mean Lawrence! He's lovely. A very interesting man. He writes books, you know. Romantic books.'

'Sex? He writes about sex? He doesn't look as if he's ever dipped his cherry.'

'He's just shy, that's all. He's teaching me to dive.'

Mairi managed to prevent her face splitting into laughter. 'Oh yes? In the pub, then?'

'We're doing theory,' Angela replied, tartly. 'I'll have to be going now. Farquhar'll be wondering where I am.'

'Didn't you tell him?'

'No. He's funny about things like that. I told him it was my Messiah night.'

'Diving, Line Dancing, the Messiah ... I don't know where you find the energy.'

'I've given up the Messiah. Half of us walked out. Murray threw a wobbly when he found one of the singers was a Baha'i.' She lowered her voice. 'One of the squatters from the castle. Murrry banned him. He went ballistic ... '

'Oh shit, I don't want to hear any more. Ministers are just suppressed terrorists, if you ask me. You're better out of it.'

'That's how I feel. Now I just want to dive.' Angela turned to look back at Lawrence. His biro was madly impregnating paper. She'd turned rueful. 'Well, back to the bastion of Law and Order for me.'

Bastard of Law and Order, Mairi thought.

Six years, eight months, twenty-six days and approximately eight-and-a-half hours. Cleghorn scratched an itch on his stomach, prised his shirt apart to make sure he hadn't picked up a tick – unlikely in December, but ticks preyed on minds as much as bodies – and checked his figures. Two thousand, four hundred and thirty-six and a bit days till his pension entitlement.

'Oh to hell.'

What level of talking to himself constituted a social breakdown? Engulfed by loneliness, he felt his eyes fill. Farquhar Cleghorn, 'Cleggy', 'Cleggy'll bite ya' standing in the playground, bare knees and bow legs, too tender, too young to defend an unpopular name. No wonder he'd joined the police. Sought the armour of uniform. Now he saw the truth. It defended you from without; made you a prisoner within.

It was a fact of police life on an island such as this that no one wished to associate with 'the Law'. If offered friendship, or, more overtly, if it bit him on the leg, he wondered if he would recognise it? Or would sycophancy, or the suspicion of it, perpetually drive a wedge between him and potential friends? The pity of it. Cleggy, in uniform, so supremely defended; still lonely.

And no wonder he and Angela had fallen into each other's arms. She'd saved Cleggy and he'd rescued Ramsbottom. Refugees. Is that all they had in common?

It seemed so. Even the dancing had disappeared. They hadn't rumbaed, sambaed or cha-chaed for years.

Would it have been different if they'd had children? Children opened hearts. They didn't understand the rules of charade, broke barriers, kept on broaching reality. Everything was back to front. It was children who understood reality. No, kids would have torn them apart. Spoilt the game. Forced them to grow up.

'To hell.' He'd work flexi-time. He picked up the phone. Dialled 828.

'Fancy a round of golf?'

Angela had lain in bed long after Farquhar had gone to work. Not sleeping. Not reading. Not for any other reason than there was no good reason to get up. Dark mornings cowed her. The great submarine adventure ebbed and flowed, sometimes grounded, sometimes fled into a distant, unbelievable mirage. She could feel herself melted, just a shapeless mass. Leaking into infinity, obscurity. And the effort of hauling it all back, dragging herself together, was insurmountable. Worse than the not knowing, was the not caring. Nothing mattered.

Claws came in. Her cat. Minx on tall legs and fish-hook feet. A tabby. Farquhar's present to her one Christmas. 'Santa Claws', he joked. She'd resented it at first. Took it personally. 'Here's the child we don't have.' That's what he seemed to be saying. As if it were her fault. Now she loved Claws. Pressed thorns to her breast. Simultaneous solace and penance.

'Oh, Claws! We've lost the means of rejoicing in the present. Of making the idle moment an opportunity to savour our existence. Unlike you.' Her hands intoxicated. Claws bubbled. 'So full of yourself. Content in your grace, secure in your perfection.'

She kissed him. 'You're such a lesson to me.'

And thought: I too have hidden perfection.

She looked for that T-shirt, and found it. Slipped into it. Cold cotton sent a frisson down her spine. She pouted before the mirror. Read the words reversed. *Behind every gifted woman there's usually a rather talented cat.*

The phone rang.

'Fancy a round of golf?'

'Now? I thought you're meant to be working.'

'I am. I'm always meant to be working on this job. And off the job. I just feel to hell with it. I'll take my afternoon off this morning. How about it?'

STUFFED LIVES *ALASTAIR SCOTT*

The last gale had abated. Left an emptiness in the air. The sea was flat, a pearled reflection of stratocumulus, yet pulled by currents into streaks like creased cling film. A raft of guillemots frolicked among sprats. Rags of mist floated low, caught on whins, left trailing threads. Millions of silver globes of dew sheathed the links. In the rough, caught on spiders' webs, they had aligned themselves into brilliant banners.

thwick. Angela's ball. Topped. A smear on the fairway.

thwok. Farquhar's ball. Soaring. A dot fading into stratocumulus.

'Nice shot,' Angela agreed. 'Pity it wasn't straight. Never find it.'

Angela played five more shots and advanced towards the hole steadily in the manner of croquet. She began the ritual of addressing the ball. Place club-head an inch behind it, jiggle shoulders, flex neck, raise club slowly, deep breath, freeze body, swing hips, eye on ball …

'FOUND IT!'

The shock caused Angela to gyrate lopsidedly. The club sank into Flabbay soil and funny-bone paroxysms shot up her arms.

'Saw you!' A sing-song voice. Cleggy Spots Cheating! 'Air shot. Counts as one.'

Angela stood on the spot hugging herself, her club discarded. Thought of racks, boots, iron maidens, and Farquhar in them. Said nothing. Muttered, *moron*. Picked up her club. *Subtracted* two as a consolation. Heard a click. Farquhar's ball streaked overhead, graceful as a swallow.

poohtuff. A flurry of sand.

'Bunker!' she yelled gleefully, welling into laughter. She mashed her chip but didn't care. Farquhar always dug himself deeper in bunkers. Years ago he'd followed the Gary Player 'Improve Your Game' strip in the *Daily Express* but he'd missed a vital month's worth on sand wedge technique. Angela was a relative beginner to the game, though she'd soon developed a knack for creative arithmetic. She watched her mishit birl over the turf trailing a peacock tail of spray, skite over the adjacent bunker and creep hesitantly into the centre of the green.

'First hole to you,' Farquhar conceded. He marked eight on his card.

She managed to halve the second, but lost six on the trot when Farquhar could do nothing wrong.

They teed up at the ninth. The short, steep 90-yard drive from Look Out Knoll down to the clubhouse. But tricky. A burn in the middle, a ha-ha of bunkers arching round the green. Farquhar allowed Angela to play first.

She felt out of kilter and changed club to a heavy-headed spoon. Nuzzled its blazed face against the ball, swung back, watched the ball change shape, hair grow into a top-knot, sealed slits for eyes, splayed nose, lips stitched together, a shrunken head, Farquhar's, after the Jivaros had had him, felt the club descend, closed her eyes, drove her arms with all her might …

'My God!' Farquhar watched the ball in disbelief. 'You struck that rather well.' And then, a moment later. 'Jesus! You're going to overshoot by … '

They saw the car change colour, dullness transformed to mirror brightness one moment, a black rectangle the next. Heard the explosion a little later, much too long to be connected, it seemed.

'Goodness,' breathed Angela, half-shocked, half-euphoric on adrenaline and killer instinct. 'Did I really do that?'

'I'm afraid so.'

'Why, it must be fifty yards beyond the hole.'

Farquhar nodded.

'I've never struck a ball so well!' Delight floodlit her face. 'Oh.' It dimmed as a realisation struck. 'Should I write that one off and play another.'

'Under the circumstances, I don't think that would be wise.'

Farquhar took a four iron, but reconsidered and chose a five, erring on the light side. Too light. Clean into the burn.

'SHIT.' He flung his club away in disgust. They heard a shout from below. Angela peered over the edge and for a while was unable to identify the strange creature that met her eyes.

'Oh, Professor, it's you!'

'Of course it's me. May I remind you, young Cleghorn, that the aim of golf is to propel the ball towards the hole, not the club. Damn near felled me, you did.'

'May I ask what you're doing?' Angela ventured.

'I'm experimenting with a new device. D'you realise, there're two things that haven't evolved since the Stone Age? Axe heads and golf clubs. That man hasn't thought of any refinements is a disgrace.'

'I didn't think golf was that old.' Angela thought of Lawrence. Wondered if she should tell him. *Arunk flunked his putt and settled for a birdie!* He'd divulged the barest outline of his plot so far. She could still only guess about the rest. The foreplay.

'It may not be, but that's not the point. I'm trying to design a brace for beginners, a support, if you like, to eliminate a whole complexity of errors. I daresay it'll revolutionise the game. Needs to. Can't have those Yanks dominating our national sport, eh?'

'Quite,' agreed Farquhar. 'Disgrace.'

'How does it work?'

Angela was enthralled by the unwieldiness of the contraption. Professor Oliphant stood within a slanting circle of metal wearing a mesh of leather straps that held the shooting stick against his stomach.

'This,' he tapped the shooting stick, 'is a shooting stick. You'll notice I'm leaning on it and it's holding me. At the bottom,' he tapped the bottom, 'this arm supports the circle of metal. Adjust it until the circle is half a club head away from the ball. See?' He demonstrated the spacing. 'You keep your club shaft against the circle – aluminium, very light – swing up and down, a perfect strike.'

'I get you,' said Farquhar. 'It's all designed to maintain consistent distances and angles.'

'Precisely.' He demonstrated on a daisy. And another. And another. A scattering of uniformly clipped heads.

'The problem I'm working on now,' he continued, 'is correlating a range-finding system with a power guide.'

'Well, good luck,' encouraged Angela. She was anxious to get to the car. Confirm it really was a Dunlop 86. Her ball. That she really had struck an outstanding drive.

'Can't see it catching on. Too cumbersome,' she confided when they were out of the Professor's earshot.

'They say he's got a brilliant mind. Almost certain to have got a Nobel prize.'

'Why didn't he?'

'A minor oversight, apparently. Cambridge Research Institute. Half the building went. Lost all his notes.'

They walked on. Farquhar suddenly emitted a feeble groan. 'Oh no! You've struck the secretary's car.'

A small crowd had gathered in the carpark. The Reverend Murdo MacLeod, the colour of cooked lobster, was extracting himself from the blizzard of glass that was his Ford Escort 1.6. He showed something to the onlookers, said something which induced nods and came striding towards them.

'I might have guessed,' he snarled. 'Bet you did it on purpose. *A Thighearna*, of all the spiteful … ' He leaned so close Farquhar could feel heat from the minister's forehead, smell breath pickled in sardines and Marmite.

'Dunlop 86?' Angela scrutinised the ball in his hand. 'My fault, I'm afraid. Sorry, Reverend. Struck it unexpectedly well … I mean … badly. Of course, we'll pay for the damage.'

MacLeod's voice came straight from the arctic. 'Oh yes, you'll pay all right.'

'Good morning, Mrs Cleghorn, gentlemen. Splendid weather for the time of year.' Miss Oliphant, in matching barracuda blue skirt and jacket. Jaunty in voice and stride. 'I trust my dedication and record over the years speak for themselves and that I can count on your vote next week?' A grinful of largesse.

'Rest assured, Miss Oliphant, you've got mine.' The Reverend MacLeod turned and stomped off.

'Reverend!' Angela's urgency froze him in mid-stride. 'May I have my ball back?'

They had a drink in the clubhouse. Farquhar, a pint of MacEwans 80/-, Angela, Bacardi and Coke.

'Of all people!' Angela giggled.

'Of all people!'

Farquhar's grin broke into a belly-laugh. She felt a rush of closeness. Not love. The opposite, really; they were accomplices in crime. But it felt good. Like a start. Farquhar felt it too. So good it was painful. He got up. Came back with a cup. The Hannibal MacFie Trophy. For the annual medal winner. Best in the club.

'I dream of winning this,' he confided. His reflection stared out, wore the engravings like scars. 'Would be my happiest hour.'

Angela nodded, sadly.

'I thee we'll have to watch you, thargeant.' Thkip, club president, on his day off, shouting from the bar. 'Thtealing our cupth.'

'Just dreaming.' He blushed. Cleggy Caught Playing Heroes.

* * *

Cleghorn sat up late at work, flexi-time. Paying for his golf. Two thousand, four hundred and thirty hours of duty to go. Angela would be out at her reading group. Or was it her Messiah night? Or had she given that up? They chopped and changed. Hard to keep track. Once again he plotted the angles and distances of the canyon between them. All these hobbies she'd taken up initially were fair enough. Then it had got weirder: mountain biking and roller-blading. She'd even talked of bungee jumping. At Flabbay Gala. Now diving. At her age! He'd given her the wetsuit she'd wanted. Handed his wife on a plate to the pervert, he feared. But he'd colluded. A seven-millimetre Typhoon. The best, apparently.

'Strange,' Cleghorn mumbled to himself. 'Never seen that before.'

Odd shadows were playing on the face of Glas Bhein above Pluckton.

Then his fax chirped to life. A clipped message. 'To Flabbay Police Station. From Mallaig Coastguard. Time: 21:21. Page 1 of 1. Can't raise the Mickle Flabbay keeper at present. Erratic light signals and shadows reported. Warning bulletin released to shipping. We'll investigate. This is for your information only. Out.'

'So, Lawrence Brodie is up to something.'

And as Sergeant Cleghorn wrestled with Vice Vice, the keeper of the Mickle Flabbay light was preparing to dive.

'Diving now,' he said with a smile, and lowered himself into her.

Hamish stumbled towards his execution, his throat a bloodknot, slipped to his stomach. Wearing white. His warders, green. For the camera.

A mat of weed shivered in a breath of air. The sea gently sucked at the sand as it retreated from the spit. The night was quiet save for the mushy creak of their boots and occasional clank of hardware from the climbers' girdles. A full moon robbed the world of half-tones. Two-dimensions. Silhouettes and enamelled edges. They surprised a heron who uttered a gralloching screech as it floated off like a pterodactyl, momentarily framed in a pillar of light.

Flash, flash, flash, flash.

Hamish fixed his gaze on the ground. He refused to look up but couldn't escape the circling spokes of light.

They paused at a shed two hundred yards from Hamish's Everest. Base Camp.

'Ye OK?'

Hamish tried to say *yes*. Opened his mouth and his stomach contracted. He felt a surge of vomit, staggered aside and fell to his knees. Nothing came. Dry heaves. He crouched, suffocating in air too thick to breathe.

'Here. Reckon ye hivnae hid enuff.' Grout handed him Rock Rose remedy (*Terror & Fright*).

Hamish took a sip. His head was two feet off the ground and doing gyrobatics. Sixty-eight would be like outer space.

'Right. Ah'll recap.' Grout threw down a coil of rope. 'Git the camera set up oan its legs. Loon and me'll scale the knob. Tak us aboot fifty minutes, gaen quietly like. At the toap, we'll fix the block an tackle. Loon'll abseil doon. Ye switch oan the camera then Loon'll tie ye in. We'll haul ye up. Aw ye hiv tae dae is stand oot frae the wall an walk.'

Hamish made a sound like a stuck record player.

'Ah've telt ye a hunner times. Ye cannae fa. Ye'll hae twa ropes on ye. They ropes kin haud a grand piana.'

With that, Hamish found himself alone. He fumbled hands over the ground until he came to resistance. Groped the shape of a stone. Another, and another. Wedged a hand in a crevice. Hauled his weight. Rose slowly and balanced, gulping chunks out of the air. Willed his heart from a battering ram to a mallet. A small rubber-headed one. Prayed.

'*Om Mani Padme Hum. Om Mani Padme Hum.*' Then: 'Our Father, Who art in Heaven ... '

He was going to need all the help he could get.

He extended the tripod. Planted its feet evenly. Screwed on the camera. Heard *tap, tap, tap, tap, tap, tap.* Then a light rain of Stevenson mortar. Then another *tap, tap, tap.* Only this time it wasn't coming from in front of him, but from behind. *tap, tap, tap.* Close behind. An echo, he thought. But he knew it wasn't an echo. This had a life of its own. His knot re-tightened.

tap, tap, tap. He was throwing up dry whimpers.

Movement. Oily black movement in the dark. Ten yards away a shag was patting a barnacle-encrusted rock with slow, dithery movements as if checking a passage in Braille.

Hamish slumped into relief. Later it was the shag's turn to suffer alarm and crane its head round one hundred and eighty degrees. Balanced uncertainly between flight and immobility, it listened without comprehension to the sounds of snoring.

* * *

An omelette blistered in the pan and uttered lisping burps. Shavings of cheese and miniature logs of spring onions were piled alongside. A plate warmed in the Rayburn, gently warbling to itself. Three fresh loaves steamed on a rack, filling the room with a yeasty aroma.

Lawrence eased his hand out of Greta. There'd been a problem. Her motor was running fast. He hoped this would be the last gynaecological operation he'd have to perform. '*HOT UP YOUR ROD AND GET YOUR ROCKS OFF!*' flagged the label. So far his rocks hadn't got off and Greta was fast losing her sex appeal. Familiarity was breeding contempt. He now regarded her as a shatter diagram of her parts, housed in a forbidden figure like that of a libidinous mother-in-law. And worse, he was afraid of her. Her *real feel pleasure pussy* now provoked the frightening image of lowering his rod into one of those kitchen sink contraptions that devoured vegetables and buckled teaspoons. He'd also sprayed half a can of WD40 into her and God alone knew what sort of a health risk that might pose to sensitive skin.

He ate his omelette and gulped back half a tumbler of neat whisky. Tonight was the night. Of Born Again Carnality. The Dusting of Genital Cobwebs. The Hotting of His Rod. The Sexual Emancipation of Lawrence Brodie. He poured another half tumbler.

Talisker 13-Year-Old Malt. Crept down his throat burning a path like lava. An infusion of heat filling his chest, stomach and rod. As the room altered perspective – skewed – he was glad he'd moved his office down from the orb during the previous night's storm. Couldn't have faced the climb. He took another swig and primed himself on his notes.

The story had leaped millennia. Arunk had performed. Fumbling through sweat and tears the Brodie Clan, passionately enthusiastic and passionately untalented to a man, had been procreating. Baffling both themselves and their women, they'd apparently begotten their way out of the late Pleistocene-early Palaeolithic, incomprehensibly sewn seed through the Neolithic Revolution, survived the frigid Ice Ages, studied pornographic cave art in the Stone Age, worshipped the stork in the Bronze, learned a thing or two at the hands of Romans, wholeheartedly swallowed Columba on Immaculate Conception and entered The Dark Ages still very much in the dark. Somehow they'd muddled through, innocently spawning sons for, Lawrence calculated, sixteen thousand, six hundred and sixty-six generations. In the face of such ignorance, it was an astonishing achievement. So void an epoch of pleasure had it been that now, in the Year of Our Lord 1040, the Brodies were questioning their orientation. They were thinking of coming out. Dramatic Twist. Everything now hinged on Macbeth.

Lawrence was aware that this was his greatest authorial gamble to date. To tinker with history and have a Brodie as a gay Macbeth might be the linchpin on which this great saga would fall. Yet his mind was set. Having swithered over whether to go with historical fact and portray Macbeth as the nice guy he really was, and his seventeen-year reign as 'The Golden Age' it really was, or go with Shakespeare's libellous distortion, he decided to side with Shakespeare. There was never any mileage in nice guys or Golden Ages.

The plot was for serial-murderer Macbeth, haunted by his victims' ghosts and the horrible spectre of his loopy wife, to reflect on a gay affair he'd once had. He vows to reignite it. On his way to the tryst he meets a seductress whose repertoire blows his mind, and everything else, to such effect that homosexuality is metaphorically out the window and the Brodies – Carnally Evolved, Full of Savvy and Unswervingly Heterosexual – are, henceforth, the bees knees in bed.

tap, tap, tap.

Lawrence poised, cocked his head and listened.

tap, tap, tap, tap, tap, tap.

A dripping tap. He got up and turned it off. He read:

Brodie Macbeth reflected on a life half-spent. He'd had it all, really. Won the jousting trophy at school. Could still picture his proud lance bouncing to the spring of his mount as he rode along. Then he'd done well in battle. Sent a few Vikings arse over tit, mashed the odd skull here and there. Won King Duncan's respect, and the Thaneships of Glamis and Cawdor. Nice spot there. Bit of boating at Findhorn. Better here, though, in the Castle of Dunsinane.

'Work hard, be honest and keep your lance in your own affairs,' had been his father's advice.

What a load of old carthorse that was! He wouldn't have got where he was today with that sort of an attitude. And now he was the crowned King of Scots!

He tossed a couple of logs on the fire.

'Great Birnam Wood logs!' he chuckled and thought back to the hags. He'd shown them. Cut the whole flaming forest down! Razed it! How glorious to bask in the certainty of defeating fate!

[Enter Seyton, an officer attending on Macbeth]

Macb: Ah, the good Seyton. Tell me, stands Scotland where it did?

Sey: Alas, poor country! Almost afraid to know itself!

Macb: What? So bad! Is there no more?

Sey: Not at present, sire. But messengers are under way. We must wait for News at Ten.

[Exit Seyton. Enter Lady M.]

Lady M [screaming]: BLOOD! Blood on the walls, blood on the carpet – the new bloody Axminster! – on my clothes, on my hands. [Thrusts fingers up Brodie's nose.] SMELL IT, BRODIE. SAVE ME!

Macb [casting her aside]: SERVANTS. [Servants swarm in.] Take her away. Witch hazel bath, jojoba massage, birch-arnica lip balm and a good dollop of Rhythmic Night Conditioner. AND DON'T FORGET THE CLARIFYING TONER AND EYE SOLACE.

She was completely cuckoo of course.

He was finished with women. He found himself remembering Banquo. Banquo and he in their late teens. Bit bloody off the battlefield. Having a dip. Glitter of sun on wet skin. An accidental touch. A jolt of energy. Their shock. Smiles. Curious hands. The jouster's urge …

He left the fire. He knew a knave. A short walk.

It was a balmy summer evening. Sun cast saffron boles of light through clouds and they held back the shadows in forest glades. Brodie walked quickly, already jousting in his mind, when three fiendish cackles erupted and near made him leap from his skin.

All Three: *All hail!*

First Witch: *Thrice the brinded cat hath mew'd.*

Second Witch: *Thrice and once the hedge-pig whined.*

Third Witch: *Harpier cries, 'Tis time, 'tis time.*

Macb: *Oh sod off! The last thing I need is your bloody rantings and crackpot riddles. Go on, piss off the lot of you.*

[Exeunt.]

No, you! At the rear. Come back. Yes. You!

[Third Witch returns. Tall. Great tits. Magnificent arse. Stunning legs. Long, black hair. Fucking gorgeous.]

Well! All that claptrap you were spouting … quite diverted my attention.

Third Witch: *Yea? Just a job.*

[She begins undressing.]

Macb: *What are you doing?*

Third Witch: *Going to give you the shag of your life.*

Macb: *But you don't understand. I've given up. I'm in to men … Oh. I thought you'd be all wrinkly.*

Third Witch: *Yea, that's what they all say. We get bad press.*

[Macbeth tears off clothes. Moves in close. Splutters.]

Something wrong?

MacB: *No, nothing. Just not used to your perfume.*

For her, for what was about to happen, he would endure any discomfort, even the unfamiliar odour of newt eye, frog toe and bat wool.

Has to be better than WD40, Lawrence mused. He refilled his tumbler again. Now he needed to go and practise a few literary turns of phrase with a bit of help. He stripped, then realised he'd forgotten to re-inflate Greta to the prescribed twelve pounds per square inch.

Warning! To inflate beyond this recommended psi nullifies your guarantee, and could result in sores or a severe reduction in your doll's lifespan.

tap, tap, tap, tap, tap.

That strange noise again. He listened hard. Nothing. Was he imagining it? No, there it was again. It was coming from outside. He threw a towel round himself. Stepped out into the cold night air and peered hopelessly into the dark. Ears skinned. Nothing but a distant car over the sea's whisper. He went back in.

He had a flash of inspiration. He kept an old wetsuit under the stairs. Splits all over the seams. He'd collapse Greta sufficiently to get her inside. Then – and this was the masterstroke! – he'd fill her with hydrogen. There was an old cylinder in the basement left over from the days when keepers had to launch meteorological balloons as part of their daily routines. And he changed her wig. Velcroed on the auburn one. ... *her shield of bronze* ... He selected *Je t'aime* from a compilation CD and put it on continuous repeat. Soon Jane Birkin's heavy breathing and moaning filled the room.

Greta came alive in his hands. *Yeah*, he thought, *Arunk's spear, Macbeth's lance, Lawrence's rod, hot HOT **HOT** ...* He fell on her, grappled her to the ground.

'Diving now,' he said with a smile, and lowered himself into her. 'Oh Angelaaaaaaaaaaaaaah ... '

She squirmed, vibrated, nudged him over, slipped from his grasp, ejected herself through the door and floated up the spiral ceiling, bouncing up the underside of steps, round and round, with low grinding squelches, she pirouetted up to the dome.

'Ahhhhhhh!' He heard her scream, deep and plaintive.

'Yee-ha!' shrieked Lawrence. 'Angela,' he sang, 'I'm coming to get you!' and burst into giggles, his excitement way off the end of the Richter scale.

* * *

'You're a chip off your mother's block, boy,' pronounced Rapsy.

'*Your children are not your children,*' Hamish responded, the words not his, but Kahlil Gibran's. '*You may house their bodies but not their souls.*'

'Wish I could instil some sense into you.'

'*You may give them your love but not your thoughts.*'

'You've always disappointed me, Hamish.'

'S*eek not to make them like you. For life goes not backward nor tarries with yesterday.*'

'How's it going with the castle?'

He watched his father's face broaden into a grin ...

'Wake up, Hame. Time tae gie it a go, eh pal. *Per ardua ad astra* an aw that.'

'What?' Hamish was aware of his body being shaken. Afraid his head would fall off and roll away. Felt his guts kink like telephone cord. Tighter and tighter until he was scared to breathe and find his lungs had nowhere to go. 'I don't think my legs'll work, Loon. I just dreamt about my father.'

'Twenny minutes an ye'll hae proved the bastard wrang. But it's nae really aboot him, Hame. It's aw aboot yersel. Ye unnerstan that? Naebody pits us ahin bars as ruthlessly as we dae arsels. An the hardest thing is tae realise the door's open, an tae step oot.'

He clapped Hamish on the shoulder. 'C'moan. Grout'll be freezin his nuts aff. Ye start the camera an step intae this harness.' Loon wriggled the loops up Hamish's body and pulled the constrictors tight. 'Snap a krab oan here, *comme ça*. Tie ye in an Bob's yer uncle, pal. Safe as lighthooses.' He paused and listened. 'Reckon the keeper's hivin a wee pairty wi himsel. Groovin tae a bit music. Y'OK?'

Suddenly a gush of vomit exploded from Hamish's mouth. He sank into a crouch and groaned. He felt a towel gently wipe his face, hands raise him upright, the blindfold envelope him, the sharp tug of knots.

'Now fer fucksakes, dinnae dae that again. Mind ah'm standin doon below, pullin.'

'Wha ... aught ... ' His teeth were chattering so loudly they sounded like chainsaws in his skull. ' ... h ... appens if ... if ... if ... y ... y ... you let go?'

'Nothin. Ratchet locks solid. An sides, Grout's haudin this safety rope. Italian hitch roond the bannister. He kid haud an elephant wi it.'

Loon gave a whistle. The safety rope tightened. 'Ye'll be fine. Ah'll jist raise ye the furst foot an we'll hang five. Pit yer feet agin the wa. Feel the rope haud ye horizontal, feel the harnesses haud ye secure.'

Hamish's senses upended. The ground turned ninety degrees. He was lying on his back but his weight was still on his feet.

'Ye OK?'

'Hm.' A rodent-ish snuffle.

'Relax. Jist start walkin each time ye feel yersel movin.'

A pull. Pressure on his chest and waist. He walked. Pull, pressure, walk. Pull, walk. Pull, walk. Felt the lumpiness of rough-hewn granite underneath. Like awkward dictionary words. Flinty words. Stevenson words ... *and find the globe granite underfoot and strewn with cutting flints* ... Robert Louis's prose on his grandfather's light. How high would he be now? Would it feel colder at the top? What if the ropes were chafing? And nobody was noticing ... *to come down off this feather-bed of civilisation* ... and strands were breaking, *snap, snap, snap* ... and the more that broke the quicker and louder the others would go ... *SNAP ... THLICK ... RIP* ... until suddenly the rope would part, race through the pulleys, a loose end falling on Loon, and he would be plummeting down, air rushing past, the earth rushing up, a mulching of blood, teeth, brains ...

'AHHHHHHH,' he screamed.

'Yer OK.'

Hamish was startled, tried to place the voice. Pull, walk. How much higher? Pull, walk. Please God, not much more. I can't take much more. When will it end? He couldn't feel his legs anymore. Liquid oozed inside his chest, the slow congesting of his lungs. Panic, mounting again. Heard a bird die somewhere in the night. Heard its grizzly shriek. Death was everywhere. Theirs. His. Heard a squeaking pulley. My God, the bloody thing's coming to bits. A breeze raked his face. Falling, he had to be falling ...

'AHH ... '

Flash, flash, flash, flash.

Hamish felt hands around his legs, his body being pulled through where the wall had been, a slight give in the rope and a solid support spread out under his back.

'Weel done, pal. Yev din it. Climbed the light. Ye wanna stan up and rest a while?'

Hamish nodded. Ropes slackened around him.

Flash, flash, flash, flash.

'Jesus. It's bright.'

'Tell me aboot it. Reckon ah've goat snawblindness. Destined fer a life in shades.'

Arms from behind hoisting him at the shoulders.

'Dinnae worry. Ah've still goat the safety rope attached. Noo, how aboot removin the bib an takin a dekko at the view. Dinnae look doon.'

Flash, flash, flash, flash.

He prised open eyes in a mask of clenched muscle. Blinked. Wobbled. Felt anaesthetised, nerves shooting out lines to locate the parameters of his body, to anchor his mind, define his being. Their signals unanswered. Thought he'd gently pitch forwards and float off but felt Grout's steadying hand.

'Easy. Tak yer time. Breathe, man.'

He breathed in air so pure it purged. Shrivelled a ghost, and like a balance, shifted its weight to his.

'How d'ye feel?'

'Like someone I don't recognise.'

'Yea. Ye'll git used tae it. Success is jist unfamiliar territory tae ye.'

For the first time Hamish took in the view. Pluckton reflected in a swath of shimmering amber. The sea an electric flow of gold, silver and phosphorescence, waves like bobbing black feathers, a vista of movement cradled between the louring permanence of the hills. A shining night. Panoplies of stars needling the vastness of the sky. The thumb of the aurora borealis tracing a fleeting smudge of green, occasionally shot through by bright slashes of some burning matter. Hamish wondered how they did it, how long they could keep it going, this guerrilla warfare of light.

Flash, flash, flash, flash.

Gingerly he turned, trying not to think of how he was going to get down. 'I suppose we'd best get on with it.'

Facing the light for the first time, his eyes began playing tricks. 'Christ, Grout. Am I seeing things?'

Grout followed his stare. Through the glass. There, repeated in a thousand prisms, some wide-angle, some outrageous magnifications, was a remarkable sight.

'Fuckin hell. A porn show.'

There were a thousand pairs of buttocks with red faces, a thousand naked men imprinted against a black woman with red hair. He bucked and she bucked, she slipped sideways and he followed, gyrating at the hips. They wrestled and tangoed, bounced and floundered until he regained control. Her arms were outstretched, and stiff, like she was drowning. Flailing hair obscured her face. Sweat glistened on white skin, smearing and darkening the black. Suddenly he withdrew his face from her unzipped cleavage, flung his head back and seemed to scream, but they heard nothing. Eyes closed, he slithered to the ground, and while she floated off he rolled over into another trick of refraction. A thousand smiles, a thousand penises.

Flash, flash, flash, flash.

'What's in there?' Hector Boyd indicated a door.

'Bulb store.'

'Show me.'

Lawrence's heart sank. It had been enough of a shock to hear a violent knock on the door at 9am after a night of fitful sleep in the dome. He'd awoken to see Greta spread-eagled against the glass canopy above him, her lust unabated, voluptuousness intact at 12lbs psi, breasts as rampant as an idol's. He was stirring to temptation when the awful banging was repeated below. In panic he grabbed Greta's ankle, dragged her down a hundred and sixty-four steps, stuffed her through the door of the bulb store, threw on the clothes discarded across the kitchen, noticed the whisky bottle, hid it behind the short-wave radio and answered the door as the handle turned and his visitor forced an entry.

The shock of being confronted by the Northern Lighthouse Board's Regional Inspector evinced a lozenge of sound from his throat, one which was as unpleasurable as it was unwelcoming. 'Mr Boyd, what a surprise … '

'Last night your sequence was out and the coastguard had to issue an emergency bulletin to shipping. We tried to contact you but your phone was off the hook. I'm sure you're aware of the consequences of negligence, Mr Brodie. So what the hell was going on?'

'Out? I wasn't aware of a problem. In fact, I spent a considerable time in the dome last night and everything went without a hitch. And if the phone was off the hook, that was entirely accidental. I'm an experienced keeper, Mr Boyd, and well-versed in the regulations.'

Lawrence had always disliked Boyd. A sneaky, crepuscular figure. Pudgy face, cod lips, neck as fat as his head. A patter of talc for hair. Wore his suit like a straight jacket. Pernickety. Lawrence bet he read nothing but Nathaniel Drinkwater and Patrick O'Brian. Steeped himself in forecastles, broadsides, press gangs and dastardly deeds on poop decks.

'I'll check the timing mechanism first, then see if everything else is in order. Get your log book ready.'

He checked the light. Found nothing wrong. Now he stopped before the bulb store.

'It's locked. I'll get the key.'

Lawrence went to rummage in the kitchen. How was he going to get out of this one? His career hung in the balance. Out of a job, home, pension. Scandalised. A laughing stock.

'Like some coffee?'

He heard a door squeaking. *The door squeaking* ...

'Don't bother with the key. It's open.'

Lawrence solidified. Cemented to the flagstones.

'Where's the light switch?'

'I ... I think the bulb's gone. Just yesterday ... '

'OK, I've got a torch.'

The seconds passed like millennia. But the Brodies were used to millennia. Used to waiting.

'I'll take that cup of coffee now.'

He hadn't seen her! Missed her! Kept his beam low! And she must have floated up! Angel!

They drank coffee.

'Well, everything seems to be in order.' Boyd stood outside, performing a final circumspection before leaving. Suddenly his gaze was arrested. 'What in God's name are those?'

Lawrence looked and saw dozens of muddy footprints ascending the tower. 'Well, I'll be ... they look like boot marks.'

'I can see that. What I want to know is, how did they get there?'

'I've no idea, Mr Boyd. Never seen that before. They're all pointing the same way. Up the light.'

He felt Boyd's glacial stare. 'I don't know how you do it, Brodie, but watch your step. Don't let's hear any more about erratic lights.' He squeezed his face into a threat. 'Or we'll have you automated two years early. Get it?'

Hamish had read somewhere that depressions went to Sweden to die. They came roiling in from the Atlantic, frenzied the ocean, stomped over Ireland and Scotland (and always Dundreary) and then, already fatally weakened, ploughed the North Sea, stumbled over Norway and expired in Sweden. A graveyard of depressions.

Attention all shipping. Gale warnings are in operation for sea areas Shannon, Rockall, Malin, Hebrides, Bailey and Fair Isle. The General Synopsis at 1200. Low Shannon 972 moving northeast to South Norway 970 by the same time tomorrow. Low Hebrides 971 expected South Utsire by the same time.

He turned up the volume and waited for the detailed area report.

Malin, Hebrides, Bailey, Fair Isle: Easterly seven, backing northerly gale eight to severe gale nine, rain or showers, poor at first, good.

He resented the way the forecaster often ended a lousy report with *good*. Seemed spiteful. ... *good! Serves you right!*

But now the weather didn't matter. He'd done the climb! No inside-out Hamish on the rocks. *Good!*

He looked out. A world on the move. Trees flayed each other, hurled branches about. Leaves zipped through castle spotlights like helpless bats. Grass, tussocks, witch-heads of heather, a blizzard of grit and soil, flashes of litter – crisp packets, Coke cans, waxed cubes devoid of their milk – an endless migration heading east, backing northerly. The slow transfer of Flabbay to Sweden.

Wind razored through floorboards, whistled through powerpoints, ejected fountains of dust. Windows moved like diaphragms, doors shuffled on the spot. Walls rippled. Even spiders panicked, sought the security of elastic cocoons, cushioned hammocks. Dundreary bent. Moaned. Old bones creaked and cracked. Tired of life. Of fighting gravity. Yearning to let go. *Ahhhhhhhhh ... rip ... rumble ... crash.*

Ming was doing an ostrich under cushions. Fran, wrapped like Amundsen, cut chicory (*Selfish, Possessive Love*) with a chopper off Madame Guillotine.

'Trasi,' said Fran. 'Now we need the trasi. Stir in the trasi, it says, cook for a minute. Did you get some?'

'No. Miss Oliphant says she doesn't stock trasi, doesn't know what it is and wouldn't stock it if she did. So I told her what you said, that it's dried shrimp paste, and she said, "If it's dried shrimp paste why don't you ask for dried shrimp paste?".'

'Well, never mind, Effie. We've a tin of anchovies. Perhaps we can do something with that.'

Nasi Goreng. Indonesian. Mrs MacFie's new fad. Nasty Goring, Nazi Goering, sounded like. With Newfoundland squid. Effie's people had always thought squid to be a starvation diet. Fit only for a dog. A shih tzu, probably. She wagered Rastafarian wouldn't touch it. What was wrong with herring and tatties, and mince and tatties, and roast lamb and tatties? Or dumplings? All this weird food, and rice that ends up down your bra or under your falsers. She preferred Fran depressed. So low a saucer of tablets and a whiff of incense made her supper. She hated these occasional highs. They'd become so rare she'd forgotten how nauseating a buoyant Fran was. Today the valuers had been, and she was definitely buoyant.

Hamish was not. He felt as low as the low. Six starched overalls – wearing their cleanliness like it really *was* godliness – prying, recording, for a whole week. Gerund's Hit Squad.

They'd been everywhere. Used architect's drawings to nose out secret chambers. Prised open chests whose keys had never been seen, found letters and diaries, drooled, *ooh*ed and *ah*ed – 'for the value, Mr MacFie, we have to ascertain *retail value*' – leered at clothing, passed their hands through underwear – 'we have to be comprehensive, Mr MacFie, who knows where family heirlooms may have been secreted?' – held up this and that, mimed a catwalk, ascertaining value, having a ball, fondling their way though private lives as thoroughly as burglars.

Strangely, they'd neglected the policies. Failed to spot the rotting trap of the vault – the newly-furnished repository of Hamish's last resort, his Pacific Island Fund.

Fran hoped they'd find the Udaipur. *Her* Udaipur. They didn't. But they valued *The Frosty Evening*. Put the restoration estimate at £5,000. Suggested a reserve of £80,000. Recommended Christies. Fifteen per cent commission.

Fingers rattling, awkward scrawls from a skidding nib, Fran did her sums. '*Yee-oow*,' she bawled. 'Sixty-three grand clear, baby.' Nasi Goreng with Newfoundland squid, but without trasi; her celebration.

Lodgepole burned in the fire, resentfully, spitting sparks but withholding heat. Hamish's fleece was zipped to his chin but he still felt cold. He rolled a cigarette and managed a few drags before it was sacrificed to the room's inhalation.

'How's he coming along?'

Grout turned to confirm Hamish's question was for him.

'Great. He's goat tae letters already. F and U. Finds K tae hard, nae the right joints fer it. We're workin on A noo.'

He was teaching Rastafarian semaphore. The dog stood upright on his back legs, leaning against a wall. He was holding out his front legs like a stiff ballerina.

'OK, Rast. That's enuff, pal.' He turned to Hamish. 'He's goat a great mind. Wish I kid unnerstand im. He kid teach us sae much.'

Rastafarian flagged S. Fooling Around. Mad Dog Patronising Humans. Easily Entertained.

'Yer looking kinda morose.'

'Yea? Since my old man died it feels like I reclaim a bit of myself every day, and yet I'm still in a hole so deep I can't see any way out.' A finger played with a spiral of curls. 'What would you do with this place, Grout?'

'Ah'd strip it doon tae the lead flashins, an flog it. Then ah'd buy a new camper an head fer Italy.'

Hamish nodded. 'My conscience won't let me sell out. This land's been neglected for three hundred years and I want to do something about it.'

Grout flounced into a chair. 'Some opportunity, pal. A crumblin castle and miles o bog.'

'It wasn't always bog. Once it was covered in lazybeds and potatoes and cereals. And before that, in trees.'

'Aye, but they dinnae mix wi sheep.'

'If there weren't subsidies you wouldn't see a single sheep here. They've always been an ecological disaster, unlike cattle. And cattle don't disturb young trees. So, we need to get rid of the sheep and replace them with cattle. And give people a stake in the land, restore the communal custodianship that was lost after the dissolution of the clans … '

'Ah hae a dream,' interrupted Grout, standing up with his arms outstretched, 'that wan day this nation will rise up, live oot the true meanin o its creed … Some speech, Hame. Aye, King wid be proud o it.'

'I'm serious about this, Grout. It is my dream.'

'Maist guys oor age are thinkin aboot girls and havin fun but ye seem tae be aye mopin aboot oan a crusade. Naw, carry oan wi the dream, pal. But tae me the biggest flaw in aw this is there's nae work, an nae hooses.'

Hamish leant forwards, his features animated. 'But I'm going to give away land for housing. We can build new communities, owned by Housing Associations to ensure they'll never become holiday homes! And we can create work! We can divide up the estate into family units. We've got to think small, and grow bigger. The key is diversification: glasshouses, veg, fruit, cheese, seafood, herbal remedies … Twenty years ago they'd treat an inflamed eye with eyebright. That knowledge is part of our culture, our strength, and it should be part of our economy.' Hamish read scepticism in Grout's expression, and chuckled. 'Maybe this is too radical even for you?'

'Sounds hunky-dory in theory but aw this costs money, Hame.'

'Yea, we're going to need finance to start things off but I believe we could do it with a reallocation of existing grants and subsidies.'

'An competition? Get real, man, there's nae way a farm here kin compete wi mass production.'

'But think what we can save on transport costs! Think what we can offer in quality! Imported vegetables are cheap because they're almost worthless. Everything's back to front. We've got to change our whole outlook.' He laughed in a humourless way. 'Here endeth the lesson.'

Grout nodded thoughtfully. 'So tomorrow, the dream, but today, yer faither's wee list o chores. Remind me whit ye've tae dae?'

Hamish guddled in a back pocket. For Gerund's letter, folded, burnished like a lover's keepsake. Typed in mock handwriting:

You are required:
1. to climb the exterior of Mickle Flabbay lighthouse, and provide video evidence of your ascent.
2. to bring about Sergeant Cleghorn's public humiliation.
3. to maintain the buildings, statues and policies in good repair, and restore the estate finances to a viable concern.
4a. to oppose the construction of a bridge — should one be proposed — to the bitter end.
4b. to produce a son.

'Numero Uno's done. Two's a piece o piss. Three's tricky ... restore the castle finances. Whit like are they?'

Hamish handed him a bank statement.

'Five thousan an forty-eight oerdrawn.'

'Monthly income: my fish farm wage plus your and Loon's dole – five hundred pounds. Monthly expenditure: twelve hundred. Overdraft limit: seven grand. Three more month's grace. Then, finito.'

'MADAME EST SERVIT,' bellowed Fran. 'Nasi Goreng is up. Come and get it. *Oh, I love to go a wan-der-ing on a fros-ty eve-ning ...* Hurrah for Turner.'

'Grout an me hiv been thinkin aboot that tae. Aw the wasted potential here. Tell ye whit, pal. Loon and me'll tak care o the finances. Ye kin nobble that Beath fulth. An if ye want help wi 4b, jist gies the wink.'

'Ye thinkin o the Byke?' guessed Loony.

'She's fuckin magic. Eftir oor wee chat, she's repentin. Chuckin New Labour. Ah'm still dreamin o er airmpits. Speaks a hale scad o languages, man. Multilingual. Oh aye, but ambidextrous.'

'Ambidextrous?' Hamish's face, innocent. 'I don't get it.'

'Ah may no either.'

Tony BLiar rearranged cramped buttocks in his chair, blew his nose, brushed a piece of errant fluff from his tie and consulted his diary.

> *11.30 Meeting with: Secretary of State for Transport, Alista Darning*
> *Scottish Parliamentary Minister for Transport, Nicol Steelpen*
> *Topic: Private Finance Initiative – Location for Pilot Scheme*

They arrived promptly. Darning, BLiar observed – for he was taking notes for his retirement autobiography – looked tired and limp, 'like a British Rail signal with nothing to report'. Steelpen was 'enviably youthful'.

They exchanged pleasantries.

'Private Finance Initiatives,' BLiar began, 'the new art of using the private sector to pay our bills. This is the future, gentlemen, and I'm sure we can not only make it work, but make it look good. Political expediency dressed as philanthropy has always been the most effective way forwards, don't you agree?' He paused to allow his rhetorical question space. 'So, where d'you think this bridge, our flagship PFI, ought to be?' He rummaged through the sheaf of reports looking for big words. 'FORTH …?'

'Not the best option, sir,' Darning ventured. 'Admittedly the current bridge is hopelessly inadequate for the volume of traffic, but the scheme would never pay at eighty pence a crossing. We'd never get a private financier at that rate of return.'

'Hmmm. Sure you're right. SEVERN?'

'Don't deserve one. Conservatives and Lib-Dems mostly.'

'Hmmm. HUMBER?'

Darning dismissed this as well. 'Very expensive. Too risky for a first. No, sir, my recommendation would be this Flabbay place.'

'Never heard of it. Where in God's kingdom is it?'

'We're not sure that it is, sir,' Steelpen joked. 'Northwest Highlands. Small island. Small project. No great shakes if it fails, but could be useful PR. *The Long Reach of a Caring Government* … helping smaller communities.'

'Thank you, Nicol. And what would this option cost us?'

'This is the tricky bit, sir. Given its remoteness, it would qualify for Objective One funding from Europe in the next round of applications in August. So it could cost us just the road construction. Well under a million.'

BLiar gave him a quizzical look. 'But it wouldn't be a PFI, would it?'

'No, sir. That's what I meant about being tricky.'

'Well that's no good. We need a PFI.' He raised his glasses and rubbed the welt on his nose, while thinking. 'August is six months away. If we sign contracts quickly then Europe would be irrelevant. Tell me, what's the local council and how's it likely to react to this bridge?'

'Highland Regional Council, sir. They've been pressing for a bridge for years. But they're adamant they don't want a toll bridge. And they're pretty clued up on European grants.'

'They'd still need government money,' Darning reminded the Prime Minister, 'even if they got the grant from Europe. I suggest we tell them there's absolutely no likelihood of money from us towards any aspect of a bridge for the next twenty years. And there's Flabbay High School. Falling to bits. Leaks all over the place. We could suggest it's a choice between the PFI bridge and the upgrading of their school, or a free bridge in twenty years and no funds for the school.'

'But the education budget's already overspent. We've no money for schools.'

Darning smiled. 'They aren't to know that, sir.'

BLiar began to smile too. 'Yes, I take your point. Well, we'll have to get cracking. Any contractors lined up?'

Steelpen gave a conspiratorial wink. 'Yes, sir. I took the precaution of approaching two companies. Milkers Civil Engineering and Madison Construction. They've got preliminary designs. Of the two, I'd suggest Milkers.'

Darning looked surprised. 'I thought it was currently a dormant company.'

'Yes, it is. Creative accountancy, and a bit of a dodge, really. But they assure me they can do this job in their sleep, ha ha ha ... ' Steelpen cut his laugh short on seeing BLiar's impassive face.

'Why Milkers?'

'They've just donated £23,000 to party funds, sir.'

'That all? Pretty paltry. And Madison?'

'Nothing.'

'Oh well, Milkers it is. What about financiers?'

'Global Bank of America, sir. Unfortunately they want a rather high rate of return. Thirty-eight per cent per annum over a minimum of fourteen years.'

'Good God! Scarcely value for money, is it? Isn't there anyone cheaper?'

'Yes, but perhaps not as solid, or as discrete. We just have to set the tolls at the appropriate level.'

'And what level's that?'

'About ten times higher than any other toll. But of course, Flabbay is ten times more remote than any other toll centre, and with one-tenth of the traffic.'

Steelpen looked worried. 'What happens if they refuse to pay these tolls?'

BLiar had regained his former cheer. 'Make it a criminal offence. Write it into the Toll Order.'

Darning felt his excitement mounting. 'Of course! The New Roads and Street Works Act, 2000. How inspired, Prime Minister! What luck we pushed it through!'

Steelpen felt his brain was doing breaststroke though treacle. 'A criminal offence? You mean they'd get a record, go to jail and all that?'

'Oh come, come Nicol. Such pessimism. I think you overestimate the level of resistance. Besides, we haven't any room left in our jails. No, no. Give a nod to the courts. Stitch them up with hefty fines. Soon whip them into line.'

'But, Prime Minister, it's not a criminal offence on any other bridge.'

'We're a pioneering government, Nicol. A government of firsts. Now what about the projected costs?'

Steelpen shuffled papers and zoned his varifocals onto the figures. 'Taxpayers' contribution, eleven million. We'll have to buy out the ferry service, say ... '

'Just a total, please. I have a lunch engagement in ten minutes.'

'Say thirteen million, and private money comes in with the rest, say another fifteen.'

'Good Lord, as cheap as that! So that's it then, gentlemen. Settled. Get the Council on side and sign a contract as soon as possible. Oh dear. I suppose they'll want a Public Enquiry. Such a tiresome aspect of democracy. That could seriously delay things, and be embarrassing.'

Steelpen moved to reassure him. 'I wouldn't worry about that, Prime Minister. We do things differently in Scotland.'

'What d'you mean?'

'We do the business on the side, *then* hold the Public Enquiry – make a show of listening, ignore the findings. Saves oodles of time. The Scots are far too divided or apathetic to mount a serious challenge.'

The Prime Minister elevated his eyebrows high above his glasses. 'Excellent! Well, gentlemen, let's adjourn. *Bon appetit.*'

As they filed out, a smile came to the Prime Minister's lips. How agreeable this PFI business was! What savings! Why, now he might be able to offer Her Majesty some encouraging news about the new *Britannia* she wanted.

Ribbons of colour flitted round The Emporium's windows, adding festive cheer to the building's dreary form. Constructed in the days of the Highlands and Islands Development Board, which awarded grants for bad taste and had rearranged the centre of Inverness as a monument to its ethics, The Emporium was a rectangular block of concrete disguised as a rectangular block of chips. 'Flabbay Emporium', stated the sign self-importantly, in gold flourishing letters against livery green, but everyone knew it as The Emporium. They had a knack for sobriquets, in Flabbay.

Noise interrupting speech in entrance to church (10).

'Morning, Miss Oliphant.' Hamish felt breezy. He hadn't slept as well for years. Nothing quite like an escape from death to make the body feel alive. And he'd done his last shift at the fish farm. Resigned, to dedicate himself to the crusade. 'Fine Christmas lights you've got there.'

'Thank you.' *ORDINATION*, she wrote. Obliquely she took in the scattering of fish scales across her linoleum.

'I see the minister's car's been in the wars.'

Big lads seen in drawers (8).

'Yes. A tête-à-tête with a golf ball, apparently. The minister's talking of suing.'

'Very Christian. Next I suppose it'll be front page of *Life and Work*.' He browsed the rack of newspapers, layered headlines blaring ill tidings. 'Oh no … '

Highland Regional Council Cave In On Tolls, said *The Herald*.

PFIs – Public Enquiry For Flabbay, said *The Press & Journal*.

Flabbay Told No Tolls, No School, said *The West Highland Free Press*.

A Bridge Too Far, Dear? asked *The Daily Mail*.

PFIs are Flabbay and Shabby! said *The Sun*.

Miss Oliphant looked up. 'I voted against it, of course. The very idea of tolling a monopoly link to an island with a European classification of disfavoured infrastructure is the anathema of decency and democracy.'

'Yea, but it seems other councillors thought differently.'

'Charlatans. The Convenor's a pusillanimous yes-boy. Feathering his own political nest. And most of the councillors don't give two hoots as long as it's not their backyard. Oh you watch out, I told them. You'll be next. Your road, your hospital, your school, they'll be the next PFIs. But they kowtowed. Swallowed the line about this PFI advancing funds for a new school. Bunkum! You mark my words, they'll build this bridge and the school'll be forgotten. Twenty-six for, nineteen against. It was disgraceful.'

'Is there any way we can stop it? What about this Public Enquiry?'

'Whitewash, I expect. No, their minds'll be made up. I wouldn't mind betting they've even signed contracts.' She returned to her paper. 'Tallboys.'

'Beg your pardon?'

'Nothing.' *TALLBOYS*, she wrote.

Endless money needed for some underwear (4).

'You'll be ordering your usual turkey this year I expect, Mr MacFie.'

'I'm afraid not, Miss Oliphant. Got to pull in the belt a little this year. Thought we'd have a couple of chickens from the garden.'

Miss Oliphant humphed. Hamish drifted off down the aisles.

The bell sounded.

'Morning Grinella.'

'Morning Dilly.'

'Did you happen to observe the wonderful *chiaroscuro* effects on the water last night?'

'Unfortunately some of us have to work, Dilly, and are unable to partake of tenebrous perambulations, and it can prove irksome hearing others gasconading about theirs. No, Dilly, I did my accounts, watched *Coronation Street* and went to bed in preparation for another hard day.'

'Of crosswords?' Realising the pun, Dilly tittered. 'Cross words,' she repeated.

'Really! You can display an extraordinary penchant for malice, Dilly.'

'My, my! Tetchy today. I suppose you're not quite yourself with the election coming up in the new year.'

Miss Oliphant sighed and ignored this. Dilly continued. 'You may be interested to know a pertinent statistic, Grinella, that in the thirty years since *Coronation Street* was first screened, four and a half million man years have been lost watching it.'

'Lost? Enjoyed, I would have said. And if I'm meant to feel guilt and remorse, I don't.'

'I'm simply suggesting that you too have a choice, Grinella, and that you might have enjoyed nature's luminous artistry as much as I did.'

Endless money needed for some underwear (4).

'The new SNH warden's arrived to look after the corncrake reserve,' Dilly continued. She raised her voice and turned in Hamish's direction. 'A lovely girl, they say, called Amulree Shaw. Isn't that a melodious name!'

'What on earth's she meant to do?'

'I've no idea. I suppose we'll all have to instal plastic nests.' She envisaged them for a moment. 'And have you heard about the Middle-Eastern gentlemen?' In her excitement Dilly put her hand on Grinella's arm and obscured the black-and-white boxes.

'Middle-Eastern? What gentlemen?'

'Ah! Then aren't you glad I dropped by after all?'

'I would be if you bought something. I suppose you're not going to order a turkey this year either?' She turned a withering glance towards the rear of the shop. 'Going to give me your economic woes or some coloratura about animal rights and Mother Earth. Everyone seems to have gone virulently green this year.' Another sigh. 'What Middle-Eastern gentlemen, Dilly?'

'Arabs have bought Fitful Lodge!'

Miss Oliphant's face doubled in length. Somewhere in the hinterland a can slipped from a hand.

'Arabs? Absurd. They like sand, not bogs. I don't believe it.'

'Arabs, Grinella. A rich sheikh has bought Fitful Lodge and all the land with it. Including the village. I daresay, Grinella, you'll have to pay your rent to him. In reyals or dinars, or suchlike.' She sniggered. 'You'll have to stock couscous, and those scarves they wear round their heads … '

'Never. Besides, I don't believe it. What would they want with Flabbay?'

'Maybe they think there's oil here. Do you think they'll bring camels? Those double-humped ones with the bristly lips?'

'Really, Dilly. Your ignorance never ceases to amaze me. The camels you're referring to are Bactrian camels from Northern Afghanistan. Nothing to do with sheikhs. Arabs use dromedaries, a single-humped thoroughbred. And if any Arab tries to import a camel here, in my capacity as councillor … '

'If, Grinella, you still are councillor.' And with that she sallied out.

Endless money needed for some underwear (4).

BRAS, she wrote.

Hamish deposited a basketful of goods on the counter.

'I trust I can rely on your vote in the forthcoming election, Mr MacFie?'

'I haven't decided yet, Miss Oliphant. I hear you've a formidable adversary.'

Miss Oliphant didn't like his wink one little bit.

Hamish drove back to Dundreary in lower spirits than he'd set out.

You are required to oppose the construction of a bridge — should one be proposed — to the bitter end.

Now the proposal was a reality. Another hurdle raised the moment the first had been cleared. Yet he'd triumphed, and the consequence would always be his. He stopped to admire the scene of his conquest. Flabbay lighthouse was washed in low winter sun. Over a livid sea it towered taller than he'd ever remembered it.

When he reached the castle Rastafarian was chasing peacocks. A dispersed ice fog had coated the trees in crystals and the birds looked down from giant candy-flosses. Iceballs dangled from Rastafarian's coat and he looked like a brush clogged with fluff. When he saw Hamish arriving, he bounded towards him, stopped, flagged an out-of-context A, and continued towards the car, leaping onto Hamish's lap when the door opened.

'Get down, boy!'

Trusting more in his appeal than the alienating effect of his ice, Rastafarian remained where he was and dispensed licks. Hamish carried him inside and deposited him before the castle's solitary fire.

'How many peacocks do we have, Angus?'

'EIGHT, AT THE LAST COUNT, SIR. IF THE DOG HASN'T HAD ANY.'

'He disnae eat em,' defended Grout. 'He jist cannae abide showin aff.' He considered this for a moment. 'In ithers.'

'Eight,' Hamish repeated. 'What's peacock like to eat, Effie?'

'YOU CAN'T EAT THEM, SIR. THEY WERE THE COLONEL'S FAVOURITES.'

'My father always ate his favourites. Effie?'

'I don't know. I'll look up *Mrs Beaton's*.'

Effie's Bible. 'Here we are. Paon rôtie. Truss, stuff, cover in bacon, roast for an hour, serve with Española sauce.'

'Sounds delicious. Let's go for two for Christmas. Grout, could you ...?'

'Naw, ah cannae face blood. Loon'll dae it.'

'Aye, ah'll dae it. Wis raised on offal, ah wis. That's why ah turned tae theology, ken.'

Angus stiffened his face and began shuffling out.

'Oh Angus. I need your help. You remember that we're all on temporary sufferance here, that in two years we may be out of a home?'

'YES, SIR.'

'Keep your ear to the ground ... ' an unfortunate choice of metaphor for the deaf, he suddenly realised, 'and your eyes peeled for any news about Sergeant Cleghorn. Any opportunity we could exploit to ... to embarrass him. Our futures depend on it.'

Angus brightened, the peacocks forgotten. 'I'LL DO MY BEST, SIR.'

Later, they played the video of the climb.

'I look like I'm doing it on my own!'

Loon nodded. 'Steven Spielberg kidnae hiv din better.'

'I'll take this to the Vulture Squad this afternoon.' He switched off the video. 'I wish we could have got some footage of the shenanigans in the dome!'

'Ken this?' remarked Grout. 'Ah'm sure ah recognised yon wumman he wis wi. Jist cam tae me. Ah'm sure it wis the Beathite's wife.'

'Really?'

'Aye. Kid be some mileage fer us in that, ken. Stitch the bastard up like crochet. Whit wid he dae if he kent that guy wis shaggin his wife, eh? Some shaggin, tae.'

'It's not a very good picture.'

Quintin Filigree scrunched his face and peered at a screen which seemed to convey images of an iron foundry and periodically filled with sparks. 'Your face looks like a bonfire.'

'Very poor,' agreed George Gerund, wiping his half-moons with a polka-dot hanky. 'You say there was no way you could have done this climb in daylight?'

'None. They refused permission so I had to do it secretly at night. Infrared film was the only way. White is hot, black is cold. So my face and hands are pure white. You can clearly make out the lighthouse as the stone is warmer than its surrounds. Much more heat up in the glass dome.'

'I had no idea we would have such dubious evidence to examine. It's like looking at moon shots. I daresay NASA would have problems.'

'But you will admit it is undoubtedly me, Mr Filigree?'

Filigree turned to compare the face before him with that of the screen. 'You do seem to share the same sense of vacancy.'

'Ever done any climbing yourself, Mr Filigree?' Hamish stared at the lawyer. A bamboo shoot of a man. Long fingers like a tree frog's. Nervously undulating Adam's apple. Mouth a ghastly mistake. Too big. Expect it to open at any moment, a long tongue to unfurl and zap a moth against the far window pane. Quintin Filigree, LLB. DIP. LP. NP. Third-generation partner of a semi-dead syndicate, secure, monied and clever, but *not* a climber. Definitely *not* a climber.

Filigree looked at him in stunned silence.

'I take it, not, Mr Filigree. Well, I've never climbed before either, and that sense of vacancy you so disparagingly remark on is because I was shit scared. But I did it. Poor quality film or not, you can see I did it.' The film was still running. They appeared to be engrossed in it. Hamish got up and went behind the screen, leant low over it and let his stare flow from one lawyer to the other.

'And d'you know the most remarkable thing about it?' He allowed them the discomfort of silence. 'The old bastard was right. You come back with a totally different perspective on things.'

He went out for coffee. Came back with a single cup for himself. Sat and drank it while they watched the film to the end, scrutinising it, he didn't doubt, for a crucial flaw.

'How on earth are you doing that?' Gerund cautiously queried. 'Looks like you've got glue on your feet and are just walking up.'

'Levitation,' Hamish replied matter-of-factly. 'A trick the old bastard taught me.'

Gerund's eyes were moons of whiteness. 'Yes, well I've no doubt you've used all sorts of invisible ropes somehow. I don't understand it, but it would appear that you have climbed the light and fulfilled the first condition.'

Filigree excused himself, slipped through a door barely ajar.

'Incidentally, we've now formally completed the sale of the Fitful Lodge property and realised sufficient assets to settle death duties and the late Colonel's debts. So you've got a new neighbour.' He smiled seditiously. 'His name is, now let me see, rather complicated … ' he rummaged through papers, 'yes, here we are. Sheikh Jasim al bu Muhammad Maziad bin Hamdan. From Qatar. Quite a high-ranking government minister, I believe.'

'So I hear.'

'Really?'

'We have a very active Intelligence Service on Flabbay.'

'Quite. Then you'll also be aware that Flabbay's bridge appears to be going ahead. Which renders Condition 4a applicable.'

'To the bitter end.'

'To the bitter end,' Gerund repeated, in the manner of a toast. 'Now, if you'll excuse me, I've a lot of work to do, and I daresay you're busy yourself.' Sarcasm smeared his face. 'Repairing the castle or producing heirs, perhaps.'

Clouds hung over the land like a dormitory of bulging hammocks. The Reverend Murdo MacLeod watched their discharge sweep across his windscreen, great splatters of rain smacking the glass, and turned his wipers to a faster speed. Still their spindly swipes were unable to cope. He cursed the weather. One day fine, the next ice, the next flood. He cursed MacArthur of Flashcairn, Calum the Post and that buffoon of a policeman. The man's only purpose in life appeared to serve the needs of the repair and insurance industries. Indeed, the Reverend himself had recently begun to wish he'd chosen a career in panel beating or body touching instead of electing to be one of Christ's generals. A veil of spray blew in through a missing piece of Escort 1.6 and slowly saturated his knees. A further tribulation in the unpalatable act of swallowing pride.

So unaccustomed was he to taking the turn-off to the National Presbyterian Church manse, he almost missed it. 'Low Church,' he breathed, and inhaled deeply in order to reduce the number of Low Church breaths he'd be forced to take during his visit.

'Murdo, how nice to see you here on my patch,' the Reverend Alexander Murray exclaimed, his air of surprise designed to be provocative considering the True Fundamentalist minister had phoned to arrange the meeting.

'It is not entirely by free choice, Alex, but I appreciate you sparing some time to see me.' He smiled deferentially at his counterpart who had ten years over him and was close to retiring. But he certainly wasn't going to be patronised. 'Especially when you've certain difficulties of your own, I hear.'

'Do come in. Tea or … tea. I've run out of coffee.' He knew MacLeod drank coffee, never tea.

'A glass of water would be most welcome.'

Murray selected a glass with a chipped rim and filled it from the tap. A shrimp-like creature dived in and he watched it flex and unfold and jerk about, before serving it. 'You were referring to certain difficulties in the National Presbyterian Church, *local* differences,' Murray stressed, 'thank the Lord. Yes, it was most regrettable to have to cancel this year's Messiah. It had become rather a proud ecumenical tradition of ours to welcome all faiths into our choir.'

'But not Baha'is, it appears.'

'Naturally not, Murdo. Completely inappropriate. Sacrilegious. Couldn't possibly allow one of these heathens under our roof. Undermine the whole fabric of our Faith. They're fanatics, these people. He was wearing an earring, too. Sodomite, I daresay. Had to fling him out. In Isaiah's day he would have been stoned.'

'I heartily agree with you. It's a sad reflection on our times that a minister's authority is held in such low regard. Have you lost many of your congregation?'

'No, no. A trifle really. Mainly the young and those with pusillanimous minds easily preyed upon. I daresay they'll realise the error of their ways and come back to the fold.' He poured his cup of tea, stirred in milk and two sugar and folded his hands around its warmth. He watched MacLeod raise his glass, take a sip and then freeze, aghast, as he noticed his shrimp. 'But I don't suppose it's to listen to my minor grievances that you've come here this morning. When your own church is burdened with a much greater predicament, one of *national* significance.'

MacLeod's lips were closed but working nervously. He dabbed a handkerchief over them, lowered his glass and stared. The shrimp was embroiled in a gymnastic field day.

'Quite,' he stuttered. 'Naturally, this is the reason for my visit.' He wondered if Murray had put the shrimp in on purpose. 'We've had our differences of opinions over the years, Alex, but when all's said and done we're both men of the cloth and worship the same God.'

'But with fundamentally different approaches. Ours, I would argue, is the more charitable, the more Christian – with a capital C – approach.' He sank back in his chair and slowly drummed his fingers on the armrests. He was enjoying MacLeod's display of humility immensely.

'I didn't come here to denigrate your Church, Alex, and I'd be grateful if you would accord the same courtesy to me. I'm sure we could both defend our convictions into Kingdom Come. On this occasion I think it would be improper for me to enter such a debate, because I have come to ask a favour of you.'

Murray lowered his eyes, dispensed pontific grace with a wave of his hand, refilled his cup and glanced to see what the shrimp was up to.

MacLeod continued: 'I find myself in the unfortunate position of being locked out of my own church. A break-away group assaulted me, stole the key and now refuse to let me and my congregation enter.'

'I assume you've reported the matter to Sergeant Cleghorn.' Murray was barely able to suppress the laughter which rollicked inside him.

MacLeod scowled. 'Not only was he a witness to the assault, I believe him also to have been an accomplice. I'm currently reporting him for professional misconduct. The riders of the Apocalypse wouldn't drag me near the man. No, the matter seems irreconcilable. Which brings me to the favour I must ask of you. Would you allow us to hold our services in your church until a solution has been found?'

Murray rubbed his hands and studied the blackness of his cassock. Of course, the request came as no surprise but, for the purpose of negotiation it would be wise to pretend it had. He radiated thoughtful doubt.

'We would naturally fit in with your own arrangements and accept the less sociable times when the church is not in use.'

Murray nodded. 'In theory there should be no problem. Of course this will entail an extra burden on our running costs, heating, lighting, cleaning, all those things, as well as wear and tear, and then there's the Fabric Fund.' He thought dismally of the Fabric Committee – Miss Gordon-Lennox, 85, Mr McIntyre, 73, Mrs Barnshot, 68-ish – preciously short of fabric themselves. 'I'm sure you're aware that for some time our Fabric Committee has been running an appeal which has still quite some way to go to reach its target … '

'How much do you have in mind?'

'Say, sixty pounds a session.'

'Thirty.'

'Forty-five. I'm afraid I really can't come lower than that.'

MacLeod sighed. It was daylight robbery. 'Forty-five, then.'

'Excellent. I think we should just confirm this in writing. You know … ' he allowed a light but genuine laugh, 'what they say about doing business with friends.'

'Yes, though I wouldn't have said this falls into that category.' MacLeod signed the paper and was leaving when Murray offered a final piece of advice.

'Far be it from me to do my Fabric Fund out of income, but why don't you knock the door down?'

'Because it's three inches thick and strong enough to repel a Roman legion.'

'A little touch of gelignite, perhaps! Well, we'll be in touch about times. A good day to you, Murdo.'

The Reverend MacLeod fumed in his car. He couldn't really have expected anything else at the hands of Low Church, but somehow he had. *Why don't you knock the door down,* he twittered, mimicking Alex's high washer-wifie voice. *A little touch of gelignite, perhaps.* Hadn't he just revelled in his superiority. Well, just you wait, Alexander Murray, it'll be my turn one day. *A little touch of gelignite, perhaps ...*

He couldn't get the phrase out of his mind. Maybe it wasn't as absurd as it sounded. A measured charge to destroy the lock, and he'd have his church back! But could it be done? He knew just the person to advise him.

He drove past his home and continued on the Dundreary road, past the golf course, up the climb until Mickle Flabbay light hove into view and coasted downhill to the quarry. As he passed between two stumps holding the rusted ends of a chain, the surface under the wheels turned to badlands. The car bucked and blundered on corrugations of sand, following a set of tyre tracks that he hoped would lead somewhere. Currently they were leading through a ghost town of portacabins and towering relics of machinery. Forces of destruction and creation which made him shiver. He didn't like this place, and reflected on the ironic twist that it was now his turn to ask strangers for help. Usually they came to him. And the awful question hit him: what support did he ever provide? Were platitudes ever enough? Could they equate to something tangible like gelignite?

Flabbay Quarry; The Reverend Murdo MacLeod's Road to Damascus. Suddenly everything fitted together perfectly: his wretchedness, his wrecked car, this wrecked landscape. But a parcel of pride still remained intact in the boot. Enough to hold the kernel of revenge.

Professor Archie Oliphant's house appeared round the next corner. An old fisherman's but 'n' ben. Hummocks of gravel had been ripped away and it stood exposed to the weather, but also to a full appreciation of the view. Cut out the quarry, MacLeod thought, and it was classic material for a water colourist. The russet roof, cerulean trail of peat smoke, dark coil of water, the background folds of hills. He could picture the old scientist in summer, in his chair on the machair, puffing on his pipe, parrot on his shoulder.

The area was littered with junk; washing machines, cement mixer, furlongs of tubes, typhoons of wire, boxes, engines, electrical innards ... more guts and decay. He parked by the Professor's Mini Cooper S with its attached trailer. Ruined his shoes in a puddle. Knocked at the door, a framed rectangle of moss and lichens.

'*fput,*' stuttered a miniature sunflower head to the left of the door. MacLeod stared at it. Thought it looked too small for its pot, then realised it was plastic and its head was a speaker. '*fput fput,*' repeated the flower and hummed. Then followed a brief screech and a nasal voice. 'In th'workshop. B'hind you, t'th'left *fput fput.*'

MacLeod turned to see a figure waving through the window of a portacabin.

'Do come in. Excuse the chaos. Mind the wires.'

'Mind the wires!' echoed a parrot standing on a vice. Its head was cocked to one side, a piercing red eye fixed on MacLeod.

'Just ignore Henry, and watch out for birdshit.'

'Birdshit!'

'That's enough, Henry.'

'That's enough, Henry. Fuck off!'

'Do apologise for his language. Had some workmen down to repair the workshop and they rather took to him. Taught him to swear unfortunately. He's got a remarkable ear. An African Grey.'

Henry blew a long, rippling fart.

'Tea or coffee?'

MacLeod felt slightly nauseous and found himself staring wide-eyed at parrot or man, whoever was speaking. It took a moment to retrieve his voice. 'Coffee, please.'

'Son of a bitch!'

The Professor filled a beaker and placed it over a Bunsen burner. 'Just ignore him. He tends to show off in front of strangers.'

'It was on the Good Ship *Venus* … '

'Henry, that's enough. I daresay you remember that one from school,' he chuckled. Saw MacLeod's collar and remembered who his visitor was, 'but probably not. Oh I'm sorry, please have a seat.'

MacLeod's nostrils curled against the pervasive stench of compost and bad eggs. He looked around. Shelves crammed with jars of powders. Colourful as a spice market. Bench tops strewn with bottles labelled with formulae, a pickled frog's head gaping through glass, crucibles, test-tubes, pipettes, scalpels, books spilling pages, a cage of rats, a perspex ant's nest, pots of foliage … and everywhere, African Grey shit. But no chairs.

'Where would you suggest?'

'Arsehole!'

'What? Oh yes. Try those magazines. Watch out for birdshit.'

MacLeod turned over the top three inches of *New Scientist* and sat on a pile two feet high. He wondered if it would appear rude if he cancelled his coffee. It now seemed likely he might receive a dose of formaldehyde by mistake.

'I hope you've not come to convert me. Atheist, you know. Was agnostic, so I've made some progress. Too late to change now. I'm eighty-nine, you know.'

'Really.'

'Motherfucker!'

'No, I expect you've come about knotweed. Tiresome. Terribly invasive.'

MacLeod watched him use a spatula to transfer coffee from a jar to a mug. Back and forwards. A steady hand. Not spilling a drop. He was small. About five foot two inches. Unusually long arms. Always moving, a simian intensity to his busyness. Bald. A red birthmark like an ink blot on his pate. A white chin-beard. Groomed tufts on his cheeks. Weather-beaten, or perhaps cured in the fumes of his own concoctions? His blue overalls, badly stained, seemed hard pressed to keep up with their owner's bursting sense of purpose.

'It's my current mission. Well, one of them.' He indicated a plant. 'Japanese Knotweed. *Polygonum japonicum*. Running rife in the Highlands. A selective poison. That's what's needed. Systemic. Leaves to roots. Only affects two species. Knotweed and brambles. *Rubus rosaceae*. Running riot here. Future curse of Flabbay. Look at Australia. Introduced brambles for jam. Gone berserk. Blue Mountains, Wonnangatta Valley, prize grazing, consumed by brambles. Then they bring in rabbits to eat the brambles. What do they find? Rabbits hate brambles, except for hiding in. But the prickly pear cactus, now that was an interesting case … '

'Professor, I haven't come to talk about virulent weeds.'

'Prick-teaser!'

'Really, can't you shut that creature up? I find it most offensive.'

'Some things can't be changed, Reverend. They just are. Have you tried getting treatment? They can cure most things nowadays, you know?'

'Treatment? For what?'

'Your perversion. Doesn't do your mind or body any good, being offended.'

'Cocksucker!'

'I am *not* sick, I do *not* suffer from any perversion. I am a normal, healthy man ... '

'Here's your coffee. I've put sugar in. Good for digestion, bad for teeth, but yours look false so that shouldn't be a problem. *Slàinte!*'

'The reason I've come, Professor, is to ask if you can help me. As you may have heard, I've been locked out of my own church.'

'Oh yes. Kneed in the balls ... '

'Balls!'

' ... very painful. Grinella told me. Schism, I believe.'

They heard hammering. The Professor looked out the window. 'There's that Braithwaite man again. Hacking away at the rock. They say he's thinking of re-opening the quarry. There'll be no peace for me and Henry if that happens. I just squat here, you know. No legal title.' He opened a jar of blue crystals and stirred a spatula's worth into his tea. Clipped his tea bag to a line to dry. 'Talking of building a bridge too. Totally unnecessary. Ruin the view.'

'Fuck the Pope!'

'I need to open the church door, Professor. It's very old, three inches thick, solid oak, studded with wrought iron.'

'Blow it!'

'I beg your pardon?'

'Why don't you blow it? Drill a semi-circle of holes, pack in a little explosive. Bang! So much easier than hacksaws or cutting torches, or any of that nonsense.'

'Do you know much about that sort of thing?'

'Good Lord, yes! Did years of research. I was involved in the bouncing bomb. You know, The Dambusters.'

'Were you really!' MacLeod sensed a flooding jurisprudence, the Lord's hand reaffirming support on a mission he was convinced was doomed. 'And could you get hold of some explosive?'

'Get hold of it? I've got some here.' He began frantically plucking bottles from shelves. 'I just need to mix it. The basic constituents are found in weedkiller and sugar. Nitroglycerine. Potassium nitrate. Bit of plumber's copper pipe, a detonator, wires and a battery, hey presto!'

'Gangbang!'
'And you'd know how much to use? Would you do the job?'
'Delighted to. Variety is the spice, they say.'
'Hard-on!'

A light dusting of snow settled in time for Christmas. Throughout the castle paper decorations hung from stuffed heads and fluttered in draughts, and the grizzly, standing in for a tree, was ablaze with fairy lights. A second fire burned in the dining-room where lunch was about to be served, when Fran made an announcement.

'I'm leaving.'

Hamish spluttered rosehip wine, scattering petals of pink stains on the table linen. They were down to his father's dregs, the cloudiest, bittiest of his home-made cellar. Fortunately most of his brews exploded during fermentation, bloodied the vaults and spared them heartburn. Rosehip was the worst. Took a bottle a week to pass through blotting paper – but the blotting paper, once dried, made excellent firelighters. Hamish had a glass to his lips when Fran made her announcement. Effie dropped a peacock. The ashet smashed.

'Leaving? You mean going away?'

'Exactly,' affirmed Fran, catching sight of her reflection in a distant portrait and rearranging her paper hat to a more rakish angle. 'Leaving. For good.'

Earlier they'd pulled crackers. Put on paper hats. Rummaged on the floor for plastic baubles, read aloud their jokes.

Fran: *What's yellow and dangerous? Radioactive post-its!*

Effie: *What did the bull say to the cow? When I fall in love, it will be for a heifer!*

Angus: *I STILL ENJOY SEX AT 71. I LIVE AT NUMBER 73, SO IT'S NOT TOO FAR TO WALK!*

Hamish: *How many psychoanalysts does it take to change a light bulb? One, but the bulb has got to WANT to change!*

Loon: *'Neurosis is awwis a substitute fer legitimate suffering' (C Jung).*

Grout: *How dae dinosaurs pass thir exams? Wi extinction!*

Cheap wine, cheap crackers, cheap laughs. Cheap Christmas.

'Where are you going?'

'AN OLD FLAME, I SUPPOSE,' Angus muttered, getting up to help Effie resurrect the peacock.

Fran fielded it good-naturedly. 'Yes, in a sense you're right, Angus. It's *my* old flame and it's burning again.' Realising Angus had his back to her and was out of the conversation, she looked at the others, biting her lip. 'When I first came here I wanted to turn Dundreary into a health spa. I think I could have made it work but your father, Hamish, couldn't bear the thought of his home becoming a business. So it never happened. But now I've got the chance to shine again. I'll tell you where I'm going after pudding. It'll give us something to look forward to.'

Behind her back Effie had succumbed to silent celebration and Angus was wrestling a bottle of brandy from her lips.

'Ah'll miss ye,' remarked Loon, 'yer cool clashes o claithes. But yer better aff oot o here. An it'll gie the phone a chance tae cool doon, tae.'

'If you were so unhappy, why didn't you leave years ago?' Hamish asked.

'Ah, yes, I've asked myself that so often,' Fran replied wearily. 'Until you've experienced the slow siphoning away of self-esteem you can't appreciate how secretly it happens.'

'Neurosis,' said Loon, rereading his paper, 'is awwis a substitute fer legitimate suffering.'

'Oh, tell me about it.' Fran threw her hands in the air. 'I'm one of those who defended herself with what's called "eccentricity", and considered "mad" for it, while the crazy-makers of the world like your father, Hamish, are revered as "great characters".' She raised a cavorting-reindeer napkin and dabbed her eyes. 'I felt I was worth nothing. Too far gone even for willow or agrimony. *The Frosty Evening* saved me.'

'I meant to ask. What did you get for it?'

'Ninety-eight, after commission. It made me think. "Well, Fran, you're no longer worthless, so maybe you aren't useless either."'

Hamish found himself staring at Fran as if he'd never seen her before. 'I ... I ... don't really know what say, except ... I admire you.' He nodded, unable to say more. He wondered if he'd miss her too, and all at once felt concerned.

'Are you sure this is wise? The money won't go far if you have to find a place to stay.'

'I've got a place to stay.' A turquoise wink flashed. 'I'll be moving in three weeks.'

Hamish imagined a Royal Circus suite, three grand a month, *The Frosty Evening* thawing before her eyes. Fran homeless and bankrupt within the lifespan of half-a-dozen pairs of tights.

Effie slopped gravy from the kitchen to the table as she served peacock with all the trimmings: Brussels spouts, carrots, parsnips, roast potatoes, gravy, Española sauce and china shards. They spent some time examining the meat and prising out little shark's teeth, then tucked in heartily.

'Very tasty,' considered Hamish. 'Like burned pheasant.'

The pudding flamed poorly. Effie had left insufficient brandy for the task. They ate it with instant custard and without fear of breaking teeth on money because Fran had forgotten and Effie cheerlessly refused to subsidise the upper classes.

Loony recalled a Christmas spent working in a zoo and his impersonation of a Vietnamese Pot-Bellied Pig set Effie off and she surprised them all with her imitation of a grouse that she'd last performed at a hen night some thirty years earlier and Hamish tried a corncrake but no one recognised it because it really wasn't very good and besides he was thinking of Salvation Army doss houses serving bowls of soup and margarined bread, and Fran sitting at their tables asking if, by any chance, they had nasi goreng or something Shinto like an aduki bean salad with taramasalata and he wondered how she'd cope with dormitory beds and her zebra outfits and plastic bags of oversized hats and no money for Rescue Remedy … until his thoughts, the charades and fragmented conversations all gradually dwindled to a natural conclusion.

Fran rose. A flurry of arms refilled glasses.

'Well, family, friends … I propose a toast.'

'To peacocks,' shrieked Effie, tossing a flume of brandy into the air, 'God love 'em. Eat 'em all!'

'Lighthouses!' suggested Hamish.

'Dunfermline!' offered Grout.

'Jung,' preferred Loon, his grasp on reality unswerved.

Fran took a large spoon and regained control by swiping an unopened bottle of rosehip.

'To Sheikh Jasim al bu Muhammad Maziad bin Hamdan. My new employer.' Her glass swung through an arc, making symbolic clinking gestures in the air. 'You're looking at the newly appointed House Manager of Fitful Lodge.'

ثاني القمارِ (٧)

For the first time in years Dundreary Castle had no first-footers on Hogmanay. Word had got around. Rosehip wine was all that was left. The Colonel's bandwagon gone dry. Hamish was glad. Glad to break the pattern of the past so he could begin to establish his own.

'I DON'T SUPPOSE YOU'LL BE HOLDING A BURNS NIGHT FANCY DRESS THIS YEAR, SIR?'

'I've been thinking about that, Angus. And I think we should.'

'Dinnae think we kin afford that,' cautioned Grout, interrupting his reading: *Grant Quarterly, The Magazine of EU Hand-Outs.* He'd prepared a budget.

'We could make it BYOH,' Hamish suggested.

'H?' queried Fran.

'Haggis. And tatties and neeps.'

'We kid mak the pairty on a theme,' Loon proposed. 'Whit aboot "Vice"? We kin pit oot press releases an git some pre-season publicity.'

Promotions manager was his new role. He and Grout had presented a new strategy, and it was all agreed; no tartan, no authentic history, indeed no authenticity at all, just sensationalism. Dundreary's Decadence & Perversion Tours. They'd fly the Colonel's dirty underwear from the battlements, dig out the family skeletons, display the lewdest letters, regale them with Uncle Hannibal's scandals, replace the boring pictures with blow-ups from *The Illustrated Kama Sutra*. Sunday openings, rip off prices, coaches welcome. They'd be sure to get a grant from Highlands and Islands Enterprise. No other castle had cottoned on to the fact that people were tired of history and privilege. What they craved were falls from grace, sex and human failings, things they could relate to. And the MacFies had a world-class collection. This was the real family treasure. They'd put Dundreary on the map.

'Yes,' affirmed Hamish, rubbing his hands as a plot evolved. 'Vice. And the highlight will be the public humiliation of Cleghorn!'

'It sounds splendiferous,' Fran sparked, already visualising her costume. 'And we'll invite Sheikh Jasim bin Hamdan.'

'Must be keen on fitba' wi yon name,' Grout commented.

* * *

ألمقابلة (٧)

They were in the landrover, driving north, on a tour to visit the quarters of the new House Manager. The road was deserted. On New Year's Day it always seemed that the automobile's time had passed, overnight, junked. They lay abandoned at strange angles to the kerb. Forsaken. And their owners dead. Struck down by the hallowed hangover. Except under a tree.

A huddled group sported umbrellas like a clump of black poppies. And on a rock nearby, the Reverend Norman MacLeod conducting his conventicle.

White horses paraded out at sea, striding purposefully across the Minch. Arriving at Claddach Beach they reared taller, white heads on necks of translucent topaz, then toppled, snorting as they thrashed themselves into foam. Flocks of sandpipers and dunlin flitted along the stain of dying surf, taking to the air as one, veering and jinxing in the unison of telepathy, landing as one. Then dissolving into their separate parts, they scurried along in endless games of dare on the ragged edge of the ocean. Further on, another conventicle, of crows dismantling the carcass of a seal.

'Poor thing,' Fran lamented.

'BLOODY CROWS,' cursed Angus. 'SCOURGE OF GROUSE. BLOODY SEALS. RUINATION OF THE FISHING.'

On their left, the great expanse of moorland. Arabian moorland. Reeds and tussock shivered in the breeze. Rusting tines of bracken waved from a dark mass of flowerless heather. Crimson fleeces of sphagnum glowed in bogs. Sheep looked up mournfully from soggy diets. Saturated breakfasts. Squelchy lunches. Waterlogged suppers. Up to their knees in peat they terrorised the plant world, severing the slightest greenery which dared to protrude, stoically trying to justify the faith on which their Common Agricultural Policy grants were based. Sheep Mountains in the making.

'Corncrake sanctuary,' announced Hamish.

'Corncrake sanctuary,' repeated Effie, Angus's amplifier.

'CORNCRAKE SANCTUARY,' extolled Angus. 'THAT QUANGO'S TAKEN OUR CROFTS FOR A BLOODY JUMPED-UP THRUSH … '

'It's a rare indigenous bird that eats pests. And Scottish Natural Heritage aren't taking away croftland. They're paying a grant for not disturbing the birds during the nesting season.'

'PAH!' Angus vented, on receiving his transmission, 'BALDERDASH! PARCEL OF CROOKS. GAVE LORD GLENNAVEL A HUNDRED AND FIFTY THOUSAND POUNDS NOT TO CUT DOWN A BUNCH OF OLD TREES HE HAD NO INTENTION OF CUTTING DOWN.'

'I agree, Angus. A scandalous misuse of public money.'

'Unless you've got a bunch of old trees on your land,' said Fran, wistfully comparing *old trees* with *The Frosty Evening*.

They passed Flabbay Hall, alone in the wilds, halfway up the island where the southern loop road joined itself and continued north around Ben Stac Mor. Scree-laden slopes, black and fissured, dropped out of the clouds. Swollen burns pulsed like twitching limbs and gathered into the rushing turmoil of Allt an Doire-daraich.

'River of Love-Making,' said Fran.

Fran always said this when crossing the bridge, adding: 'That's what it means in Gaelic.' She refused to believe that the words actually translated as 'River of the Oak Grove'. To her it was always the 'River of Love-Making' and everyone respected the myth in case, privately, it wasn't.

They continued to circumvent Ben Stac Mor's lordly proliferation, swung round its northern flank and saw ahead of them its secret entrance, a sea loch whose narrow opening the Vikings never discovered. Here Somerled, Lord of the Isles, built a stronghold and hid his fleet of galleys. Here his successor, Sheikh Jasim al bu Muhammad Maziad bin Hamdan would do whatever sheikhs did with Highland Estates.

'Whit the fuck's he gaunnae dae wi the place?' Grout asked.

'Gae deep intae debt, ah expect,' Loon replied.

'Coming from where he does,' Fran stated authoritatively, 'one has a deep interest in, and fascination for, water. I suspect that has something to do with it. And I think he's interested in breeding.'

'Aren't we all,' Grout agreed.

'Horses. He's going to establish a stud. Thoroughbreds.'

They came to a sign.

PRIVATE – KEEP OUT

Fitful Lodge was a balanced structure of six towers rising into turrets. The corner ones had bay windows, the central ones the main entrances. Supported on pillars, a canopy extended into the drive to protect guests from the weather when their carriages halted underneath. It was slightly smaller than Dundreary but better proportioned and in better repair.

'That's where I'll be staying,' Fran said, pointing to a cottage whose dark stone matched the lodge.

'The old keeper's cottage,' remarked Hamish, raising his eyebrows. He didn't add that it was reputed to be haunted.

'HAUNTED,' announced Angus. 'THE GREEN LADY. YOU'LL NEED YOUR BIBLE, CROSS AND GARLIC THERE HA-HA-HA.'

'Be quiet, Angus. I'm sure Mrs MacFie'll be very happy there,' Effie cut in, frightened Fran might change her mind. 'You can cook Nasi Goreng to your heart's content.'

'YES, THAT'LL SEE EM OFF BETTER THAN GARLIC HA-HA-HA.'

'Those are the new stables,' Fran pointed out, 'for the thoroughbreds.' Work was in progress, a skeleton of struts and rafters.

'Fer horses?' Grout queried.

'For horses.'

'Big buggers, eh?'

Fran rummaged in her bag, and handed Hamish an envelope. Incipient tears ringed her eyes. 'This is for you.'

He held it suspiciously. Opened it. A fox-hunting card. A voucher. Ten two-hour sessions, signed 'Amulree Shaw'.

'Sessions? … with the corncrake warden?'

'Amulree's resigned. Horses are really her thing and she's coming to manage the sheikh's stable. She'll teach you to ride.' Her tears were flowing freely now. 'It may not be enough, but it's a start.'

'Are you sure you know what you're getting yourself into, Father?'

'I haven't been a scientist for sixty-five years without learning something, Grinella. I thought you'd have more confidence in me by now.'

'You're scarcely the epitome of success, I must point out. Your inventions aren't exactly household names, are they? Oliphant's Autolung bagpipes, for example. Damn lucky you weren't sued when that poor man suffered valve reversal and almost lost his tongue. Oliphant's Midge Repellent, if I recall correctly, was said to be "like wiping yourself with a skunk, and probably less effective." And, I need hardly remind you about what was left of the Institute when your contract was terminated.'

'Skunk!' Henry was listening intently.

'That's in the nature of my business. Risk. You have to risk failure to gain success. No one appreciates the nature of success, it's only achieved through failure because we pioneers have to abandon conventional wisdom, dare to think differently and leap into the unknown. I just need a break.'

'That's exactly what concerns me. You seem to get plenty of them.' Grinella tidied away the groceries she'd brought. 'Here's your laundry.' She indicated a pile, neatly ironed. 'Those overalls look festering. Off with them.'

'Festering! Skunk!'

It was only later that he realised his calculations for the church explosives were on a scrap of paper in the overalls his daughter had removed. He rewrote them from memory and set to work.

That evening he telephoned MacLeod.

'You're all set?' Enthusiasm raised MacLeod's voice to a tinny alto. 'Praise be … near caught my death of pneumonia, I have. These outdoor services. One inside, one outside, all we can afford. Tonight then?'

'Jolly good! What fun!'

'It won't make much of a bang, will it?'

'No, no. Like a shotgun going off. Maybe two.'

'Oh. As bad as that. I'll come and collect you. Discretion being advisable … would midnight be too late?'

'Not a bit. Never in bed before two. Insomnia. Curse of old age.'

MacLeod arrived on time. They drove to the church.

'Festering skunk!'

'Did you have to bring that bird?' MacLeod was feeling edgy. A dereliction of God's attention.

'I take Henry wherever I go. He likes cars. He's quite safe in his cage.'

MacLeod parked well away from the church and used a discrete pen-torch to light the professor's way to the door. He was carrying the wire and battery, and treated them as gingerly as if they were the explosives. Not since National Service had he felt so fragile.

'Terribly simple,' explained the Professor. 'It's a sort of homemade semtex. I've sealed it into tubes. We drill six holes in the wood around the lock, insert the tubes, attach detonators and wire, apply an electrical charge and, bingo, no lock!' He threw the tubes onto a concrete step. MacLeod let out a strangled cry in the expectation of instantaneous disintegration, his mind already a blitz of light, fire, shrapnel and pain.

'Inert. Without a detonator, utterly inert. Crush them. Burn them. Nothing.'

He took a brace, inserted a bit like an oversized corkscrew and drilled. Hammered in the charges with a mallet, screwed on the detonators and attached the wires in parallel. With MacLeod holding the axle and the Professor spinning the cable drum, they unwound sufficient wire to reach a safe refuge at the rear of the building.

'I've got a carpenter and locksmith arranged for first thing in the morning.' MacLeod felt the need to say something reassuring to himself.

'Excellent.'

'You're quite sure you've worked everything out properly.'

'Absolutely. It's all a question of counter-balancing specific densities with the relative coefficients of expansion. Wood, copper, the charge, they're all scientific constants. You just apply formulae. Any fool could do it. You could do it.'

'Let's get it over with.'

'Right-ho. One, two, three ... '

He touched the remaining wire to its terminal.

There were two explosions on Flabbay on Friday, reported Scoop MacKenzie in *The West Highland Free Press* of 8 January, 2004. *The first occurred shortly after midnight at the former Fundamentalist (now True Fundamentalist) church, an historic building erected after the 1892 schism.*

The blast removed the southern gable of the church and one-third of the roof. It blazed a trail of plaster and slate to the sea, scattered hazardous chunks of masonry across the road, blew in the windows of the manse as well as those of two neighbouring houses and demolished a pensioner's greenhouse. The minister's Ford Escort was rolled twice and left upside-down in a culvert, and flying débris caused considerable damage to the police car parked at the nearby station. Hymn books were found as far as two hundred yards from the blast. Mrs Jessie Troutbeck found one in her field. 'It was right queer,' she said, 'there it was lying open at Hymn 528, "I feel the winds of God today". Gave me quite a turn, it did.'

The only reported casualties were two dead bantams, a lame Lonk tup (belonging to B&B owners Bill and Gladys Braithwaite) and a parrot. The parrot, a twelve-year-old African Grey called Henry, was inside the minister's Escort at the time of the explosion. Miraculously Henry was found to be unharmed in his cage. When asked whether his pet was suffering from shock, Henry's owner, Professor Oliphant replied, 'Shock? It's a wonder he didn't come out in slices.'

The Professor was most upset about Henry's reluctance to talk after the experience. 'He used to have such an extensive vocabulary,' he said, 'now all he says is "Bang".' Professor Oliphant explained that he had lent the bird to the minister who was depressed as a result of the recent split in his church and a recurring pornographic disorder. He thought the minister could do with some company and Henry would cheer him up.

The minister, the Reverend Murdo MacLeod, great-great-grandson of legendary preacher and colonist, the Reverend Norman MacLeod of Achmelvich, was too distressed and unavailable for comment yesterday. He had recently been locked out of his church by loyal adherents of the Fundamentalist Church (Continuing) who had refused to join his break-

away order. 'It's quite knocked the wind out of him,' lamented one of his congregation. 'We thought he was a chip off his great-great-grandfather's block, but he's quite gone to pieces. I don't know what'll happen to us.' However, the former precentor took a more optimistic view. 'Half a church is better than no church,' he said.

It is estimated repairs will cost between £70-90,000. As a result of the tendency of insurance companies to invalidate ecclesiastical claims on the grounds of 'Acts of God', the building was uninsured.

After inspecting the damage Sergeant Cleghorn put the cause of the blast down to a gas leak in the church's outdated hot water geyser. This was disputed by the Reverend MacLeod's rival congregation who suspected vandalism.

The second explosion occurred later in the afternoon. Though of a very different nature it still sent shock waves through the community. In the local elections long-standing councillor Miss Grinella Oliphant suffered a surprise defeat at the hands of newcomer, Ms Mairi MacLeod. Miss Oliphant has held the post for the last twelve years and was expected to win by a comfortable margin. Ms MacLeod said she was honoured to hold the community's trust and put her victory down to the people of Flabbay 'voting out fuddy-duddyism, voting in kick-ass activism.' The Free Press *offers its congratulations to Ms MacLeod, and condolences to Miss Oliphant.*

Flabbay Community Hall hadn't experienced a capacity crowd since the Grand Fête and Games held in 1952 to celebrate the coronation of Her Majesty, Queen Elizabeth I of Scots – a day sadly marred by a blocked drain and a partial boycott of the Sack Race by parents protesting against the 'parochial designation of Queen Elizabeth II'.

'Well, well,' muttered Calum the Post, for whom Flabbay Hall still evoked happy memories of his triumph in that Coronation Sack Race when he narrowly out-bounced Grinella Oliphant. 'Never thought a bridge enquiry would have brought so many out of the woodwork.'

'It'th not often we thee a government minithter on the island,' replied Thkip. 'I wonder how many toeth they have.'

They looked through the doorway and saw car headlights scythe the darkness and illuminate the angel. She was kneeling, a soldier slumped against her, his head in her lap. Her left hand rested on his brow but it was too late for him and the fifty-eight names below, and she was looking up at the laurel wreath held out in her other hand, wings open, ready for take off.

'Look! The dethecrater.'

The Reverend Murdo MacLeod's scrawny figure appeared in the entrance, nervously looked about, saw them and made for the far off corner where the Reverend Alexander Murray was already sitting. They continued watching the spectra of inhabitants drift in. Their shoes rumbled the hollow-sounding boards, echoes drifted through the roof's matrix of metal beams. A series of gas grills along each wall glowed with serious intent but little effect and their heat rose to disappear among the echoes. On the stage stood a lectern sprouting a microphone, four chairs and a table decked with MacFie tartan, glasses, a jug and the winning arrangement of the WRI's 2003 Silk Flowers & Foliage Competition.

The influx ceased. The doors were closed. The lights dimmed and four figures walked out of the wings and took their seats. The only one immediately recognisable to the majority present was Councillor Mairi Ban MacLeod. She'd dyed her afro-frizz day-glo green.

'Fuddy-duddyism. *pah!* The insolence of the woman,' fumed Miss Oliphant. 'Pride comes before a fall. And she's got a long long way to fall. But fall she will, Dilly.'

'She's looks quite the part tonight. Never seen her in a long skirt before. Very nice. I'm looking forward to seeing how she performs.'

'*pah!*'

Two rows behind, Grout dug Loon in the ribs. 'Ah Loon. Haud oantae me, pal. She's fuckin stunnin.'

Mairi Ban got up and went to the lectern: 'Good evening, folk, and may I offer you the warm welcome the heaters are failing to provide. We're here to discuss the proposed bridge, or, to give the Order its correct title, "The Invergarry-Pluckton Trunk Road (A87) Extension (Flabbay Bridge Crossing) Toll Order (Variation)".' She paused and surveyed the sea of bemused faces. 'That's just the name they've come up with. Wait till you see the design.' The panel exchanged glances and shifted in their seats as a simmer of laughter died. 'During this enquiry all views are welcome and, I'm told – though I don't believe it – will be given due consideration. So, without further ado, I'll introduce the panel. On my left, the supposedly impartial Scottish Executive Reporter, Miss Harkum.'

She nodded. Applause.

'In the middle, that rarest of Hebridean visitors, a Secretary of State for Transport. The Right Honourable – we hope – Alista Darning.'

Nod. Applause.

'And last, Mr Watch-My-Lips "No Tolls". But of course, that was two weeks ago. An awfully long time in the subservience industry. Mr Peter Chough, Convenor of Highland Regional Council.'

No nod. No applause.

'Kick-ass activism,' Dilly whispered, and tittered.

'She's an insult. Her libellous disregard for basic courtesies is scandalous.'

'I think she comes over very naturally at the microphone. Some don't. Just seem to blow bubbles.'

Mairi Ban exaggerated a bow. 'Mr Darning, over to you.'

The Transport Minister rose, placed a sheaf of notes on the lectern and put on spectacles. The speakers, as if to illustrate Dilly's point, issued froggy *blorps* as he fumbled to raise the microphone. He had a long face and jaws that looked strong enough to shell almonds. A hand ran over his head and smoothed an oily sheen of hair.

'Good evening, Ladies and Gentlemen. I'm not sure whether to thank Councillor MacLeod for her unusual introduction, or whether I should simply leave now.' To his relief this raised a laugh. 'Naturally Westminster politicians wish they could travel round the country meeting people more often, but believe it or not, we are busy people doing our best for the nation. And New Labour is delighted to be doing something very special for you people of Flabbay, providing you with an overdue fixed-link with the mainland. No more ferry queues, no more disruption by storms. A bridge will be good for business, good for employment, good for tourism.'

'Good for the Bank of America,' someone heckled. The remark was ignored.

'John, the first image please.'

From some unseen recess an overhead projector threw up an artist's impression of the proposed bridge. Badly wrinkled by the cream curtains which substituted as a screen, a curved boomerang of concrete rippled across the width of the hall.

'The plan is to extend the road along the coast from Pluckton – here – construct this outstandingly elegant bridge to the lighthouse island of Mickle Flabbay – here – privately owned and available for purchase, and run a causeway to Flabbay – here – just before the quarry, on land owned by the MacFie family.'

'I WON'T SELL,' Hamish shouted.

'Next, please John.'

'The favoured bid is that put in by a joint venture of Milkers Civil Engineering of Edinburgh and Docker-Huff and Woodmann of Munich. The latter have a patent on vital aspects of the technology. It will be … ' he consulted his notes, ' … a balanced cantilever bridge of pre-stressed concrete, main span 250 metres, two-lane, eight degree gradients.' He continued with more statistics, praised the expediency of New Labour policy in advancing Private Finance Initiatives, promised no action would be taken until all local issues had been resolved, gathered his notes, thumped them on the lectern, made the speakers *blorp* and sat down.

Mairi Ban asked for questions.

'Looks like Hitler's Revenge,' called a high-pitched voice. People laughed and turned to see whose it was. Miss Stewart's. Zimmer parked alongside.

Miss Oliphant was first to her feet. 'As former councillor for Flabbay, Mr Darning, I voted against a toll bridge, as Mr Chough can verify, on the grounds that we are a remote community with European Objective One status. As you are aware that means our economy and infrastructure are disadvantaged. What we want is a toll-free bridge' – volleys of agreement sounded from the floor – 'so why don't you give us one?'

'Impossible, I'm afraid. There's no guarantee of European money and we've limited money in the pot. Not enough for a bridge, upgrading your school, your roads.'

'How long will tolls last?' This was Calum the Post.

'Fourteen years. Eighteen at the absolute outside.'

'How high will the tolls be?' Calum persisted.

'It is envisaged they'll be about the same as current ferry fares.'

Thkip MacQuarrie immediately rose to his feet. 'That'th outrageouth. The Flabbay fareth are artificially high to croth-thubthidith other Hebrideth routeth. That'th robbery to maintain them. And what'th going to happen to the ferrieth, and thirty jobth. Anthwer me that.'

The Transport Minister looked embarrassed and turned to Mairi Ban. 'What Captain MacQuarrie said was … ' and she furnished a translation.

'Naturally the ferries will have to stop. The price of progress! We will continue to subsidise other ferry routes and about half the redundant ferry workers will be offered posts as toll collectors.'

Questions continued for an hour, a sense of gloom pervading the hall. Of a world out of kilter. Of the government's negotiator in a Chieftain tank, and they, the people, with nothing but damp powder and rubber bullets. Scoop MacKenzie sat at the back slashing shorthand into his notebook.

Grout was amongst the last to speak. 'Ah've been readin yer New Roads an Street Works Act, 2000. Furst ah'd like tae tell ye tae try writin English in future. A Madagascan marmot wi a smatterin o words kid hae made it mair intelligible. Secondly, section forty-three pairt two B sais tolls kin niver be imposed oan a trunk road where there's nae viable alternative access. Kin *niver* be imposed, ken? So, where's wir viable alternative?'

'You have a ferry from Grimport, do you not? To Benbecula. With a connection to Oban. I think you'll find that satisfies the relevant criteria.'

'That's a two day trip an two hunner smackers … '

'Then I'm sure you'll find the tolls extremely good value for money.'

Hamish was next. 'My name is Hamish MacFie. As you correctly said, I own the land on this side. And I repeat. I'm not selling.'

'Then we'll exercise our powers of Compulsory Purchase.'

'I'LL FIGHT THIS TO THE BITTER END,' Hamish shouted.

Mairi Ban moved to conclude the evening. She walked to the lectern. The Transport Minister took a step back and stayed beside her in anticipation of adding a final word after her note of thanks.

'Thank you, that appears to be it.' She turned to the Minister.

In his seat towards the rear of the hall a prescience of foreboding swept the Reverend Murdo MacLeod but before he could articulate a warning, it was too late. Mairi's movement caught the minister by surprise. His legs buckled and crossed, his mouth fell open, spilling a low, ululating groan before he rocked backwards and collapsed into a writhing heap of knees, feet and elbows.

'I trust you'll keep your word, Mr Darning.'

'Aw, jist let me at her,' Grout drooled. 'Mairi, *mon amour.*'

* * *

Within a week bulldozers moved into an abandoned gypsy camp on the edge of Pluckton and a colony of portacabins grew as tall as the trees. In the *Press & Journal* a notice appeared: 'Labourers Wanted, Pluckton Area' over the banner of Milkers, Docker-Huff and Woodmann. The project was not specified.

Farquhar watched Angela doing her makeup. Storm of powder from a fluttering puff. Delicate strokes of mascara. Dabs of shadow. Patina of rouge. Slate-purple smears to pouting lips. Contorted face, alien colours. He watched portrait turn caricature, wife turn stranger, life go grotesque, saw her doubled in the mirror's reflection, twins, mouths agape like a pair of hungry pelicans. And he, feeling like fish. Small fry.

'You still haven't told me what you're going as?'

'A frogwoman.' She pointed at her wetsuit. 'I'll carry the flippers.'

'Frogwoman? What on earth's that got to do with vice?'

'It's all in the mind.' The beaks expanded. Silently Laughing Pelicans. 'I see you're going as yourself. Sergeant Cleghorn. Very original.'

'All I could think of. But it fits the theme. Very odd choice.' He fondled his baton. 'Very suspicious, if you ask me.'

'Couldn't you make *some* gesture, for God's sake? At least put on a funny hat, *or something.*'

They drove to Dundreary in a rattling Uno shell. Wind warbled through an absent windscreen and two other empty frames. Under the bonnet a dozen piglets were being slaughtered. Uno engine in mourning. A trailing exhaust fired extravagant volleys of sparks into the air. Uno decibels exceeding legal limit. Uno atmosphere, Third Ice Age.

Unable to kick the habit, Angus Dalrymple was re-peppering the castle walls when they arrived. Dressed in leathers with steel embroidery, chains and swastikas. Reluctantly borrowed from Grout. Teeth still gritted.

'You told me to wear a funny hat,' protested Farquhar, when Angela erupted on seeing what he'd chosen.

'I didn't mean my good Jaeger beret.' She put on her flippers and slapped her way to the door.

'EVENING MRS CLEGHORN. SERGEANT. DOG'S PISS.' Angus held up the pepper by way of explanation.

'You look really cool,' Angela cooed, and clattered her way into the hall. A sheikh broke off his conversation with a witch as she approached. The witch turned. Her day-glo hair was a give-away, even among fancy dress.

'Hi Mairi!'

'Hi Angie. My! Don't you look good in all that tightness. A real little "vice" you've got there!'

'Thanks, Mairi. I thought you were great the other night. You've a real way with words.'

'And knees,' added the Arab.

Angela waited until the Arab had drifted off. 'Any idea who that was? Obviously a woman from the voice.'

'Amulree Shaw, the sheikh's stable manager. Sorry Angie, I should have introduced you. Delicious girl, and what an athletic body! She says those stallions are a bit of a handful. Aren't they all, though?'

'I suppose they are,' Angela replied uncertainly. She felt the rub-aah effect, an all-over tingling, and didn't know how to begin. 'Mairi, there's something I've been meaning to ask you.' She glanced around to make sure no one was eavesdropping. 'I'm not very experienced … you know … with men.'

'You want to sleep with me? Well why didn't you say so years ago?'

'No, Mairi, that's not what I mean.' Angela was aware she'd turned scarlet. 'No, it's me and Lawrence, I was thinking about.'

'You mean you haven't screwed that guy yet?'

Angela winced. 'You make it sound so crude, Mairi. I think we're aspiring to something higher … ' her eyes drifted up, ' … possibly even transcendental.'

'Well that's great, honey, but I suggest you start with a plain simple good old shag.'

Angela's eyes descended to Mairi's. 'That's what I wanted to ask you. About starting. It may seem silly but over the years I've sort of lost my confidence, and Lawrence, he's so shy.'

'Shy but hanging out for it, darling. Believe me, I can see it in his walk. But you're going to have to be proactive, Angie. His ma probably sewed him into his underpants to protect her boy. Force an entry and go for it. Subtlety won't work.' The possibility of teaching evening classes flashed through her mind: Refresher Courses in Sex.

'Really?' Something jolted inside Angela. She felt her old sense of daring return, a flush of liberation. 'Thanks, Mairi.' She leant forward and kissed the witch's lips.

'Any time you'd like a demonstration, honey, just call. And remember, shag first, transcend later.'

Angela scrabbled into the *mêlée* of figures. Searching. Colours, pressing bodies, knobbly appendages, burbling conversation, someone saying 'Bang!' ... Eventually she found him.

'Snap!' she said, touching his shoulder.

Lawrence turned. 'Snap!' he said, his face lighting up. 'Only you've flippers, and I haven't.'

Father Benedict, loosely modelled on Flabbay's war memorial, looked on enviously.

'Good to see you, Father,' greeted a new voice.

Father Benedict jumped. A single wing, made from recycled coat-hangers and starched crêpe paper, juddered behind him. The voice came from a sheep's skull. Algae verdant along its seams, horns like long, gnarled toenails. He searched for clues to identity in the living eyes, the black cape and dangling tail, but found none. The wellies, painted with claws, had to be a man's.

A hand tipped back the skull and revealed the face.

'Ach, Hamish! That outfit's a little too realistic for comfort.'

'I like yours. Why only one wing?'

'I was hoping someone would ask,' he beamed. 'Fallen Angel.'

'Rather a lot of Arabs here tonight.'

'Can't see what Arabs have got to do with vice, myself.'

'I think it's just Flabbay's innate xenophobia coming out. First the Vikings, then Lowlanders, then English, now a sheikh. Always nice to have a change of hate. Incidentally, I sent Sheikh bin Hamdan an invitation. Fran said he might turn up. If he's here, it'll come as a bit of a shock to find twenty-two other sheikhs as neighbours. But I suppose if he's in fancy dress, he'll be in a kilt.'

'I don't suppose he's that man dressed as a pirate, is he? With the bird on his shoulder.'

'No, that's Professor Oliphant. The Mad Professor. And Henry?'

'Oh, is that him? I'm very fond of parrots. Must go and say hallo.' He moved off, the wing wobbling in his slipstream.

'I assume that's you under there, Mr MacFie?'

Hamish turned and felt his heart sink. 'Very smart detective work, Sergeant.'

'It seemed an elementary deduction that the host would dress as the Devil.'

'Sorry to be so predictable. Your hat's very fetching but work clothes don't count.'

'I have to remember my position, Mr MacFie. And I would like it on record that I strongly disapprove of the theme for this party. It encourages everything that I and my uniform stand against.'

'In most circles, Sergeant, it's called *fun*.' Hamish wished Loon would come to his rescue. He couldn't wait for Cleghorn to see *his* outfit. 'If you really felt so strongly about it, you could have chosen not to come.'

'I have my wife to think about. Have to protect her from *what might happen*. I'm sure you know what I mean.'

'I haven't the faintest idea.' Then a smile broke out under his skull. He thought of the climb. Mrs Cleghorn in rubber. A thousand penises. He knew exactly what the poor sergeant meant.

'Besides, I consider it my duty to attend,' Cleghorn continued. 'Doesn't hurt to get around the place. Keep your eyes open. Never know what you'll find. Some little snippet that could assist in future enquiries.'

The policeman's voice was developing a sinister confidence. Hamish registered its playful menace. It could only be leading to something unpleasant.

'You see, Mr MacFie, there's been a recent spate of hoax calls to the police station, body found here, break-in reported there, that sort of thing. Serious offence wasting a police officer's time, and hoax calls, well, minimum two years usually. I've also had my car vandalised and I daresay, Mr MacFie, that whoever did it thought it was what you'd call *fun* … '

'Sergeant, you happen to be in *my* home at *my* party. If you want to give me a lecture, save it for … '

'The point I am making, Mr MacFie, is that this upsurge in crime coincides with the arrival on this island of those two hooligans you give refuge to in this castle. I took the liberty of having a wee walk around the place. You have two greenhouses at the back, don't you?'

Behind his mask, Hamish blanched.

'In the walled garden. Just happened to shine my torch inside. Interesting crop you're growing.'

Hamish said nothing. Imagined the well. Deep. Dark. Hidden under moss. *Searchers Abandon Hunt For Missing Policeman.*

'Cannabis, unless I'm very much mistaken.' He withdrew a crumpled green stem with fleshy leaves from inside his jacket. 'I'll be sending this off for analysis in the morning with a full report. Do enjoy your party, Mr MacFie, but don't have too much *fun*. The law might take a very dim view of it.'

A tenth of an acre of cannabis, and Cleghorn had stumbled on it. He searched for Grout and Loon but they were nowhere to be seen. Shit! He could kiss goodbye to the castle, to ambition. The evening was going horribly wrong.

'WARLOCKS AND WITCHES,' a voice announced. Everyone turned to see Hell's Angel Angus. 'PLEASE TAKE YOUR SEATS FOR THE SERVING O THE HAGGIS.'

Effie, stuffed with bolsters to represent Gluttony but just looking like Very Fat Effie, followed by a squad of plumped-up nieces and nephews, appeared with trays of BYO-haggises, tatties and neeps that had been reheated in the castle oven. People shuffled through to the dining-room where, as an exception for the evening, a second fire blazed ruinously. Hamish made his way to the top table to deliver the traditional address. He caught sight of Grout at the back of the room, and Gertrude eating the curtains. If he was losing the castle, at least he was losing it in style, he thought. He surveyed the bizarre banquet and felt like an extra in some film set crossed with a bad morality play. *Lawrence of Arabia, directed by Hieronymus Bosch.*

'WILL SOMEONE GET RID OF THAT GOAT,' Miss Stewart shouted. 'I CAN'T THINK FOR THE SMELL, LET ALONE EAT.'

No one was surprised to see Miss Stewart at the party. It was a matter of pride to her that she'd attended every one since she was eighteen, including Hannibal MacFie's elite and esoteric debaucheries. Now in her ninety-fifth year, she wasn't going to miss one even though they'd become such staid, tame affairs. Why, in Hannibal's time parties went on so long people were regularly reported missing, and no one ever came back in the clothes they'd arrived in. Most of the guests considered she'd done very well with her costume, considering the restrictions of the zimmer. Buried in flouncing pale-yellow ruffles, she'd come as crumpet.

Grout detached himself from the seat next to Beelzebub and led Gertrude to a half-ton Eagle On A Bough in bronze, a *cire perdue* from the late Ch'ing dynasty, and tethered her to one of the eagle's feet. Grout was dressed entirely in white. White turban, bangle earrings, shirt with jabot, Aladdin baggies, jester slippers with curled toes. Scimitar hanging from cummerbund.

'Very odd outfit he's wearing,' commented Miss Oliphant. 'Can't make head nor tail of it. Still, I suppose with the education he's had, "vice" is something he does naturally without knowing the meaning of it.'

Dilly, who'd consulted her thesaurus and come as Vice Versa, had scribbled poetry over an old parchment-coloured dress and stuck a couple of quills in her hair, was tiring of her friend's grumpiness.

'If you're determined to wallow in a kippage, Grinella, I'll find some other company. I think his costume is both natty and clever. Sinbad. I overheard him telling someone. Quite erudite, actually. Sin-bad.'

'Thank you, Dilly. I got it first time.'

'Bang!'

'I swear I'll shoot that bird if he says that one more time. Wish Father would leave the wretched thing at home.'

Dilly noticed the continued stares in their direction. One of the sheikhs appeared particularly interested.

'I have to say, Grinella, and I know compliments make you fractious, but I wish to make it clear that a kilfud-yoking is the last thing on my mind.' She paused, waiting for Grinella to respond.

'A *what*?'

'Kilfud-yoking. Isn't it a marvellous word? I just discovered it today. Of course, being a compound rules it out for Scrabble, which is a pity. "A fireside disputation". Look it up if you don't believe me.' She waved her napkin to dissipate the fire's heat. 'I think you've stolen the show this year, Grinella. Your Boadicea, while perhaps not ingeniously in context, is brilliant. Bold, shocking and really *very* sexy.'

Hot red was her colour. A fiery boa was wrapped around her head with a conical crown of cardboard coated in gold glitter. Her earrings – and she'd got the idea from the louts – were red mackerel lures without the hooks. Over a velvet gown was a veritable fetish of leather thongs – various harnesses and trappings borrowed from Flabbay Pony Riding 'N Treks – emphasising the fullness of her frame. At the front her gown parted and ponderous breasts jutted out, encased in a bra which her father had fashioned from family-sized baked beans tins and buffed so that the entire banquet was reflected in them. The gown fell away into culottes with high slashes, and ultimately to riding boots. Tied at the waist was a Nazi sword, a chance find at a Sally Army shop.

'Well, thank you Dilly. Compliments so often, in my not inconsiderable experience, come dressed in sarcasm or ulterior motive. Abuse is so much easier to deal with. You know exactly where you stand. But I won't argue with you on this occasion. I just thought, "Grinella, you show them." Fuddy-duddy indeed. Play that little strumpet at her own game.'

A movement at the top table caught her eye.

'O Lord, there's that performing dog again.'

On a podium Rastafarian was signalling.

'Whit naebody realises,' Sinbad explained to the witch, 'is Rast's sayin Q-U-I-E-T. He's a fuckin marvel that dug.'

'Fair fa' your honest, sonsie face,' recited the Devil,

'Great Chieftain of the Puddin-race!

Aboon them a' … '

'Just look at Fran MacFie,' whispered Grinella. 'A Lawson's sausage, I suppose. Ridiculous! And Gladys Braithwaite looks like she's fallen off a Greek vase. Really! It's not in the spirit of these parties to *look* glamorous, if that's what she's trying to do.'

'Don't forget, she had that accident,' recalled Dilly. 'Two years back. They say she still gets migraine from it. Probably trying to get her confidence back. It's a wonder she can even face haggis.'

It had been in all the papers at the time. A gift to journalism. Everyone had found it so funny, which, quite aside from concussion and migraine, had been particularly hard for Gladys Braithwaite to bear. *Floored By A Flying Haggis!* ran one of the less sensitive headlines. Haggis hurling had long been one of the highlights of Flabbay Gala and to withstand an afternoon of heavy landings the haggis had to be frozen. Mrs Braithwaite, it was reported, was standing with her back to the arena and was buying her niece and nephew toffee apples at the time. Hector Ross, a local youth on his second toss, *had whipped himself into an Olympian birl* – Dilly could remember that bit, a nice description, she thought – when the haggis prematurely slipped from his grasp, *flew a not-to-be-sneezed-at fifty yards* and struck Mrs Braithwaite a glancing blow to the back of the head. There'd been talk of litigation but the Gala committee had managed to smooth things over by sending Mrs Braithwaite a bouquet of roses, an apology on Gala headed paper and – somewhat callously, many felt – a leftover box of haggis.

'Ye pow'rs wha mak mankind your care,' Hamish was concluding.

'And dish them out their bill o' fare,

Auld Scotland wants … '

A sudden flash filled the room. Everyone turned to look up at the minstrel's gallery. Loon was smiling behind a Sinar 5 x 4 and a battery of umbrellas. Sheet film, large format for the cover of the new Dundreary brochure. *Dundreary Castle – Five Hundred Years of Sin, Scandal & Shame.*

People strained to make out what he was wearing, then to find significance in it. His pale blue sports shirt was ripped and hung off in shreds. In parallel lines across his chest were blazed the words **CORNBEEFIES** and **BRAZIL NUTTERS.** Most onlookers remained unenlightened. They correctly guessed that the secret could be solved by reading the words written on about twenty balloons floating from strings in his left hand. From that distance the words were indecipherable. Loon now reached for a cord and tugged it. A banner unrolled to the floor, a copy of the words for all to see.

Before any of them could take them in, Sergeant Cleghorn leapt to his feet, whipped out his baton and shook it at the gallery. 'YOU INSOLENT BASTARD,' he screamed.

Flash!

'I'LL GET YOU FOR THIS. YOU WON'T GET AWAY WITH IT, YOU … VERMIN.' He delved inside his jacket and withdrew the plant. 'SEE THIS. IT'S GOING TO PUT YOU AWAY FOR LIFE.'

Loon turned, dropped his white shorts and mooned him, **THE PARS** neatly printed across his buttocks. Cleghorn turned to Angela. 'I'll wait outside for you,' he said, ripping off the Jaeger beret and striding off.

'I don't understand,' exclaimed Fran, dressed as a femidom, 'why he's so upset? He always spoils things. And what was he doing stuffing mint in his pocket?'

'It wasn't mint, it was cannabis.'

'Really! I never knew he did drugs.'

'He's full of surprises, our friend the sergeant. He's also a football fan. Of Cowdenbeath. Apparently the team's nicknamed the Blue Brazil and the big rivals, Dunfermline Athletic, are known as the Pars. That,' he nodded to the writing on the banner, 'is a listing of the Blue Brazil's defeats over the last two seasons.'

He raised his glass in the air. Traditional sign to eat. Knives stabbed. Skins popped, haggis erupted and oozed. There was a clatter of cutlery like the workings of a woollen mill. They ate.

Lawrence Brodie sweltered in his outfit. It had been Angela's idea for them to come as frogpeople. She said she wanted to wear rubber. She used the word a lot and always said it in a strange way – *rub-aaah* – unnaturally drawn out like she was combining it with a yawn, or something more exciting. They hadn't seen much of each other and at the table Lawrence found himself next to Mairi Ban. Her choice of a witch's costume was appropriate, he thought, considering he'd almost come as Macbeth, and her reputation for having the Second Sight.

'Have you had any visions recently, Mairi?'

'Oh yes,' she spoke softly, as if in no doubt that Time and Reason both honoured her words. 'One very troubling one. I've had it three times now. That's usually a sign, you know.'

'A sign?'

'That it's going to happen. Once, you don't take much notice. Twice and you think, *hey, this is a repeat.* Third time, *you know.*'

'May I ask what it was about?'

'I see two people dancing. Forehead to forehead, in a slow intimate tango, a contact of harmony. Perfectly synchronised. I hear the music, you know, that Argentine squeeze-box thing ... '

'Bandonion?'

'Yes, yes, that's the one. I can hear it, and those sounds, oh such sensuous sounds, of leather glissading over wood. I can see their limbs intertwining and unlocking, discipline effortlessly judged. So beautiful. They strut and spin, double and feint, this way and that, she on the edge of the abyss and he always there to catch her. The artistry of kindred spirits. But all the time their faces are hidden and it's only at the end that they turn and both catch the light. And then I see it, clear as writing. Hers is the face of trust, his the crafted façade of treachery. You know the next time, he's going to drop her. But,' she stared him hard in the eyes and a hint of smile curled her lips, 'she wins in the end. I can read that too.'

Lawrence felt his spine tingle. His throat blocked. He swallowed. He and Angela. She was talking about *them.* He found some saliva to free his tongue. 'Do you know who ... these people are?'

'Oh yes.' She leaned closer. 'He's Man. She's Nature.'

Lawrence exhaled heavily in relief. Mairi realised he didn't understand. 'The bridge,' she hissed. 'Something's going to happen.'

There was a scream, followed by another and people began ejecting themselves from the table in a wave of panic. A chain-reaction like some unseen electrical current causing violent contractions. Chairs toppled and figures were soon sprawling on the ground. Gertrude suddenly burst from under the tablecloth and vaulted the top table to complete a flying assault on Rastafarian. He nipped behind a dragon *cloisonné* vase which exploded into fragments a moment later. Gertrude stood there faintly stunned but clearly satisfied. She'd never managed to do that to a dog before.

'Marvellous party, Hamish. Haven't had as much fun for years,' the Pirate enthused. 'What a clever party piece to arrange for the goat to do that stunt!'

'Fuck off!'

Professor Oliphant turned to Henry, then back to Hamish, his face alight. 'Good God! Did you hear that? Must have been the vase that did it!' He turned back to Henry and smothered him in kisses. 'Henry! That's my boy! Feeling more our old self, are we?'

The band struck up for a Strip the Willow, tables were pushed aside and everyone formed sets. As the night wore on, the number of dancers diminished and gravity shifted. The Fall of Man entered its final act. Someone was trying to revive the exciseman, the head of the local Licensing Board by fanning a beermat in his face. But the man was beyond ministration and was indulging in cavernous yawns during which his falsers closed with a *clunk*. Then came the sounds of drunken singing. A duet. Sinbad and the witch had discovered a mutual interest in Burns's lewdest songs. Raucously out of tune, they bawled:

> *Come rede me, dame, come tell me, dame,*
> *My dame come tell me truly,*
> *What length o'graith, when weel ca'd hame,*
> *Will sair a woman duly?*
> *The carlin clew ...*

* * *

At some time during the early hours, probably with assistance, the Roman monopede lost his remaining leg and crashed to the ground.

rede, advise; *graith*, gear; *ca'd*, driven; *sair*, serve; *carlin*, old woman

'Sergeant, I wish to complain about the noise. And the traffic. It's preposterous. This road was never built with these vehicles in mind. It's also immoral, a flagrant breech of a promise. The Minister of Transport has hoisted himself with his own petard in this instance and it's up to us to see that he's called to account for it. Before hundreds of witnesses he promised that nothing would be done before the results of the Public Enquiry were published but here we are, within a fortnight, it's all gung-ho and up with a bridge. *And* he said no decision would be taken without further consultation ... '

Cleghorn let Miss Oliphant rabbit on. And on. And on. At appropriate moments he grunted and hummed. If there was one thing he had learned in his job it was not to interrupt Miss Oliphant when she was on her soapbox.

'Furthermore, they've no right to work on the Sabbath. Not that I'm one of these Scripturalists – sensibly National Presbyterian, as you well know – and neither do I wish to be ... be ... '

'Fuddy-duddy?' He regretted the reference the moment it came out.

'*That*, Sergeant Cleghorn,' she snapped, 'is as nefarious and reprehensible a remark as it is impertinent.' She glared at him. 'What I was going to say was *prim*. I don't wish to appear *prim* about Sunday working but I regard it a basic human courtesy and a foundation of civilisation that one respects the views of others, and there are many whose piety is deeply offended by the deafening workings at the quarry. First the endless lorry loads of equipment and now the constant churning of borers and buckets. My father can barely have a conversation with Henry any more. I demand you get Health and Safety down to that place at once.'

Cleghorn waited to ascertain whether the pause was a full stop or a comma. It proved to be a comma.

'And where on earth did that Braithwaite man get the money to open the place up? I don't recall any advance notices being posted, applications for planning consent. For twenty years my father's as good as owned his place there, and now he'll be driven from his home. An old man at that. It's iniquitous.'

Full stop.

'Miss Oliphant, the facts as I understand them are these: Mr Braithwaite has signed a private contract with the owners of the quarry, Bluewater Ltd. The quarry has never officially closed, the original planning consent was based on tonnage of material removed and as that figure was never reached, the original consent is still valid. I believe Mr Braithwaite has received a substantial grant. Your father appears to be squatting in the quarry but if he believes he has legal rights, he should see a lawyer. There is no actual law against working on a Sunday. The vehicles using the quarry are all operating within legal limits, and Health and Safety have inspected the works and issued an operating certificate.'

'That's just the sort of response I would have expected from you. Well, let me tell you,' she placed both fists on his table, bent her arms and leant towards him bulldogishly, 'if Henry suffers a recurrence of shock or my father has a heart attack as a result of your contemptible apathy, then I shall publicly expose you as an insensate huckster and a charlatan. Good morning, Sergeant.'

The door slammed behind her. Two Ruth Rendells fell. *A Sleeping Life* and *A New Lease of Death*

Good morning! When had there last been one? Two days ago the half-page colour photograph in the *Free Press*. Angela had come running in with a copy, almost helpless with laughter. He looked a complete fool standing there in her idiotic bonnet, shouting and brandishing his baton at a crowd of lunatics. From his complexion and unfortunate expression, he appeared to be sozzled. And worse, he looked as if he were singing an aria and actually enjoying himself. The caption did nothing to redress the impression: *Flabbay's policeman, Sergeant Farquhar Cleghorn [lower left, in the funny hat] entertains the crowd at the recent Burns Night Party at Dundreary Castle.*

Yesterday Chief Inspector Harlaw phoned with another acerbic reproach for the continuing spree of damage to the car, mentioned an official complaint from the Reverend MacLeod and made snide remarks about spending less time bringing the Force into disrepute by fooling around in ladies' hats. On a brighter front, Harlaw acknowledged receipt of the plant which had been sent to the labs, and confirmed that the system for tracing calls had now been installed. In view of the island's analogue exchange the trace time would be around six hours.

He'd concluded: 'You aren't exactly flavour of the month, here. You *will* catch these hoax culprits soon, *won't you*? And there *won't* be any mistakes this time, *will there*?'

Cleghorn found the juxtaposition of positives and negatives a little confusing but the message was clear enough. The Sword of Damocles was up and fraying.

And then yesterday's mail. The envelope was still on his desk. Flabbay postmark. Newspaper cuttings. Adjectives highlighted … ***disgraceful*** … ***pathetic*** … ***toe-tied*** … under the heading … **Dunfermline 5 Cowden-grief 0**.

The phone rang. He took the message and thought: Well, well, right on cue! What perfect timing! That familiar, muffled voice. Not a body or a break-in this time. But a brawl. Grimport again. Somerled Bar. Knives involved. Looking very serious, the voice said. 'Please hurry.'

He lifted the receiver and dialled. 'Trace that last call, please. Six hours? That'll be fine.'

Cleghorn smiled. Lay back in his chair wallowing in one-up-manship. The tables had turned. He opened a drawer, withdrew the handcuffs and clipped them to his belt. He rose, locked the office and got into the car. As he drove off he noticed the Dundreary landrover parked by the road, and Angus Dalrymple inside. He appeared to be doing the maritime equivalent of trainspotting. 'Not quite the full shilling that one.' And Cleghorn looked the other way and pretended he hadn't seen him.

This latest hoax, coming so opportunely after the recent run of bad luck, had dispelled his morning depression and he felt in jubilant spirits. He'd get them. No, not in Grimport. He wasn't going to Grimport. He was going to the scene of the crime. Dundreary. To see what they might be up to. As a diversion, he drove in the opposite direction for several miles and waited an hour.

An overnight frost veiled the land in satin. Rabbits had scored motorways over the golf course. Clumps of daffodil shoots were poking resolutely through the roadside verges and already the first snowdrops were in flower. The sea was taut, as if to dip a toe in would sound a note, C sharp, probably. The gods, Cleghorn felt, were smiling.

He didn't feel possessed of, or by, a God. In his youth, God had a tough time in the Chicago of Fife. He'd sunk into a talisman-taboo figure connected with extremes – miracles and death – only natural among miners working deep underground, and women waiting for their return.

You wanted to be in with God but you didn't want His attention, until it was usually too late. He couldn't win. After a time, it seemed, He no longer tried. He became a secret, someone Cleggy supposed was still there but who remained disconnected from Beath in general, and from policemen in particular.

Yet today he felt – in general, secular, metaphysical terms – that the gods were smiling.

A T-Rex dumper swung out of the quarry entrance and suddenly blocked the road in front of him. He swerved into a passing place, brakes screeching and smoking, narrowly avoiding a collision. He sat there in the dumper's blizzard of dust, cursing, wondering if he should pursue the driver on a carelessness charge, but the inconvenience of turning and suffering miles of dusty turbulence decided him against it. He turned off his engine and waited for visibility to return. Heard rattling machinery, saw rock being crunched, graded and jirbled into baby mountains. Vibrations shook the ground. The air trembled. He noticed a figure like some dreadful holy vision, a cross encircled by a silver halo. He watched the figure revolve and a white dot rise and arc towards a stamper battery on stilts, hitting its sides and bouncing off, and realised it was the Mad Professor taking revenge. He suddenly understood how he felt, and Miss Oliphant's indignation. Yet he felt more than sympathy. Envy. He wished *he'd* thought of opening the quarry. Make a bloody fortune with the bridge contract on the doorstep.

He drove on, sneering at Lawrence Brodie who'd soon have motorbikes and caravans and artics and Wallace Arnold and rubbernecks, all conceivable traffic, passing his dome and gawping into his privacy … then he saw something that instantly expelled all thoughts of spite, hooligans and his current mission. He stamped on the brakes and sat staring at it.

Angela's bike, protruding from bushes.

Lawrence was angry. His view was ruined, his privacy destroyed, his peace drowned. Everything he lived on Mickle Flabbay for had suddenly gone. And it would get worse. He glanced through *North Beam*, the magazine of the Northern Lighthouse Board. With all the closures as a result of automation the *Situations Vacant* column had closed too – head office had more expended keepers clamouring for work than it had posts to fill. But there was an occasional *Exchange* column for those in work. Lawrence read the only entry.

> **Cape Wrath**. *Exchange offered in this building of outstanding beauty and antiquity. 187 steps, anti-clockwise. Would make an interesting change for anyone currently in clockwise …*

Lawrence wasn't interested in Cape Wrath. With a bombing range over the fence, unexploded missiles littering the bogs and a regular summer schedule of tourists, it was scarcely an improvement on Flabbay. No, he'd come out of the job. With the royalties from his book …

Now, in his striped knickerbockers, Paisley lace ruffles and ostrich-plumed bonnet, William Brodie found it hard to believe he hadn't always been dressed like this. But it had only been a week since he'd heard about the job. He'd been having his hair cut in an up-market salon on the Royal Mile. Instead of the customary dull magazines like Wench's Weekly, Proletariat's Friend, Hovel & Plot, *this salon had reading material he'd never seen before:* Palazzo & Villa, The Tittle Tattler *and* Ello! *The barber, Cuttabene, turned out to be Italian and a great friend of Riccio, secretary to none other than the queen herself. Through Riccio, Cuttabene had heard that the palace was looking for a young groom. William had applied without delay.*

'Well, wot ave we ere?' exclaimed Mary Queen of Scots on seeing him.

William bowed so low he buried his face between his knees.

'Wot an ear-ot-eek pair-form-ance, n'est-ce pas?' Mary Queen of Scots scratched her left boob and nodded thoughtfully. 'And you know ow to faire good service, oui?'

William had spent a day practising and had learned six French words. Faire was one of them. 'Bien sûr,' he replied, perfectly.

'Awh! Parfaitement! You ave a beeg wone?'

'I beg your pardon, Queen Mary, of the Scots. I do not understand.'

'I am ask-eeng eef you ave a beeg wone? A beeg vocabulaire of zee French?'

'Unfortunately not, ma'am. Just a little one.'

'Awh! But I am sure you are beeg in other ah-ree-ers, mais non?'

It was then that William took the biggest gamble of his life. To lose ... to the chopping block. Generations of unborn Brodies looked down nervously at this impetuous youth dangling the ancestral testicles on the line.

'You have beautiful melons, ma'am.'

Mary Queen of Scots rouged. Looked aghast. As if she might explode and cover the room in bits of damask and whalebone. She raised a hand.

Blown it, thought William. She's going to call the guard. William Brodie, beheaded 1651, without issue. A withering end to the family tree.

She giggled. Her face suddenly dimpled, like the first spots of rain after drought, then she smiled, and all doubt was banished, replaced by her promise of favour. The hand rose, bent, rummaged in her cleavage and pulled out a silk handkerchief, a taut flow of white. When it ended, with an elastic bounce, she drew it over her lips. Then she tossed it at him.

He smiled and collected it. As he was repeating the sequence in reverse, Darnley, the queen's husband, entered. The queen's eyes leap-frogged a chaise-longue and then all the life seemed to drain from them.

'Strange way of interviewing staff,' he observed. Cattily. 'I suppose that's how you do it in la belle France. And what a gormless-looking boy, you are ... '

'Ee as plenty of gorm, and you will not interrr-fear. Ees my new groom.'

And so, William Brodie, descendent of the Cave (3 [lfl]) of Arunk, entered the Royal House of Stuart, with a new uniform, board and keep, a salary of 10 pounds Scots per annum and a spanking opportunity to lay a sovereign.

And that was another root of his anger. He'd lost the plot. Couldn't concentrate. Even wax earplugs and industrial ear defenders were unable to block out the massacre at the quarry. Muffled and marooned in his tower he felt very cut off. Lonely. He longed for Angela to arrive. They were going all the way today.

'Hi Law!'

She'd taken to calling him Law. A perverse satisfaction because she was married to it.

'Hi Angel!'

'I've brought the ratatouille!'

'I've made a feta salad!'

They had lunch.

'Shall we get going then?'

'Ooo yes. I'm so excited.'

She began undressing.

He began undressing.

She glanced round. Giggled. Caught his eye. Knowing smile.

He raised a hand. Made a hole with thumb and forefinger. Pointed. *I'm all right! And you?*

Another hole, her thumb and forefinger. *I'm all right!*

Inverted thumb. *Going down?*

She nodded, laughed silently, in the language of looks, as if underwater.

No need for privacy, or words. Where they were going. Together.

On with the rubber.

'I think ten pounds should do you. We'll try it out. Can always add more.' He helped her into her weight belt. 'Easiest way to carry it is to wear it.'

The tank felt heavy as she walked to the water's edge. Her reflection looked like a mermaid. Or an Angel. With one wing, like Father Benedict's. He sat beside her. She felt the roughness of barnacles hold her. He rinsed his mask, left a dribble of water inside and spat, swirling froths of saliva round the glass.

'Stops it misting up,' he explained. Dappling of stubble on his chin. He looked safe, professional, manly. Angela dribbled saliva into her mask. It seemed such an intimate thing to do in his presence.

They purged their valves. Hisses of air, mists of ejected water. Inserted their mouthpieces. Angela heard her heart thumping. She was sure the beat had to be showing through her suit. Its pounding was deafening, and she realised how frightened she was.

Just breathe, Law signalled. *Slowly. Take your time. Rhythm. Remember, nice and even.*

She had no idea how much time she was taking, sitting there fighting off panic, convincing herself that she wasn't suffocating. It would be no different underwater, Law had assured her.

Relax. Concentrate on rhythm. In. Out. In. Out. Good … keep it steady.

She'd been fine during their practices but now she was about to slip below the surface, her confidence was faltering. She wanted to call it off.

I'm OK! You?

Her arms felt like lead. *I'm OK!*

He helped her slither down the rock. Held her as she felt the seeping infusion of cold creep up her skin. Felt him still holding as water rushed over her head, a darkening, a tinselled muffling of sounds. Her breaths shortened and sharpened. Urgent gasps for air. She felt she was drowning, spinning down, down, down. But then so must he be, for his arms were still there. Strong arms. She opened her eyes for the first time. Blinked uncertainly as she took in the unusual colour, the oily thickness, and found his reassuring eyes.

Just breathe. You're doing fine! Take your time.

And she vowed, if she ever got out of this, she'd love him forever for the tenderness in his eyes. There was so much of it. All for her.

She began to relax. Looked about. It was snowing! Snowing sand and particles of weed stirred up by their feet. She was underwater, but breathing! It was like conscious dreaming, a miracle of possibilities! She lowered her head, opened her arms, felt herself flying. She kicked, saw the particles surge towards her and part. Two more kicks and she'd broken through. Into a green-amber world. Shoals of minnows darting and hovering, minute fins fanning. Shafts of light slanted from the surface, bars so clear she could count them ... sixteen, seventeen ... in shades of grey like far-off mountains, and below, a moving garden of kelp. She cruised through fronds, felt them caressing her legs, watched their hypnotic sway, spotted a miniature lobster, almost transparent, squatting on a perch conducting a symphony with his feelers, then, too close, a blurred spasm and it was gone. All fear vanished. She was oblivious of everything except this unknown universe she'd suddenly slipped into. Where the only sound was a sussurance of moving air, bubbles struggling to break free and the echoes of her breathing. She'd never seen anything so full of beauty, or mystery, never felt her curiosity so deeply aroused. She wanted to know what lay beyond that rock, what strange creature might lurk in the next glade, what colours the sky could cast next ...

She felt a tug on one of her fins. For one terrible moment she thought it was a shark. It was only Law. And she laughed, inwardly, at how she could have forgotten him so quickly.

He drew alongside, tapped his depth meter. She read the figure. Thirty-eight feet. She'd gone too deep. He indicated another direction where the seabed rose and then levelled. They swam side by side. When he glanced at her and their eyes met, she could tell he was happy for her. They surprised a velvet crab which paddled rapidly under a rock, and a less-athletic but enormous brown crab which rose on its points, hoisted a couple of fearsome shears and reversed on tiptoes. Law spotted a flounder concealed in the sand and Angela got a fright when it suddenly burst cover and skimmed away. Blood red anemones adorned the reefs like exotic flowers. Best of all she liked the rays. They curled their wings and flew as gracefully as any bird, gliding in a mesmerising elegance of symmetry.

'Oh, Law, it was so wonderful,' she enthused when they were back on land. 'I never thought anything could be so beautiful. The whole experience, I mean. You don't get that from TV.'

He nodded. He knew, of course. 'It's never something you can explain to people who've never done it. They just think it's a murky, dangerous place. I'm glad you know now. That it's something we can share.'

He helped her off with her flippers. They walked back. Sat in towels by the stove, drinking tea. She felt slightly awkward now. The freedom of water had given way to the barriers of land. Of known boundaries. You had to watch your depth even more on land, she realised, than in water.

There was a knock at the door.

Lawrence looked at Angela. *Who could that be? Strange! Maybe you should go and get changed.*

She disappeared. He opened it.

Sergeant Cleghorn filled the doorway.

'Is my wife here?' His voice bristled with indignation.

'Yes. She's just changing. Just had her first dive. Did really well. Took to it like … '

'She won't be coming for any more *lessons*, Mr Brodie.' He ran his eyes distastefully down the hair on Lawrence's chest and thought of his own meagre endowment.

'I would have thought your wife might have some say in the matter.'

'And don't you think I, as her lawful husband, have any?'

'People are not objects, in my view. We do not own them. We have no right to control them.' Apart from resenting Cleghorn's intrusion, he resented him letting the heat out. 'Why don't you come in. The house is getting cold with the door open.'

'I wouldn't wish to defile myself by entering your house.'

He waited. Watched the keeper towel himself, keelhauling his back dry, and pull on a sweatshirt. Felt the outflow of warm air.

Angela appeared. He pretended not to notice her, leaned forwards and snarled a whisper. 'You filthy little pervert. I saw you with that *other* woman of yours.'

He caught sight of Angela's eyes widening and knew he'd scored a victory. 'Angela, we're leaving now. And I've told Mr Brodie you won't be coming back. The lessons are over. I have some disclosures about your *teacher* that will turn your stomach.'

Angela looked confused. Too confused to resist. Behind her husband's back she blew Law a secret kiss, and let herself be led out.

Sitting in his office later that afternoon, Sergeant Cleghorn regretted his actions at the lighthouse. It was the sight of the bicycle that had inflamed his worst fears and impelled him to make a stand. For his pride, promotion, marriage and, he assessed ruefully, his sex life. With a matter of minutes remaining before the results of the trace call were due, he ran over the two statistics he kept religiously.

Two thousand, three hundred and twenty-nine days remaining until his retirement.

Five hundred and forty-six days since he last had sex. One year, five months and thirty days ago. 23 August, 2002.

Once, he'd read an article on the Southern Right whale. *Eubalaena australis* gathered in pods off the coast of Argentina each summer, it said, and immediately after the cows had given birth to their young, they let the bulls mate and then they all swam off. Same time, same place, next year. Poor buggers, Cleghorn had thought at the time. Getting it off once and having to wait *a whole year* for the next time! Now he looked at their record with envy.

That afternoon had done nothing to advance his copular cycle. Angela had been furious in the car. Accused him of having a 'sickly suspicious' mind. And how dare he interfere in her private life? He told her about the sex doll but she'd have none of it.

'You'd stoop at nothing to blacken his character,' she ranted. 'I think you're despicable.'

And that was how it had ended. He'd parked the car, noticed how the Dundreary landrover hadn't moved and tried to think of more cheerful things – like trace calls – as Angela slammed the door and strode off in the opposite direction. How could he tell her it was for Love? But was it? Was it more about wedding vows and the myth of How It Should Be?

'Here's your post.'

'Thanks, Calum.'

The report from the lab on the Dundreary Castle sample. A single sentence. He'd expected at least a couple of sides of analysis. He skipped to the last words and felt his heart dive.

' … *Mentha arvensis,* more commonly known as Garden or Spear Mint.'

The telephone rang.

'Flabbay Police Station. Sergeant Cleghorn speaking.'

'You requested a trace on the call received at 1406 hours today?'

'Yes.' He grabbed a pencil.

'The number that called was Flabbay 828.'

He wrote 828, then paused. 'Did you say 8—2—8?'

'That's correct.'

'There must be some mistake.'

'I can assure you, Sergeant, there's no mistake. I have it on the screen here before me. Now the name listed against that number … '

'Thank you,' he interrupted. I know whose number it is. He took the longest time to replace the receiver. Lowering his eyes to the large graphite digits, he stared at them. 828.

No mistake, she had said. His own number. That could mean only one thing.

'Angela?' he breathed.

The Barmaid's Armpits did a blustering trade on Friday evenings. On alternate weeks The G-Strings crooned country western and RotyaSox hammered out rock. Tonight The G-Strings were on and unrequited love bounced about on lumpy banjo notes. The Armpits' new glitter ball had been installed that afternoon and the patrons were being relentlessly stabbed by a galaxy of lights.

'*Òbh! Òbh!* Th'nough to bring on epilepthy.'

'Right enough, Thkip. The younger generation seem to go for glittery things,' replied Calum. 'Like mackerel. And magpies, for that matter.'

'If there'th one thing worth than having to lithten to men in pain, it'th having to watch them.' He jerked his head towards The G-Strings. 'Acting like their willieth are thnagged on the back of their guitarth.'

'GEE-tars,' Calum corrected. 'Not guitars. They call them Gee-tars.'

Thkip found this remark petty and ignored it. 'Very bithy tonight. Lotth of thrangerth.'

'All these bridge workers. It's a disgrace. They said there'd be work for everyone when construction started. Then they said no one had the right certificates so they've brought people in for all the good jobs.'

'Thcoungrelth. Mairi wath quite right. Need a regular knee in the gooleyth, tho they do. *Hoigh*! Mairi,' he yelled. 'Another round here!'

Mairi appeared five minutes later. Looking shot. Skin hanging like scads of bats below her eyes. 'Holy Mary Mother of Jesus,' she said – watched Calum wince – 'it's buggered that I am. Worked off my legs with all these new lonely boys. Two Cuillin an a double Grouse, five ninety-six, that'll loosen your barnacles, ta Captain, *moran tang*.'

'Don't know how thee doeth it.'

'I'd prefer not to know.'

They drank. Were bathed in lyrical tears. And blitzed.

'Heard any word on MacLeod?' Thkip asked.

'Still in the loony bin. Nerves shredded like a flag in the wind, they say.'

'Thame.'

'Charlie the Brick says he should have stablised the walls by the end of next week. With scaffolding and a tarpaulin, we should be able to use the church again soon. I'm sick of flogging over to the hall.'

'I've thtill got the key. Funny having it, and no lock. No door. No gable, even!'

'*Slàinte mhath!* I was hearing from John Ruaraidh … '

'Who?'

'You know John Ruaraidh, Angus Mor's son, brother of Coinnich the Fank? Yes, you know him, married to Fiona MacCrimmon's grand-daughter who runs The Scissors … '

'Oh John *Ruaraidh*, yeth, yeth. Iain the Tractor'th nephew, liveth bethide Alathdair the Thparkie.'

'Well, I was speaking to John Ruaraidh and he said he's come out of retirement. Two weeks ago. The sheikh's asked him to be his stalker. For thirty thousand a year!'

'Thirty thouthand! Thtalker!'

'Quite. But that's the half of it. You know they've altered the stables and have all those thoroughbred horses? Millions of pounds worth, they say. Well, guess what else has arrived?'

'The harem?'

'A camel.'

'A camel?'

'A camel, no less. Huge creature. Got a hump on it like Stac Mor. Eats hay, just like a sheep. Spits when it's angry. Well, John Ruaraidh laughs when he sees it. Then the sheikh says he's to use it for stalking, for retrieving the kills. "An f-ing camel", he says, and the sheikh, whose English is pretty good, I believe, says "no, not when she's f-ing because there's no one for her to f with. Take her after she's eaten". This camel's a cow, you see, or a bitch or whatever they call them.'

Thkip was clutching his stomach and shaking.

'Now John Ruaraidh's signed the contract, you see, and he's not going to throw away thirty thousand like that and besides, he thinks, it's only a short stalking season so if he's going to be spat upon by this bolshie cow of a camel, he can put up with it. Then he thinks, well, what if this camel won't work? Then he can go to the sheikh and say she can't do it. Needs sand under her feet, she does. What she's used to. Not bog. Then he can ask for ponies like he's used to. So he thinks he'll give her a trial spin. So he gets

someone to show him how to rig her up with a halter – *o, mo chreach*! …
that's a bit I forgot, her name … ' he dug Thkip in the ribs, 'wait till you hear
this! … her name's Sultana Fatima!'

'Thultana.' Thkip wheezed and dissolved into a series of whoops.

' … so he leads Sultana up the hill and gets a few spits down the neck
and all the time he's thinking he'll get her stuck in the deepest bog and haul
her out with his uncle's tractor when suddenly he realises she's breathing
right down his neck and *he's* the one that's bogged down, right down to his
knees and he looks at her feet and there they are standing on top of the bog,
almost dry. So he frees himself and walks on watching these feet and he can't
believe his eyes. In mid-air, between strides, these feet shrink to this … '

Calum extended one hand with all digits held tightly together.

' … and just before they land they go like this … '

He placed both hands on the table six inches apart, thumbs and fingers
splayed.

'"*A thì*, Calum!", he said to me, "those camels. *They're unbelievable!
They're perfect bog-walkers*".'

Calum slapped a thigh and was speechless with mirth. Thkip felt it was
only his jacket that was holding him together. For five minutes they
laughed, oblivious to a particularly excruciating rendition of *You picked a
fine time to leave me, Lucille*. Though a slow process of giggles, sobs and
grin paralysis, they recovered.

' … *blay-anne-khet oun the gray-hound* … ' drawled The G-Strings and
finally killed the last remnants of pleasure.

'*Thlàinte mhath*!' Grouse chased Cuillin. 'The thargeant lookth
particularly morothe tonight.'

Sergeant Cleghorn sat at the edge of a table of strangers and stared into
a relief map of Scotland so coated in nicotine it looked more like a framed
kipper.

'Not surprised. What with his wife having it off with the lighthouse
keeper.'

'Really? Brodie? Bonking her?'

'Fornicating like rabbits, I hear. Up the light, under the table, on the
beach, in the water. Everywhere, they say.'

'Thee ith rather tathty.'

'Poor man been driven to order surveillance equipment. Should be
here in a month. I'm keeping an eye out for it.'

'Really? Thurveillanth equipment! I wouldn't half mind thurveying her.' Thkip thought of Angela at the party. Beautiful perky breasts outlined in rubber. 'How d'you know all thith, Calum.'

'Angus told me. The telescopic ear.' He nodded to the west bay window. 'Did I ever tell you about the hand, Thkip, the parcel with the lady's hand?'

In the west bay, Rastafarian dipped his tongue several times into Hamish's pint and the level dropped a thumb-breadth. Hamish, preoccupied with Angus's recital of the day's events, didn't notice.

'What sort of equipment has he ordered?'

'SOME SORT OF RADIO TAG … '

'SSSSHHHHH,' Hamish hissed. 'Keep your voice down. He's over there.'

'I *AM* KEEPING MY VOICE DOWN,' Angus brayed. 'SAYS HE DOESN'T KNOW WHAT THE LATEST THINGS ARE BUT HE WANTS A BLEEPER THING THAT LETS YOU FOLLOW SOMEONE PLANTED WITH SOMETHING. DIDN'T MAKE MUCH SENSE TO ME, SIR.'

'Who's he wanting to track?'

'DIDN'T SAY.'

'Did you get anything else?'

'NOT MUCH, SIR. ONLY GETS ONE SIDE OF THE CONVERSATION. AFTER A WHILE HE SAYS, "DELAY? A MONTH?" AND LOOKS DISAPPOINTED, BUT SAYS IT'LL HAVE TO DO.'

'A month … ' Hamish drummed his fingers on a beermat. 'Wonder if Calum the Post would help?'

'ALREADY ASKED HIM, SIR. ON MY WAY HOME. SAYS HE'LL LET US KNOW WHEN HE'S ANY PARCELS FOR THE STATION. CAN'T INTERFERE WITH THEM, OF COURSE, BUT SAYS HE'LL LET US KNOW.'

'Excellent. So we can relax for a while.'

'Ah wonder how the grass analysis is gaen?' Grout ventured.

'Probably sent it aff tae the FBI fer carbon datin an finger printin an aw,' replied Loon.

'Mebbe git lost in the post, eh?'

'Yea, that I'd be so lucky.' Hamish tossed back a dark tress. Wrapped in blue smoke, he looked more like a holy icon than ever, Grout reflected. 'I can't understand why he's taking so long to charge me.'

'HAD A ROW WITH HIS WIFE THIS AFTERNOON. RIGHT BELTER BY THE LOOK OF IT!' Angus suddenly proclaimed. Bored with a subject he didn't understand.

'Nae much news in that, eh pal?'

Angus conceded a grunt but was reluctant to lose the lead. 'YOU'VE HEARD ABOUT THE CAMEL, I SUPPOSE? CALUM WAS TELLING ME.'

They knew nothing about the camel.

'A fuckin camel! Here on Flabbay!' Grout hooted, after hearing the John Ruaraidh story.

'Nae a fuckin camel, pal. Yer nae listenin. There's naebody fer it tae fuck wi so cannae be a fuckin camel … ' And as Sultana Fatima was doubling her mileage with every telling, Rastafarian was finishing his second pint.

February passed, as February always does, quietly, quickly, but everyone felt the burden of winter shift. Especially Grinella Oliphant, still reeling from her first valentine for thirty-six years:

Boadicea

My desire

X

March brought crocuses and blazes of daffodils defying sporadic coverings of snow, and erratic bursts of sunshine lathered the land in colour and light. Tree buds swelled. Hares boxed and capered. Skeins of geese cut chevrons in the sky as they traversed Hebrides, Bailey, Fair Isle and headed for spring breeding in Iceland. Littering the air with metallic honks they caused people to look up suspiciously, doubting their ears. Miss Stewart was reported to have heard a cuckoo but as it was Miss Stewart, no one gave it credibility. Attention-seeking, the cynics decreed. It was well-known Miss Stewart always claimed the first cuckoo.

Plucktonites heard little of spring arriving. An invasion of earth-movers had trundled in and were shifting the landscape to the north of the village. By day the air was filled with straining engines, rumbling loads and yielding rock as a road was bludgeoned along the coast. Below Lawrence's light a flotilla of pontoons were moored in the channel and pile-drivers hammered sheets of steel into the seabed. New words muscled into the landscape. Caissons, tremmies, chamfered piers. No hole, it seemed, was too big to fill with concrete and 4,600 tons were poured into the feet alone. Legs appeared. The monster grew.

Lawrence watched the geese with envy. The saga stuttered on but he knew it was foundering, could never survive the growing swell of doubts. Unknown, unpublished, he could only think, 'who'll care?' Some days he gave up hope altogether, let coffee dregs in half-a-dozen unwashed mugs usurp his desk, sat there, eyes glazed as the *krunk-krunk-krunk* drove piles into his soul. Grammar, style, plot, pace, repetition, cliché … each a lethal self-criticism penetrating the heart of creation. Saga and author were slipping under. Cupped fingers tapping mouthpiece. *I have no more air. I have no more air.*

' ... and who cares?'

But he knew Angel cared. He no longer lived for himself but for her. For their 'water flights' as she called them. The purity of her pleasure, the flowering of her confidence brought him the greatest joy he could imagine. He craved nothing more. His novel, he realised, and five hundred millennia of Brodies, had completely missed the point.

She'd come back twice since her husband's intervention. Both visits brief, stolen in fear. She was afraid of Farquhar now, she admitted. She had to plan carefully. She suspected her line was bugged and had to use a call box. But twice, they'd flown together.

The sounds that were murdering Lawrence carried across the water and juggled echoes in the crevices of Dundreary. They needled Hamish until he felt as fragmented as the monopede.

'Loon an me'll pit the Roman back taegither, dinnae worry, pal. Hae im lookin good fer they tourists, eh?'

'Thanks Grout. I'd appreciate that.' He sighed. 'That noise is really getting to me. What the hell are we going to do about it?'

'Guerilla warfare.' Grout rubbed his hands. 'We'll hae tae form an army. Whit'll we call it? Need a good acronym.'

'How aboot FLAB?' Loon proposed. 'Flabbay Against the Bridge.'

'FLAB! Nae exactly yer Tamil Tigers, all claws an teeth, is it?'

In a lean week, Scoop MacKenzie reported the formation of FLAB.

It was in mid-April, the start of unusually balmy weather, when Calum the Post tipped them the wink.

Angus was back on watch that afternoon as Calum handed over the parcel, franked with the logo of 'Sensory Perceptions Ltd', and obtained a signature for it. He watched Cleghorn go back to his desk. Polystyrene shells spilled as he withdrew what appeared to be a small radio. He examined something too small for Angus to identify and began reading a booklet.

Angus watched the man's brow crease in concentration, then flatten over a grin. A further period of reflection followed and then the sergeant rose and looked through the window towards his house. A moment later he appeared outside and went to a bicycle propped against the fence. He took something from his pocket and fiddled with it under the bicycle's seat. He checked his watch and passed through the garden gate to his house.

Thursday morning. A blip in the weather chart and a real scorcher.

'My line dancing day today,' Angela remarked over breakfast.

Farquhar grunted behind his newspaper.

Angela thought of lowering her voice and saying through her sleeve: *There's a body on Grimport Pier, Sergeant ...* or of tossing the cannabis specimen at him, just for the sake of provoking some reaction. She tried to imagine where, behind the paper, the exact spot between his eyes would be at that very moment. Stared at his abandoned bowl of Bran Flakes with brown, crispy coracles floating round the whaleback of a prune. Thought of Moby Dick, discoloured, with Farquhar attached within a tangle of harpoon lines. At the empty shell of his boiled egg. Witch's boat. Smashed skull. She sighed. Looked at her yoghurt curdling on grapefruit and muesli.

Threw down her spoon. *klat-klat-inkle!* Scared Claws. Made the paper drop.

'Might as well be brick as paper.' She stuffed some Twixes and clothes in a day-pack. 'I'm going now.'

'I didn't think dancing started till two.'

'Two-thirty, actually, like it always has for the past two years. I'm going cycling. If you're remotely interested.'

Oh, yes, he thought, I'm interested. Make no mistake about that. I'm very interested. Cycling, my foot ...

He gave her an hour and a half's start while he caught up on paperwork. Then he packed map, binoculars and camera, and switched on the Sensory Perception Locator. An LED display lit up like a radar screen with ten concentric circles, each representing a mile. These were overlaid by a compass face. A flashing dot, accompanied by a weak *bleep*, indicated that the target was on the outer edge of contact. Range: nine point six miles. Bearing: 063° True.

That would be about right, he thought. Low tide. She must have cycled right up to the lighthouse. He took a fresh notebook. It even felt tacky. The Adultery Diary. He hated what lay ahead, but there were pride and honour to consider. He'd make sure there was no fuss, no contention. He'd have all the evidence to support his case. A silent settlement. He climbed into the Uno and turned the ignition. A silent Uno. Exhaust fixed. Ready for the hunt.

He pulled up after a hundred yards, opposite the landrover, and wound down his window. Daft Dalrymple. Eyes reduced to slits, pupils wrenched into the corners. Slithery reptilian eyes; hiding-watching.

'What on earth are you up to, sitting here day after day?'

Angus turned slowly, widening eyes, centring pupils, his face the supercilious expression of one whose space has been invaded by the tiresome. 'MARKET RESEARCH,' he boomed, wearily. 'CASTLE'S GOT A NEW TOURISM STRATEGY THIS YEAR, IF YOU HAVE TO KNOW.'

'Well you've an hour to wait for the next lot of visitors. Ferry's having its monthly safety drill.'

'FINE BY ME, SERGEANT. IT DOESN'T TAKE *ME* LONG TO WAIT AN HOUR.'

Cleghorn drove on, his ears still ringing. 'Market research!' he repeated and the absurdity of the old man even knowing the term kept him chuckling until he reached the track to Mickle Flabbay. He hid the car in a disused lay-by, and switched on the Locator. The bleep was considerably stronger now but to his surprise, the target was not even remotely where he expected it to be. He'd been certain it would lie due east, at the lighthouse, but it was showing at 340°, north-northwest. Range: three miles.

'Well, very interesting indeed. A lovers' tryst at Loch Papil, is it?' He was glad he'd thrown his wellies in the boot at the last moment, and put them on. A peat-cutters' track led off into the moorland and he took it, as a landrover streaked past and left a blue ribbon of smoke.

The market researcher. 'By Jove! It certainly didn't take him long to wait an hour!'

For two miles the track was studded with stones and yielded no telltale tyre marks or footprints. He still found it odd that there was no sign of recent disturbance. He began to sweat and loosened his tie. What a day! Peat hags stretched away on both sides, islands of mud waiting to be skinned and diced, their edges straight and scarred, low black-brown cliffs above a sunken sea of moss. One cut to a family. Each cut a hallowed acre of tradition, etiquette and right. Never a transgression. Never a theft. It was, Sergeant Cleghorn reflected, a model of self-administrating, unwritten law.

Here and there were piles of last year's harvest, stored in blue and white meal sacks discarded by fish farms. Golden plover piped and flitted through the tussock. Peewits sang their names as they flew crazy aerobatics, skimming so low over the ground Cleghorn feared they'd catch a wing and cartwheel into destruction. By contrast, meadow pipits appeared novices of the air, mimicking larks and falling with wings held out as parachutes until they ran out of space and had to give up the pretence and behave normally. Had he not been chasing his own mate, Cleghorn might have been happy. As it was, he'd run out of colour, posture and dance in the mating ritual. He wasn't out to impress. All he hoped for in future was a better record than the Southern Rights. In fact, now that he thought about it, all he wanted was his *conjugal* southern rights.

BLEEP! BLEEP! BLEEP!

The signal was strengthening. Range: one point six miles. Bearing: 300°.

He consulted his map, 300° would be smack on Loch Papil. It was a renowned and popular picnic spot among locals in summer, and he wasn't surprised Angela had chosen it. 'My line dancing day today,' he parodied, and realised that throwing her spoon down and walking out early hadn't been a spontaneous act at all, but part of a premeditated plan. And what a shock they were about to get when he burst in on their little secret!

At the end of the peat moss the vehicle track suddenly dwindled into a narrow path. Now any evidence of recent traffic would be obvious. There was none. This didn't unduly worry Cleghorn. Angela and Brodie might have used the alternative path to the east of Loch Papil. It took longer to reach it as you had to drive to the start of Claddach Beach, but the path itself was a mile shorter. One thing was certain. Angela was up ahead and he was closing in on her.

He reached the loch at eleven. To his chagrin, he still appeared to be half a mile behind Angela. The bleep lay off the far end of the loch, at 320°. They must have been on the far side and were now wandering into the heather. To make their little love nest. He increased his pace. He'd long since removed his tie and jacket, and now opened his shirt to the second lowest button. A dollop of flesh pushed through the gap. Sweat flooded the material, great welts of grey devouring the white, under the arms, across the chest, between the shoulder blades. The sun beat down relentlessly. It had to be 26°C. In April! He felt himself melting. Molten Farquhar flowed down his face, gathered in his eyes, made them sting.

The loch was surrounded by sand. It squeaked underfoot. His trousers stuck to his legs like hardening plaster casts. Waterboatmen dimpled the loch's surface; so calm, you could spot an insect's footprints! Further out it shimmered a painful blue, dazzled unprotected eyes. He suddenly felt dizzy. His heart was working like foundry bellows. His chest was tight, a shoal of needling pains trapped inside. He wasn't used to this level of exercise. His vision swayed and blurred. *Heart attack*! flashed through his mind. This is how they started, didn't they? Chest pains, dizziness, heavy legs. *He overdid it …* A rest. He had to rest. He was almost at the end of the loch, on a jut of land opposite islets. He had time. He turned the bleeper's volume low. Switched on. He was close now. Range: quarter of a mile. Close enough, if he needed help.

He lay down and counted to a hundred, felt the earth cradle him, his heart relinquish the race. Too hot. Had to cool down. He began undressing. Walked in naked. Felt the water's coldness burn his legs, his thighs, that gasp of shock as his genitals submerged, splashed his chest to prepare for the worst, sank suddenly to his knees uttering *ooh-who-aah-waa*, carefully, controlled, despite the glacial voltage to his nerves, so as not to disturb his wife's love-making. Slowly he felt relief, the water warming, its beautiful, tingling aliveness. He went under, to let the loch clean his eyes, charge his brain. He swam breaststroke round an eyot of rock and heather, lay on his back and fanned his arms, floating, suddenly laughing at the absurdity of it all, once again finding himself the poorer replica of whale.

Then the cold got to him. Wriggled into his bones. He swam ashore, and stood in the sun, his skin drying and thrilling.

He went for his clothes. They had gone.

At first he thought he'd mistaken the spot, must have swum round the eyot and lost his bearing. He went back and forth, quartered the ground, but always returned to the original place. He knew this was the spot. It felt right. And there was the flattened grass where he'd lain down. Then he found the Locator. Slipped into a recess among the heather. His wellies and socks had been discarded several yards away. The truth slammed home. *Someone had taken his clothes …*

Hastily he pulled on his boots, looked about and ran onto the nearest knoll, but there were knolls everywhere. Easy for someone to disappear. Yet he knew he had no option but to run, run for all he was worth to cover the ground and hope he'd chance on the culprit. And he ran. For twenty minutes until the chest pains returned. Then he stood there in his wellies in the middle of a moor, naked from the knees up, the sun already burning his flesh, his sole possessions a map in one hand, an electronic bleeper in the other. Crusoe Cleghorn, he thought, and wanted to cry.

cuckoo-cuckoo!

He searched for the sound, convinced it was human. A joke. His persecutor teasing him. Then he saw a blue-grey undulation, the graceful sickle wings, heard *cuckoo-cuckoo!* once more but found it no less hurtful for being real. For a while he was so confused he couldn't think what to do. His only hope was to catch up with Angela and Brodie. He checked on the Locator. Half a mile, north-west. Of course he'd have to change his tune a bit, now he had no camera. Adopt an air of leniency and conciliation, he figured, in exchange for the loan of some clothes.

He walked steadily. Danced through a patch of dwarf willow with a hand cupped under his scrotum to protect it from the higher sprigs. His boots chafed rings round his legs. Several times he stopped to drink, sinking his face into the coolness of a burn. Up and down hummocks, in and out of a labyrinth of bogs. Amazing, he observed, how much a willie flaps about on a simple task like walking!

Almost there. Range: tenth of a mile. On the other side of that hillock. Close to the crest he dropped to his knees and crawled, parting the heather to the left and right as if he were back swimming breaststroke. Slowly he raised his head and looked over.

At a goat.

A white goat. The white goat, he recalled, that had assaulted him at the louts' camp. He closed his eyes, despair draining his energy. He'd been duped. Well and truly duped. Set up for this mad ruse, and he'd fallen for it. It dawned on him just how naïve he'd been. Up until reaching Loch Papil, it had all been plausible. He should have realised that no one could be pushing a bicycle through this clutter of vegetation. He looked around to see if he was being watched but no one was visible. Just a naked land. Yet they had to be out there, somewhere. And he could *feel* eyes on him. Incapable of registering wit or irony, one word scrabbled in his mind.

scapegoat

He rose and walked towards her, a nanny trawling a bag of teats. She was chewing, jaws moving sideways in jerks. She spotted him. Stopped chewing, tilted her head and eyed him. He could see a loop of insulating tape round her horn, and once, it gave a metallic sparkle. He wanted his tag back.

'Good girl. There's a good goat … ' he crooned, slowly advancing.

She turned to face him, backed, began pawing the ground, lowered her head. He stopped, looked for safe ground, then heard her snort. The next moment she leapt into the air, kicked her back legs and cantered out of sight.

He sat down and spread out his map to try and work out which of the few alternatives would be the least unpleasant. Turning up naked in Flabbay was out of the question. Turning up naked at Dundreary would be playing into the hands of the louts who were undoubtedly at the bottom of this. His eyes scanned the contours and alighted on Flabbay Hall. The words brought a jolt of relief. Flabbay Hall! Of course! It was only about three miles away and was as close as anything. His spirits were rallied by the knowledge that at this time of year the hall served as Public Toilets for tourists and was left open, and not only that – he knew there was a cupboard at the back storing remnant costumes from Flabbay's now defunct Amateur Dramatic Society.

A mile later he was following the sinuous gabble of Allt an Doire-daraich, again musing on a willie's antics once freed from the constraints of underpants and wondering how the great apes coped, when he suddenly heard a snort. He froze, fearing the goat was stalking him. Ahead was a junction of gullies and approaching from the right, still out of sight, came curious sounds.

splick, splock, splick, splick.

He sank into the undergrowth.

splock, splock, splick, splock.

A camel walked by with a man sitting on its withers, leaning back against its hump. A saddle was visible, and the man's legs were supported by stirrups.

Cleghorn stared wide-eyed, thought he had to be hallucinating, heat stroke tricking his brain. The whole day felt like some terrible nightmare he couldn't escape from and which just got weirder and worse. Only he knew this was real. *splick, splick, splock, splock.* Was hearing it with his own tympanic membrane, was inhaling rancid mammal, was witnessing hard evidence of flying blots of Flabbay and cloven-hoofed scars in the peat.

He hurried down to the hall, afraid of what might bear down on him next. He'd lost all concept of time. Close to the hall he waited while two cars passed. Checked all was clear, and ran to the door. It opened. No one was there. Relief made him laugh. It was going to be all right! He went backstage, found the cupboard and wrenched it open.

Only one costume was hanging there. He'd been sure there would be several but now only a bonnet and a pleated frock, drab grey, with a cream-coloured pinafore attached at the waist hung from a peg. He recognised it. Flora MacDonald's, from the 1995 production of WB Pratchett's satire on cultural tourism, *Will Ye No Come Back (And Spend Some More) Again?* Dismally he held it up. There was no alternative. Moths had devoured a series of holes up each side and these sheared as Cleghorn slid the dress up his frame. A mouse had made a nest in a fold at the left breast and had munched away the walls. He looked at himself in the mirror. Sleeves too short, fabric stretched taut, left breast showing, side flab showing, flouncey bonnet and black wellies. He improved the image slightly by hiding his nipple behind toilet paper. At least the bonnet could be pulled to cover most of his face. Now to try and hitch a lift home. He'd make a joke of it. Say it was a prank for charity!

He stepped out into the hall but stopped dead at the sound of a car door slamming. He heard voices approaching and soon they filled the vestibule. He backed into the changing room, held the door shut and when hands tried to open it, he resisted, placing one boot on the wall and locking himself against their pull.

'That's very strange,' said a voice on the other side of the door, 'it's never been locked before. OK girls, we'll just have to change out here.'

Oh my God! he thought. The Line Dancers.

* * *

Once Angus had ascertained that the policeman's likely destination was Flabbay Hall, he compacted his telescope. The uniform and bits and pieces bundled under his arm, he headed back to his landrover, his lank wiry frame striding easily over the moor with the ease of a lifetime's practice. When he reached Dundreary he immediately got Effie to make a phone call.

'Scoop, please.' She waited until she recognised the voice. 'Hallo Scoop, Effie the Castle here. Think you should pack your camera fast and get to the hall. Our police sergeant's there and he's in the pink, so to speak. Having a spot of bother.'

Then Angus put the clothes in two disposable Emporium bags, drove to the police station and left them on the doorstep.

* * *

By the time Angela reached the hall it was already half full. She'd enjoyed the cycle run, peddling slowly to take in the view. There was always less traffic on the western side and she wasn't so familiar with the road. She stopped at the Old War Camp beach and on an impulse, stripped and walked naked on the sand. Her body felt younger afterwards, invigorated by the sense of daring. And yet, not for the first time, with it came the sad realisation of how she'd allowed that very sense of daring, so active in her youth, to be stifled by convention. Policemen's wives didn't walk naked on beaches. Angela Ramsbottom did. Angel Ewe would. Angela Cleghorn couldn't. How absurd it was; you put limits on yourself and they cut you off from the stimuli of youth – risk, fear, daring, thrill, wonder, happy-go-luckyness. We grew old, she decided, because we thought old. She vowed she'd walk naked on beaches more often. Dare more.

'Hi Angie!'

'Hi Doreen!'

Another chorus of *Hi Angie*s rippled out from others.

'Hi everyone!' She smiled.

The Flabbay El Alamo Line Dancers had been started by Doreen Williams two years earlier and regularly attracted a troupe of forty. Some went the whole hog and wore cowgirl hats, patch shirts, string ties, rawhide trousers with full-leg fringes and branded knee-boots with platform soles, while others came in skirts, jeans, and depending how cold they expected the hall to be, anoraks. Angela went half the hog and sported the boots and the shirt. She enjoyed the sessions and the company. It was a club. A home, even.

'You can't use the changing room, Angie,' someone called. 'Seems to be locked. Have to see the caretaker about it.'

Five minutes later Doreen pressed the button on her ghetto-blaster.

'OK ladies, we'll warm up real gentle and slow, now you just loosen up those limbs … ' a snare drum *zthittered*, two gee-tars struck an up-beat tempo, were joined by blue-grassish fiddle and a lonesome cowboy, ' … shake those bits you love shakin an don't forget those bits you just wish weren't there, yee-ah, give it some, swing those hips, feel the beat, ye-ye-ye-ye-yeah that's the way, don't be afraid to cover the ground, girls, move the arms, twist the back, bend, let it all flow, don't do no pushin, nice an easy that's the way … '

Behind the scenes, Flora MacDonald still had his welly against the wall in case a latecomer might take him by surprise. As the warm-up progressed cramp forced him to relax his defence. Each twang of music, each yelled instruction, jangled his nerves and added to his ordeal. He wasn't sure how much of this he could take and racked his brain to try and recall how long Angela said the classes lasted. He had a horrible feeling it was two hours. Two whole hours … and besides, now he was out of the sun he was rapidly chilling. But there was no way out. The only windows were in the hall and the only exit was through the hall.

'OK, OK ladies, I see some of you are just beginning to perspire so that's great. Don't want to run out of steam before the fun starts. So here we go. Elsie's favourite, *Waltz Across Texas*, wait for the music now,' the tape recording had faded into an indigestion of snuffles and hisses. Suddenly the band returned, 'one, two, three, grapevine to the right-AND-grapevine to the left-AND-grapevine to the right-AND-grapevine to the left, stepball change-FAN-stepball change-FAN-AND-turn-grapevine to the right-same as the start ladies-and again to the right, this time no fan but a chug, two, three-CHUG-swivel-hitch right, turn, hitch left-FAN-AND-FAN, stepball change, and back to the start, AND-grapevine to the left-AND … ' they continued grapevinin, hitchin an stepballin, ' … grapevines now and don't forget that final stomp, AND-grapevine-to-the-left, heel dig, heel dig – STOMP …

… Whee-ew! Well done ladies, you've come on real good on that one. You've got it fine, Linda. Catch your breath everyone, we'll have a wee pause before *Trashy Women*.'

They danced *Trashy Women*.

Followed by *The Dink*.

Followed by *Cowboy Shuffle*.

Then *Gallopin Alabama*.

By the time they reached *Cruisin Feet* Flora could take no more. He was shivering and almost driven insane by fans, swivels, chugs and stomps. He had to make a break for it. Gently he turned the handle and opened the door a few inches, enough to catch with his toe. He pulled the bonnet low over his face, reached each hand across his chest and gripped the ripped sides of the frock, thereby covering toilet paper and nipple with his arms, took a deep breath, jerked the door open and walked out into the hall.

Cruisin Feet happened to be the shortest dance and the music ended before he'd covered five yards. He heard someone scream. Then more screams. Was aware of everyone staring at him, some shying away. He walked as hurriedly as his limited vision allowed, squinting through a gap in the bonnet which was fixed on the distant door. Suddenly he felt a hand on his shoulder.

'One moment, please.'

Flora slowly turned, still hunched over and gripping his frock, panning the gap to see who had stopped him. The gap was filled by Scoop MacKenzie, camera to his eye. Flora should have abandoned all pretence and fled but in that critical split-second when a decision had to be made, he could think of nothing to do but curtsy. He curtsied. A blinding light erupted, and Flora rushed for the door, his only thought to steal a car and disappear.

'Thank you, ladies,' Scoop announced. 'And thank you, Sergeant Cleghorn.'

'D'ye think we should gie im the one leg or two?'

'One. Mind whit ah telt ye, Grout. Perfection's trade, flaws is class.'

They had the Roman monopede restored in time for the opening of the new season. Gave it a new head. A manly face. Maggie Thatcher's, with a Roman nose. But still no arms. Still crippled (in case she came back to life). The rhododendrons had been cut back to allow coaches access, an enlarged parking area had been created and the old Massey Fergusson had hauled trailer loads of gravel from Braithwaite's quarry to fill a quarter of a mile of potholes. Ill-advisedly, Eagle Star was offering one million pounds Public Liability cover against such mishaps as food poisoning, gargoyle fatigue or a visitor taking a flier on a wonky step, all of which were real possibilities with the castle filling up with the unwary, and stomachs ungalvanised against Dundreary bacteria.

The first coach rolled in at 10am. The new sign was out:

Welcome To Dundreary Castle
Home of Decadence & Perversion

Coaches Welcome! Open 10-6
Guided tours only, on the hour
Over 18s, Unsuitable for Puritans
No Cowdenbeath supporters (or refunds)
Sex Shop, Peep Shows, The Flabbay
Chippendales (Apr-Sep except during
sheep shearing), Lap Dancer Bar
& Effie's Kitchen

'KEEP MOVING FORWARDS, PLEASE, LADIES AND GENTLEMEN,' Angus called.

He was collecting admission money, dressed in the studded leathers which he'd taken a fancy to since the Burns Supper. The hall had been redecorated with a papier-mâché chastity belt, the Sebastopol bridal (labelled *Bondage item, 1854*), a Roman hot water bottle designed to fit a specific part of the male anatomy (*[replica] Excavated at Birrens Fort,*

courtesy of The National Museum of Antiquities) and an assortment of 'medieval' cod-pieces knitted by the local branch of the WRVS who were under the impression it was a contract for teddy bear stuffing.

'Ma name's Grout an ah'm yer guide fer this tour. Noo, this castle's perhaps nae sae auld as some ye've seen, an perhaps nae as authentically restored as ithers. But whit ye hae tae mind is the difference between a museum an a hame. Tween new and auld money. This is the real thing; aristocracy, class, a hame. It's nae vulgar, it's sick. Rest assured, ye kidnae find a mair genuine or sordid family seat oanywhere this side o the Marquis de Sade.'

'The furst MacFie mentioned in oany records is Alpin Bentknee MacFie wha we reckon hid the rickets or wis jist plain shagged oot. Here's ... '

He pulled a cord. Curtains opened and the crowd emitted a common gasp.

' ... a life-size statue of auld Alpin Bentknee exercisin his right tae deefloower a serf's bride oan her weddin nicht. Wis ca'ed *jus primae noctis* if oany ye's interested. This way, please.'

'Frae this early portrait ye kin see the effects o years o in-breedin an an English education. Aw the girls wearin frilly frocks in this picture are in fact boys. Recent research shaws that maist landlords the day are transvestites wha buy up tracts o Scotland where they kin indulge their fetish wi oot drawin tae much attention tae themselves, hence the popularity o the kilt.'

'Arranged around the room is the MacFie transvestite an langerie collection. Here we hiv nurses' ootfits, school girl uniforms, wigs, lace an latex wear.' A bewildering array of saucy underwear was pinned to the walls, whilst the most titillating items were modelled by shop dummies. 'The split-crotch rubber kilt is in the MacFie huntin tartan. The items wi red labels are modern replicas an kin be purchased in the shop eftir the tour. Now if ye'd like tae move along straight aheid tae the Drawin Room ... '

'The MacFies spent maist o their lives in the military. The particularly useless were made commanders an sent tae India, leadin frae the rear wi a buffer o men proportional tae their incompetence. This left their women at hame fer prolonged periods an in this room ye kin see the extraordinarly lengths they went tae, tae entertain themselves.' He swung an arm extravagantly around the laden shelves. 'The MacFie dildo, sadomasochism and sex toy collection.'

'This is disgusting,' shouted one man. He pulled his wife away and slammed the door behind them.

The others shuffled round *ooo*-ing and *aaa*-ing and nudging and sniggering and blushing. 'Course they didnae hiv batteries in they days but it's amazin whit ye kin dae wi clockwork.'

They moved into the Morning Room where a model Rapsy, naked except for a pair of crampons, was suspended by climbing ropes from the ceiling, buttocks-side down. Above him, also suspended by ropes – buttocks-side up – were two Alpine beauties in the flimsiest of dirndls.

'The main exhibit's the twenty-third Laird, the current laird's faither. Bit o a wanker, really, an a Gaullist tae boot. Born in India, he founded the Rajput Lower Caste Orphans Mission – or, tae phrase it mair correctly – *his* wis the foundin member. Aye, quite a lady's man. Dabbled a bit in hillwalkin up the Jungfrau in his youth. Goat a few intae trouble. Alpenstock Jock they ca'd him.'

He allowed them time to take in the details. The models had been very expensive but, Grout conceded, well worth it. Even he'd been shocked.

'Ye'll notice the pictures here are unner black drapes. That's because the content's o a particularly sensitive nature.'

'What do you mean *sensitive*?'

'Jist step this way.' Grout led the man to a picture and pulled back the awning sufficiently to let the man glimpse underneath.

'Well dang! I'll be … ' and blood flushed his face.

'Quite,' Grout added. 'Now fer those o ye wi a robust constitution, an that excludes oany wi pacemakers, at the end o this tour ye kin come back an look unner the covers fer a modest additional chairge o fifty pee. Weel worth it. Perk up yer sex life nae end.'

'This is the library. Maist o the world's obscenities are here. The virgin copies are classics, unread. Those wi cracked spines ye kin guarantee are works o outstandin randiness, the dirtiest passages easily traced by dugears and fingermarks. Oan the toap shelf oer there's a complete set of *Lovecare* mail order catalogues since the process of vulcanisin India-rubber wis invented in 1839. The fat volume oer there's a collector's piece, only iver issued the once, the *1929 Whore's Who*. Hiv a wee ogle here, nae extra charge.'

Next came the Red Room.

'This is ca'd the Red Room cos it's awwis been red. On display here is the MacFie's obscene photie collection. The large print oan the wa here shaws castle life in modern times,' he pointed to a photograph of the Burns Supper, 'one o the present laird's little swurrays. In the centre o the picture ye kin see oor local polisman, Sergeant Cleghorn. Lovely man. Very lonely. If oany o yers is iver passin the polis station be sure tae drop in fer a cup o tea and say hallo. Walkin encyclopaedia on botany, that man.'

'The picture tae ma left's a print o Turner's *The Frosty Evenin*, the original of which used tae hang oan this very spot but it hid tae be sold tae pay fer the bills o the current laird's stepmother's psychotherapist. The large canvas tae ma right's by Sir Peter Lily, the famous portrait pinter. It shaws Lady Caroline, mistress o Charles I – of whom it's famously said, "she gave im head an he lost it" – during his short peregrinations in Scotland. Nae gaein tae fast, am ah?'

Loon came in. 'How's it goin, pal?'

Grout lowered his voice to a whisper. 'Ah'm fuckin knackered. Ah cannae hack a hale season o this.'

'Jist think o the tips.'

'The rest o the pictures,' Grout resumed, 'are frae McGonagall MacFie's time. He wis the sixteenth Laird excommunicated fer dealin in hardcore goache an oil. As ye leave this room look oot fer two life-sized figures. Oan the left's a suit o armour, sixteenth-century Spanish, made in Hong Kong, an oan the right's Sharon Pairty Doll. Feel free tae wander aboot but dinnae fiddle wi oany the exhibits.'

The tour lasted an hour.

'Noo,' Grout rallied, 'if ye'd like tae proceed tae the cafeteria an gift shop, it's doon these stairs in the basement. We've peep shows, hardcore movies, the Flabbay Chippendales and the Dundreary Lap Dancin Bar. Ye kin visit the chapel oan yer right o the drive as ye leave, an say a wee prayer fer ma girlfriend who disnae fancy me cos she's lesbian. There's votive candles at twenny-five pee a piece, an ah'll need aboot half a dozen. That's awfie kind o ye. Thank ye fer yer attention an ah hope ye aw enjoyed yersels.'

He smiled and nodded as hands pressed coins and notes into his hand.

'Which way did you say the cafeteria is?'

'Doon they stairs, ma'am. Look oot fer the sign.'

Two flights down was the sign.

EFFIE'S KITCHEN

Teas, Coffee, Home Baking, Light Snacks

Today's Specials:

MacFie Aphrodisiac Soup w/ buttered roll
Sergeant Cleghorn's Celebrated Haggis
Effie's Nasi Goreng with Trasi and Coconut Rice

* * *

'Ah wis thinkin, Loon,' Grout blurted out, while counting money that evening, 'that if we hid tae extend th' exhibits tae include the twenty-fourth Laird, oor Hame, we'd be scunnered. How kin ye come frae a long line o sexual gorillas an be aboot as sexless as a fence post?'

'Aye, beats me. Mebbe he's jist a late developer, but ah think he's oan the camp side, masel.'

'Naw, ah bet he's screwin that chick wi the horses. Ridin lessons, eh? Ah widnae mind a ride wi her.' He heard footsteps in the corridor. 'That'll be him noo, Bentknee MacFie, Junior.'

'How did it go?'

'Crackin. Some geysir tried tae steal the Roman hot water bottle,' Loon griped, still thistley with indignation. Sucking a pipe, cocooned in Sweet Apricot. He paused from looping rubber bands over bundles of notes, his arm resembling that of a bangled Rajasthani. 'Kin ye credit it? Wis makin oot he wis jist tryin it oan. Ah sais he kid keep it if he kid prove it wis a perfect fit.'

'Rast did weel buskin an aw. Thirty quid. But that's fer his ane accoont.'

'How did Angus make out in the shop?'

'He wisnae that keen tae begin wi. Practically hid tae lash im tae the coonter. An at the end o the day ah couldnae get im oot. Hid tae drag im hame tae Effie. But he's nae worth a toss at pushin the sexy undies. Nae is fortay. We kid dae wi the polisman's wife. That randy Angie, ken. She'd shift it. Hae a word wi the sergeant next time, eh?'

'We've nae finished the tally yet,' Loon added. 'Eight coaches, aside frae aw the cars. Three grand in gate dosh, fifteen hunner in the cafe, an Grout's

jist tottin up the shop. Sold a hunner postcairds o Cleggy at the pairty. Yon book *The Nudists Guide tae Hebridean Beaches* sold weel.'

Hamish was sidetracked on mental arithmetic. 'You mean … you took around five and a half thousand? In one day?'

'Aye. We dinnae piss aboot whin it comes tae work, ken. Unlike some.' Grout cast a sideways look at Hamish.

He blushed. 'I was working too. I had some business to attend to at Fitful Lodge.'

'Telt ye, Loon,' said Grout triumphantly. 'Whit did ah say? Workin oan the son an heir bit wi that Omelette or Amulet, or whitever her name is.'

'Amulree,' corrected Hamish. 'I had my second riding lesson with her, actually, but I had business to attend to as well. I went to see the sheikh.'

Loon raised his eyebrows and shunted his jaws in opposite directions. 'Hampden?'

'Hamdan. We're going into partnership together. Doing a little bartering.'

'Tell us mair, eh?'

'No, not yet, it's too soon. We've both promised not to tell anyone.'

'Whit's he like, this sheikh?'

'What you'd expect. Rich. Suave. Shrewd.'

'Say nae mair. Ah weel, milk the bastard fer whit ye kin git.'

'In this case, it's not money I'm after.'

'Curiouser an curiouser,' quoted Loon.

'Ach, aw life's a riddle tae me at the moment. Ah'm worn oot bein nice tae folk. Nae used tae it. S'killin me.'

'Me tae,' agreed Loon. 'At least we hid a laugh. Mind that man wha went ballistic. Threatened tae ca the polis.'

Grout chuckled. 'Ah telt him tae gae right aheid. He'd find the polis in drag. Shawed him the *Free Press*. That shut im up.'

'I haven't seen a paper yet. Grimport had sold out. What's it like?'

Grout slid the newspaper across the table. 'Ah dinnae think Bonnie Prince Chairlie wid hae gien er a kiss. He'll nae talk is way oot o this in a hurry. Ah'd say Condition Two's stitched up nicely.'

Hamish looked at the picture. Front cover. Soaking the issue's entire colour budget. Under the title, ***Police Sergeant in Transvestite Furor***. The camera had caught the policeman in mid-curtsey but it looked more like he was trying to conceal a physical impediment by folding his stomach over his groin. Except for one eye, his features were clearly recognisable through the gap in his bonnet. The visible eye leered at the camera while his mouth, ravaged by conflicts of horror and politeness, was twisted into a lurid rictus. Quite clearly, it was the face of a maniac. Flesh showed through the sides of his dress and his bent posture caused a fold of material across his chest to fall into an impression of a voluptuous bosom.

Serious questions were being asked in Flabbay this week about the suitability of the island's only police officer, Sergeant Farquhar Cleghorn, to continue holding his post following the revelation of his fetish for dressing in women's clothes. The scandal broke last Thursday afternoon during the weekly practice of The Flabbay El Alamo Line Dancers at the community hall.

'We arrived at the usual time,' explained El Alamo organiser, Doreen Williams, 'and were surprised to find the door to the changing room locked. It's never normally locked so we had to change in the hall. We never suspected a man was in there spying on us.' The dancers had been going through their steps for about an hour before the mysterious voyeur emerged. Mrs Williams relates what happened next.

'We were just coming to the end of Cruisin Feet *which is a short dance when the changing room door flew open. Well, talk about shock! I happened to be looking in that direction at the time and you could have knocked me down with a pair of tights. Suddenly there it was swinging open and this ghostly woman emerges. You could tell it was a man at once, and then we all recognised him. We couldn't believe it. Our policeman! Sergeant Cleghorn. It's his wife I really feel sorry for. Angie's been one of our regulars since we began. And we'd always thought he was a quiet, nice man. But there he was in this frock which he'd ripped up the sides and stuffed with paper to make boobs. It was obscene. I felt sick.'*

Following a tip-off, Free Press reporter Sorley 'Scoop' MacKenzie went to the hall with his camera and caught Sergeant Cleghorn trying to sneak out. 'If Scoop hadn't been there,' dancer Jessie Troutbeck believes, 'no one would ever have believed us. Not in my wildest dreams could I have imagined Sergeant Cleghorn doing something so perverted. Our children won't be safe on the machair as long as he's on the loose.' Mrs Elsie Inglis, who was also present, agreed. 'What really upset me,' she added, 'was that he stole my car. He just ran out the hall and drove off in it. Of course he later denied it. Well, if you can't trust your policeman, who can you trust?'

A good question and one the Free Press *put to the Northern Constabulary. 'The matter is under investigation, that's all I can say,' responded a spokesman. 'Any comment at this stage would be speculation and prejudicial to the enquiry.' Sergeant Cleghorn refused to speak about the incident beyond saying there had been a 'gross misunderstanding' and that this was all part of a charity fundraising initiative in aid of the Police Dependants' Fund. He refused to reveal more details, adding that he'd revealed more than enough already. Mrs Cleghorn was not available for comment.*

Local councillor Ms Mairi MacLeod said she could well understand the sergeant's hobby but stressed it was paramount for people in positions of trust and responsibility to separate their public and private lives. 'If they're paid to do a job, they should be out there doing it,' she said. Local laird Hamish MacFie said this scandal didn't surprise him after recently seeing the sergeant wearing a lady's beret.

'Great,' said Hamish, reaching for a pair of scissors.

Tool in place of immoral practice (4)

'Ha! That's easy!'

Miss Oliphant was talking to herself.

VICE.

'What about three down now?'

Arab in icebound skating, caught out (7)

'Has to be an anagram. Whose one is this? Oh, Doollan. Might have guessed. Keen on his anagrams is Doollan. Now let me see … '

She shattered *icebound* into a random circle of its letters. The doorbell jangled, like little Hare Krishna cymbals. A troupe of tourists, followed by Dilly.

'Afternoon, Grinella.'

'Bedouin,' replied Grinella.

BEDOUIN.

'Afternoon, Dilly … '

The old soldiers with one Arab (6)

' … most peculiar! So many of today's clues seem relevant to Flabbay, Dilly, that I'm wondering if Doollan – he's the composer – isn't resident on the island. That's two mentions of Arabs in one crossword.'

'Anything I can help you with?' Dilly asked, leaning over, reading the clues upside-down.

Grinella blinked and delayed opening her eyes in the hope Dilly would read Intense Annoyance. Dilly didn't. 'I shouldn't think so and I'd prefer you not to even think of attempting it. If there's one thing worse than someone talking while you're doing a crossword, it's someone trying to imply intellectual superiority by beating you to an answer. Plagiarising the fruits of your earlier ingenuity in the process.'

And, triumphantly, she wrote *YEMENI*.

'Is that a new perfume you're wearing, Grinella?' Dilly made a show of sniffing. 'A bit *loud*, isn't it?'

'I happen to think it discrete but distinctive. You're probably just not used to *good* perfume. It's very expensive.'

'And since when have you taken to wearing expensive perfume?'

'Since my last expedition as Boadicea.' A Grinella grin. 'It was a present. I seem to have made a secret conquest.'

'Thkip,' pronounced Dilly. 'He could hardly keep his eyes off you at that party. That's who it'll be.'

'Don't be absurd, Dilly. I've known him for years and he's never shown any interest at all. Besides, I can't imagine Thkip would know *good* perfume from deodorant. I'm not that convinced he's acquainted with the latter.'

'You could do a lot worse than Thkip, Grinella. At your age.'

'I won't rise to such a rancorous remark except to say that jealousy ill becomes you, Dilly.' She raised a limp wrist and inhaled her perfume.

'I was talking purely from a pragmatic point of view and my seniority entitles me to. You will recall my saying at the party that I thought you were the hit of the evening. It seems I've been proved right. I just hope it doesn't turn out to be the Reverend Murdo MacLeod. Maybe he's turning his thoughts to matrimony. Doesn't have much else to look forward to at the moment, being a housewife!'

'Murdo MacLeod! Don't be ridiculous. He'd no sooner buy perfume than pray for the Pope! And what d'you mean, *housewife*?'

'Thought you'd have heard. The new policeman. Sergeant Fyffe. He's got lodgings at the manse. MacLeod's doing Bed and Breakfast.'

'Bed and Breakfast! My, my! Didn't know the new sergeant was staying there. I've only seen him the once. Funny looking creature. All neck and chin. Eyes look loose in their sockets. He has a hard edge.'

'I just can't understand what possessed Cleghorn to dress up like that and go spying on ladies dancing. And how did he get there? He didn't have a car. No one's answered that yet?'

'I suppose that's why they've let him stay. Nothing quite adds up. Mind you, never did with that man. So he's on probation. Madness if you ask me. Lucky not to be locked up.'

'I wonder how Sergeant Fyffe'll cope. I daresay this arrangement with MacLeod won't last long.'

'Oh MacLeod would drive anybody mad. We'll probably end up with two sergeants sitting there in dresses.'

Dilly changed tack. 'I see you've expanded your range quite considerably: couscous, basmati rice, ghee, tamarind, *trasi* – whatever that is!'

'Trasi happens to be dried shrimp paste. I'm doing quite a good trade in it with the castle, though naturally I don't condone those *disgraceful* tours. And as for the other exotica, well Dilly, one has to move with the times.'

'Excuse me,' interrupted one of the tourists. 'Do you have any newspapers?'

Another Prolonged Blink. 'I think you'll find about ten square yards of newspapers and magazines over there by the entrance.' She turned to Dilly. 'It doesn't matter what you put where, it's never good enough for some people.'

The tourist examined the papers. 'These papers … they're yesterday's!'

'That's perfectly correct. What papers were you wanting?'

'Today's.'

'In that case you'll have to come back tomorrow.'

Hebridean Holiday Off To Shaky Start, the tourist turned and walked out.

'I suppose it'll change with the bridge,' remarked Dilly. 'There won't be a last ferry for the papers to miss. Everything will seem more urgent, closer. I don't like *new* news. It doesn't seem so important when it's old news. More like history.'

'Quite.'

Aristocrat one's seen in pubs (8) - A - - N - - -

'And this anti-bridge demonstration young MacFie's planning, you know, FLAB's, I hope it won't turn violent. I daresay your father'll enlist in the front line. How is he, by the way?'

'Oh indefatigable. They're quite terrified of him at the quarry. He's threatening to contaminate the place with knotweed poison. Ruin the cement mix. He's convinced it's a fight to the end. The bridge or him. I'm afraid he's right.'

'Baroness,' said Dilly. 'Sixteen down. It's *BARONESS*.'

Cleghorn pulled at his pipe. Experimentally. A New Hobby. Felt smoke curl on the edge of his throat, exhaled, watched a dragon unfurl, stretch out feet and writhe in the air. Inhaled too soon, before the tail was fully out. It wriggled in his chest. A violent fit of coughing, pipe spat to the floor, dragon blasted into the stratosphere. He retrieved the pipe, tamped down the charge, wiped off fluff and dottle from the mouthpiece and tried again. Then he picked up the note and read it once more, even though he knew its contents by heart. As if the umpteenth rereading might throw up new meaning. Nothing could reverse the message, but some overlooked nuance of kindness might lessen the pain.

Farquhar,
I'm leaving. Don't try and find me. There's no point. We've never understood each other and it's too late to try now. This latest scandal is more than I can bear. Either I have to accept you are a transvestite or were the victim of a prank while spying *on me. Either way, my trust is shattered. I accept that I failed you as a wife and companion, and you failed me. What each of us wants, we can't bring out – or find – in the other. We are who we are. We made a mistake. People should grow in a marriage but in ours, we were shrinking. It's sad, but better to get out while there's still something left. I've taken Claws, and the picture of you on the beach. In the Force Six. It seems like it never died down.*
Don't try and find me. I'm gone. It's over.
I wish you well.
Angela

There it was:
I've taken … the picture of you …
Not much, but a nuance.
But then twice: *Don't try and find me.*
He went to the lighthouse first thing the next morning. Didn't tell Fyffe. Didn't care what he, or the Northern Constabulary, thought. Set as they

were against him, it would make no difference that this would be the first time in his entire career he'd be late for work. His cell was open. He had to go and find out.

But the lighthouse door was locked. No sign of life through the window. The glass was cold. *Mentha arvensis* waved in the breeze. Taunting. In the sky above him the last chamfered segment was being lowered into place. Flabbay's missing link. An island no more. Everywhere, ends and beginnings.

It was Lighthouse Inspector Hector Boyd who forced the door. Bursting in with Sergeant Fyffe on his heels, fearing the worst. But nothing. No note, no clue. Everything in its place. Jackets on pegs, clothes folded in drawers. As if the keeper had simply slipped out for a while. To check a mooring. Or something. The Coast Guard searched the waters, back and forth, back and forth, just in case. Inspector Boyd announced that the light had now become the Board's most urgent priority. Work on automation would begin at once. The Mickle Flabbay keeper would not be replaced.

It was Calum the Post who started it. Rumour or fact, no one could be sure. Two dead seals had been found on Mickle Flabbay. Skinless. Below the house, on the beach closest to the door. Nobody skinned seals, but plenty people still believed the selkie legend. That people came from the sea and returned there when they could reclaim a selkie's skin.

Sergeant Cleghorn didn't believe. Yet every night after work he walked high above Mickle Flabbay, looked down into the light, saw her face in a thousand reflections, then leant on a bar of scaffolding which served as a temporary railing, and trained his binoculars on the sea.

'Aye, *taigh na Galla*! It'th an ugly bugger, right enough. For all their cleverneth concrete thtill jutht lookth juht like concrete. Liquid thabbineth, I call it. And thabbietht the moment it thetth.'

All spring and summer Thkip had watched Hitler's Revenge take shape from the bridge of the *Flucker*. Now it slashed the panorama like a great pavement in the sky.

'It's got a right bend in it, so it has,' observed the mate. 'I'll be damned if it's not the humpiest bridge I've ever laid eyes on. Chust why, for heaven's sake, did they have to put such a hump on it?'

'The reathon ith thimple,' Thkip elucidated. 'It'th a thort thpan and it hath to be high enough for the talletht thip. And, I hear you athk, what thip would that be? Well, I'll be telling you. *Britannia*. The new Royal Yacht *Britannia* ith rethponthible for it being the humpietht bridge in the world. Thee may never go under it but that'th not the point. The point ith, it may one day pleathe her majethty to theek an amuthin diverthion to Balmoral tho that if thee chootheth to come under Flabbay Bridge, neither thee nor the corgith will be dithappointed.'

'You're surely joking, Thkip … '

'Abtholutely therious. The bridge wath raithed two meterth to allow *Britannia* thafe pathage underneath at Mean High Water Thpringth. Put an extra million on the cotht, but what prithe the royal view, eh?'

'So there's a million. And the government'll pay Calmac one and a half million each year in additional subsidies for the loss of the *Flucker*, the most profitable ferry in Scotland. And Bank of America wants fifty million back in tolls to pay back the loan. It chust doesn't make sense.' The mate considered the figures dismally. 'We'll be redundant in a month. Any idea what you're going to do?'

Thkip shook his head. The mate thought he caught a glint in the captain's eyes.

'Me neither. I reckon it's not going to work, you know. Highest tolls in Europe, they say. Five pounds twenty for a car. *Single*! And no reduction for residents. Seventy-five pounds for a coach! Tourists may pay that for a ferry, for a *voyage*, but not for a road. Makes Flabbay look like Berlin. Checkpoint Charlie, so it does. All those barriers. No, I don't think it'll work.'

'Criminal offenth if they don't pay. No alternative actheth. They wouldn't get away with it in London. Thtick a five-pound-twenty toll on Wethtminthter Bridge. *Pit!* There'd be a forth-ten revolution. But they don't give a thit about uth.'

'I'm joining that demo on Opening Day. Should be a right good shindig.'

'I hope it'th jutht a thindig, not a thivil war.'

They looked down to the deck where attendants sheathed in electric lime were beckoning, fingers fluttering as they coaxed cars and coaches to nestle within inches of each other. 'More trade for the Emporium and Dundreary.' Thkip spoke his thoughts out loud. 'It'th been a good theathon. The latht and betht.'

It had indeed been a rare summer. The best since '76, most considered, and in Flabbay if there were two things people remembered, genealogy was one, weather was the other. Aggie MacAskill, whom everyone knew better as Aggie 'Boer' on account of her grandfather, Captain Alasdair MacAskill, VC, a gallant scourge of Kronje's forces at Paardeberg, rated it even better than '45 but not quite as good as '36. And Aggie was held as *the* authority. Loch Papil dropped ten feet and was the constant destination of picnickers. Hose restrictions were imposed – and ignored – in Grimport. Private water supplies dried up and strange bugs, previously unknown over Flabbay except at Dundreary and the National Presbyterian manse, scuttled out of taps. Sea-front benches ('Presented in loving memory of Dr Archibald Dunn, RIP, *Don't rush though Life's enchanting isles – but stop, sit doon and rest your piles*', etc), normally little used, now became busy rest stations where travellers and shoppers mopped brows and shared communion as fellow sufferers. Radio Nevis broadcast sunstroke and ultraviolet warnings, the Emporium shifted unprecedented quantities of sunblock and calamine lotion, and memories of winter were redressed in nostalgia and fondness. People blamed all sorts of things: Pollution; Gulf Stream; God; Absence of God; Global Warming; *El Niño*; Saddam Hussein. But most put it down to one thing and one thing only; The Camel. In Sultana Fatima they invested the plague of desert.

Claddach Beach turned Bondi. Inspired by *The Nudists Guide To Hebridean Beaches* – so it was popularly held – a colony of naturists set up camp among the dunes, provoking widespread *tut-tutting* and rumours of some surprising converts among the island's more distinguished citizens. An alleged sighting of Grinella Oliphant was universally condemned as scurrilous but no one felt immediately inclined to dismiss an account of Miss Stewart's involvement. The corroborating evidence was convincing. A zimmer was seen, and zimmering nudists were unquestionably rare. That Thkip MacQuarrie had joined as a day visitor and regularly strutted his stuff on free afternoons could not be confirmed – for no 'witness' ever claimed first-hand knowledge of such sightings – but the possibility surprised no one. The captain certainly looked healthier. But so did everyone. The sun filled in the emptiness of that very northern, very Scottish, below-the-neck pallor. Turned flesh lusty.

And nowhere was flesh presented more lustily than at Dundreary. **The Decadence & Perversion Tour** was condemned as 'disgusting and offensive' by The Scottish Tourist Board who immediately ostracised the venture and banned promotional literature from its outlets. Yet tour operators seized on Dundreary as something novel among a numbing tedium of factory shops, heritage centres and 'cultural experiences'. Their clients loved the perversion tour. Bought sexy underwear. 'For a friend,' they usually said, and sniggered. 'Haven't had such a laugh for years,' they added, 'and that amazing dog should be on TV!' The word spread. Coaches poured in. A new parking area had to be created, new staff taken on. These and the core team, Angus, Effie, Grout and Loon, retained their northern, Scottish, below-the-neck pallors. But they were making money.

3 (*... to restore the estate finances to a viable concern*) was progressing a treat.

Culicoides impunctatus were the most prolific flaws in the summer. They didn't come down taps but came from everywhere else. Midges. The Highland piranhas. The hope that the prolonged drought would purge their numbers proved ill-founded and on still evenings the ferocious black clouds descended. Praised by sunlight, cursed by midge, Flabbay amply demonstrated the conundrum of Highland life: paradise in hell, hell in paradise. Despite the reassurance of concerned B&B proprietors – 'A wee bit troublesome, right enough, but I'm sure it'll be better this evening. More breeze. They don't like the breeze, you see. And it'd be a shame to miss the north end. "Jewel of the Minch", that's what they call us. And I see there's rain forecast for the east' – despite this concern, the piranhas bit and bit, drove hardened locals to dementia and drove softer targets to curtail their tour of the Jewel and take their chances in the east. How the nudist colony fared no one could imagine but assumed principles were waived and replaced by clothes.

Midges didn't trouble Amulree's protégé. First at a walk, then at a trot and finally at a canter (short bursts only), Hamish's riding lessons continued. He began to merge with the rhythm, blend into the gait. He learned about halters, bits, girths and martingales; how to control with the reins, when to press with the heels; how to distinguish laziness from fatigue, obstinacy from his own failings in communication or technique.

And he had other business to attend to ...

He had climbed the light, humiliated Cleghorn, restored the family's finances and opposed the bridge ... but it wasn't enough. The castle was slipping away. Of course, this was his father's plan. Lure Hamish into the fray and crush him one more time. Make him feel defeat the more keenly for having fought the harder to avoid it. There remained one slim hope and on this he staked everything. He arranged an appointment with the Vulture.

* * *

And one evening, in the uncertain time of that summer, from his vigil on the bridge, Sergeant Cleghorn sees her. He steadies his glasses. Push-pulls the focus to gain the slightest edge on sharpness and knows it's her. Far away and drifting further, *but it's her*. No mistake. He phones the Coast Guard, heart pounding like it did that day on the moor.

In Church Street the office staff appeared to have been freshly-starched – Mrs Sumo wearing her deadliest arsenal of skewers. Gerund greeted Hamish with barely camouflaged disdain. Read his T-shirt: *Comedy is simply a funny way of being serious. Peter Ustinov.* And when he'd passed, on the back:

> *Dundreary Castle*
> *Seriously Funny*

'You've come about the bridge, I suppose, try and convince us you've satisfied the term *to the bitter end.* The Board of Trustees has considered the matter at length. It could be argued that your actions so far have satisfied the terms of the requirement *literally*, but we feel they fall a long way short of the spirit of your late father's wishes. In this regard the Trust is not acting under *jus sibi dicere* or *jus respicit aequitatem* but its rights under *jus tertii.* Something a little more assertive … '

Hamish studied Gerund's nylon socks with their harlequin pattern – about as wild and as exciting as Gerund got, he imagined. Heard his words as babble and his voice a distant engine, like some weekender in a speed boat playing in his own wake. George Gerund playing with words, a fifty horsepower wank.

'I didn't come about the bridge.'

Gerund's lips pursed in impatience and he made no attempt to hide it. 'Then what did you come about?'

'To tell you that I'm gay.'

Gerund dropped his pen and stared at Hamish, eyes large behind his glasses, chair reversing on its wheels. 'Homosexual? You are stating clearly and unequivocally that you are homosexual?'

'I think you'll find that is, literally and spiritually, a correct interpretation.'

'I have to establish your precise meaning. If this is your idea of a prank, it's a very foolish one. You will recall that under the terms … '

'You have to sell Dundreary. Go right ahead.' Hamish rose. Leant over Gerund's desk and peeled a sheet of paper from a pad. 'Sell Dundreary,' he wrote with the solicitor's fountain pen. The nib caught and added its own embellishment of blotches.

To the bitter end …

'To the highest bidder,' he added, and signed his name.

Monday 16 October dawned sailor's-warning red.

Malin, Hebrides, Bailey: Southwest 5 veering westerly 6 to gale 8, rain then showers, moderate becoming good.

The Grimport fleet eyed the barometer and decided to stay at home. *992, falling more slowly.* Great Brillo pads of cumulus came scudding in on the back of the wind, drawing black smears of nimbostratus in their wake. Rain clouds. Leaking badly. Thkip, steering the *Flucker* into Pluckton for the last time, watched drops spattering on his window with spiteful satisfaction. If anyone was intending celebrating the end of his career, he was glad they'd get drenched in the process.

In Flabbay's Marine Hotel the Right Honourable Alista Darning, looking as if his breakfast sausage had lodged sideways in his mouth, grinned off the gloomy forebodings of his Scottish Parliamentary colleagues and made a joke as raindrops the size of Tuscan grapes exploded against the dining-room windows. 'A soft day in the west, I believe they call it'.

Inwardly, he blew raspberries, wishing he'd drawn Minister of Defence in the cabinet lottery. So much easier to shoot at things than compliment them. Then he thought of galoshes, his gabardine raincoat and an expense claim for an inside-out umbrella.

At 10am, an hour before the official opening, FLAB met round the back of the Armpits. A gaggle of oilskins and macintoshes bantering under umbrellas. Placards wrapped in plastic held up as roofs. John Ruaraidh, now with chapped thighs and a Butch Cassidy walk, cassidied up to an open window, and called through:

'Mairi, let's be seein you. What time you openin today?'

'Eleven.'

John Ruaraidh looked at his watch, saw there was an hour to go. '*Mo chreach!* In that case,' he said, 'we'd better have another while we're waiting. So that's one for Iain, Coinnich and Malky too.'

Mairi passed out four pints. 'I hope Sergeant Fyffe's not snooping around,' she whispered. 'Interfering busybody, he is.' She dealt with the money. 'I've been thinking, John. Maybe Sergeant Cleghorn was a blessing we failed to appreciate.'

John Ruaraidh gave the possibility consideration. 'No, not a blessing, Mairi. But I'm thinking maybe a very tolerable curse.'

'Well I sort of miss him,' Mairi confessed. 'In my professional capacity as a businesswoman I always felt liberated by the knowledge the law was in Cleghorn's hands. But this new man, Fyffe ... ' she spat an imaginary lump of phlegm past John Ruaraidh's right ear.

'Quite,' he said, suddenly concerned for the integrity of his drinks. 'Quite so. Better go and fortify ourselves for the march. *Slàinte.*'

At ten to eleven the rain eased to a drizzle. On a signal from Pipe Major Bill Braithwaite, Flabbay Pipe Band swelled their cheeks and thumped their bags. Drones groaned, warbled, squealed and settled into a concordant hum. Drumsticks clattered a beat and fourteen chanters skirled into a set of marches: *Daft Donald, The Crisis, Hot Punch* and *The Road to Sham-Shui-Po*. All eyes were on the Pipe Major's saucy swagger that turned his kilt into a breaking wave, waiting for his special trick. Many had considered it an embarrassment to have a Yorkshireman as Pipe Major, but he'd been the only applicant and over the years had developed considerable prowess with the mace. Six foot four, chest pouting like a hippopotamus's, he was resplendent in the rear-end remnants of the MacFies' safaris – bear skin (busby), leopard (tunic), beaver (sporran), gerfalcon (claw kiltpin) – and an Edinburgh Woollen Mill travelling rug pinned to his shoulder with a brooch.

As the band moved off, a ribbon-bedecked Daimler with a Union Jack chattering to itself on the roof pulled up behind the band and followed at a discrete distance. The band had moved on to a medley – *The Price of a Pig, The Hen's March to the Midden, Oh Hag You Have Killed Me* and *The Clumsy Lover*. They paused on the crest of the bridge and, as the heavens opened, they finished off with the funeral march *The Flowers of the Forest* as a mark of respect for the now defunct *Flucker* that was tied up at Pluckton pier and hooting like a dyspeptic owl. A final roll of drums was followed by a clean edge of silence. A small throng of bystanders clapped. Pipes collapsed into limp tartan octopi and were stuffed into black bin liners. Drums disappeared under elasticated covers.

Daimler doors opened and the official party climbed out. The Transport Minister struggled with an umbrella in New Labour red, jumping back when its canopy suddenly flared, turned inside-out and disappeared over the parapet. Reinstating his sausage grin he held up the spindly frame for the benefit of the TV camera and said into the bedraggled ball of fluff at the end of the soundman's boom, 'I believe this is called a soft day in the west.' His companions smiled generously.

Rain came hurtling down. The Minister felt it dragging his hair over his ears, fill his eyebrows, seep down the back of his neck, shrink trousers against shins, draw cold razors down his ankles. He walked up to a microphone weighed down by concrete blocks.

'Ladies and Gentlemen,' he began, 'unaccustomed as I am to drowning in public ... ' The microphone quonked, caused the speakers to emit an electronic belch which looped and reverberated for a full minute until water penetrated some vital circuit and induced a thrombosis. Then silence. There was a delay while a technician attempted WD40 resuscitation.

Sergeant Fyffe stood rigid as a stanchion as he presided over a troop of policemen – including Sergeant Cleghorn – guarding the symbolic ribbon spanning the width of the bridge. Nervously at first, then with growing alarm he watched the approach of an unscheduled vehicle. No other vehicle was permitted on the bridge during the opening ceremony. Yet one was approaching, a Ford Escort 1.6 whose repainted body failed to conceal facets of dents. Sergeant Fyffe broke rank and marched towards it. Realising it wasn't going to stop he threw himself out of the way at the last moment. The Escort stopped fifty yards later, between the Daimler and the closed ranks of the band, now looking like a colours wash awaiting spinning. The Reverend Murdo MacLeod got out as Fyffe bore down on him.

'Sorry, Sergeant, mercy mission,' he shouted, ignoring the official party gathered around the dead microphone. Before Sergeant Fyffe could speak, the minister had opened his boot and was handing out capes to the band.

'Gladys sent me over with these,' he explained.

Gladys Braithwaite was caretaker of the band's uniforms. Within this select corps of volunteers it was unanimously agreed that hanging, drawing and quartering was a preferable fate to facing Gladys with a tear or stain derived outwith the arena of performance.

'She also gave me these,' added the minister, passing round cups, thermoses of coffee and a tin of biscuits.

'Good old Gladys. Three cheers for Gladys. Hip Hip ... '

' ... HURRAH ... '

The dignitaries looked on enviously at the steaming cups as two more hip-hip-HURRAHs sounded.

'While I'm here,' the Reverend MacLeod suddenly announced, 'I'd like to offer a prayer and blessing on this auspicious occasion.' He turned to the official party. Steeped in misery and no longer caring that events were conspiring to hijack the occasion, the Transport Minister bowed and gestured approval with a revolving flourish of the hand.

'Let us pray,' decreed the Reverend MacLeod. 'Dear Lord God Almighty, we thank Thee for Thy bountiful provenance which has brought all this concrete into one place and we thank Thee that the place should be ours. We praise Thy mastery of design which holds it all together as a path over the waters just as once Thee provided a path for Thy chosen people through the Red Sea. I call on Thy great prophets Isaiah, Jeremiah, Obadiah, Zephaniah, Haggai and last but not least, Malachi, to bless this bridge. May it be a path of progress for the just and righteous, and a bitter testimonial to Thy wrath for transgressors, blasphemers, fornicators, transvestites and all others sinful in Thine eyes. Hurl them from its heights into our seas and eternal damnation as punishment for the iniquity of their ways. We further pray that the same spirit of speedy construction, as well as any superfluous materials, will attend and assist those currently labouring on the restoration of Thy house in Flabbay. We humble ourselves before Thee and ask this in the name of the one and only purified Faith, the True Fundamentalist Church. Amen.'

A murmur went through the crowd. A hard-boiled egg from someone's picnic narrowly missed the minister and smashed on his windscreen.

'Pharisee!'

'*Thalla is cac!*'

'Pillock!'

The crowd surged towards the ribbon but the police linked arms and held them back. They watched the Ford Escort reverse and disappear.

'Ladies and Gentlemen,' the Transport Minister began again, this time without amplification. He paused. Distant shouts were approaching from the Flabbay end of the bridge. 'Today is an historic occasion ... ' and he extolled PFIs, mentioned 'progress' six times, muddled his bridges twice and finally declared what an honour it was to be cutting the ribbon.

On that cue Mr Peter Chough stepped forward with a cushion brocaded in gold on which lay a pair of scissors. The Transport Minister took them and snipped the ribbon.

'I now declare this bridge open!'

Some people cheered. Most were more interested in the leeward ribbon which the wind had whipped round Sergeant Fyffe's neck.

The shouts were growing louder and were now unmistakable as chants.

Next to speak was Jack Milker, Chairman of Milkers Civil Engineering (Dormant) Ltd. He wittered on about obstacles and challenges, and risked a joke about thanking God for his help but his engineers had also put some thought into it. No one laughed, but there again, he consoled himself, no eggs were thrown. The final speaker was Sir Earn Nobble, a Pluckton landowner who was a vociferous opponent of the bridge until offered the nominal chairmanship of the toll-collectors. Mercifully he considered one minute of praise sufficient to justify his £40,000 salary.

'WHEN DO WE WANT IT?'

The chants were now close enough to hear, and the leading protesters close enough to recognise. The Transport Minister felt a bullet of panic and his thighs tighten. A splurge of day-glo hair was approaching.

'NOW!'

His eyes assessed the distance between them and scanned the sodden schedule in his hand.

11.10 Gaelic Airs, sung by children from Pluckton and Flabbay Primary Schools.

11.15 Pipe Band marches to Toll Plaza followed by officials in their car. Car passes under barrier. Proceed to Lochree Hotel for lunch.

Five minutes. It wouldn't be enough.

Resembling a stance of penguins, children in oilskins and Sou'westers sang their airs. Thin monotonous voices. Cold wee souls as yet oblivious of the *we-were-there* aspect of history and yet intuitively critical of the sense in singing lullabies to bridges. They opened with *Tiugainn gu Flabbaigh / Welcome to Flabbay* which Miss Lennox (Flabbay) chose, and concluded with Mrs Dragnet's (Pluckton) controversial choice but one that she had successfully argued for on the grounds of its pleasant melody and its link, albeit tenuous, to the bridge's builders: *Till an Crodh Faidh an Crodh / The Milking Song.*

'WHAT DO WE WANT?'

'NO TOLLS!'

'WHEN DO WE WANT IT?'

'NOW!'

'WHAT DO WE WANT?'

Sergeant Fyffe led his men round the group of officials and they linked arms against the advance of protesters.

The Transport Minister read the slogans waving in the air:

Free the Flabbay Bridge

Damned if we pay – Damned if we don't

We toil, the Bridge tolls

*Perfectly F****** Iniquitous*

Although the rain had eased, Pipe Major Braithwaite, mindful of his wife and the risk of damage, announced that the band would not play until they reached Toll Plaza. They set off at the double, relieved to get their circulations going again, and this greatly accelerated the proceedings. The ministerial car was able to depart just ahead of the protesters and the chain of policemen dissolved without the need for confrontation.

The band reached Toll Plaza just as a shaft of sunshine broke out and a rainbow parodied the bridge's hump. The barriers were down for the symbolic first crossing. A much larger crowd had gathered here, transferred from the jollification at the pier. Pipes were brought out and drums exposed. Bill Braithwaite stole a fly swig from a flask and raised his mace. A breathless hush fell. This ritual heralded the most daring act of his repertoire. The drums began beating. Bill sized the rhythm, heels stamping new asphalt, knees matching each other for height to within a gerfalcon's toenail. Pace and distance timed to fall precisely on the beat, he marched to the Daimler and back bouncing the mace, measuring its weight and integrating this new factor into his calculations. Suddenly he lowered his arms, simultaneously bent his knees and launched the mace into a blurred spin high above his head. A gasp ran though the crowd. Instead of being pitched forwards to land in front of him, the mace had gone straight up and Bill was now marching *away* from it. He couldn't see it! Hadn't any idea where it was! Higher and higher the mace rose, its head carving a silver O in the air. Bill marched on unperturbed ... left, right, stop, knees scuffing Daimler, smidgin of oil on kilt (OK by Gladys, part of performance), stamp, turn, left, right, left ... and there was the tail of the mace, swinging down to where his hand lay reversed on his chest. It smacked securely home. Shrieks, cheers, whistles, applause and then a surge of sound as the band launched into *The Mucking of Geordie's Byre, Sow's Lament for the Tatties, The Diel's Awa Wi the Exciseman* and a particularly moving rendition of *G Company's Welcome to Kuala Kuba Bahru*.

'That was some display with the mace, sir,' suggested Peter Chough.

'I wish they'd get a bloody move on,' the Transport Minister retorted, eyeing the advancing protesters.

'Soon be away, sir. That's them rounding it off now.'

'Good.'

The Daimler moved forwards towards the barrier. The Transport Minister wound down his window and waved at the crowd, then to the TV camera which he noticed beside the toll collector's window. The Daimler suddenly jolted to a stop. The Transport Minister's face crumpled against the chauffeur's headrest.

'What the devil's going on?'

'Barrier should have gone up, sir.'

'Five pounds twenty, please,' said the collector.

The Transport Minister, aware that the camera was back on him, laughed. 'Ah ha!-ha!-ha! ... '

'You can laugh if you like, sir, but that's the charge.'

'Open the barrier,' yelled Peter Chough.

'Certainly. Once you've paid. Five pounds twenty.'

'Look, you fool. We're the official opening party. This is the Secretary of State for Transport, the Right Honourable Alista Darning ... '

'Can be Bugs Bunny for all I care. If you don't have a disabled badge, you pay. That's the rules.'

'Good God,' groaned the Transport Minister. 'He's serious.'

'WHAT DO WE WANT?'

'NO TOLLS!'

'WHEN DO WE WANT IT?'

'For goodness sake, Peter, go and sort it out and be damn quick about it.'

Peter leapt out of the car. 'Raise this barrier at once, d'you hear?' he demanded. 'This car's on official business ... '

'Did you, or did you not, cross the bridge?' asked the collector.

'Of course we did. We've opened the bloody ... '

'Then you pay the toll. Regulations … '

'Don't you quote bloody regulations at me!'

'Don't you tell me how to do my bloody job.' He slammed his window down on Peter Chough's fingers, waited for them to withdraw, and snibbed it shut.

'WHAT DO WE WANT?'

'NO TOLLS!'

'WHEN DO WE WANT IT?'

'NOW!'

… and round and round the circle went, round and round, on and on … they advanced on the Daimler.

'Stop them, officer!' The Transport Minister yelled as he leapt from the car.

Sergeant Fyffe ran towards the phalanx of chanting crofters, housewives, children, grannies and grandpas. Cleghorn followed him but for a very different reason. He knew these people. Some of them well: Miss Oliphant, Miss MacDonald, Father Benedict, Marion Black, Iain the Tractor, Coinnich the Fank, Charlie the Brick, Malky the Fence … Others he knew by profession or reputation: teachers, a retired trade union leader, a computer genius, some nurses, a doctor, the school country dancing tutor, the VAT inspector, Gaels, non-Gaels, locals, incomers … he heard a high-pitched nasal echo … *WHAT DO WE WANT?* … oh, yes, sir, he knew them all – this had been his patch for so long – you didn't get to identify the myriad elements of a society overnight, oh no, sir – it took time to place them, rank them in order of trouble or danger, know when to rush in and when to hold back … *FUCK OFF!* … *BANG!* … oh yes, sir, anyone can *see* it's a parrot but the trick was learning *who comes with* a parrot, *who comes with* that cute looking goat, with day-glo hair – *it takes experience to read danger, sir …*

'WHAT DO WE WANT?'

Hamish and Mairi were in the lead. *JUSTICE*, read their banner.

Grout and Loon followed with Gertrude.

Sergeant Fyffe lead the opposition.

Sergeant Cleghorn followed, trying valiantly to save him.

Loon thought Fyffe carried The Charge of the Light Brigade in his features. Grout thought him stupid. Gertrude couldn't believe her luck.

'STOP WHERE YOU ARE,' Fyffe bellowed, baton raised, his face as threatening as a pug's. Fifteen yards behind, Cleghorn saw it was futile. Too late. 'AS AN OFFICER OF THE LAW' was as far as Fyffe got before he chanced upon Mairi's knee. By an uncanny quirk of fate he fell in the direct line of Gertrude's approach. Flexing her neck she drew her weight back and launched herself at him, timing her butt to combine with her momentum as she brought her skull down on his. Slightly disappointed that policemen didn't disintegrate as easily as dogs, Gertrude dipped down and gently carried off his cap, her teeth already sawing into the fabric. Fyffe lay on the ground, out cold. The doctor and nurses gathered round.

Cleghorn stepped aside and let the throng pass, and his fellow officers followed his example. He had tried, but in failing to save his superior he couldn't help smiling. He could already see the list:

One pair regulation issue trousers, torn & stained   30.00
One regulation issue jacket, – ditto –   58.00
One regulation issue cap, eaten   37.50

'NO TOLLS!'

'NO TOLLS!'

His desperation mounting, the Transport Minister withdrew a tenner and waved it at the collector. The window opened.

'Five pounds twenty, thank you.'

'Keep the change,' the Transport Minister yelled, already half into the car.

'Not allowed to do that, sir.' He glared at Chough. 'Against regulations.'

'Just open the bloody barrier,' the Transport Minister screamed.

'Four pounds eighty change, thank you. Have a nice day.'

Suddenly everything went dark in the car as bodies pressed against it.

'NO TOLLS!'

'NO TOLLS!'

People began peeling off oilskins, relieved to be out of them, and draped them over the car.

'My God!' exclaimed Jim Milker, 'what are they going to do to us?'

'Heaven knows,' replied the Transport Minister, 'but they seem to be in a pretty ugly mood. I know from personal experience how violent they can be.'

They felt the car tilting and shuddering. Bottles clattered in the fridge.

'Why don't the police do something for Christsake?' The Transport Minister found himself pitched into a sobbing Sir Earn Nobble.

'Into the thee with them,' they heard someone yell.

'Oh God! It's not that wretched minister again, is it?' Jim asked.

Then the car lurched the other way.

'Ransom them!'

'Let me bludy well through,' bellowed a Yorkshire voice. 'Sum folk's got work to do. Tryin to make honest livin's ard nuff wi'out yoos blockin bludy bridge. Clear off.'

They heard a scuffle, bodies knocking against the car, figures wrestling, placards descending on heads …

'ALL RIGHT, ALL RIGHT, BREAK IT UP.' A voice of authority. 'CALM DOWN EVERYONE. YOU'VE HAD YOUR FUN, NOW IT'S TIME TO GO HOME. JUST BE ON YOUR WAY AND SEE THERE'S NO MORE TROUBLE.'

The car stopped moving. Visibility returned as oilskins were removed.

'You OK in there?' Sergeant Cleghorn asked.

'Yes, thank you very much, officer. Things were looking very nasty for a moment.'

'Just a little bit boisterous, sir. I'm sure there was never any danger. They just have to be allowed to make their point and then they're happy.'

He noticed Bill Braithwaite's cement mixer, driven by the son, slopping concrete from its rear. 'Hey, you. Use the wide lane. Over there.'

'TWENTY-SEVEN NINETY,' yelled the toll collector. 'HGV'S TWENTY-SEVEN NINETY.'

'URD YE FIRST TIME,' Cyril Braithwaite yelled. 'NOT BLUDY DEAF.'

He handed the fare to Sergeant Cleghorn who acted as go-between and raised the barrier by hand. 'Hope you haven't spilled too much of that stuff.'

'Must ave spilt bludy half ton wi all that stop-start-stop-start nonsense. Bludy demonstrators. Commie bastards.' He roared off in a typhoon of fumes, depositing a huge cement pat at Cleghorn's feet.

The TV crew moved in on the Daimler. The Transport Minister tried to gather himself and salvage some self-esteem from the occasion.

'Minister,' the presenter said, holding the microphone to himself, 'people are saying this has been a bad deal for everyone except the banks, and if you'd delayed a few months European money could have funded a free bridge?'

The Transport Minister waited for the nod to speak. 'Absolute rubbish. They don't know the facts.'

'Having just experienced the full brunt of local anger against what people consider an exorbitant level of tolls, and projecting this into a broader context, are you not worried that PFIs might just break your government's back?'

'That's an absurd suggestion. Any dissatisfaction is minor, and misplaced.'

'Is it not, at the very least, an embarrassment ... ' the presenter persisted.

He paused while the cameraman reacted to a prearranged signal.

' ... being Secretary of State for Transport ... '

The angle of view widened to include the whole car sitting on the ground on its hubs.

' ... and to have lost your wheels?'

For Sale by public auction on 20 October 2004. Historic castle and outbuildings with approximately 42,000 hectare of sporting estate ... Would benefit from some upgrading ... Currently a popular visitor attraction and viable business (many extras included) ... a rare opportunity ... early viewing advised ... Bids opening at £700,000 ... contact selling agents Rut, Funk and Knightly ...

The advert had run on the web and in the national press for weeks. Such was the level of interest that Rut, Funk and Knightly had reprinted the brochure twice and Frank Rut had come out of partial retirement to conduct the proceedings himself. A small marquee had been erected on the castle lawn and seats had been laid out for an optimistic attendance of fifty. Elevated on a stage, Frank Rut stood on an inverted beer crate and still looked small behind a walnut lectern. He had bushy grey eyebrows which registered bids with grasshopperish spasms. He turned to make sure his staff – a recorder and two spotters – were ready, then gave a questioning nod to the front row.

George Gerund signalled the go-ahead and, smiling, inclined towards Quintin Filigree. 'Excellent turnout. Surpassed my best expectations.'

'First rate. Not even a seat for the owner!' He chuckled. 'The MacFie boy's having to stand at the back!'

'Should have spared himself the discomfort. Can't think why he turned up.'

After Rut's introductory preamble, the bidding got off to a brisk start. ' ... Eight hundred thousand? ... thank you ... eight hundred and fifty ... eight hundred and fifty ... yes we have eight hundred and fifty ... who'll give me nine hundred ... nine hundred ... '

Hamish had watched the tent fill with a mixture of despair and amusement. His hope that Dundreary's dilapidation would deter widespread interest had proved a fantasy. The aspiring Country Set had arrived – parodies of each other in immaculate tweeds, Barbours and *Gumboots de France* – stepping down from Range Rovers and Discoveries into pantomimes of courtesy and posture. Their faith in their 'country camouflage' and understated wealth made him laugh. He recognised the *nouveau riche* in them and despised their attempts at belonging. Then there were the others in uncompromising business attire; agents or property speculators, he guessed, and again his heart sank at the thought of what funds these people might have at their disposal.

Among those who were clearly out for an afternoon's entertainment Miss Stewart came as no surprise, but Father Benedict did.

'Hey Loon, djay think he's goat a bid frae the Vatican up his cassock?' Grout asked.

'Tae make a basilica oot o the chapel, mebbe?'

'Two million, three hundred, thank you on the left ... Three hundred and fifty ... thank you at the front ... four hundred ... Who'll give me four hundred ... do I hear four hundred ... it's too cheap ... am I bid four hundred ... '

'It's slowin doon noo,' Loon remarked.

' ... No? Then I'm asking three hundred and sixty, Ladies and Gentlemen, and you're getting a bargain at three hundred and sixty ... three hundred and sixty ... '

'Jist a jiggle short o twa and a half million. Fuckin insanity.' Grout turned to Hamish. Noted the rigid back, narrowed eyes, shallow breathing. Saw his fingers crushing Sweet Chestnut (*Extreme Mental Anguish When Everything Has Been Fried and There's No Light Left*). Read his T-shirt: *Too much of a good thing is wonderful. Mae West.* Knew it was all over. 'Weel, bin good knowin you, pal. Nice try and aw.'

Hamish made no response. Paralysed with Sweet Chestnut's foe, heard only the auctioneer's voice.

' ... three hundred and sixty ... yes we have it ... what about three hundred and seventy ... three hundred and seventy ... three hundred and seventy ... ' His words hung in the air. 'This magnificent castle and estate going for two million, three hundred and sixty thousand pounds ... going ... '

A profound hush fell. The spotters scanned the ranks, ' ... going ... '

'Five hundred.'

A gasp ran through the crowd. Everyone turned to identify the bidder. For the first time the auctioneer's demeanour betrayed uncertainty.

'I'm bid two million, five hundred thousand ... who'll offer me five hundred and ten ... five hundred and ten ... five hundred and ten this is your last chance, Ladies and Gentlemen, going ... going ... GONE,' and the gavel simultaneously struck wood. 'Sold ... ' his voice was thinner and higher-pitched now, ' ... to Mr MacFie.'

Dundreary's leaves wrinkled and shrivelled in flamboyant death throes. Sycamores dyed themselves a Fran-lipstick vermilion, horse chestnuts blushed maroons and pinks, the ginko went purple, oaks yellowed, beeches rusted and birches – resisting – lightened to caterpillar green. As colours faded and spiralled to the ground, and trees turned skeleton, roosting peacocks became easier to spot. They'd had a good season, three successfully-reared chicks. Despite the spectacle of their raised tails and the autumn festival, the castle appeared gloomier than ever. More wind-ravaged slates lay crooked on the roof, more gutters hung useless or were missing, more moss stained its walls, more wood showed through flaked paint. The rhododendron jungle was encroaching. Potholes had reappeared. The parking lot looked like the aftermath of a Bangladeshi monsoon. The Roman Monopede stood as a fitting figurehead for the estate: patched, repaired, balancing on his single leg where a gangrenous discolouration announced he had contracted water on the knee.

'Ya thinkin whit ah'm thinkin?' Grout asked.

'Yea.'

They made a sign and nailed it over:

> *NO CAMPING*
> *KAMPING VERBOTEN*
> *NON CAMPÉ*

> *Dundreary Castle*
> *Tours cancelled due*
> *to unexpected family*
> *bereavement and insurmountable debts.*
> *Don't even think of knocking.*

Then they joined Angus and Effie in the kitchen, ate as much goreng and haggis as they could and split six bottles of wine.

'Who's died?' Hamish asked on his return from Fitful Lodge. He started on seeing Effie lying below the table.

'PISSED,' explained Angus.

'Gertrude's missin,' said Loon.

'Reckon Cleghorn's nailed er. Spiteful bastard.'

'WE'RE HOLDING A WAKE FOR HER.' Angus raised his glass.
'HERE'S LOOKING AT YOU, GOATEE.' His fingers rippled over an
imaginary chanter as he hummed the slip jig *Kid On The Mountain*. Then
he fell to the ground.

'Maybe she's just wandered off?'

'Naw. Cleghorn's clocked er. Ah'm sure o it. He kid awwis find er wi that
gadget. Ah should hiv taken that tag aff.'

'So you reckon that's it for the season? I thought there were still a few
daily coaches?'

'Aye, but we're pissed aff wi it. If ah iver see anither tourist, ah'll murder
em.'

'Sides,' added Loon, 'whit's the fuckin point. Weze made more money
than Fort Knox. Seven hunner and fifty grand clear. Course oor salaries an
bonuses hiv yet tae be paid. Thirty grand fer each o us. Say, seven hunner
grand in the bank. So weze jist a smidgin short o the twa and a half million
Yer Knobship's goat tae fork oot next month. C'moan, man, pull yer heid
oot the sand. Yer bankrupt. This heap's gone.'

'Aye, an ken this, ye niver deserved it. Fuckin djaysus, while we've
shagged oor guts oot here tryin to save yer miserable castle, whit hiv you
been daen? Skivin aff oan riding lessons an dein fuck all tae earn a sou.'

Hamish swept a hand through his hair, scattering curls, and stared
Grout in the eyes. 'You're wrong and I'm just about to prove it. All I need is
three days, and ten thousand pounds.'

'Ah'm sick o yer secrets ... ' Grout cut himself short as a realisation
dawned. 'Ah get it. Horses.' He shook his head. 'Yer thinkin o layin ten
grand o oor money oan a fuckin horse?'

'Remember I said I was going into partnership with the sheikh? The
Forthlinks Grand National takes place on Saturday. I've entered it.'

Grout and Loon stared at him, disbelief lengthening their faces.

'Ye've entered it? Ye mean yer ridin?'

'Yes.'

'Ye've goat tae be jokin. Taks fuckin skill tae be a jockey.'

'He's lendin ye a horse?' Loon whistled. 'A fuckin thoroughbred! Frae
the maist expensive fuckin stud in the country? Ah dinnae believe it.'

'Me neither. Why wid he dae that? Gie a million quid horse tae a fuckin punter.'

'It's a loan.'

'Whit's he gettin oot the deal?'

'The one thing he hasn't got, which I have. A title. Twenty-Fourth Laird of Dundreary. He wants it.'

Grout shook his head. 'Ye'll brak yer neck at the first fence. No way am ah haen oanythin tae dae wi it. Fuckin madness. Money doon the drain.'

'Answer's no,' Loon added. 'N-fuckin-O.'

But later, after Hamish had gone, they found he'd stolen the previous week's takings. And left a note. *Gertrude sends her love. Back Sunday.*

* * *

Hamish revved the engine against the steepness of the bridge and noticed the HIGH WIND warning signs were activated even though there was no wind at all. The landrover juddered over frequent ruts, low sastrugi of concrete.

'Van and horsebox, twenty-seven ninety, please.'

'Your sign says HIGH WINDS,' Hamish pointed out, 'and there's no wind.'

'We're aware of that, thank you,' replied the collector, and for the forty-eighth time that hour he explained that they had no control over the warning signs. 'They're operated by a computer in Newcastle.'

'You're kidding!'

'Absolute truth. Must be windy down there. Twenty-seven ninety, please.'

'I'm afraid I'm not paying.'

'Fair enough. I'll have to call the police, though. Would you move your car to the side, please.'

'Certainly.' Hamish pressed the accelerator to the floor and surged forward. Bits of barrier erupted around him and, in his rearview mirror, he could see plastic fragments scuttling in his wake.

* * *

By 8pm that evening Sergeant Cleghorn should have been home, but, he reflected, what was there to go home for? Besides, he was enjoying having his office back to himself, and had more than enough work with these reports on the toll refusers. Refuseniks, he called them. Some had gone on and on about their 'reasonable excuse', and every word had to be recorded and typed out. If he were an Inspector, he thought even more wistfully, he'd be entitled to a secretary.

Inspector Farquhar Cleghorn's Secretary
INSPECTOR Farquhar Cleghorn's Secretary
INSPECTOR FARQUHAR CLEGHORN'S SECRETARY

Now it seemed unlikely he'd ever have to make the choice.

There was a knock at the door.

'Come in.'

Roddy Mayday entered, still in his Coast Guard's uniform.

'About that body you reported, Sergeant … '

Cleghorn leapt to his feet. 'Yes?'

'We found her.'

'Her?' His blackest fears rampaged through his mind.

Roddy Mayday nodded. 'That's correct. Took us two days. When I say "us" I mean a Nimrod, two Sea Kings, two lifeboats and our own launch. Quite an operation. Estimated cost, about a hundred and twenty thousand pounds. Of course we don't mind when a life's at stake. Pity about this one. I've left the body outside.'

'Dead …?'

'Dead.' He turned to go but paused in the doorway. 'If you spot any more of them at sea, Sergeant, next time don't call us. Try Highland Council. Protective Services as I believe they call it now.'

Cleghorn felt his body turn to lead. Like a heavy somnambulist he shuffled across the room. He heard Roddy Mayday drive off. Opened the door and let his gaze float down and across the grey sea of gravel.

She was lying by the side of the building, her arms out as if to welcome him. He knelt beside her. Felt her auburn hair and stroked it even though it was unfamiliar to his touch, too dry and lifeless and gritty. Ran his fingers over the contours of her wetsuit the way he'd seen her do so often.

'Angela … ' he whispered.

And he heard her answer.

I'm gone. It's over.

'No,' he sobbed. 'He's got her.'

Then he carried her home. She was all he had. It was all he could do. Made him feel better. To hold a hostage, half of a bargain. One day …

… one day …

… was that the cant of hope, or self-deception …?

… one day he might be an Inspector …

… one day there might be an exchange …

… one day she might be back …

On the morning of the race Hamish woke with butterflies blundering around his stomach. Frightened of sabotage as a result of the controversy his entry had provoked, he'd slept in the stable, and slept badly. Snorting, whinnying, the staccato clogging of nervous hooves and Gertrude's eructations had prevented any sleep at all. Rubbing membraneously opaque eyes, he looked through the half-door. The sky had turned turtle, drizzle peppered the ground, dented puddles with puddocks' peep-rings. That cheered Hamish. He turned to his mount.

'We'll do it, girl.' He stroked her muzzle, kissed her, silently suffered the sharpness of her bristles.

Five hours to go. He checked everything was in order. Amulree would be down later to relieve him. It had been a condition of the loan that she had to be here and he was immensely glad to have her. He'd undertaken this as a joke at first, without realising what he was getting into. He'd fancied it as a David and Goliath scenario, pictured himself the winning underdog. Hero! Wee Man from Flabbay Does It! Now the prospect terrified him. Win or lose, it now seemed, he could only lose. What was a laugh to him was a ruthless business to others. He was dabbling in a mafia of odds-rigging professionals who knew the game and controlled its rules. They gambled everything on being right, stakes of awesome magnitude in which fortunes, reputations, careers and even lives hung on the outcome of a single race. They didn't like outsiders trespassing on their patches. They hated surprises. They took defeat particularly badly.

Stable hands, other jockeys and badged officials began to mill around hoping to catch a glimpse of 'Sheikh Hamdan's Prodigy' as the papers were calling him, so he closed the door on them. Amulree arrived at ten. Hamish breathed in the relief her presence always induced, steadied himself on the predictability of her mood and appearance. Sixty inches of infectious confidence in a Scottish Hockey XI tracksuit. Short, black, bobbed hair and equine eyelashes and a face that could swivel from elfin delight to Kublai Khan threat as rapidly as any situation required. Not that it was required often. She was all grace and dignity, as if contained within was an amphora of life with more than enough to pass around.

'Hi, Hame. You're causing quite a stir. How d'you sleep?'

'I didn't. I feel like the cavalry ran over me.'

'Ah you'll be fine. The adrenaline'll pick you up. How're the gals?'

'OK. They don't seem to need sleep. Think beds are for eating.'

'There was talk of cancelling. Waterlogged course. But they've just had an inspection and decided it's good enough. Soft going, that'll suit us. What we're used to.'

'Think I'll walk the course. Check the height of the jumps.'

The squishiness underfoot surprised him as he crossed the spectating circle, but once on the track itself he could feel the difference. A base of sand combined with an intricate drainage system produced a much firmer surface. The going might be soft for his rivals but by Flabbay's standards it was a desert. He felt the first twinges of excitement as he was now on the hallowed ground he'd been dreaming of for so long. Scotland's Aintree! Taking part in the premier steeplechase of the calendar – The Forthlinks Grand National. Three laps, each ten furlongs. Just under four miles. Months of training for four miles! He'd studied the course on maps and videos. Knew how the gates worked, the curvature of the bends. They'd marked out a replica on Fitful's fields and rehearsed their strategy. He knew every detail of the regulations, what was permissible, what would result in automatic disqualification. Like missing a jump, for example. There were four each lap. He came to the first. A box hedge erected for the day. Four feet six inches high.

'Good,' he murmured. His information had been correct. The success of the plan depended on it. He measured the remaining three and found they were identical.

'Place yer bets, place yer bets.'

The bookies had already set up their blackboards, chalked up the fields and were touting for custom. Money bags bulged at their groins. Raptor's eyes darted everywhere as they tracked business and scouted for semaphored warnings.

'Place yer bets, place yer bets.'

Hamish had already placed his the previous day. Ten grand on himself, to win. At 300:1. The longest odds ever placed on a Grand National runner. Now he noticed they'd shortened.

Mr Golightly	2:9	Unfortunate	8:1
Chasing the Bride	2:5	Pridewood Fuggie	19:1
Buggerme	6:1	Your Agoodun	12:1
Light The Fuse	2:7	So Willing	2:1
Inthemeantime	11:1	Done and Dusted	18:1
We're Not Stoppin	18:1	Timeforadream	16:1
Never Can Tell	12:1	Colossal Dick	16:1
Rushin Romeo	3:1	Sultana Fatima	250:1
Nowt Flash	8:1		

Never in the course's two-hundred-year history had a camel entered a race. Sultana Fatima of Wadi Hari IV's true identity had only come to light three days earlier and had precipitated an emergency meeting of the Forthlinks Race Club committee. The Club presented an imposing Edwardian façade to the external world, and the immutable face of fogyism to its internal one. Sheathed in the bounty of Empire, teak from Burma and mahogany from Siam, it was the glory of bargain opulence in the dying days of craftsmanship. Time lay pickled under crystal chandeliers, Bihar carpets and acres of plush. Brass signs identified every door. They used the definite article pointedly, for the one permitted species. *The Gentlemen's Bar. The Gentlemen's Cloakroom. The Gentlemen's Dining-Room*. Not until 1978 were women permitted inside. New, longer signs appeared. *The Gentlemen's Guests' Cloakroom. Bar for The Gentlemen and Guests*. The possibility of Guests becoming Members was never discussed. In The Club, two concessions in one century would be unthinkable.

'It's outrageous even to consider this application,' expostulated The Gentleman Chair. 'Everyone knows only horses are eligible.'

'Quite,' agreed A Gentleman Board. 'I contacted The National Hunt Committee and they said they'd never heard of anything so ridiculous. The regulations expressly prohibit it.'

'Alas,' The Gentleman Clerk replied gloomily, 'I've checked everything. Constitution, Charter and *our* Regulations. Apparently they're quite unique. They used to explicitly state "horse", but it was amended. Some pranksters dressed up as one for a wager and had to be allowed to run. In 1888. So they changed the wording from "horse" to "integral quadruped, minimum fourteen hands". I'm afraid that unquestionably includes camels.'

'Can't we change them? "*Bona fide* horse." Something like that?'

'Only at an AGM. Impossible at short notice.'

The Gentleman Chair suddenly raised a finger and smiled. 'Surely we can have it banned on health grounds?'

'Nothing to help there. All its papers are in order.'

'You mean … we're going to have to let a *camel* run the Grand National?'

'I'm afraid so, sir.'

'Good God. We'll be a laughing stock.'

The newspapers were of the same opinion.

Red Faces Over Camel Ruse, said *The Scotsman.*

Camelong for the Circus! said *The Evening News.*

Hump to Jump Grand National, said *The Daily Record.*

'Hey you,' someone shouted, 'you're wi that fuckin camel, incha? Fuckin heidbanga!' Then laughter. Hamish quickly slunk away and disappeared into the crowd which had been steadily building.

'There seem to be a lot of hostile punters out there.'

'They'll soon fall for our baby. Everyone loves her.'

Sultana Fatima looked down from the stable rafters and continued chewing. Seven feet lower, Gertrude interrupted her own industry and basked in reflected glory.

'She's certainly not pining for home. Looks like there's a serious friendship going on here.'

This had been another condition of the loan. Camels removed from familiar surroundings must have company or they pine. Hamish had suggested Gertrude, and it had worked.

They decided to forego the jockey's parade, and a warm-up. Sultana Fatima didn't need one and Hamish wanted to spend the least possible time airborne. They checked her girth for tension, secured all the race accessories to the hump, Hamish climbed up a step ladder and settled into the saddle. For a long sickening spell he felt his head go dizzy and watched Forthlinks tilt to one side. He concentrated hard, fixing his eyes on the distance and fought to overcome a flash recurrence of vertigo. The greater part of his training programme had focused on suppressing this phobia and he believed he'd conquered it. The thought of losing to it now was more than he could bear.

They walked to the start. Suddenly they were surrounded by a mob of journalists and photographers.

'Why are you running?' asked one.

Amulree fielded the questions. 'Camels don't run. They pace. Different gait. The legs on each side move forwards and backwards in unison.' She smiled.

'Ya? I'll rephrase that,' a tired journalist's voice. 'Why are you taking part *on a camel*?'

'To win.'

'What speed can a camel do?'

'Seven miles an hour, at a push. They prefer five.'

A gale of laughter. Scribbling hands.

'How long will the course take you?'

'About an hour and a half.'

Another wave of guffaws. A woman from *The Daily Express* whooped hysterically until she felt hot breath on her neck and her collar was ripped off.

As planned, they were the last to enter the field. The remaining jockeys were already in the starting boxes. The first problem to manifest itself was the discovery that Sultana Fatima was too wide to fit into a box. This caused some consternation until it was decided she would have to stand behind the line of tails to reduce the chance of a false start. Horses stamped, kicked and tossed their heads. Nostrils flared and snorted. Mr Golightly, a previous winner, vibrated his lips and white strings of slaver plastered his snout. Sultana Fatima gazed at the crowd with interest and chewed contentedly.

Bang!

The gates flew open and out charged the sixteen thoroughbreds, their jester-coloured jockeys bent double, wobbling, arms flailing as they thrashed stocks through the air. Hamish, in a blue boilersuit, tapped his heels. Sultana moved off with a fringe of grass hanging from her mouth. All along the barriers he could see figures helpless with mirth. He tapped again and Sultana accelerated.

Left, left. Right, right. *splick, splick.*

Pacing.

5mph.

Hamish adapted to the swaying rhythm and tried to forget how high off the ground he was. He began concentrating on the first jump. The rest of the field were almost on it, already two furlongs ahead. They jolted into the air as if a great carpet beater had smacked the turf beneath them, and were gone. Hamish and Sultana were on their own. Left, left. Right, right. Slowly but steadily they approached the jump.

'Jumping's the problem,' Amulree had warned when he first broached the subject. 'Unfortunately camels aren't inclined to jump outwith the *musth,* or mating season. And they need someone sexy to jump on. No, we'll have to find another solution.'

It was Charlie the Brick who hit on the idea. 'And why don't you use a stile? A portable stile's surely the answer?'

They'd checked the regulations and there was nothing to say a stile couldn't be carried. The rules only stipulated that a jockey could not receive outside assistance during the race. They'd experimented with designs and materials and found a welder in Inverness who had knocked up a prototype in an aluminium alloy. It was light, strong, quick to set up and dismantle and came in two folding sections. After her initial distrust had been overcome, Sultana had quickly mastered it. Hamish was nervous she might suffer a change of heart in front of a crowd.

From the siderail Amulree watched anxiously. She knew this first fence would be crucial. She nodded as Hamish began the agreed routine. He steered the camel to the far side of the hedge then turned her, and forced her to walk along its length so that the foliage brushed her flank. He then worked her back to the centre, where she toppled forwards onto her knees and rocked back into a lying position. Hamish dismounted, unclipped the stile and soon had it in place.

'Go for it, girl, go for it,' Amulree urged.

With bated breath she watched Sultana heave herself up. They approached the steps. Just short, Sultana stopped. She leant over, swiped a mouthful of leaves and then, despite having lost all momentum, turned to the crowd, and clambered over.

By this time the leaders had completed the first lap. Approaching at 35mph were the favourites, Mr Golightly and Chasing the Bride, slightly ahead of So Willing, Nowt Flash and, rank outsiders, Pridewood Fuggie and We're Not Stoppin. As they bore down on the fence which Hamish was just leaving – the stile having been safely stowed against the hump once more – spectators began to sense that something was wrong. The pattern of the race was changing. Those accepted hallmarks of discipline and dedication that drove the pack and thrilled the crowds could be seen to disintegrate.

The horses closest to the centre of the track began shaking their heads and slowing. So Willing appeared to suffer a coughing fit and began weaving erratically, veered into Nowt Flash, and they both stumbled to the ground. Unable to avoid them Unfortunate lived up to her name and landed a cropper on top. Mr Golightly misjudged the angle of the jump and sheered over the siderail into instantaneous disqualification, while Pridewood Fuggie and We're Not Stoppin seemed oblivious to any fence. Fragments of hedge exploded around them and they left two large holes partially filled with their jockeys. Chasing the Bride scraped over on the outside edge, and was followed by Rushin Romeo, Light the Fuse and Done and Dusted. Buggerme swerved to adopt their line but suddenly lost nerve, stopped dead and pitched his jockey into the wake of the camel. Spooked by the *mêlée* of writhing horses, latecomers Colossal Dick and Inthemeantime spun round and cantered back to the start. Timeforadream, Your Agoodun and Never Can Tell trailed long after the others and wisely picked the now vacated holes in the fence.

Amulree rubbed her hands in glee. One lap down and half the field scratched.

Her digestion loosened by this unexpected burst of activity, Sultana was emptying her bowels of that morning's intake. As he approached the second fence Hamish now adopted a new course, zigzagging from side to side to lay a trail of steaming pats across the full width of the track. He was particularly keen to clear the second fence before the remaining runners overtook him on their final lap. Once again he got Sultana to smear her scent along its length.

It was his grandfather's diaries that had inspired this strategy. In 1938 Sir Hector had been sent to Bikanir in Rajasthan to form the Camel Corps.

While the efficacy of camels as beasts of burden in the desert has long been known, today I was most fortunate in witnessing their effectiveness on a battle front. The results astonished me! My host, the Maharajah of Bikanir, has for some time been plagued by a band of dacoits raiding his supply routes. Disguising his Corps as a trade caravan he lured them into an ambush. The thieves, mounted on horses and suddenly finding themselves trapped by the line of camels, had no alternative but to charge and try to break through. This they attempted and I was sure they'd succeed for the horses were fast and the camels well spaced. But the moment they scented the camels, all hell broke loose. They ran amok! They tossed their riders, turned so quickly they fell and every one eventually fled. The Maharajah said it is well known that horses are afraid of camels. Even the smell of fresh excrement will cause panic and drive them away.

'Go Sultana go!' someone yelled.

Just as the race's ragged survivors appeared in the distance, she descended the stile and the second fence was conquered.

Chasing the Bride was first to arrive. She'd slowed to a canter and was carefully considering where to place her feet. Her jockey was whipping her relentlessly but then he desisted, leant forward and folded in her blinkers. This had the desired effect and she returned to a gallop, leaping the fence cleanly. The next moment a camel filled the narrow slit of vision. She bucked violently, cleared the baggage from her back, lurched round and set off back to the fence. As she hurled herself over it a second time, she met Light the Fuse on the very spot she herself was heading for. With split-second reactions Light the Fuse aborted take-off, collapsed his undercarriage and avoided a head-on by diving into the fence.

Rushin Romeo was next to approach. Confused by the sight of one horse embedded in the hedge and another charging towards him, he forgot to jump and another dramatic burst of foliage and spread-eagled jockey took to the air. Yielding to an inevitable force he couldn't understand, Done and Dusted's rider pulled on the reins and steadied himself as the gelding vaulted the siderail into the quiet of the park. Timeforadream, Your Agoodun and Never Can Tell never reappeared.

Left, left. Right, right. Left, left. Right, right.

5mph. Two and a quarter laps to go.

They negotiated the remaining two jumps calmly. No more need for urgency. The competition had been wiped. All they had to do was finish.

At the completion of the first lap they were assailed by a deafening wall of boos. Hamish tried not to think how much money the punters had lost. Instead he thought of William Hill, Leith. The money Mr Hill was going to have to fork out. The only bookie who wouldn't be celebrating.

Left, left. Right, right.

Still 5mph but the laps were going more quickly now that several competitors had generously provided camel-sized holes in fences 1 and 2. No need for the stile, and plenty of time to indulge a light snack.

The fear of retribution still haunted him. A shot to Sultana's legs ... a tripwire ... a poison dart ... what lengths might they go to stop him winning? A race with no finishers would rank null and void. Bets would be returned.

By the time he completed the second lap, the majority of the crowd had dispersed. Bored. Slow and Steady wasn't the way they liked it.

Left ...

Right ...

Never had four miles seemed so long. Never had thirty furlongs taken so long. Then at last the finishing line.

Now the engraver could set to work. Below,

2003   My Baba   7:43.3

a new entry:

2004   Sultana Fatima of Wadi Hari IV   1:28:57.9

They loaded Sultana and Gertrude at once, asked for the £50,000 cheque to be posted and left. That night there occurred another first in the history of Forthlinks Racing Club when the winner's chair remained empty during the prize-giving and celebratory dinner – a vacancy that brought relief to The Gentlemen's Board, but disappointment to The Gentlemen's Guests.

Sergeant Cleghorn feels something gnawing at his insides. He can't identify it or even place it. It's just there. Like a voice calling, but too quietly to be sure. Or like that presence he felt on the moor *of being watched*. None of it makes sense but of one thing he's certain. He has tuned in to a warning.

Something is wrong …

Something is about to happen …

He's restless. Can't settle. Can't hit a straight drive. Knows it's bigger than any vice he ever imagined. And worst of all. He knows he *should* know what it is. He's seen a clue. It's in his mind but he can't find it. Some apparently harmless and innocent happening that is now flagging danger.

He taxes his memory. Retraces his steps, re-enacts conversations. It's been an unusual fortnight since the bridge opened, since he watched Sergeant Fyffe's boots disappear into the ambulance. He's booked a hundred and twenty-eight people for toll offences. He's misdirected an invasion of journalists hunting The Camel. He's attended his vigil on the bridge. He's met Gladys Braithwaite. The weather has been ridiculously hot.

Hot.

    Braithwaite.

        Heat.

            Braithwaite.

                Bridge.

'My God …!'

He's got it.

The clue.

It's still only an intuition but he's got to act. Fast.

He phones Toll Plaza.

'This is Sergeant Cleghorn. STOP ALL TRAFFIC ENTERING THE BRIDGE. IMMEDIATELY. THIS IS AN EMERGENCY.' In his excitement, he's shouting. He calms himself. 'Do you understand?'

The manager repeats the instruction.

'NO EXCEPTIONS,' he adds.

He replaces the receiver, knocks over his chair and runs to the Fiat Uno. Checks the cordoning tape is in the boot. Drives to the Flabbay end of the bridge. Parks his car broadside across the road. Knows it's a risk that neither an Uno nor Harlaw can afford to take any more. But this is different. Runs snarling tape back and forth. A cat's cradle in red and white. Cars build up. It's eleven-fifteen. It's hot and getting hotter. People ask what's wrong.

'The heat,' he explains. 'I pray to God I'm in time.'

He's not explaining it well. They don't understand. 'Anyway,' he's about to say. 'It's just a hunch. Nothing concrete ... ' but catches himself in time. Of course, it's *all* concrete. That's what's wrong. They don't understand that he feels bad for having taken so long to grasp the danger.

'Concrete expands,' he adds.

They know concrete expands. Everyone bloody well knows concrete expands ... They're angry. They've got businesses, errands, routines, schedules. It's a brand new fucking bridge, ferchristsakes. He's a fool. Everyone knows about concrete and everyone knows about Sergeant Idiot Flora MacDonald Cleghorn. They're demanding to be allowed over, shouting abuse, but Sergeant Cleghorn can take abuse, oh yes sir, he's served his apprenticeship in abuse, can take any amount of it, he can ...

... and suddenly there's a deafening noise, a black cloud and ripping and breaking and a rush of wind and the Uno turns on its side and people are hurled here and there and they scream and stones and bits of things fall around them and then everything goes quiet except for moaning and whimpering and a nurse is there – was there all the time – and asks 'How are you?' and says 'You'll be fine, I'll just put a dressing on it' and on to the next and the next and miraculously no one's seriously hurt and a shocked silence descends as people take in a new, unfamiliar landscape. The bridge is still standing but one lane is missing, one edge ragged. Bent metal bars protrude, like fishhooks. From the ends of some dangle lumps of concrete, like bait.

'That's what I was trying to tell you,' says Sergeant Cleghorn, appalled by the scale of his vindication. 'Concrete expands. And Braithwaite's lorry spilt heaps of it. Into the expansion joints. Bunged them solid.'

But they soon realise that's just the half of it. Concrete with nowhere to go doesn't explode. It suffers phenomenal stress. It buckles. It cracks. But it needs something else to make it *explode*. So they follow the bent trees to the blast's epicentre and find a black patch of ground, a pall of smoke over lingering smoulderings, scattered masonry, shrapnel, the petal of a plastic sunflower, a few grey feathers. The air smells of dead fire and weedkiller.

'It was just a feeling I had,' Sergeant Cleghorn says, 'an extraordinary stroke of luck.'

And later, philosophically, Grinella says: 'Well, Father had a good innings.'

'And a fair outing,' adds Dilly.

They stand in silence for a while, each lost in their thoughts. Dilly is the first to voice hers. 'I wonder what Henry would have made of *that* if he'd survived.'

'I shudder to think.' And then she shudders involuntarily. 'At least it would have been quick.'

'And saves troubling the crematorium,' Dilly mentions, in case it helps.

'You know, he was never really cut out to be an inventor.'

'No. It seems the knotweed won. His final straw, so to speak.'

The Global Bank of America realises, too late, that it has neglected to insure the Bridge and is legally responsible for its repair. It is at the receiving end of no less than three litigation suits for misconduct and misappropriation, one of them filed by the world's sixth largest economic unit, the State of California. Very Serious. Flabbay Bridge seems a long way off and is a problem it could do without. A deal is done. Flabbay bridge changes hands, it is rumoured. Repairs begin, but to a new design.

Among the chief criticisms of the old bridge – as it is already being called – was that it imported a fast pace of life alien to Flabbay's culture. The ferry had slowed things down. People had to wait for it to arrive. Friends unexpectedly met friends. They had time to blether, catch up on news. The new bridge will adopt a distinctly Highland solution to restore this quality. It will be single-lane with passing places, and have wide grass verges for the flock of sheep that is to be installed permanently along its length.

'I wonder who owns the bridge now,' Dilly muses in the Emporium one afternoon. She's alarmed to see a box of Durex Featherlites discretely stored behind the counter.

'Wouldn't you like to know,' replies Grinella.

The omission of the question mark stirs Dilly's curiosity. Grinella doesn't loosely discard them, which means it wasn't a question, it was more of a rhetorical nature. A jibe, even. Full of Smugness.

'You think you know?'

'I know I know,' Grinella says.

'You do?'

'I do.'

Dilly hesitates, wondering if she is going to be told or if she'll have to ask and risk being snubbed. Some friendships are never easy.

'*I* do,' Grinella repeats, with a change of emphasis.

'You do what?' snaps Dilly.

'*I* own the bridge.'

Dilly stares at her in disbelief. Then she bursts out laughing. Grinella is not known for her sense of humour and so it is to be encouraged. Dilly laughs and laughs.

Grinella doesn't. Resents the insinuation by Dilly that she, Grinella could not own, would never be worthy of owning, a bridge.

'Your father's life insurance …?' Dilly asks tentatively.

Now Grinella laughs. 'Never had a policy.'

Dilly's mind stalls.

'You'll recall,' Grinella concedes, 'I had a mystery admirer after that splendid party at the castle? The expensive scent? Yes? And you, dismissively, suggested it was Thkip MacQuarrie. Well it wasn't. It turned out to be someone immeasurably more attractive. And the more I refused his advances, the more generous his gifts became. Until eventually, poor man, in desperation he asked what he could give me that was my heart's desire. And, jokingly, I said, "The Bridge". So he bought it for me! *I own the bridge*, Dilly.'

'The sheikh?'

'Hurrah!'

'You're going to marry the sheikh?'

'Who said anything about marriage? No, no. That would be unthinkable. I daresay he's got a dozen wives back home. And besides, who'd want to marry a man who squanders his money on expensive derelict bridges?'

'But surely you're going to have to *do something* for these presents.'

'Receive, Dilly. Receive gracefully.'

Thkip has a reprieve while the bridge is reconstructed. The *Flucker* lives again. For a few months at least. Until the Re-Opening Ceremony and Dedication. Sheikh Jasim al bu Muhammad Maziad bin Hamdan is unable to attend, called away suddenly on Gulf business. Grinella wears an Armani camisole, jacket and skirt – impractical but stunning – and – in deference to conservationist principles – an imitation ocelot coat.

She has been practising microphone control. No bubbles. No quonks.

'I name this The Archibald Oliphant Memorial Bridge,' she announces, 'and declare it open. Passage is free … '

She is interrupted by shouts and cheers.

'There's going to be a catch,' Dilly whispers, to Miss Stewart. 'If I know Grinella. Things are never straightforward with her.'

'Free, that is, during the hours worked by the former ferry. Outwith those hours tolls set at the previous exorbitant levels will be charged. The new Toll Supervisor – enjoying a change of bridge! – will be Thkip MacQuarrie.'

'I told you,' says Dilly, as she joins everyone in singing *For She's A Jolly Good Fellow.*

Sergeant Cleghorn receives a letter of commendation from the Northern Constabulary. He reads it with pride. His eyes glaze over, soggy in the corners. He's not used to things going well. Even Cowdenbeath manage to beat Dunfermline 1-0 (in extra time) that week. He clips the article. Sends it to the castle. The following day, receives notice of his promotion to Inspector. He acknowledges it by return. He's finally settled on uppercase Copperplate which conveys quiet authority without being too flashy, and in no way suggests that the process of selection has been a detailed preoccupation.

INSPECTOR F CLEGHORN

Strength in understatement.

He does not order the new plaque. Leaves the old one there

`Sergeant Cleghorn` (dull Courier on plastic)

but unscrews

`Sergeant Fyffe`

and throws it in the bin. A week later he tenders his resignation. Signs it in the space between Yours Faithfully and Inspector F Cleghorn.

'What the devil's going on?' fumes Chief Inspector Harlaw at Northern HQ. 'One week you accept promotion, the next you resign … '

'I'm resigning, sir.'

'My God, Cleghorn, I rue the day I ever had anything to do with you. Why? On what grounds?'

'Personal reasons, sir. Being a police officer is incompatible with Life. I have other ambitions.'

'What other ambitions could you possibly have?' Piqued, Harlaw is resorting to sneer.

'The Hannibal MacFie Trophy, for one.'

Harlaw splutters indignation. 'Then why the hell did you accept promotion?'

'For the pension, when it comes.' Inspector Cleghorn puts the phone down on Chief Inspector Harlaw. It's immensely satisfying.

Two thousand and sixty-eight days to go until he is eligible for an Inspector's pension!

The other statistic is even better.

Three days since he last had sex!

He'd forgotten how invigorating it felt! How uplifting!

Bill Braithwaite has been thrown out of his house. Gladys caught him on the job with a secretary. 'Gettin is bludy rocks off in quarry,' she fumes with bludy-shovel matter-of-factness. 'Nowt mooch o a marriage at best o time,' she confides to Farquhar. 'What we im never bludy there.' And Farquhar deflates Angela's effigy, puts her out with the wheely bins and moves into Gawthrope Guest House with its weird bunch of sheep.

Must have been a consequence of the haggis, people say about Gladys, tapping their temples. *Soft In The Head* …

Or Cleggy's haggis, some joke.

They don't really know what they mean.

It just seems funny.

Like he's always been a joke.

But Inspector F Cleghorn, Retired, doesn't care. He's got his golf, and is already one up on the Southern Rights.

An unexpected glut of mackerel swims into the Minch. Mairi Ban is worked off her feet. The upshot is a marked improvement in her Latvian, Estonian, Lithuanian and Bulgarian which, the way the European Union is breeding, will come in handy if she makes it as a MEP. MSP, however, remains her preference. New Labour lose the election big time. BLiar and Darning don't care, not now, with life membership of the crony circus, fat cat tricks to perform; memoirs to write, Chairs to grace with their status, After-Dinner Pearlers to dispense as liberally as anyone pays them. Mairi Ban joins the SSP. She needs larger arenas and more important groins for her talents.

Hamish has doubts. Doubts about the Scottish Parliament. Doubts about the land. Knows Scots have grown used to watching others succeed or cock it up. Is frightened they prefer it that way rather than risk failing themselves. Intimidated by freedom, wary of opportunity: inferiority's scars. 'Better the Devil … ' they say. Too long, caged.

'S*tands Scotland where it did?*'

'*Alas, poor country! Almost afraid to know itself!*'

He reads this in a new book. Understands. Knows it'll take time to *re-know*. Knows he has to try.

The new book – *A LONG TIME COMING, A Saga of Clumsy Love and Misconceptions* by Greta Sex – hits the Emporium's shelves and shocks Flabbay. They are shocked because they never expected a history of the Brodie family to find a publisher, and because they'd never have thought that such a nice, quiet man would have come out with such filth. No one has any doubts who the author is, despite the pseudonym. Those better informed, like Hamish and Grout who have seen him stripped to the core a thousand times, are more certain than others. The pseudonym is popularly believed to be a pun on 'Greater Sex'. It is not. It would take an intimate knowledge of Lovecare Ltd's catalogue and an anagrammatical mind like Grinella's, Dilly's or Loon's to understand it. The reviews are poor. But who cares? Greta's ex has come good.

Grout's been spending a lot of time feeding the peacocks – for ethical reasons; sharing, nurturing – and watching the garden grow.

'Tae mony folk's forgotten the pleasures o simple things,' he says. To a peacock. 'See us, we tak wirsels sae seriously, man. Goat tae work, produce, achieve. Christ! Whit fuckin arrogance! Like we're so special we hiv tae prove it the hale time. Egotistical, man! Jist live. Be. If we cannae enjoy the noo, wiv only goat niver.'

The peacocks strut, peck. One's taken to standing on the monopede's head. A pigeonish stunt. But they're safe. It'll be vegetarian next time.

The family's split. Gertrude has found permanent lodgings in the stable of Sheikh Jasim al bu Muhammad Maziad bin Hamdan, twenty-fourth Laird of Dundreary. So they're moving on. Cutting loose. He and Loon have bought a new van, their sole divergence from the alternative wealth of poverty. Painted a flower. Grout, top left. Loon, top right. Rastafarian, centre bottom. Dunfermline below.

'What ye think, Rast?'

Rast exercises The Right To Be A Normal Dog. Farts. Goes to sleep. ·

Goodbyes.

'GOODBYE,' says Angus, '*SLÀINTE MHATH.*'

'Keep the claithes.'

Effie presses a bag of scones into Loon's hands. He is her favourite, although she's fond of both. Dabs her eyes with her apron. Like losing sons.

Formidable lady whichever way you look at her (5) thinks Loon, already working on next month's composition. *Madam.*

Hamish is last.

They hug. Cry.

'Thanks,' says Hamish. 'I'll miss you.'

'Yea.'

'Good luck wi the revolution.'

'Djaysus, whit ye gaunae dae wi this place?'

'Kill the woodworm. Put a new roof on, and then I thought to myself, what would my dear father want me to do with it?' His face is serious. Looks older. Not old Jesus, old Judas. 'And that decided me.'

Grout and Loon waiver. Class Distrust Rears Ugly Head Again.

'To turn it into Scotland's first gay hotel. That should make the old bastard foam in his water.'

A joke. The decision is no longer his. A Community Trust is in the making and may go for a conference centre or spiritual retreat, perhaps –

something much less controversial and longer-term, it is hoped, than the Perversion Tour – but there'll be space set aside for running evening classes, artisan workshops, a youth club … and already there's talk of establishing a Rural Skills Training Centre. Hamish is moving to a cottage with outbuildings where the witchery is to be installed as an eyebright factory. The land is being divided into plots. Suspicion is yielding to possibility, and responsibility.

A month later another MacFie tradition ends: for want of the Udaipur, Hamish has to buy Amulree a ring.

Locals aren't speaking to incomers, incomers are deriding Gaels, Gaels are into closed-shop Gaelic, the Fundamentalists (Continuing) are shunning the True Fundamentalists and being shunned in their turn, the 'pro-Baha'i's-in-the-Messiah' National Presbyterians have given up church altogether and condemn those who haven't as dyed-in-the-wool blackfaces, the Catholics are the butts of Protestant jokes again but don't care because they go to the confessional and enjoy a life – 'Thank the Lord!' – free from Calvinist guilt, the heaven-sent cure and curse of tourism is renewed, B&B owners are back to their back-stabbing and switching signs, xenophobes are xenophobing, the ever-vigilant Rural Eye is censuring and gossipers gossiping, yet partner-swappers swap, Grimport cruisers cruise, grant-grabbers grab and the Flabbians drink themselves flabbier. Vice Vice VICE Uice Vice *Vice* Vice **Vice** *Vice*

Life is back to normal again. They can live with that. It's change that's upsetting.

Kittiwakes call, tuning their wings to the breeze.

They walk their island. Hand in hand. Feel sand shift and harden underfoot. Walking, into their world.

It's so beautiful.

No regrets?

None.

I'm OK!

I'm OK!

Let's fly.

Forever.